BOOK ONE OF THE FOURLINE TRILOGY

GATEWAY TO FOURLINE

BOOK ONE OF THE FOURLINE TRILOGY

GATEWAY  TO FOURLINE

PAM BRONDOS

SKYSCAPE

SKYSCAPE

Text copyright © 2015 Pam Brondos

Published by Skyscape, New York

www.apub.com

Amazon, the Amazon logo, and Skyscape are trademarks of Amazon.com, Inc., or its affiliates.

ISBN-13: 9781503948358
ISBN-10: 1503948358

Cover design by Chelsea Wirtz

Printed in the United States of America

To Peter

CHAPTER ONE
Fourline

Barba stood by the side of the stable, chewing on the delicate meldon flower pulled from her small supply. She swallowed the bitter petals, then looked west toward the last orange glow of the day. A light breeze played with the curly red tendrils of hair poking out from beneath her hood. She stepped away from the stable and listened. There it was—a faint, high-pitched warble coming from the gully behind the farmhouse. Annin was waiting.

Barba shoved two more petals in her mouth. *A little extra protection from Nala venom never hurt,* she thought as she unclipped her cloak. She fingered the tightly embroidered vines that covered the fabric. She paused, bringing the material closer to her face. Her pointed nose twitched when she smelled the manure. Retrieving her fist-sized orb from a pocket deep within the garment, she rolled the cloak into a tight ball that fit neatly into her saddlebag.

"Don't wait up," she whispered to her mare. She rubbed the white diamond of fur between the mare's eyes and headed into the night, away from the safety of the farmer's stable.

Sweat soon covered Barba's forehead as she ran toward the meeting spot. Too many days and nights in the library and not enough time training had made her soft. The ground transformed from grass to rock, causing her to lose her footing. Loose gravel followed her down the side of a gulley. She righted herself and peered into the half-light. Annin's girlish figure appeared from behind a cottonwood tree, and the two ran silently and swiftly over the rocky ground. After several minutes, Annin slowed and motioned Barba to follow as she deftly scrambled up the side of the gully. Once out, the girl crawled through the tall autumn grass to the edge of an insignificant hill.

"Three Nala and two dozen soldiers, Sister," Annin whispered as she parted the grass with a slender hand. A semicircle of torches blazed in the valley below them. No fewer than fifteen soldiers stood in the ring of fire. Barba counted five soldiers with drawn bows.

"I recognize that one." Annin pointed to the nervous figure standing in front of the soldiers. "He was Lord Mudug's emissary to the Healing House."

Barba studied the odd grouping. Why was Mudug's man risking his life to meet with the Nala?

The Nala stood in the darkness away from the flames. One crawled forward, its pointed forearms brushing the ground. A flare licked the air around its bluish skin. The creature straightened and stood surprisingly erect, but its powerful back legs twitched as if ready to spring. It swiveled its bulbous head toward the flames. The torchlight reflected off its faceted silver eyes. Barba refrained from looking at the row of sharp teeth protruding from its mouth.

The emissary stepped forward hesitantly. He gestured to the guards around him and cleared his throat. His voice was low. Barba could barely make out what he was saying to the creatures in front of him. She put her hand on Annin's arm and pointed to a fallen trunk near a grove of trees about halfway down the hill.

The two crawled slowly through the grass until they reached the collapsed trunk. Barba peered around the jagged edge of wood. Two human archers, with arrows trained on the Nala, crouched a few yards below the trunk. Barba flattened her body against the ground and listened as snippets of the conversation floated up from below.

"Lord Mudug is keeping his word. You must do the same, or we will have to change the terms of our agreement. The last Warrior House will close within the week." The emissary's voice trembled slightly as he spoke.

"We promised safe passage on two conditions," the Nala said, its words rising through the air like steam from a boiling pot. "You have met neither."

"The Houses are closing; the Sisters are out of your territory. As for the other condition, it's not as easy."

The Nala let out a breathy hiss. "What? Human, can you not tell the difference between one of us and one of your own?"

Barba lifted her head ever so slightly. The emissary was now surrounded on three sides by his guards.

"They do not live openly among us." He spoke quickly. "Our reports say there is a settlement east of your forest. If you would provide assurances, we—"

"Fool." The Nala leapt toward the emissary, the pale sheen of his face reflected in the smooth blue skin of the Nala. Barba heard the creak of bows tightening. "Do you think we would not have them if they were near our territory?" the Nala hissed.

"Touch me and you will die," the emissary barked.

The Nala stepped back, shaking its head and rubbing its pointed hands together. "So much that is worse than death." It paused, then straightened its slender body. "Bring me the halflings, or your precious routes may encounter unexpected visitors. Without your Sisters, you have no protection."

"Do not underestimate Lord Mudug, spider," the emissary spat. "Nothing good will come to you if you renege on your promise."

"Maybe, human." The Nala's eyes widened, elongating the facets, and the emissary took a sudden step backward. "But ask Lord Mudug, does he want hundreds of Nala hunting him down every night of his life? Bring me what I want." It turned and scurried into the darkness, followed by its two companions.

A moment passed. The emissary shakily stepped backward into the center of the torch holders. The soldiers scanned the dark beyond the torchlight. The two archers near Barba and Annin stood and slowly made their way down the hill with their bows still drawn. By the time they rejoined the remaining soldiers, the emissary was far down the valley. Barba heard a nervous string of horses whinnying in the distance.

Annin pressed her hand hard into Barba's back. Barba could feel the girl's thin fingers trembling. She turned and looked up in the direction Annin was pointing. Two silver eyes peered through the dry autumn leaves above them. The Nala crouched on the branch, ready to spring. Barba reached for her dagger and scrambled to her feet. The creature tilted its bulbous head and moved a spiky hand toward a lower branch. Barba positioned herself between Annin and the tree, freed her companion orb, and sent the glowing ball hurtling toward the Nala.

"Leave now, Nala. Join the others," Barba commanded in a low voice.

The Nala waved its arms wildly at the orb as the sphere circled its body and repeatedly slammed against its blue skin.

"Do nothing to violate the Rim Accord." Barba's voice grew louder.

The Nala hissed but backed up onto its original perch. "There is no violation known if you are gone, Sister." It leaned forward, narrowing its silver eyes to focus on the markings on Barba's uncovered arm. "Not even from the Warrior House, just a Wisdom Sister." It made a harsh barking sound and opened its mouth. Little droplets of venom dripped from its fangs onto the branches and dried leaves below.

4

Barba held her dagger in plain sight of the Nala. "You cannot kill me with your venom, spider."

"Other ways to kill, Sister, but since you are no Warrior Sister, tonight I shall spare you and abide by our accord. Call off your orb." The creature darted to another branch, and Barba pivoted. The orb continued to strike the Nala. It swatted at the orb, then froze as its eyes met Annin's. It leaned down, one pointed hand curved around the branch, and hissed again.

"The Sister has a duozi." The corners of its mouth curved upward.

Annin jumped to her feet with her own dagger drawn just as the Nala leapt to the fallen log. The girl stepped to the side, and Barba brought her dagger down into the base of the Nala's skull, crushing it. The creature crumpled at Annin's feet. Still clasping the dagger's hilt, Barba crouched over the dead Nala. Her breath came in sharp gasps. She'd never killed a Nala, let alone been attacked by one.

She felt Annin's small hand on her shoulder. "Its head, Sister Barba," Annin said.

Barba nodded, remembering her training from years before. "Turn away, Annin." Barba glanced at her, taking in the girl's one human and one Nala eye. Annin shook her head, her black curls escaping her loose hair tie.

"It's not a choice, Annin. Shut your eyes," Barba ordered. Annin reluctantly obeyed. After a few moments, the girl opened them to see Barba wiping her hands on the tall grass near the body of the headless Nala. A discarded arrow stuck straight out from the Nala's soft abdomen. Annin leaned down and examined the arrow. She looked at Barba questioningly.

"Let them think Mudug's men did it." Barba sheathed her dagger. "We must leave now. Mudug's guards may not have noticed us, but the Nala will track down their missing member and us as well unless we're careful. We can't risk getting caught up in a confrontation with more Nala, not now."

Annin stood above the creature's body. She pulled up the sleeve of her tunic, exposing a thin forearm. The blue skin matched the skin of the Nala.

Barba touched the girl's arm. "Annin, let's go."

Annin exhaled and dropped her arm. She stepped back, and her foot landed with a thud alongside the dead Nala.

As they retraced their steps to the gully, Annin seized a clump of ramp weed and broke two thick stalks with a quick motion of her hand. She squeezed the end of one stalk, and a green liquid oozed into her hands.

"Sister Ethet says this covers any scent," she said.

"Does she?" Barba held out her hands, and Annin smeared a bit of green ooze into each palm. Barba spread the sticky goop on her cheeks and neck. A strong fragrance of mint filled her nostrils. "Good memory."

The pair scrambled down the side of the gully through the tall grass and rock. When they reached the rocky bottom, Barba caught her orb floating next to her. It instantly emitted a faint light, and she released it. The sphere hung in midair for a moment, then zoomed ahead. Barba and Annin followed the orb as it raced over the rocky ground, leading them up and out of the gully. It sped so quickly through the crest of the grass that Barba momentarily lost sight of it until it popped up in the distance. The sphere bobbed up and down impatiently before taking off again.

Barba turned once to find Annin easily keeping pace at her side. The girl was fast—faster than most her age. Her speed reminded Barba of the Nala. She quickened her pace and kept the faint glow of the orb in her sight. The sphere led them far away from the valley to a broad hill where it weaved in and out of the tall grass. The glowing ball rolled to a rest near the base of a pointed leafy bush. Barba fell to her knees and reached between the shaggy branches to retrieve her orb. Sweat and sticky resin covered her arms. Annin knelt beside her, breathing only slightly more heavily than normal.

Below, about a half mile away, lay the farmhouse, the stable, and their horses. Barba sighed and pulled the orb close.

"Shouldn't you go down, Sister?" Annin asked. "If the farmer finds our horses but no one in the Sisters' quarters, he will tell someone."

"No. I'm more concerned with the Nala than the farmer. If they come tonight, it will be from the east, closer to the forest. I'd be able to see them approaching far better from here than from down there." She turned away, hoping Annin believed the partial lie. The encounter between the emissary and the Nala and the attack on Annin had her mind in tangles. She wasn't about to leave the girl alone, and every horse but Annin's would kick up a fuss if she brought the girl near them.

"I am going to need all your senses tomorrow, Annin. Sleep. The orb will let me know if trouble is coming tonight."

Annin stared at Barba for a moment, then reluctantly lay on her side in the tall grass and pulled the folds of her cloak around her. Barba sat crosslegged in the tall grass, staring at the farmhouse and wishing she could will her cloak out of her saddlebag, up the hill, and over her shoulders.

She pushed the question of why Mudug's men were meeting with the Nala from her mind. She had more pressing issues to consider, mainly the safe passage of Estos. If everything and everyone were on schedule, she and Annin would meet up with the new regent and his retinue midmorning on the Meldon Plain. Then, it was simply a matter of convincing him to pass through the membrane. After that, he would be safe, unlike his sister. They could sort the rest of this mess out later.

Annin's strange eyes were open when Barba looked over at the girl.

"Annin?"

"Yes, Sister."

"Have you heard the word 'duozi' before?"

"Yes," Annin replied.

"Do you know what it means?"

"It means someone like me."

"Hmm. Go to sleep, Annin." Barba brought her hands gently over the girl's halfling eyes, willing them closed. She pulled the edge of the cloak tight around Annin's shoulders and wondered why the Nala had gone after her.

CHAPTER TWO

Six Years Later on the Other Side

It sounded like a freeway with cars swishing past. Nat listened as she waited for the red light to turn off. The stainless-steel door then slid open, and a swell of steam enveloped her face. Another load of clean dishes rolled down the line in a lime-green crate. She touched the edge of the crate to keep it from falling off the rolling track.

"Naaaaat!"

The dish-room matriarchs shook their heads as Nat's roommate, Viv, danced toward her. A zebra-patterned hairnet held back Viv's moss-green hair. Nat tucked a strand of straight brown hair behind her ear with a damp finger as Viv danced in circles next to Nat, pointing to Nat's green eyes in a spastic disco move. She patted her stomach in a drumroll before pulling out an earbud.

"Shift's over, Nattybumpo," she sang and removed the dish and dish towel from Nat's hands. "My notes from chem class are on your desk." She replaced the earbud, and Nat mouthed, "Thanks," knowing the spoken word was pointless.

"Hey!" Viv called.

Nat turned.

"Your mom called." Viv wiped a dish as she yelled, "Not that I mind talking to your mom, but try turning your cell phone on once in a while."

"I know, I know, but ignorance is bliss, right?"

Viv gave her a wide smile. "I can't hear you, but I know you just made some smart remark. Make me proud—call your mom." She turned her back on Nat. A noise like a bellowing baby seal filled the air. Viv's green ponytail bounced inside the hairnet in time with her singing.

Nat walked past the long line of sinks and tossed her wet dish gloves in the last sink, the rubber slapping against the side of the basin. Viv's singing reached a crescendo. Nat glanced into the dishroom and shook her head at the sight of Viv belting a song to a dirty soup ladle. Even after living with Viv for more than a year, Nat was still amazed by her less-than-normal appearance and overt gregariousness. The two had made peace long ago with what was obviously a twisted joke by someone in the housing office. Or she sometimes wondered if the psychology department had deliberately put the two of them together as an experiment, like lab rats, except without the whiskers and tails.

Nat swung the dishroom doors open and walked by a line of students picking through the salad bar. Buzzing voices from the cafeteria replaced the sound of Viv's singing. She paused in front of an information board plastered with flyers and scanned the colored sheets.

"Don't need tutoring, can't afford a new computer," she said under her breath. Failing to find any "Help Wanted" ads, she pulled a tab off an advertisement for singing lessons. *Viv could use this if she'd ever pull herself out of the art studio,* she thought. Viv's sketches and sculptures always boggled Nat. She could barely draw a stick figure, let alone shape clay into anything beyond a pathetic-looking bowl, while Viv could create a detailed miniature of a person in minutes. A small portrait of Nat's little sister, Marie Claire, hung above her desk. Viv had given it to her after she'd met Marie Claire during a visit their freshman year. The sketch captured her sister's sweet, eager face.

A squirrel climbed up the metal exterior of a garbage can directly outside the doors of the Student Center. It dived its paws into the overflowing can, retrieving a half-eaten sandwich. Nat watched it scamper away toward the Science Center. A trail of students streamed into the building. She dug through her backpack for her phone, wondering how she was going to squeeze in the extra labs her biology professor had just assigned her class. She loved her biology major, especially her Plant Morphology class, but she needed more work-study hours, not more lab hours.

A red bar flashed on the screen of her phone. Low battery. *Need to make this quick,* she thought, feeling slightly relieved she couldn't talk long. She passed the Science Center and jumped over a pile of leaves onto the concrete path leading to the library. She paused below the safety lights and dialed home.

She hadn't spoken to her mom or dad since the rushed visit to the hospital two weeks before. Her father, always trying to do too much, fell from a ladder while pulling a grain bag from the barn loft. It wouldn't have been so bad, except he'd landed on a scrap heap of barbed wire. A broken leg and sixteen puncture wounds later, he was now laid up with no one to help him with the farm chores or with the orders from his small woodworking business.

She couldn't be home to help, and neither of her parents had asked. But that reality did little to relieve her guilt. A cluster of students, hands shoved in their pockets, passed her. She watched them as they disappeared into the library, wondering what it would be like to worry only about her classes. She skipped onto the sidewalk leading to the Speech and Theater Building, adjusted her backpack, and listened to the phone ring.

"Hello?"

"Hi, Mom. You sound tired."

"Natalie, I've been trying to reach you all day." Now her mom sounded exasperated and tired. Nat's guilt level deepened.

"Sorry, Mom, I've been in class and then work. Viv told me you called her. What's going on?"

"Your dad's back in the hospital. Nothing serious, I think. He has an infection of some sort. Dr. Bitty had him admitted this morning." Nat cringed, remembering how she'd ignored the call earlier in the day.

"I can be home Friday." She didn't mention the lab she needed to catch up on or the work shifts that she couldn't afford to miss. She'd figure that out later.

"No, don't, Nat. He's going to be okay, he just needs to get this infection cleared up. I've got Gary, Jim Harris' boy, coming over every day to help with the farm while I'm at school. Marie Claire is helping so much. She had dinner made when I got home from work last night." Her mom let out a little laugh. "It was mac and cheese with celery sticks on the good china. Lots of people are pitching in. Even Cal is helping out. She's been on the phone calling Dad's customers, letting them know about the delays." Her voice had a false tone of lightness to it.

"Cal should be doing more than calling customers. She can help Gary with the sheep at least." Nat imagined her middle sister holed up in her room, talking on the phone while her mom prepared lesson plans, Marie Claire made dinner, and Gary tried to handle the farm. Cal never did a lick of work unless bribed or coerced.

"Lay off Cal, Nat, she's trying," her mother said testily. Then she sighed. "Honey, given everything that's happened, it's going to be difficult to come up with the money we were planning to send to help with tuition. With paying Gary and the doctor bills, and no money coming in from Dad's business, I'm not sure what you can expect from us."

"Don't worry about me. I knew it wasn't going to be easy for you and Dad, so I already looked into it and have it covered." The lie sounded fairly convincing, and she hoped her mom bought it. "The last thing you need to think about right now is my tuition. Tell Dad I love him."

"I never need to worry about you, do I?" Her mom sounded relieved. "Thanks for being older than you should be. I know none of this has been—"

"Mom, really, you have enough on your plate," Nat interrupted, not wanting the conversation to continue. "I've got to get to class, but I will call Dad."

"Thanks, Nat. I love you."

"I love you, too."

Nat hit "End" on her phone and stared at the bright light spilling out of the Speech and Theater Building's glass doors. The smell of rotten crab apples hung heavily in the air. Her parents didn't know that she was already trying to cover the tuition increase for her sophomore year on her own. She pushed open the doors leading to the foyer. She turned right and climbed up a worn set of wooden stairs, wondering how long the college would let her attend class if she stopped making tuition payments.

A little of her stress seeped away when she walked into the dark, circular theater. Something about the room, with its high-arched ceiling and mini–flying buttresses, pleased her. It was the exact opposite of the auditorium and labs in the biology department, where she spent most of her class time. Strips of silken fabric in the deepest hue of blue adorned the honey-colored walls. The octagonal stage looked like an island amidst the surrounding audience chairs. As much as she groused about having to take this Acting for Nonmajors class to meet the fine-arts requirement, she loved the peaceful atmosphere of the small theater, especially when it wasn't her turn to take to the stage.

Chairs creaked as students claimed seats around the scuffed-up stage. Nat glanced at her watch; Professor Gate was late as usual. Normally this didn't bother her, but she felt frustrated as her thoughts slipped back to her tuition problem. She dropped her backpack on the floor next to her seat, accidently bumping the leg of the boy sitting next to her.

"Thanks. Now the eye patch is all wrong." Butler, one of Viv's friends, had a drawing pad cradled in his arm and gestured to the pencil sketch. He erased a crooked line. "I call it *Pirate Annin*." He held up the pad, revealing a harsh sketch of a young woman with long, wild hair, a discolored right arm, and a lopsided eye patch. Her other hand held a thin sword.

Nat immediately recognized the subject of his inspiration. Annin sat in a high row of seats on the opposite side of the stage. Nat tended to forget she was in this class, because she rarely attended and never spoke except during required performances.

"Aside from being cruel, it's not bad." Nat held the pad in front of her, glancing quickly at Butler's subject. "The sword suits her, I think, but you have the other arm wrong. She's got a line . . ." She looked up. The young man Annin always sat next to, Estos, was staring at her. His blue-gray eyes unnerved her, and she glanced away. He whispered something in Annin's ear. Annin lifted her chin and shot a cold look at Nat. Thick coils of black hair hung over her uncovered eye. A creepy shiver ran down Nat's spine, and she dropped the pad into Butler's lap.

"Next time you draw her, make sure she's on the other side of campus, not the other side of the room. She gives me the creeps," she said. Butler shrugged and slid the pad into his bag as Professor Gate came hurtling down the theater stairs. He pushed a wavy lock of black hair away from his thick glasses and spread a sheaf of papers across the edge of the stage.

"Pull up your syllabus, and note the two assignment changes," he said as he hopped onto the stage. His lanky frame cast a long shadow over the wooden floor as he listed the new due dates for monologues.

"Do you know of any jobs on campus that pay more than the caf?" Nat asked Butler as she powered up her old laptop. Professor Gate looked in her direction.

"Ask Bloomers. Regan found a job through it a few weeks ago." Butler peered at Nat's computer screen. "Maybe you need to ask Bloomers for a winning lottery ticket, too." He pointed at the thin blue stripes marring her screen. "That thing isn't going to last through the semester."

"Yeah, well, it doesn't have a choice," she said, thinking Bloomers, the campus-wide search site wasn't a bad place to start a job search.

"Ms. Barns, you seem chatty tonight." Professor Gate eyed her from the center of the stage. "Why don't you and"—he spun around and pointed—"Annin start us off with an improv exercise. I'll set the scene. Come, come." He gestured to her, and she groaned inwardly. She hated improvisation.

She handed her laptop to Butler. He smirked at her. "Don't let her break your leg," he whispered.

Nat shot him a nasty look over her shoulder and climbed the stairs to the stage. Annin stood across from her with her arms folded defensively. She brushed her hair away from the patch that covered her eye, and Nat glanced at the floor, trying hard not to stare. *Of all the people, why her?* Nat looked briefly at Butler, whose amused expression only increased her irritation.

"Ms. Barns, you are traveling on a packed train in a foreign country when Annin attempts to lift your wallet from your bag. Let's begin." Professor Gate clapped his hands and strode toward the edge of the stage. She took a deep breath and stepped hesitantly toward Annin.

The college's logo moved slowly across the computer monitor's screen. Nat stared blankly at it and yawned. Like her laptop battery, she was drained. She glanced at the clock hanging above the library shelves. It was only eight thirty p.m., but she felt exhausted as she thought about her day, which had started with an early morning run and ended with that stupid improv exercise. She still had a study group and at least an hour's worth of work to finish up the extra biology lab her professor had asked her to complete. *And I need to find another job,* she thought and sighed.

Nat scooted her chair closer to the library's computer monitor and typed in "Bloomers." She clicked on the link, and the sunshine-yellow Bloomers home page popped up. She glanced around the empty table, thankful she was the only one using the public computers. Most evenings, this corner of the second floor of the library was packed. *There must be a game tonight,* she thought and tried to remember the last time she'd managed to catch one of the college's sport events.

Nat scanned the site, clicked the "Sellers" tab, and scrolled through the responses linking campus buyers to sellers and providing advice from the unknown entity "Bloomers." One response read: "Xeon: Contact Carrie in Kierk Hall. She needs a bike. Milo's 8 downtown is best for consignment."

Nat thought a moment if she had anything to sell. She needed her laptop, as close to death as it was, and her bike was home collecting dust in the barn—not that anyone would want to buy either. She clicked the "Help Wanted" tab. She typed her name at the prompt, pressed "Enter," and then typed her query: "Looking for a job on or off campus that pays more than $8/hr."

"Excuse me."

Startled by the low voice, Nat jerked away from the keyboard and knocked her textbooks off the table. A hand reached out and caught the books.

"I didn't mean to startle you." Estos dropped the books next to the monitor. Up close, his eyes were more gray than blue. He scratched his head, leaving a clump of dark-brown hair sticking up at an odd angle. A frayed power cord dangled from his hand. "You left this in the theater." His voice had an odd inflection.

"Thanks . . ." Nat wrapped her fingers around the cord.

He sat on the table and flipped through the pages of her morphology textbook. "Thank Annin, she found it," he said without looking at her. "Impressive improv, by the way. Very convincing."

"You're kidding, right?" Nat shifted in her seat and wondered how Estos had found her in the library.

"No." Estos placed the book next to her hand, crossed his arms, and gave her a curious look. He was tall enough to make Nat feel dwarfed sitting in the computer chair. She shoved the cord into her bag and pushed away from the monitor. She realized the "Help Wanted" tab was still open and closed it with a click.

"Looking for something on Bloomers?" he asked and nodded toward the garish yellow home page.

"No, I like reading the advice," she lied, not interested in talking about her job search with someone she barely knew.

He drew his dark eyebrows together and looked at the battered watch wrapped around his wrist. "You have a Plant Morphology study group in ten minutes, and you're wasting your time reading those responses?"

"How do you know I have a study group?" Nat pressed her back against the chair, feeling uneasy. She tapped the side of the keyboard.

"I know one of your study partners." Estos grabbed another one of her textbooks and opened it to a page filled with her notes scribbled along the margins. He traced her writing with his finger as he read the notes. She was just about to grab the book back when she noticed a long, thin scar running from the base of his ear down his neck.

Estos set the book on the table, leaned over her shoulder, and examined the screen. She smelled the faintest hint of fresh pine. His arm brushed her neck when he clicked open the "General" tab. Nat tensed.

"She gives odd advice," he said after reading a few responses.

"How do you know Bloomers is a 'she'?"

He shrugged. "Where I come from, most of the people who give advice are women. They seem to have all the answers. This woman, I'm not so sure about." He scrolled through more responses, and she caught herself staring again at his scar. The line ran right near the location of a jugular vein. *He's lucky to be alive,* she thought. She glanced at the clock.

"I need to go. Like you said, I have a study group." She cleared her throat and pointed to his arm blocking her way. He dropped it immediately. "Thanks again for the cord."

"I'll make sure Annin knows how grateful you are," he called as she jogged toward the stairs. Estos leaned against the table, watching her go. She took the stairs two at a time, wondering about the odd encounter.

It wasn't until Nat was out the library doors that she realized she hadn't pressed "Enter" to post her job query.

CHAPTER THREE

The fabric on the chair in the financial-aid office irritated the back of Nat's legs. The day was weirdly warm for the beginning of October, and she wore a pair of frayed shorts. She picked at the pilled upholstery, waiting for her turn to speak with an adviser. Numbers, interest calculations, and payment dates ran through her head.

The student in front of her was taking forever. Nat puffed out her cheeks and let out a long breath. She rummaged in her backpack for her phone and dialed home, knowing a follow-up call to check on her dad was long overdue.

"Hello?"

"Hey, Cal," she said to her seventeen-year-old sister. Nat heard the clacking sound of typing in the background.

"What do you want?" Cal said tersely. Nat bit her lip. Her sister was possibly the rudest, most self-centered person she knew. The clacking sound grew louder.

"What are you working on?"

"I'm writing a paper." Cal used the same tone when she spoke with an ex-boyfriend.

"Really? You're writing a paper?"

"Is this an emergency? Are you dying or something? Because otherwise, I've got better things to do than listen to you crab out on me."

"Are Mom and Dad there?" Nat said in a clipped tone.

"They're out at some school thing for Marie Claire."

"How's Dad?"

"Sick, stressed."

"Mom?"

"The same."

"MC?" she asked, using her nickname for Marie Claire.

"A twerp."

Nat's frustration grew. "You're helping Mom and Dad out?"

"No, I'm just enjoying myself while my parents face financial ruin because their eldest daughter turned down a full ride to the U so she could go to some snooty private school." Cal slammed the phone down.

A short white-haired woman beckoned Nat to her desk. Nat shoved her phone into her backpack in anger and took a deep breath. The woman smiled as Nat settled into another itchy chair and slid a small piece of paper across the desk.

"I need to check my account status, please," Nat said.

The woman turned toward her computer, her white hair swinging back and forth. Her fingers flew over a worn keyboard. She glanced at Nat.

"Something wrong, dear? Your face looks a little, well, beet red."

"No, I'm fine, just the heat, I guess." Nat took another deep breath. It didn't help. She still felt like throttling her sister.

"Your account shows $6,524.39 due for this semester. We have a scheduled payment in two weeks. Is there a problem with that payment date?" She turned the computer monitor so Nat could see the screen and pointed to the amount.

"No, no problem." *Big problem*, Nat thought. "While I'm here, can you give me the amount for next semester, too?"

The woman typed something, and Nat heard a printer come to life.

"Here." She took a highlighter and circled a figure at the bottom of the printout. "The top figure is this semester, and the second figure is next semester. Assuming your financial-aid and scholarship information remains the same, this is the total for the rest of the year." She tapped the figure with the tip of the marker: $13,759.02.

"Couldn't you just round down to make it easier for everyone?" Nat muttered.

"Are you all right, dear? Now you look a little pale."

"I'm fine." She felt like throwing up all over the desk. Her palms were slick with sweat as she clutched the printout. Where was she going to come up with six thousand dollars, let alone thirteen thousand? Her parents had planned on covering four of the six thousand for this semester, but that wasn't going to happen with her dad out of work.

"Um, can I make an appointment with you to go over loan options?"

"I've got a few moments right now."

Nat glanced at her watch. Thirty minutes before her Plant Morphology class. She nodded.

Twenty-five minutes later, Nat pushed open the administration building's doors and took off across the quad toward the Science Center. She and the adviser had submitted an application for two low-interest loans totaling three thousand dollars. She hated loans but had no choice. In her bag, she had an application for an additional scholarship for one thousand dollars, which she had a chance of getting. Now she needed to find another job, keep her grades up, and hope something miraculous happened before next semester.

The cavernous library reference room was quiet until Viv pushed through the glass doors. She dropped her bag across from Nat. "I've got some—"

"Just a sec." Nat held up a finger while she finished an equation. She looked up. Viv's hair was no longer moss green but aqua. "When did you do that?" she asked. Her roommate's hair changed color more often than a chameleon.

"Yesterday. We were experimenting with fabric dyes, and I tried some on my hair. I had a shade picked for you if you'd been home at a reasonable hour. You missed out."

"Lucky me."

"Probably, my pillowcase was kind of disgusting this morning. But you wouldn't know that since you were gone when I got up. Where have you been?"

"I took another work-study shift." Nat flipped a page.

"Shh!" A boy with a spiky shock of red hair glared at the pair.

"Shh?" Viv repeated.

"This is a library." His face turned as red as his hair.

"No, you must have missed the memo. This room"—she waved her hand in the air—"is the romper room. You romp in this room. You don't 'shh.' If you want a quiet place to study, find a tidy table on the third floor next to the little boys' room."

He slammed his books shut and shoved them into his bag. "Grow up, freak," he snarled.

"Bathroom's on the third floor!" Viv yelled after him. "Hope you get that problem taken care of!" He blew by the tables and slammed into the door.

"That was unnecessary," Nat said. Her eyes traveled down the room to see who had watched the outburst. A few tables away, Estos leaned back in a chair, the front legs tipped up. Annin shuffled a sheaf of papers across from him. Her mouth moved as if she were talking to herself. Estos set his chair back down and pointed to what looked like a map.

Annin pushed her curly hair away from her face. The eye patch didn't hide her scowl. Nat stared at Estos. He gestured to a corner of the map with his long fingers, his attention focused in front of him.

"Viv, what do you know about those two?" Nat asked in a hushed voice.

"Who?" She turned. "The townie twins?"

"They're not townies, and they're definitely not twins. Impossible."

"Are too. At least townies. They're related to one of the professors in the theater department. I don't know anything about her other than she has a bizarre tattoo on her arm and is channeling an inner pirate. Estos was in my physics class last semester. I switched lab partners so I could watch his angular velocity." She winked at Nat, then curved her lips into a smile. "Are you interested in him?" Her chin jutted forward.

"No," Nat answered defensively. "He's just different."

"Caviar on cheese in a can is different, Nat." Viv rolled her eyes. "Ask him out." She nudged Nat's textbook. "It wouldn't hurt you to pursue a life."

Nat glared at Viv and stuck her face back in her book.

Viv shoved the book gently aside. "Who cares about them? You're making me forget what I wanted to tell you."

"Which is?"

"Okay, good news or bad news first?"

"Bad news."

"Your turtle is dead."

"I can live with that, especially since it isn't or wasn't my turtle." Nat began reading the next page.

"I know, but I can't bring myself to dispose of him. Since you have all that circle-of-life farm-girl experience, will you take care of it?" Viv leaned against the table and inserted her head between the book and Nat.

"Fine." Nat knew the pestering would continue until she gave in. "I'll do it this evening. But you have to do my laundry this week."

"Deal. Maybe you should do it this afternoon, because the aquarium is starting to stink."

"I was wondering what that smell was. What's the good news?"

Viv held out a bright-yellow sticky note. "I was surfing Bloomers and saw your name." Nat snatched the paper from her finger and stared at Viv's scribbling.

"How did this . . . ? I didn't even submit my query."

"The response is for you. How many other Natalie Barnses do you know? I wrote it down word for word." Viv read the note in a deep voice. "'Natalie Barns: See Barba Gate in the costume division of the theater department.' Are you looking for a Halloween costume? I'm offended you didn't come to me first."

"No, I was looking for another job, but I didn't post my search, unless . . ." She looked across the room. Estos and Annin were gone.

"What are you waiting for? Go find"—Viv grabbed the note—"Barba Gate. The costume department could be a sweet job." She handed the note back to Nat. "But you probably want to take care of our turtle first."

CHAPTER FOUR

The door in the bowels of the theater department was slightly ajar. Angry voices erupted from the other side. Nat knocked gently. The voices stopped.

"Come in," a female voice responded in a high, light tone.

Nat pushed the door open and walked around a packed clothing rack. She paused when she saw Estos standing next to a woman with loose red hair who was perched behind a wide white cutting table. She wore a green tunic and held a brown garment in one hand and a needle and thread in the other. She looked vaguely familiar. Estos was leaning toward her, his hands flat against the end of the cutting table. He straightened when he saw Nat. She stared at him for a moment and had a suspicious feeling that his presence was not a coincidence. She cleared her throat.

"I'm looking for Barba Gate," Nat said. "I was told I could find her here." She suddenly remembered where she'd seen the wisp of a woman. She'd been in Nat's theater class at the beginning of the semester when they were working on set design. She'd watched Nat and Butler construct a complicated pyramid set and helped them locate a materials reference book in the small theater library.

"I'm Barba Gate." She placed the fabric on the table and extended a hand. The movement exposed the markings of two entwined green vines on the inside of her right arm. Nat hesitated. She adjusted her books, stepped forward, and shook Barba Gate's hand. Barba held it longer than Nat expected.

"Natalie Barns," Nat said.

"It's a pleasure to see you again."

Nat returned her smile, surprised the woman remembered her.

"I assume you're here about the position?" Barba resumed her work, eyeing Nat between stitches.

"Yes." Nat glanced at Estos, who picked at a chip in the corner of the table. *Did he see my job search query and tell her?* Nat wondered.

Barba turned to Estos as if suddenly remembering he was there. "Estos, let's finish our conversation this evening, with the others."

"I can come back later," Nat said, backing away.

"No." Estos rounded the table. "The Sister and I are done." He paused in front of Nat and regarded her with his pale eyes. "Good luck."

A look of irritation crossed Barba's face when Estos slammed the door behind him. Nat waited. Barba pursed her lips and resumed sewing.

"Professor Gate, I—"

"Just Barba, I'm not a professor. You know my husband, Professor Cairn Gate." Nat nodded. "I have a costume shop in town and help with the costumes and set design when the department needs me."

"Is the job with the theater department?" Nat asked.

"No, it's in my shop. Here, write your name and e-mail on this." She handed Nat a crumpled brown paper sack and motioned to a pen on the table.

"You're a biology major, aren't you?" she asked as Nat wrote her name.

"Yes," Nat said brightly, hoping Barba Gate wasn't wanting a theater major.

"Good. Ethet will appreciate a similar mind. Do you have any skills?"

"Do you mean work experience?" Nat handed her the brown paper, wondering who Ethet was.

Barba examined Nat's signature, then corrected herself. "Yes, work experience."

"I work in the cafeteria." Barba peered at her. Nat moved on quickly. "Before I came to school, I helped my father with his woodworking business, I waitressed, and I had my own business selling eggs and fresh produce." None of that had anything remotely to do with costumes, but Nat was proud of it. She'd made decent money. If Cal had been willing to actually work instead of complain about working, she could've taken over the business and kept it going after Nat left for college. Now, MC delivered the occasional dozen eggs but could handle little more.

"You lived on a farm?" Barba interrupted Nat's thoughts and brought her back to the interview.

"Yes." She nodded.

"How old are you?" Barba took a closer look at Nat.

"Nineteen."

"I assume you are familiar with computers?"

"Yes."

"I've heard you run." Barba wiggled the fingers of her left hand in the air.

"What? Run? Yes, I run." *What does that have to do with anything?* she wondered.

"Can you run far?" Barba placed the brown fabric on the table and smoothed the finished seam with her hand.

"I suppose I can." Nat thought back to the three miles she'd put in before Viv woke up, before classes, before work. It was one of the few things that kept her sane. "Is running part of the job?"

"Not really. Can you sew little things like buttons?" Barba held up a knobby-looking button.

"Yes, of course." Before Barba could begin another barrage of strange questions, Nat continued, "Profes—Mrs. Gate, I'm not exactly sure what the job is. I am quick to learn. But . . ." She paused. "Before I waste both our time, I need something that pays more than the $7.81 I make an hour in the cafeteria." Nat knew the next bit wasn't going to go down well but thought it was better to be honest up front. "And I may also have to study part of the time while I'm working to keep my grades up, so I don't lose my scholarships. If the pay and study requirements don't work for you, I understand." She braced herself for rejection.

"You're honest in your intentions. A refreshing change from some of my previous apprentices." Barba placed the button on the table. "Let me explain the position, and then you can tell me if it will work for you."

"Okay." Nat let out a little sigh of relief.

"Several of my . . . relatives work with me in the shop. Some will be gone during the Halloween rental season. Those who will be there are not the most adept at dealing with customers and computers. I need someone during the busy season to handle front-of-house duties. October and the beginning of November will be very busy. You may not have much time to study at work right now, but you would after early November. I promise to keep you on at the same hours and the same rate of pay after Halloween if everything works out." Barba placed her hands flat on the table. Nat noticed the marking did not extend over her forearm.

"What hours?"

"Assuming you don't have evening classes, I could use you a few weeknights and Saturday. And I would pay you fifteen dollars an hour." She picked up the brown garment and started ripping out a hem.

Nat did not hesitate. "I'll take it." *But I may not sleep between now and mid-November,* she thought.

"Good. Come tomorrow after your classes. Take the bus into town to the last stop on Grand Street. You'll need to walk a few minutes from the bus stop. The shop is at the end of Grand next to a warehouse." Barba drew a crude map on the brown paper and ripped it off. Nat took the paper and waited for a moment.

"Go on, then," Barba said and gestured to the door.

"Thank you," Nat managed to respond as she hurried out the door quickly, hoping the stroke of luck was real.

CHAPTER FIVE

The next day, Nat boarded the old maroon van that served as the college town's bus. It made six lurching stops before reaching the end of Grand Street. She stuffed her Plant Morphology notes into her backpack, jumped off the bus, and unhooked Viv's bike from the bus's bike rack. Viv had agreed to let her borrow the bike as an additional favor in return for her disposing of the dead turtle.

Nat rode down Grand Street parallel to the river until the street curved north toward a limestone cliff. Solid gray clouds spread across the sky. Her cheeks stung slightly in the chill wind as she cycled past car-repair shops and small warehouses. She adjusted the strap of her backpack and scanned the mishmash of buildings along the road. In the distance, she spotted an illuminated oval sign that said "Gate's Costumes" jutting out from a stucco building. The sign blinked erratically, and a tall warehouse loomed behind the building's facade. The backside of the warehouse appeared to be built into the cliff wall. In the shop's large plate-glass window, a zombie playing chess with an angel peered out at her.

A harsh chime rang as she opened the door. The shop smelled of musty clothes.

"Hello?"

No one was behind the glass-case counter. Nat walked past two changing rooms separated by a full-length mirror and display shelves laden with accessories ranging from wigs to glowing red teeth. Row after row of long garment racks, heavy with costumes, filled a room to the right. Another door behind the counter was closed.

"Hello?" she called out again and turned. A mannequin wearing a bear costume, a chef's hat, and a checked apron loomed in a corner of the shop. The mannequin next to it wore leather lace-up boots, leggings, a belt, a sword sheath, and a sand-colored tunic trimmed with a vine pattern.

"Do you need something?" the mannequin in the tunic said.

Nat jumped. "You startled me! I thought you were just a dummy dressed up." She laughed but stopped when she saw the man's expression. A neatly trimmed beard and mustache surrounded his frown, and his blond hair was slick with sweat.

"Natalie." Estos popped his head from behind an open door. He turned to the man. "Andris, this is Natalie, the woman Sister Barba hired."

Andris wiped his brow. "Another mistake." He turned and stepped into the room with the costume racks. "You have thirty minutes, Estos." A door slammed shut in the distance.

"Don't mind him," Estos said. His cheeks were red, and the front of his shirt was drenched with sweat.

"I see what your sister meant about needing a little help with customer service." Nat tilted her chin in the direction Andris had disappeared.

"My sister?" The flush drained from his face.

"Mrs. Gate. You called her your sister," Nat said quickly, sensing she'd said something very wrong.

"No, she's not my sister. She's my aunt. Where we come from we call some women 'Sister.' Like Sister Barba. It doesn't mean she is my actual sister." Estos took Nat's backpack from her hand and carried it behind the counter.

"Where are you from?"

"Canada." He shuffled a few papers on the counter.

"Canada? Really?" She leaned against the glass top of the counter and tried not to stare into his eyes. "Not what I would have guessed."

"It's a big country." Estos shrugged. "Barba's tied up right now. She asked me to show you around."

As Estos began explaining the rental system, Nat pulled out a green spiral notebook and started scribbling.

He paused. "What are you writing?"

"What you're telling me."

"Why?"

"So I don't forget and have to ask someone."

"I always ask, at least two or three times a day," a deep voice boomed behind Nat. She turned. The squarest-looking person she'd even seen stood in the doorway leading to the room with the costume racks. His head was as bald as a plastic block and nearly the same shape. He wore a loose brown shirt embroidered with a vine, a bird, a sun, and a sword. The vine was the same pattern she'd seen on the inside of Barba's arm.

"Natalie, Oberfisk." Estos gestured between them.

The stocky man took a step forward and enveloped Nat's hand with his, his meaty fingers squeezing tightly. "Nice to meet you." His smile was wide and warm.

"You, too," she said, returning the smile.

"Oberfisk will help you when you're busy up here." Estos pointed to the empty shop.

Oberfisk continued to grin. "Come with me, Ms. Natalie. I'll give you the tour." He extended a thick arm. Nat hesitated, then placed her hand in the crook of his arm. "Estos, you're needed in the back." He nodded to Estos and his grin disappeared.

Estos vanished through the doorway without another word. Nat remembered Barba's comments. Maybe the entire family, including Estos, were lacking in social graces.

The front door chimed. A short woman holding a gnome costume entered the shop.

"Perfect," Oberfisk said, dropping Nat's arm and rubbing his hands together. "Watch me run through this one, and then you can do the next on your own." She followed Oberfisk around the counter. He limped slightly. Nat watched and scribbled more notes in her notebook as he accepted the costume return.

"Clear?" Oberfisk asked after the woman departed.

"Clear as mud," Nat responded, smiling. Oberfisk's face fell. "No, it really is clear. I've got it." Nat tapped the notebook.

"All right, then," Oberfisk said, looking relieved. "Let's move on. The room to your right has all the costumes." He limped to the doorway. Rows of costumes greeted Nat when she peeked through the entrance. She ran her hands over the gaudy fabrics as they walked past.

"It's all alphabetical." He pointed to the crudely laminated paper hanging from the end of each rack. A sign with a thick black *P* hung from one rack. "That's the pirate rack. Needed a whole row for them. Never understood the allure myself." He rubbed his bald chin. "*Q* through *Z*"—he pointed to the remaining rows—"ending with some fellow named 'Zorro.'"

Nat pulled a fake foil from a Zorro costume and flicked her wrist, making a *Z* in the air.

"Why does everyone do that?" Oberfisk asked.

She dropped her hand and blushed. Oberfisk continued in his booming voice. "This door leads to the laundry room behind the counter." He pointed to a door across from the row of pirate costumes. "And that door"—he gestured to a thick metal one at the back of the room— "leads to the workshop where Professor Gate and his assistants work on sets and special costumes for productions and such. The rest of the area back there is basically our house. If I'm not out here and you ever need any help, just ring the bell under the counter or knock on that back door. Someone is always on guard. No reason for you to come busting through there." He laughed nervously.

"On guard?" Nat asked, wondering why they needed a guard.

"Well, er, Sister Barba and Sister Ethet are a little protective of their costumes and sets," Oberfisk responded before turning toward the front of the shop.

That was the second time Nat had heard the name Ethet. The fact that they guarded their costumes was a little weird, but Nat could put up with a little weirdness for fifteen dollars an hour. The door chime interrupted her thoughts. She hurried to catch up with Oberfisk.

CHAPTER SIX

As Halloween approached, customers streamed in and out of the store, reserving and picking up costumes and buying accessories. The moment Nat passed through the shop's door, it was a flurry of pulling costumes, writing rental tickets, ringing sales, and mending anything that needed mending. If she was lucky, Oberfisk would be behind the counter to greet her with a cheerful "Huya," load her down with pull orders or mending, and send her into the back room with a slap on the shoulder. She'd slip on her earphones and replay a lecture while she pulled costumes, or she'd reread class notes while she mended, washed, and ironed.

The timing on other days was not so opportune. Three times she arrived to find Andris lurking near the door to the costume room. He would glare at her with his mud-green eyes for a few minutes and then disappear, leaving her to handle the store on her own.

On her first Saturday at work, Cairn—Professor Gate had told Nat to please call him by his first name—walked in laden with bags from a local drugstore. An even taller silver-haired woman was close on his heels. Nat recognized the angular woman with ebony skin immediately. She'd been introduced as a visiting professor during Nat's freshman chemistry class and had observed a handful of Nat's labs, including one where Nat had substituted for an absent teaching assistant. The lab was one Nat had conducted during high school and was simple enough to teach, but the woman had grilled her after class, questioning her on every detail of the experiment. After the barrage of questions, Nat had steered clear of the woman.

"Another trip to the greenhouse should provide all we need. At least, all I can get here," the woman said as Cairn held open the front door. She paused and looked at Nat with her round brown eyes behind half-moon glasses. Nat felt like she was standing in the principal's office. The woman kept her keen eyes on her as Cairn fumbled with his bags and shut the door.

"Natalie, this is Ethet Nightswain." He gestured to the woman, who gave Nat a slight nod of acknowledgment. Nat noticed a small sun pattern on Ethet's inner arm when she reached to relieve Cairn of a bag he was about to drop.

"Do you need help?" Nat asked, but Ethet and Cairn were already out of earshot. Nat heard the metal door to the workshop area slam shut.

The faces of Barba's relatives became more familiar as the month passed. Besides Barba, Cairn, Ethet, Estos, Andris, and Oberfisk, Nat knew that at least two other men, Kroner and Riler, lived or worked in the back. They would quietly leave the store with Cairn or Barba and then return with groceries or other supplies.

One afternoon, as the sky was beginning to darken, Estos walked into the shop from the costume room. A puffy red welt encircled his right eye, and he favored his right leg as he rounded the counter.

"Oberfisk, Andris is ready for you," he said in a strained voice.

Oberfisk took off the reading spectacles he used when he rang up tickets. "Fine, then. And I'll remind him to go a little lighter next round." Oberfisk gestured to Estos' leg.

Estos laughed. "Do you think Mudug or the Nala will go easy on me, Oberfisk?"

"It's not going to do any of us good if you go in injured." He glanced at Nat, crossed the room, and was out the door before Estos could reply.

"Go in where?" Nat snipped the end of a thread she'd used to sew up a small hole in a raccoon costume.

"Martial-arts competitions." His pale eyes darted from her to the door and then to the counter.

He was lying. She set down the raccoon costume she was brushing. Estos' back was to her as he mindlessly scrolled through costume orders on the computer.

"Do all of you compete?"

"In some form or another."

"Is that what you do back there in the warehouse? Train for competitions? I thought it was for Cairn's sets."

"We use the warehouse for a lot of things." Estos faced her. "Andris likes creative anachronism and period fighting. He trains us in sword fighting, close combat. We use some of the space for that kind of thing." He turned back around, punched the keyboard, and printed a list. "Barba wants these costumes pulled and ready for tomorrow." He stepped aside, allowing her to go ahead of him. "Lady before the limp."

Nat shook her head and slid off her stool. She crossed in front of Estos just as he took a step. His leg buckled, sending him stumbling into her. She grasped him around the waist. He grimaced and pressed his hands against the counter.

"You can let go, Natalie," he said, looking down at her arms. She dropped her hands and hustled into the costume room before he could see her cheeks burning.

Estos limped behind her. "Let's see, one Zorro and two medium zombies." He started down the row, holding the list.

Even though she knew he'd lied, Nat felt some sympathy for his physical state and put a hand on his shoulder to stop him.

"You tag, I'll retrieve." She squeezed down the narrow row, pulled the three costumes from the tight rack, and hung them on an empty rack by the door. "What's next?"

"Large umpire and a transient."

She worked her way down the next packed aisle. "Is Annin at a competition?" She held the umpire costume. *Is he going to lie again?* she wondered. "I haven't seen her here or in class for weeks."

"No. She had to go back to Canada to care for an ill Sister. She should be back soon." He glanced toward the door at the back of the room. The scar below his ear stretched thin and pink.

Canada. Martial-arts competitions. Creative anachronism. She hung up the costumes and dusted off her hands. "How does she pass if she misses so many classes?"

Estos studied the list and answered without looking at her. "Sometimes she watches a podcast of the class. But she usually doesn't take her classes for a grade. Medium tarantula, small taco."

She pushed her way down the next aisle and flipped through the hangers.

"Do you like working here, Nat?" Estos asked.

The question surprised her. "Sure."

"I know we're a bit different." He sounded apologetic.

She hung up the taco and held out the tarantula costume for Estos to hang on the next rack.

He stepped back, holding up his hands. "I'm not much for spiders."

"Come on, Estos, spiders? They eat insects and are easy to kill." She dangled the costume in front of him.

"Not where I come from."

"One of these days when I'm not working two jobs and going to school, I'd like to visit where you're from. Weird accents, big spiders. Sounds like paradise." She hung the tarantula costume on the rack.

"What's next?" She waited for a response. "What's the look for?" He had a funny expression on his face.

He smiled. "I was just imagining you in my home country."

"I've been to Canada before. I hate to burst your bubble, but it's not that different from here." She leaned against the end of the costume rack. "Where exactly in Canada are you from?"

"North."

"North, that's pretty specific." She rolled her eyes.

"You wouldn't recognize the name," Estos countered. He shoved costumes to the side, the hangers grinding against the rack. "My home is beautiful. Like nothing you've ever seen." He gave Nat a challenging look. Her lips parted, but something about his expression stopped her from saying anything. He dropped his head, his voice breaking. "Some nights I dream that I'm home, and I can hear the horns from the trading boats, the bells of the Wisdom House, and my sister Emilia calling me to come in from practice." He brushed his hand across his eyes.

Nat looked away, toward the massive metal door. After a moment, she took the list from him and made her way down an aisle. "Is Emilia your sister? Or a sister like Barba?" she asked, trying to keep the interest out of her voice. She knew he wasn't lying to her about his home this time.

"Emilia is my sister." He cleared his throat.

"Does she still live in Canada?"

"No, she moved on," he said in a cheerless tone. He limped down the aisle and yanked another costume off a rack. They worked side by side in silence. When all the costumes were pulled, Estos asked if she could watch the front by herself.

"Of course." She leaned against one of the racks, watching him limp toward the metal door. He paused with his hand on the worn knob.

"You would like my home, I think," he said with his back to her. The door clanked shut behind him.

CHAPTER SEVEN

"Nat! Wake up! Get up *now*! You have a midterm in thirty minutes!" Viv hung over her, a halo of magenta hair surrounding her face like a cloud of cotton candy.

"What!" Nat sat upright in her chair and scanned the room for Viv's creepy cat clock. It grinned at her. "Nine thirty! Why didn't you wake me earlier?" she yelled at Viv and scrambled up.

"I just got back from breakfast. You were still sleeping at your desk when I left, and I didn't want to wake you since you were up so late. I figured you'd be up and gone by now." Viv grabbed a granola bar and rummaged in the minifridge for an energy drink. She flipped the tab and shoved the drink into Nat's hand. "You didn't get back from wherever you were until midnight. Here." She placed the unwrapped granola bar in Nat's other hand. "Rally, zombie girl. If you fail this one and lose your scholarships, I'll have to find a new roommate when you get kicked out." She tossed Nat a sweatshirt. "It took me too long to break you in to have to go through that again."

"Thanks for the words of encouragement." Nat clipped back her hair while shoving her feet into a worn pair of sneakers.

"Don't mention it. Seriously, though, after you get through this exam, maybe you need to rethink your work-life balance. I've hardly seen you this month except when you're drooling on your pillow—or your desk." Viv handed Nat her backpack.

Nat quickly riffled through its contents, then swung it over her shoulder. "Don't have much choice right now," she said, her mouth full of granola bar. She zipped up her blue plaid coat. "They can kick me out just as easily for not paying the rest of my tuition. I've got this exam down. Don't worry."

"Yeah, I'm worrying. Don't forget, you're coming home with me for the weekend."

Nat stopped with her hand on the doorknob. "Viv, I'm sorry, but I've got to work tonight, tomorrow, and this whole weekend."

"All right, fine." Viv blew the bangs from her face with an exasperated breath. "I knew you were going to bail on me. Bad news for you is I'm taking my bike back to get the gear fixed. Get going." She pointed to the door.

Nat nodded and headed out the door. A burst of cold wind stung her skin and pushed her slightly to the side as she left the dorm building. She pulled up the collar of her coat, then shoved her bare hands into the fleece pockets. The weather woke her up quickly. She hastened through the quad to the thick glass doors of the Science Center. She paused while looking at the reflection of a hollow-eyed girl clutching the neck of her coat. She could sleep later. Now she needed to push everything but this exam out of her mind, including the late-tuition notice she'd received in her mailbox yesterday. Her cheeks puffed out as she exhaled and opened the door. *Let's go nail this and move on,* she thought.

Two customers were waiting with returns when Nat rushed into the shop, her head pounding. She felt like little fingers were digging into her forehead. She brushed the light snow off her shoulders while averting her eyes from the bright fluorescent light that hung from the ceiling. Andris stormed in from the costume room.

"You were supposed to be here fifteen minutes ago," he growled.

Her cheeks burned. "I told Estos I would be late. I had to walk from the bus stop."

Andris ignored her excuse, dumped a load of costumes in her arms, and stormed off.

"I'll be with you in just a minute," Nat said over the pile to a young couple holding two matching starfish costumes. She dropped the load on the worktable and shoved her coat and bag under the counter. The back door in the costume room slammed shut. *Good riddance,* she thought. She'd rather work alone with her head about to explode than be subjected to Andris' icy glares and guttural responses.

A few more customers trickled in with costumes to return. She accepted them with as little interaction as possible. The headache was unrelenting. She dug through her bag, found an old bottle of painkillers, and swallowed two pills dry. They stuck in her throat, sending her into a coughing fit.

When the store quieted, Nat reluctantly turned her attention to the packed return rack. She replayed the morning's exam in her mind as she halfheartedly checked the costumes for stains. Five questions with two lab experiments. She knew she'd failed at least one of the labs by mistakenly using vinegar to distill the plant oil from the unidentified leaf she'd been given. The vinegar corroded the sample and caused the lab to reek like a pickling plant. How could she have made such a rookie mistake? If she received anything below a B on the midterm, she'd have no room to breathe for the rest of the semester. She had to maintain an A to keep her scholarships.

She sat back, surveying the heap of costumes, and sighed. Thanksgiving break was coming. The thought of going home brought her headache surging forward. Her family was a train wreck right now, and there was not a single thing she could do about it. She couldn't heal her dad or meet any of his work orders. The last time she'd tried his lathe, she'd nearly lost her thumb. Conversations with Cal led to nothing but arguments. Her mom was already on her about how she was treating her sister. Nat fumed. Her mom was blind to how Cal manipulated her and wheedled her way out of any responsibility or chore. She couldn't help herself. Someone had to get her to step up.

Nat laid her head on the counter and considered her options. The best thing for her and her family would be if she stayed on campus over break and tried to catch up on her studies. She gazed absentmindedly at the front door as she imagined her mom's reaction to her not coming home. Splatters of snow covered the gold lettering painted onto the glass. The chime sounded, and Nat jerked awake. She feigned a cough to suppress a yawn as the customer walked into the store. Snow blew in, leaving a light cover on the doormat.

At seven p.m., Nat locked the front door and flipped the "Open" sign to "Closed." She pressed her face against the glass. She was so tired. The glass fogged around her face. The sky was already dark, but she could see heavy snow whipping against the door. If she left now, she would have to wait for the seven forty-five bus in the snow. *I may as well get through more of this pile before I go,* she thought.

Nat separated the costumes that needed washing or dry cleaning, started a load of laundry, and began returning other costumes to their racks. She glanced at the back door of the costume room and remembered Andris' tantrum. Hopefully someone other than Andris would come to lock the shop behind her as usual.

At seven twenty-five, she pushed the button under the counter and waited near the back door. The knob remained motionless. She glanced at her watch. She was going to have to run to catch the bus. A thin line of light shone underneath the door. Her knock was soft at first but then grew louder. She tried the knob and to her surprise it turned.

The door opened, revealing an empty hallway. The unadorned walls led to the most intricately carved doors she'd ever seen. Thick and made of dark wood, they stood like sentinels at the end of the hall. Carvings of vines, swords, birds, and suns covered their surface, and the handles were shaped like enormous flowers with their petals curved back. She could barely close her fingers around the handles, but they turned easily. She stepped into a foyer with a stairwell at one end and a smaller open door covered with entwined vines at the other end. The smell of rosemary and roast meat filled the room. Nat's mouth began to water.

"What are you doing here?" Andris appeared in the doorway. A thin shirt of chain mail covered his broad torso, and a sword at least a yard long hung from a thick leather belt strapped tightly around his waist. The vein in his neck bulged. Nat took a step back.

"It's time to close up the shop. I need to go home."

"Go, then!"

"Someone needs to lock up after me."

"You came back here to tell me that?"

Nat bit her lip and took a deep breath. "I'm leaving to catch my bus. Do what you want with the shop." She slammed the metal door to the costume room on her way out. She pulled her coat from under the counter. The door chimed dully as she burst out of the store with an arm in only one sleeve of her coat. Snow pelted her skin, and the cold brought her back to her senses a little as the anger faded.

"Stupid Nat," she muttered, pulling her coat tight. "That's going to get you fired." She trudged through a thick blanket of snow covering the sidewalk, cursing herself. Work, school, her family—it was all too much. Maybe she should take next semester off and work full-time. She could get a job at the restaurant back home where she waitressed in the evenings during the summer. She'd always been able to pick up odd jobs, and she could help her dad with his woodworking business and the farm. If she could keep her scholarships, she'd have enough money saved up by next year to come back and not stress so much.

The street was deserted as she continued her trek toward the bus stop. The streetlights gave off a foggy glow, and she slowed momentarily as she passed underneath them. The road and sidewalk were now indistinguishable. She pushed back her coat sleeve and checked her watch. 7:40. She quickened her pace and then broke into a run. Her sneakers were already soaking wet, and her feet were more than cold. If she missed this bus, it would be a long, nasty climb to campus.

Andris opened the door and watched Nat disappear into the storm. He turned and surveyed the quiet storefront, a line of worry set deep in his forehead.

"Andris, I heard yelling. What's going on?" Estos emerged from the costume room.

"The girl came into the back. She almost made it into the kitchen before I caught her sneaking around. She won't return after tonight. We're better off without her around. It was foolish for you and Barba to hire her and bring her so close to the entrance. We've got enough problems on our hands without having to worry about that one."

"What do you mean she won't return?" Estos asked.

"She doesn't seem to like my manner. She bolted into that storm like it was a spring day on the banks of the Rust River." Andris smiled as he scratched his blond beard.

"You let her leave on foot in this weather?" Estos looked out the window. White flakes splattered the glass.

"She mentioned a bus."

"She's not going to catch it. Everything is shut down because of the storm." Estos pulled a heavy felt cape off a mannequin and opened the door. "Lock up behind me, we'll come around to the side entrance."

"We?" Andris asked, looking at Estos as if he'd just gone mad.

"And tell Ethet and Barba that we are having company for dinner," Estos called out.

Nat brushed snow off her watch. The bus was late. She shifted her weight from foot to foot. The road was a smooth layer of white. She looked through the falling snow to the Italian restaurant across the street. A "Closed" sign hung crookedly in its dark window. She straightened as she saw a pair of headlights in the distance. The vehicle slowly turned onto a side street. She shoved her hands deeper into her pockets. Viv was gone, and none of her other friends had cars that could handle this road. Calling anyone was pointless. She had just decided to walk downtown when she heard her name.

"Natalie!" The snow and dark obscured Estos until he was right below the halogen glow of the streetlight by the bus stop.

She squinted into the snow. "What are you wearing?"

Estos pushed back the hood and held up a snow-covered panel of his cape to examine it. "I think it's from the Robin Hood costume. I was in a rush to catch you. Come on, this weather is getting worse." He grabbed her arm and started to pull her back the way he came. Nat resisted and Estos let go.

"I'll find a ride back to campus."

"No, you won't. Not in this."

"Yes, I will. It's not that far to town." She wiped snow off her eyelashes so she could see better.

"I'm not trying to be difficult, Natalie, but they shut down the hill road. If you haven't noticed, nothing is moving in this. Please come back with me. We have plenty of room for you to stay, and dinner is on." He held out his hand. Snow plastered his hair. She looked through the swirling storm, down the dimly lit street toward downtown, then back at Estos.

"You win." She sighed. "I'm so tired right now, I don't even know if I could make it downtown. I'm not sitting next to Andris at the dinner table, though." She gave Estos a sideways look, hoping he'd take it as humor and not offense.

"Fair enough." They walked a few moments, then Estos added, "Don't take Andris' behavior personally. He's stressed and preoccupied right now."

Nat held her tongue. Andris must always be stressed and preoccupied.

They walked silently through the snow past the car-repair shops and auto-parts stores until the outline of the costume shop came into view. She slowed as they reached the entrance, but Estos took her hand, gently this time.

"There's another entrance around the side. It's not much farther." They walked along the warehouse wall. Flurries of snow fell in waves from the gutters high above them. Nat heard a faint humming. When they reached the far corner of the warehouse, Estos pulled her round to a small door. The snowdrifts were knee high. Nat wiggled her toes, trying to regain some sensation in her frozen feet. Estos quickly punched buttons on a keypad and spoke into a snow-covered intercom. The door clicked, and the two stepped inside.

They walked into a dark, cramped room that smelled faintly of pine. The humming sound grew louder. Estos leaned toward another door and spoke again into a screen. The door clicked, and they proceeded up a set of enclosed metal stairs, which led to a high narrow walkway made of metal grates. Snow melted off of Nat's shoes and dripped between the slats. She looked over the railing and stopped. The tips of thick evergreens touched the edge of the walkway. Half of the warehouse was filled with towering trees. Skinny, faceless blue dummies floated above them, suspended from the ceiling of the warehouse. At the other end of the building, she saw a small greenhouse and neat rows of plants. Fiber-optic cables coiled down from the ceiling to the roof of the shed. A patch of dirt was adjacent to the garden and greenhouse. Long spears, swords, clubs, and other weapons lined the wall in the corner.

"Come on, Natalie," Estos beckoned from farther down the walkway.

"What is this place?" She reached out and touched the tip of a pine tree, rolling a needle between her fingers.

"Think of it as one big movie set." Estos grinned in the wan light. An open door greeted them at the end of the walkway. Estos closed the door and moved swiftly past Nat down another set of stairs, his boots thudding against the metal. When she reached the bottom of the stairs, she realized she was on the other side of the second carved door Andris had come through earlier in the evening.

After a few more steps, they entered a galley-style kitchen. Oberfisk and the tall, muscular man named Kroner sat at a long wooden table next to Barba. Cairn was hunched over a sink, steam encircling his long arms. Pots, pans, and dried herbs hung from ceiling racks above the table. Oberfisk stood quickly, knocking over his stool and barely missing bashing his head on a low-hanging pot.

"Bit foolish going out in the weather without letting us know, Estos," he chided as he took Nat by the elbow. He pulled out a chair. Nat sat directly across from Barba.

"I let Andris know," Estos replied coolly.

"Cairn, would you get the girl a plate? She looks like a starved, wet rat." Oberfisk accepted a plate from Cairn and plopped it in front of Nat. "No offense meant." He smiled down at her, the kitchen lights reflecting off his bald head.

"None taken." Nat inhaled the rich smell of roast beef and mashed potatoes covered in gravy.

"You can get your own." Oberfisk pointed to Estos and then sat down with a thud. Estos loaded his plate, and he and Cairn joined the four already sitting at the table. Barba leaned forward slightly with her arms crossed. Her eyes never left Estos. Nat glanced at him as he shoved a forkful of potatoes into his mouth. No one said a word.

After a few minutes of silence, Nat said, "Thank you for the dinner, Professor Gate, Mrs. Gate. I don't mean to impose on you like this." She twisted her napkin underneath the table.

"Don't give it a thought," Oberfisk answered. "It's our fault we kept you late during such a bad storm. We were just a bit busy back here and forgot all about the store. Guess that's why we hired you, isn't it?" He chuckled, looked at Barba, and clammed up.

They continued to eat in silence until Estos got up for a second serving. Nat wondered if Oberfisk was the one person in the group designated to speak until Barba suddenly spoke up.

"Estos, show Natalie to the spare room upstairs. She's exhausted, and we all have matters that we must attend to." Barba gave Nat a gentle smile, which disappeared when she turned to Estos.

"Please don't." Nat held up her hand. She'd broken some strange taboo by merely sitting at the table with this group. "I can walk downtown and catch a ride up to campus." She stood and slung her sopping wet bag over her shoulder. "Estos, if you would just show me out, I'll be on my way."

Barba rounded the table. In one fluid movement, she took Nat's bag off her shoulder. "Don't be ridiculous, come with me."

Nat looked back at Estos, unsure what to do. He nodded encouragingly toward Barba. Nat reluctantly followed her out of the kitchen. Wisps of red hair had come loose from the tight bun high on Barba's head. Nat thought she looked like a petite lion. They walked through the room where Andris had yelled at Nat.

"I have seen too many students in my time not to recognize when you're about to fall down from exhaustion," Barba said as they reached the base of a staircase. Nat thought Barba didn't know the half of it but nodded in quiet agreement. The stairs creaked slightly underfoot. She doubted she would be able to sneak back down without anyone hearing.

"Sleep here tonight," Barba said as she flicked on the light in the last room at the end of the long hallway. The room contained a dark-blue chair, an ottoman, a small daybed covered in a down comforter, and a tall wardrobe. On the wall next to the single window hung a painting of hills swathed in golden-yellow flowers.

"The bathroom is across the hall." She placed Nat's bag by the door. "Estos will come get you in the morning. Have open dreams, Natalie." "Thank you." The door clicked shut. Nat kicked off her wet shoes and lay on the bed, staring at the painting. Her eyelids drooped, and she was soon asleep, dreaming of golden fields.

CHAPTER EIGHT

"It was premature to have brought her here, Estos," Barba scolded the young man. Oberfisk and Kroner stomped down the hallway in front of them.

"Tell me when the time would be right, Sister? We're running out of options. You've been assessing her for more than a year. How much longer do you need to watch her? She's mentally strong, physically capable, and meets all your other criteria," Estos replied, his tone full of exasperation.

Oberfisk and Kroner halted in front of a door emblazoned with carvings of a vine, sword, bird, and sun.

"She can be on her way tomorrow knowing nothing if you prefer." Estos tilted his head, listening to the muffled voices on the other side of the door. "When did they get back?" he asked.

"Shortly after you left to get Natalie," Oberfisk replied. "Couldn't really mention it with her in the room." He and Kroner grabbed the door handles. "After you." They bowed slightly as Estos stepped across the threshold into Ethet's laboratory.

"Two weeks, and you couldn't deliver a simple message?" Andris was stomping back and forth in front of an opening to a rough limestone corridor in the corner of the bright room. Ethet and Annin were bent over Riler, who lay on a narrow table opposite Andris, moaning in pain.

"They were tracking me, you dolt," Annin said. "What did you want me to do, lead them straight to your brother and the rebels? They knew Riler was through, too." She pointed at Riler, and the blue skin on her arm rippled under the light. "They're tracking all of us." Annin's wild hair flew in all directions. She stopped when she saw Estos. He brought his hand to her cheek.

"It's good to see you," Estos said. A look of relief washed over his face. Her blue eye glittered like shattered glass. The patch over her other eye hung crookedly.

"I tried, Estos. I'm sorry."

"It's okay. At least you're back safe," Estos said. Oberfisk cleared his throat, and Estos dropped his hand.

"How were you able to stay two weeks, yet Riler was attacked after just half a day?" Andris stepped in front of Estos. Spittle from his mouth landed on Annin's cheek. She wiped it away and gave him a murderous look.

"I assume it's because I am, as you're always reminding me, a 'duozi.' We're harder to track than you." She shoved him slightly aside and grabbed a glass-stoppered vial from a high wooden rack.

"The Nala and Mudug's men have been a day behind me ever since I crossed over. I've spent the last two weeks trying to find your brother or the Northern Warrior Sisters. Get out of my way." She pushed past Andris again and stood next to Ethet. Andris clenched his fists, and Estos moved protectively between him and Annin.

Ethet dropped the scissors and pulled layers of blood-stained fabric away from Riler's thigh. She inspected the long gash and took the now unstoppered vial from Annin's hand. The wound sizzled slightly as the clear liquid fell from the vial onto Riler's ragged piece of skin. He arched his back and groaned.

Ethet leaned over the wound and sniffed. "It's clean." His body relaxed, and everyone in the room except her and Annin let out a collective breath.

"Annin, mallow salve and threaded needle. Have the bandages ready." Ethet gently inspected the rest of Riler.

Estos pulled up a stool while Ethet irrigated, then sutured the wound. "Tell us what happened," he said calmly. He laid a hand on Riler. "Annin, you first."

"I waited in the portal before I crossed over. Nothing was in the forest when I made it through." She had an odd look in her human eye.

Barba interrupted. "Did the membrane push back?"

"Not when I was leaving. I was caught coming back. I had Riler past the barrier, but it took me more than a minute to pull myself through." Annin turned her attention to Riler's thigh. Ethet brought the curved needle up in tight, efficient strokes, securing and cutting each suture before starting another.

"Did anyone see you?" Estos asked.

"No." Annin kept her head down, swabbing the wound lightly as Ethet worked. "At least I don't think so." Her voice held some hesitation.

"Go back to the beginning," Barba demanded.

"I traveled northeast out of the forest along the edge of the Meldon Plain."

"In the opposite direction of where we told you to go." Andris looked up at the ceiling and pulled his beard. "Why didn't you go straight to Benedict's house?" His face was a shade redder than normal. Estos looked at his friend and held up a cautioning hand.

"You told me to go to the Hermit's house, Andris—no one else did," Annin shot back as she scowled at the soldier. "I'd never go near that rat traitor. He'd turn me over to the Nala faster than Mudug's men."

"You and your imaginary conspiracies cost us time and almost cost us Riler." Andris placed one hand on the rough limestone archway and gestured to Riler with the other. "He went in to find you and do the job you should have done weeks ago," he said accusingly, narrowing his eyes and twisting his mouth.

"The rebellion will not hold if they think Estos is dead. It's been almost a year since Oberfisk delivered the last message for Benedict, and we don't even know if that made it to the right hands. I knew from the beginning it was a mistake to send in a duozi. No one would have believed a word you said, even if you had managed to pass the message on. We've wasted all this time!" Andris kicked a small waste bin. The metal clanged as it hit the limestone.

"Enough!" Estos shouted. The room fell silent. "Annin, you said they were tracking us. What do you mean?"

Ignoring Estos' question, Annin ripped the patch from her face. An eye like a faceted silver disc focused on Andris. He instinctively stepped back.

"Annin," Estos said, impatiently.

Annin glared at Andris a moment longer, then responded to Estos, "Do you remember when Oberfisk tried to go through about nine months ago?"

"Do I!" Oberfisk exclaimed from the corner. "Nearly got my head pinioned to a tree by Mudug's lackeys when I came out on the Meldon Plain." He patted the side of his head.

Annin nodded. "And Barba and Kroner, similar thing. When they tried last year, they were attacked by the Nala." Barba and Kroner nodded, looking grave.

"We all know this," Andris said grimly. He addressed Estos. "Just let me go in, Estos. I can find my brother and ensure the rebels are ready for your return."

"You'd be dead before you reached Daub Town, not that it would be much of a loss in your case." Annin's voice was vicious.

Andris opened his mouth to speak.

"Let her finish," Estos said, again holding up his hand.

"Two days after I passed through, I knew someone was following me. At first I suspected it was the Nala, but then I had a run-in with one of Mudug's men when I was traveling north looking for any fringe Sisters." She paused and glanced at Barba. "He ambushed me, but he was alone and easy enough to take down."

Andris scoffed.

"You forget what happens when I'm in Fourline. I don't need her potions to keep me strong." She gestured to Ethet.

"Annin, what happened after the attack?" Barba asked.

"I did a dream-speak and learned he was tracking me, receiving messages about my movements. He was under orders to kill me, to kill all of us."

Silence settled over the room.

Barba and Ethet exchanged glances. "Did you see any signs of the Sisters, Annin? Any healers?" Ethet asked.

"No," Annin replied softly. "Perhaps they are afraid to openly help but are healing in other ways."

"We must touch to heal." Ethet sighed, finished her last suture, and cut the thread. "No, they are either dead or so frightened that they refuse to use what they know. Healing House was never known for its courage or strength like the Warrior House. I'm afraid the Sisters and their knowledge have faded over the years we've been here."

"Did you find the rebels?" Oberfisk asked, turning the topic away from Ethet's sad musings.

"Just a ragged band of sixteen men living north of the mines. I dream-spoke one of them from a distance." Annin smiled broadly.

"Really? How far away?" Estos asked, leaning in to listen to his friend.

"Far enough not to spook their horses. The band was planning an attack on a small section of a mine in a few days' time. Mudug was mining something odd—not copper, something else. The men were trying to stop the mine's operations. I couldn't confirm if the men were with

Andris' brother Gennes, but I sensed they were. The one I dream-spoke was well trained, and it took all I could do to get him to open up about their plans. I left him with the impression you were well, Estos."

"That should take care of it," Andris scoffed. "I'm sure my brother will find great comfort in a grunt telling him he knows that King Estos is alive because some duozi told him in a dream-speak."

Annin gripped the edge of the table.

"Andris, no more interruptions," Estos said in a calm but commanding tone. He gestured for Annin to continue.

"I moved south, trying to outpace whatever was tracking me," Annin said. "But Mudug's men caught up with me between Rustbrook and Daub Town. Barba, do you remember where we saw the meeting between Mudug's emissary and the Nala?"

"It's a night not to forget, Annin."

"I fell asleep on the hill above that farmer's house and woke early. A pack of Nala and Mudug's men were riding past the farm. I could barely make out the riders, but I sensed at least five Nala. I took off toward the Meldon Plain and stopped after a few miles near the edge of it to keep watch, then I made my way back to the portal by following the last section of the path. That's when I found Riler and two of Mudug's men."

Riler turned his head to the right. Bits of dried leaf still clung to his beard. He took up the story.

"I stayed in the portal for a bit and came out right as the sun was coming up." Ethet taped a gauze pad over his wound. Riler winced. "I could hear the birds and figured that was as good a sign as any that none of the Nala were around. I never saw any Nala, but I got ambushed about halfway to the Hermit's house by two of Mudug's guards."

"You let two of them take you down?" Oberfisk's face soured.

"I'm not proud of it, Oberfisk," Riler replied sharply. "But I did break one guard's arm and left a nasty gash on the other's face. I thought at first they meant to do me in right there, but they argued with one another about bringing me back to the capital. They even knew my name. One kept referring to me as 'the traitor Riler' while he trussed my arms."

Ethet gently pushed Riler back down on the cot. "Settle down, Riler, you'll undo all my work," she said.

Riler let out a slow breath. "I heard Annin's birdcall when they were leading me to the edge of the forest. So I pretended to trip, and she fell out of the tree and knocked out one of them. I managed a good kick to the one with a broken arm, and he went down like a sack of bricks. Passed out cold." Riler smiled.

"We pulled them off the path." Annin resumed the story. "I dream-spoke the one with a broken arm. He knew each and every one of us. But they knew Riler and I were near the Meldon Plain."

"How is that possible?" Andris asked. Estos shook his head and let the interruption pass.

"It was the same with Mudug's other guard. They were receiving messages about our location somehow." Annin paused for a moment and looked down the tunnel beyond the limestone archway. "They knew a general region to look, but not a specific place. I guess that's one thing to be thankful for." She glanced at Riler. He gave her an uncomfortable look. "What?" she asked.

"Nothing." He turned away. "All right, it's the eye. Gives me the shivers. Could you cover it up?"

Annin pulled the patch over her disc of an eye. "Don't worry, Riler, I don't bite like the Nala." She smiled.

"Annin, that's enough," Ethet scolded her apprentice.

Annin shrugged and continued. "Anyway, I tried to confuse both soldiers so they'd forget what had happened. Riler and I traveled as quickly as we could down the path and waited just long enough to know we weren't being watched before we came back through." She sat back on the stool, leaning against the long table behind her.

Other than a slight pulsating hum, the room was quiet. Barba and Estos walked to the entrance of the tunnel and stood next to Andris.

"We have a problem," Barba said as she stared into the grayness.

"I expected a little less of an understatement coming from a Wisdom Sister." Andris leaned against the limestone and crossed his arms.

"Don't be so derisive, Andris." She pointed a finger at his chest, then turned quickly to Annin. "What about Cairn, do they know him?" she asked.

"They do. They know all of us who have come through or been over," Annin said without emotion.

Everyone in the room watched Barba pace. Finally Estos spoke up.

"Barba, I know you're thinking the same thing I am. We tried our theory with Annin, and it didn't work. We need to see if she'll go in for us." He spoke directly to Barba as if no one else were in the room, but everyone looked at them quizzically.

"It's too soon." Barba walked to the door with a concerned look on her face. "What if she . . ."

"We don't have a choice. Not only do we now need to get a message to Benedict that I am—that we all are—indeed alive, but we need to find out how Mudug is tracking all of us."

"What if it has something to do with the passage, what if they pick up on her, too?" Barba challenged the young king.

"If that were the case, they would have been on Annin and Riler immediately. No." Estos shook his head and ignored the bewildered stares of the others. "It has to be something else. She's the only one we can use," he said. His eyes held a look of certainty.

"What lure do you suggest?" she asked, conceding to his decision.

"She'll do it for money," Estos said.

"Who in the blazes are you talking about?" Oberfisk turned around with his arms open wide. Annin spoke up.

"Natalie. He's talking about Natalie."

Everyone erupted into argument, drowning out Estos' words, but Barba made them out well enough.

"She'll do it for money," he repeated to the Sister.

CHAPTER NINE

The rain sounded like thousands of small firecrackers as it hit the barn's metal roof. Nat's three ewes paced in their pen, stomping at the dirt as she approached with a load of fresh hay. Her father bent over the hydraulic lift of the tractor, pale green and rusted with age. His slicker dripped water, a puddle forming by his left foot. She could hear the drip even over the incessant pounding of the rain. He turned and said something. She couldn't hear him, but she still heard the drip, drip, drip. He opened his mouth again and thrust a finger in the air, pointing to a spot behind her. Drip, drip, drip . . .

"What are their names?" Estos startled Nat. He looked over her shoulder.

"Blue, Wally, and Rump." She handed him a pitchfork. "Feed them since you're here." Estos dumped a hay flake in the wooden trough. "Why are you here?" she asked, suddenly aware how out of place he was.

"Your father needs you to come with me."

"I doubt that, I still have to clean out their pen." Nat laughed as she extended her hand to retrieve the pitchfork.

"No, he needs our help." Estos' voice took on a tone of urgency. Nat looked over her shoulder. Her father no longer stood by the tractor.

The base of a ladder appeared at her feet. Her father hung by one hand from the top rung.

"Climb!" Estos yelled. She jumped onto the lowest rung, and the dirt floor around her disappeared. Her free leg dangled over a black pit.

"Estos!" she cried.

"Keep climbing." His voice was distant.

She climbed another rung, and the barn walls disappeared.

"Daddy!" she cried and looked up. Her father kicked frantically at the air above her. She clambered up the ladder and grasped his feet, guiding them to the rungs. The moment they touched the cold metal, her father faded away. Nat stared at the empty space.

"You're at the top. Jump over and invite me in." She felt Estos' breath on her cheek. The ladder was leaning against a dark ledge. She slapped her hands on the barrier and scrambled over.

"Take my hand and invite me in." Estos hovered on the opposite side of the ledge. Gray light illuminated the darkness around him.

"Come in?" Nat asked, confused by his request. He grasped her hand and jumped over the top of the barrier as if he weighed little more than a feather.

"Where's my father?" She peered over the ledge. A thick gray cloud obscured the ground.

"He's fine, Natalie," he said dismissively. His pale eyes looked almost luminescent. He glanced around the dark space. She sensed he was questioning something.

"Do me a favor, think of your favorite room."

The honey-colored walls of the theater erupted from the ground. Colored light filtered over the stage and seats. She looked up and gasped at the delicate flying buttresses floating above them.

"Interesting choice," Estos said as he perched on the edge of the stage. He gestured for her to sit.

"What just happened?" she asked him with her eyes still locked on the floating ceiling.

"You filled your dream space. Please sit, Natalie."

"My dream space?" she said in a confused voice. She ran her hand over the edge of the wooden stage.

"It's a place that protects you from dream manipulation." Estos leaned forward and placed one hand perpendicular to the other. "My left hand is your dream." He wiggled his fingers. "The dream stops where it meets my right hand. Above my right hand is your consciousness, still in a state of sleep, but out of the dream. Only you can find the access point to your dream, and only you can invite others in." He clapped his hands together as if the explanation were obvious.

She settled onto the stage next to him. "Your explanation doesn't make sense. You're part of my dream, so you shouldn't be here," she said, trying to follow his logic. She thought back to her dinner. She must have eaten something weird that was causing this dream. The walls around them grew transparent.

"Focus, Natalie. Think of the theater." The walls took shape again. "I'm not a figment of your dream. I have training that enables me to interject myself into a dream and move about freely." He leaned closer to her. "I'd like to show you something." He pulled a small folded paper from his pocket and smoothed it against the stage floor. A three-dimensional map appeared. Nat's eyes widened when she looked at the tiny snow-covered mountains, forests, and a rust-colored river that cut through the heart of the map and poured into an ocean.

"That's amazing." She ran her fingers through the clouds swirling above the map.

"Would you like to see it up close?"

She nodded, hoping she would remember at least a fraction of this dream. He took her hand, and a forest of ancient pine trees towered above them. She brushed her hand over a bough. The needles felt pliant, almost soft.

"Run with me." He clasped her hand in his, and they stepped onto a faint path covered in short grass and tiny blue flowers that grew low to the ground.

"Fast, Natalie!" He dropped her hand. She chased after him. Her feet fell onto the narrow, overgrown path that wound its way past a red boulder, then an enormous tree trunk. Long branches formed arches over the path and let in only thin shafts of light. She ran and jumped over roots and fallen branches. Her feet were light. Even in her best race, she'd never run this fast before. Estos flew past the trees in front of her until he disappeared. The forest became less dense. She slowed her pace and found him leaning against a crooked tree at the edge of a wide field surrounded on all sides by the forest. He took her hand and brushed it over the rough bark.

"Do you feel that?" he asked. She traced an elongated hole in the bark and nodded.

"Remember it," he said, then vanished.

Nat whirled around. "Run back to the rock cliff where we started." His voice was a whisper in her ear, but she couldn't see him. She searched the branches of the tree, but only its leaves fluttered in the wind. She backed away from it and found the path into the forest. Her breath was easy and relaxed as she made her way along the trail. She could see Estos' figure in her mind as she traced her way over the faint path. Her mind and feet were in perfect harmony.

"Easy enough, then. I expected nothing less from you." Estos hopped off the rocks as Nat came ripping around the red boulder and stopped at the base of the cliff. He took her hand and in one step they were back in the imagined theater. "Have a seat, please." He placed his hand on the small of her back and gestured to the front row.

I have to remember this, Nat thought. She watched him as he settled into the seat next to her. He couldn't be much older than she was, but something about him seemed aged. She blushed when he caught her looking at him. "I hope I remember this dream. I'll have to tell you about it," she said, looking at the colored light streaming from the stage lights.

"Natalie, this is not a dream." His tone was as somber as the expression on his face.

"Right, my little superwoman marathon through an unknown forest just a second ago really happened." She laughed, unnerved by the seriousness in his gray eyes.

"It did, in your mind. It won't be like that when you enter the real forest. It'll take much longer. About an hour to get there and back, if you run hard and don't have any problems. I've seen you run at school—you're fast on an empty track, but this will be different. Your head knows the path now." He tapped her forehead lightly. "As much as I can remember it, anyway. There will be new branches and roots and . . ."

She pressed her fingertips against her forehead, completely confused.

"I've gotten ahead of myself," he apologized. "When you wake up, I need you to take a small piece of paper and tuck it into that opening in the crooked tree. Would you do that for me?" The earnestness in his face stopped Nat from asking what he'd put in her dinner.

"Okay, let me see if I have this right." She sat up straight. "You're asking me to take a piece of paper, run through a forest, shove the paper into a tree, and then come back."

"There's a little more to it than that, but basically, yes." He nodded in agreement.

She laughed. "Asleep Natalie is a little more open-minded than Awake Natalie. I have a strong feeling Awake Natalie is going to say thank you for the dinner and use of the bedroom and make her way back up to campus as fast as she can." Nat relaxed back into the comfortable seat.

"Would Awake Natalie agree to do it if we paid her?" Estos asked quickly.

"Pay me? How much?" The offer brought back the sick feeling of insecurity she carried around on a daily basis. She knew she sounded desperate, even in a dream.

"How much do you want?"

Nat laughed again. He still looked so serious. She stopped laughing. "Thirty-five hundred dollars." The math was easy. A month's mortgage payment for her parents and the rest she owed for this semester's tuition. *This is a dream, right? Why not ask for dream wages?* she thought.

"You agree to do this for thirty-five hundred?" Estos leaned toward her, hand extended.

"Yes. Why not? It will help you as well?" She took his hand.

"You can't even begin to imagine." His hand wrapped around hers. "Agreed, then." He dropped her hand. "When you wake up, Sister Barba will be in your room. She'll draw a pattern on your arm sort of like the one she has." He looked at her for acceptance. "It shouldn't be permanent."

Nat nodded. The theater walls faded and the lights flickered. She looked toward the ledge that she and Estos had climbed over to get into her dream space. Gray clouds swirled behind it.

"After Barba's done and you're dressed, you'll go," Estos said with a look of relief. He rose from the seat.

"Can't wait," she said, feeling a funny sensation that her dream was coming to an end. She smiled wistfully. "I just wish all of this were real."

CHAPTER TEN

The bed was warm and snug, but a light shone somewhere nearby, aggravating Nat's attempt to return to sleep. She pushed the comforter away from her face and sat up. A lamp burned brightly above the bed.

"My apologies for the light. I find it's the best way to gently pull someone from sleep." Barba sat next to a small round table Nat didn't remember having seen in the room earlier. She rubbed her eyes, feeling a little disoriented.

"Are the roads clear?" she asked and looked out the window, thinking it was a benign way to respond to Barba being in the room.

"No." Barba poured a few ounces of green liquid into a bowl and began to stir with what looked like a metal chopstick. An earthy smell filled the room. Nat's nose crinkled. Barba watched Nat carefully. "The smell will go away. Ethet had to come up with something that wasn't permanent, and unfortunately, it smells like decaying leaves." The metal stick scraped against the bowl as she continued to stir. "I need you to dress before I start with this." She gestured to the wardrobe. A long green shift with slits, green leggings, and a cloak embroidered in leaves hung on the door.

"It's an old cloak given to me by a Sister from the Warrior House. I thought it best that we present you as a novice of the exiles, or a 'fringer.' It may keep certain elements away from you." Barba stopped stirring for a moment and waited. Nat remained in bed, confused. It was only a dream. This must still be a dream.

"The conversation with Estos was real, Natalie," Barba said, as if reading Nat's mind. "Your money is right here." She pointed to a thick envelope next to the bowl. "Are you still willing to go now that you are awake?" she asked while holding the metal chopstick over the bowl.

Nat slid her feet to the floor carefully, as if the surface might give way. She walked to the table and picked up the envelope. She flipped through several hundred-dollar bills with her fingertips. Staring at the money, the image of the forest surged to mind, as if the path Estos had shown her was now a permanent part of her memory. She looked at Barba in disbelief, feelings of wariness and unease growing inside her. "You need me to deliver a message, that's it?" Nat put the envelope down and crossed her arms.

"More or less." Barba failed to meet her eye.

"It's the 'more' I'm wondering about," Nat said. "Aside from the whole entry into my subconscious, it's a lot of money for just delivering a message." Nat waited for a response, expecting a catch.

Barba tapped the end of the stick against the bowl. "We haven't asked you to do anything illegal."

Nat wondered if she was reading her mind. If they could get into her dreams, could they get into her thoughts?

Barba continued, "None of us can deliver the message, but for reasons that will have no effect on you or your ability to do so. I know we have little history with each other—certainly nothing upon which you can honestly base any sort of trust. But that is what I am asking from you, Natalie—to trust us. This is a simple errand for which you are receiving generous pay, nothing more."

Nat sensed there was much more she wasn't being told. She glanced at the fat envelope of cash. The amount was generous—absurd, in fact. No one would pay her that kind of money to deliver a message unless she was still dreaming.

"Please dress and drink this. I'll explain a few things while I mark your arm." Barba handed her a cup of what smelled like herbal tea. Nat took a sip. It smelled faintly like marigolds but tasted buttery. She placed the cup on the edge of the table and eyed the clothing. After opening the wardrobe, Nat slid off her pants and unbuttoned her flannel shirt. She watched Barba through the crack by the door's hinge. Her back was to Nat as she dipped the chopstick back into the metal bowl.

"All your garments must come off, Natalie. Undergarments are tucked under the leggings. No jewelry."

"I don't have any jewelry on," Nat responded, blushing. She would have preferred to do all of this in the bathroom. "What is this thing?" She flung a thin, fibrous piece of clothing that looked like a unitard over the door.

"The undergarment. It's made of a material that can deflect sharp objects. Not that you'll need to worry about that," Barba added hastily.

"So it's like body armor?" Nat stepped into the material, and it instantly conformed to her shape. Why she needed body armor to deliver a message was a question worthy of an answer.

"Stronger and more flexible. Now come out where I can see you." Nat stepped out from behind the door. The shift brushed the top of her knees. Barba leaned back in her chair and studied her. "I'll need to pull your hair back. No Warrior Sister would wear her hair down. Come and sit down, please."

Nat sat on a backless stool in front of the table. Barba took her right arm, turned it over, and pushed up the sleeve. Nat placed a hand on her forearm. "Before you start marking me up, look me in the eye and tell me that I won't be in any danger."

Barba smiled and gently pushed her hand away. "You won't be in any danger placing a message in a tree. Good enough?"

"I guess." Nat chewed her lip as Barba began to draw thin entwined lines on her forearm with the tip of the metal chopstick. The color changed from bright green to a faded sage a few moments after the metal pressed against her skin.

"These markings are from a very old House. They should wear off in a few weeks." Barba drew six lines interspersed with tiny spears. "If they don't, you can take it up with Ethet." She finished the last spear, and Nat held up her arm, examining the markings.

"My mom is going to take it up with Ethet. She's not much of a tattoo lover." Nat imagined her mother's response if she came home for Christmas with this on her arm. No presents under the tree would be just the beginning.

Barba removed a brush from the top drawer of a bureau. "Your mother's a librarian, isn't she?" She began arranging Nat's hair in a tight topknot.

Nat winced. *How does she know about my mom?* she wondered. "Yes. Will I be back in town by tomorrow night?" she asked, trying to move the subject away from her family.

"You will be back in a few hours. Finish this." She handed Nat the cup of tea, completed the topknot, and motioned for her to stand. She fastened a worn leather belt around her waist and a cloak around her shoulders. The leaf pattern on the cloak looked like a kind of camouflage. Barba fingered the border of the cloak. "The thought of someone else wearing my cloak is a little off-putting, but I have to say, you look the part." She patted Nat's shoulder as if to say "Good enough."

"Am I supposed to be a nun of some kind?" Nat asked.

"A nun?" Barba repeated, astonished.

Feeling foolish, Nat said, "Everyone here refers to you and Ethet as 'Sister.' If I'm wearing your cloak . . ."

Barba chuckled. "No, a 'Sister' is a woman who has shown she is a master of a specific set of skills or abilities. It's an honorific. Only those who study, apprentice, and prove their skills are entitled to be called 'Sister.' I am a Sister from the Wisdom House, Ethet was the Head Sister of the Healing House."

"And I am pretending to be what?" Nat asked, looking down at her garments.

"You are from an old Warrior House, or rather a new House that has taken on the old ways. Come, we need to go."

Nat followed her out the door and down the hallway. "So my area of study is how to be a warrior?" She tried to walk alongside Barba but had to follow at an angle.

"It is more complicated than that, Natalie. After mastering certain required skills, you choose a specific area. Your markings tell your skill. Yours are the markings of a Keeper of the Accord." They descended the stairs.

"What does that mean?" Nat asked, growing more confused. They passed through the kitchen and down a hallway she hadn't seen before.

"It means you keep the bad element at bay." They entered the room where Riler had been the night before. It was empty, and the makeshift gurney was gone. Steam rose from small flasks sitting above burners that were situated on a long table across from Ethet's wall of herbs and medicines. Nat felt a vibration through her borrowed boots. She swallowed and shuffled slightly. Looking around for another door that might take them to a garage, her eyes landed on an archway to what looked like a tunnel.

"Are you the one taking me to the forest?" Nat asked, wondering where Estos was.

"No."

Nat fiddled with the edge of her sleeve, waiting.

Barba asked, "What will you do with the money, Natalie?"

"I—" Nat looked down, not interested in meeting her gaze. "It will help solve some problems. Where does this lead?" She pointed down the tunnel.

"It leads to where you need to go next. You will find an odd door at the end. Just press through. I'll be here when you get back." She placed a small dagger and a piece of paper in Nat's hand. "The dagger is for show, but hide the paper until you reach the tree."

"If it's for show, I don't really need it, do I?" Nat tucked the paper into a deep inner pocket in the cloak, then examined the dagger in Barba's outstretched hand. Her hands trembled with nerves.

"Take it."

"None of this is real, anyway, right?" She clipped the dagger to her belt. "I'm still in a dream."

Barba stepped forward and tucked a loose strand of hair behind Nat's ear. "Good luck, Natalie."

Nat took a few tentative steps toward the tunnel. Barba nodded in encouragement and then walked over to a shelf laden with glass vials. Nat waited a moment, watching Barba arrange them. *Time to go, then, I guess,* she thought.

The vibrations increased as she approached the entrance to the tunnel, which appeared to be carved out of solid limestone. She touched the side and felt the vibrations travel through her fingers. Her eyes quickly adjusted to the dim light. As she walked farther, the tunnel narrowed and the ceiling began to slope downward. The path continued to turn to the right. No lights hung from the ceiling or walls, but she could still see where she was walking. The source of the light remained a mystery until she rounded a last curve to find what looked like an opaque plastic sheet. Diffuse light filtered through its surface. Nat placed her palm against the sheet. It vibrated slightly and flexed away from her. She searched the edge for a place to peel it back or open it, but found none.

She stepped back. Barba had said to press through. A movement on the other side caught her attention. A long, thin object moved back and forth along the top of the sheet. Nat placed her palm on it again and pushed hard.

Barba stopped pacing when the small orb zipped through the opening of the tunnel and landed in her palm. Ethet looked up from the table where she was chopping up a greenish root.

"She's through, then?" Ethet asked.

"She's through." Barba had told her orb to return only when the girl had crossed over. Now all they could do was wait. Ethet resumed her chopping. Barba, orb in hand, strode over to the wooden door and pulled it open. Oberfisk nearly landed on his backside but quickly righted himself.

"A little notice would have been nice there, Sister," he said.

"My apologies, Oberfisk. I wasn't expecting you to be taking a nap against the door." She brushed past him and looked around the hall. Annin, Cairn, and Kroner stopped talking. "Come back in. She's through. Where are Estos and Andris?"

"Estos is talking to Riler in the sick room, and Andris went to the training ground after he and Oberfisk almost came to blows," Annin said as she passed by her into the room. Kroner and Oberfisk took position on either side of the entrance to the tunnel.

"That one's not my fault," Oberfisk said to no one in particular. He flicked a speck of lint off the tip of the spear he was holding. "He just needed a reminder that this isn't his personal fiefdom. We're living in a democracy here, and if he doesn't like it, well, he can head on into the forest, then, and see how well the Nala like his whining."

"It does us no good to get on each other right now, Ober." Cairn took a mortar and pestle from Annin and began crushing some of the green root Ethet had chopped earlier.

"I know, I know, but he's not the only one going crazy here. There isn't a waking moment that goes by that I don't think about going home and fighting Mudug," Oberfisk said. "Andris needs to focus on the here and now." Kroner nodded in agreement, and Oberfisk tapped the base of his spear against the floor.

Barba shook her head. She'd heard this preachy diatribe against Andris too many times to listen to it again. She whispered to her orb, which shot past Oberfisk's head back down the tunnel.

Oberfisk paused long enough to take a breath and then continued. "We've all lost our homes, our families . . ."

"Let me do that, Ethet." Barba reached for the metal spoon Ethet was using to scrape the sides of a heavy stone bowl. "If I stand here with nothing to do while we wait, I might come to blows with Oberfisk." Ethet smiled and handed her the spoon. Barba scooped a portion of Cairn's green mush and added it to the bowl.

"You never were interested in listening to others, even when you were a student. It's a good thing you chose Wisdom House. I would have had you living in the garden shed if you'd chosen Healing House." Ethet looked over the rim of her glasses at Barba.

"Funny how it worked out, isn't it, Ethet," Barba said quietly. She watched her old friend add a few more ingredients. "I dedicated my studies to trying to understand how his father got out." She looked at Cairn. "And now we are trying to figure out how to get back in."

"'Funny' isn't the word I'd use." Ethet sighed, remembering their flight through the membrane.

"Is this going to be enough?" Barba asked, peering into the bowl. "If she has more than one bite, we will need multiple poultices."

"She won't get bitten," Ethet said, then added, "Did she drink the tea I gave you?"

"About half. I don't think she liked the taste that much," Barba said.

"This will be enough. The tea was almost pure meldon juice. I'm surprised she kept any down." Ethet raised her silver eyebrows, creating perfect arches.

"She's polite but curious. She'll be full of questions when she gets back. We'll need to decide what to tell her, if we tell her anything at all. Or maybe it will be best for her to forget."

"Messing with memory is my specialty." Annin bowed slightly, her mass of hair falling forward. She opened her mouth to say more, but Oberfisk's booming voice interrupted her.

"Take King Estos! He lost his sister, but you don't see him trying to take down his compatriots every time the wind blows against him," he said.

"Thanks for the compliment, Oberfisk." Estos shut the door behind him.

"Sorry, my lord." Oberfisk said, then grew oddly quiet.

Estos walked to the tunnel's entrance and turned to Barba. "She's over, then?" he asked.

"Fifteen minutes and counting. She would have been back by now if she'd changed her mind," Barba said. "Whatever you told her worked. Either that, or she still thinks she's riding a dream."

Everyone in the room thought of at least one other reason why she wouldn't come back. Estos verbalized it first. "If the Nala leave her alone, she should be beyond the red boulder by now. She's fast."

"Let's hope she's fast enough," Annin said.

CHAPTER ELEVEN

Nat moved swiftly across the forest floor. She jumped over an ancient moss-covered log without even looking at it. The sensation that her feet knew the way unnerved her. *Dreams are so odd,* she thought. Her hood got pushed back, tangled in a branch. She recognized a cluster of trees from Estos' map. *Halfway there.* Flashes of green and brown blurred her vision. She'd been exhausted yesterday. Or was it the day before? She couldn't remember. Her stress and fatigue had to have caused the crazy dreams, including the one reeling through her mind now.

Another low-hanging branch raked her cloak, but she kept her pace. The forest thinned out. The path widened but kept her inside the line of trees. She found herself glancing constantly to her right, expecting to see something or someone. Birds burst out of a branch above her. Her feet anticipated the turn before it came, pushing her toward an opening in the trees. She looked up to see a field peppered with scraggly shrubs. The crooked tree looked like lightning had split its upper trunk in two. A ring of a half dozen saplings encircled the tree, thick, pointed needles covering their branches. Nat paused. She wondered if she would remember any of this when she woke up. She reached down to push a sapling aside and jerked her hand back. Three needles stuck out from the fleshy part of her palm. Her hand puffed up as she pulled each needle out, wincing in pain. Cradling her throbbing hand, she rounded the crooked tree. The saplings made a perfect ring, almost as if someone had planted them. They were too tall to jump over.

Nat walked around again and stopped next to a tall aspen. One of its branches bent down over the crooked tree. She unhooked her cloak and placed it on the ground. After two unsuccessful jumps to reach the lowest-hanging limb, she grasped the branch and climbed up the trunk. When she got to the overhanging branch, she stopped with her arm wrapped around the trunk. She could make the jump, but getting back was the problem. The eye in the tree wasn't high, but if she fell, it would be right into the pointed needles of the saplings.

Nat jumped and scraped her throbbing hand against the rough bark as she grasped for a handhold. The pain was unlike any sensation she'd ever had in a dream. A thick branch stuck out like a ladder step about three feet above the eye. She encircled the branch with her legs and swung upside down. Her left hand barely reached the hole in the tree, and her fingertips strained to push the folded paper into the opening. A corner of the paper stuck out. She swung toward it and flicked the paper in. Satisfied that nothing more was visible, she pulled herself back up and sat on the branch while the blood drained from her head. The drop was a good seven feet. That, plus the distance needed to clear the saplings, was not going to make for an easy jump. The last thing she wanted was a twisted ankle or broken leg. She'd felt pain in dreams before, but her hand was really throbbing. A twisted ankle would be worse.

She was looking around for any option that would get her to the ground in one piece when the sound of low voices and snorting horses traveled across the open meadow. Three riders had appeared from a cluster of trees directly across from her. Their thick blue coats fell to their stirrups, and white circles were emblazoned on their coat sleeves. She squinted to get a better look. They all had pointed beards like Andris.

She pressed her back against the trunk of the tree and listened to their voices. Estos had a reason he wanted this paper hidden, and the riders didn't look particularly friendly. The bark scratched the back of her neck as she tucked herself tightly into the branches.

"Huya," a rider urged his horse into the meadow. It swung its head and stomped at the ground.

"Yah!" one rider yelled, digging his heels into his horse. The horse twisted to the side, nearly unsaddling the rider. The horses high-stepped in nervous circles. After two more attempts to press the horses forward, the riders retreated into the forest.

Nat sprang from the branch and landed in a heap beyond the saplings. The ground, soft with decaying aspen leaves, buffered her fall. She tested out her legs and ankles. Besides another long scrape on her arm, everything felt okay. She scooped her cloak off the meadow floor and ran for the tree line.

Her heart pounded like she was running a race. She glanced behind her. Gnarled trees lined the edge of the forest. She jumped onto the forest path. Branches laden with triangular-shaped leaves raked her cloak. Her foot caught on a root, sending her sprawling onto the forest floor. Dirt and soggy leaves clung to her throbbing hand. She pushed herself up and jogged a few steps before running hard into the woods.

Her breath was coming in ragged gasps when she reached the red boulder. In the distance, the tops of two trees swayed back and forth, but the trees around her were still. When she looked at the distant trees again, a blue object flew from the top of one of the trees to another. Growing larger, the blurry shape transformed into a lean figure. Adrenaline surged through her body, and she sprinted to the rocky cliff. Where was the entrance? Her mind remembered every step of the path, but she couldn't remember where the entrance was. A strange light shone from between a crack in the cliff. Jagged rocks scraped her arms, but she plunged toward the light. An opaque rock pulsated in front of her. The surface gave under her fingers. She flung her body at the rock and tumbled onto the floor of the tunnel. A strange glass ball floated above her.

CHAPTER TWELVE

Nat stumbled behind the glass ball and out of the tunnel.

Oberfisk greeted her with a giant smile. "I knew you could do it!" He clapped her on the shoulder, sending her flailing into the room.

"Oberfisk, be careful. Bring her here." Ethet motioned to a low bench along the wall. She and Annin rolled up Nat's sleeves, inspecting every inch of skin. Annin examined her swollen hand carefully.

"Annin," Nat whispered, her voice urgent.

"What?" she asked as she turned Nat's hand over.

"Am I dreaming? Because all of this is too real, but it was totally surreal back there."

Annin stopped and looked up at her. Nat trembled as their eyes met. A look of sympathy briefly flashed across Annin's face but disappeared as quickly as it came.

"You're not dreaming, Nat. And you're not crazy, at least not yet. Welcome to the family, Sister." A silver arch appeared above Annin's eye patch as she gave Nat a little smile. Nat slumped against the wall and looked around at the people in the room.

"Porc tree, nothing else other than a few scrapes," Ethet announced. Everyone in the room except Nat let out a breath.

"What do you mean 'nothing else'?" Nat pulled her hand back.

"No other wounds is what she means." Annin stood swiftly. She accepted a small bowl from Ethet, which she thrust at Nat. "Here, rub this on your hand. It will help with the swelling."

Nat took the bowl, then watched Annin move around the sterile room. She darted from place to place like a hummingbird, standing still only long enough to put something away before she moved again.

"You delivered the message without any problems, then?" Barba hovered at Nat's side, her red hair frizzier than usual.

Nat regarded her for a moment. Barba had lied. Estos had lied. Who were these people? She began rubbing the salve onto the tender skin. The instant the salve touched her hand, the pain began to recede, but her agitation did not. She needed to get away from them and that tunnel.

"Well?" Barba asked.

Nat waited several moments, savoring the anxiety building in the room. *How do they like it?* she wondered with a little animus. *How do they like being kept in the dark?*

"Depends on what you define as a problem," Nat finally said, her voice low. "I had a problem being in a forest where there shouldn't have been a forest. I had a problem when my feet were more in control of me than my head. I had a problem with the ring of prickly trees piercing my skin." Her voice continued to rise. "I had a problem seeing three armed men that looked like him"—she pointed to Andris as he walked into the room—"pass too close while I was stuck in the stupid tree." She took a deep breath. "I had a problem with something blue chasing me through the tops of the trees on my way back. And did I mention that I had a problem with *wherever it was you sent me?*" she yelled and pointed to the tunnel.

"The blue thing—was it far behind? Did it see you enter the cliff?" Ethet asked, ignoring Nat's hysteria.

"What?" Nat shook in little spasms of anger. The bowl tumbled out of her hand.

"Was the blue thing far behind?" Ethet shook her head and bent her long frame to retrieve the bowl.

None of them seemed the least bit fazed by Nat's outburst. She looked from face to face. Oberfisk looked away. Barba held her hands at her side. Estos and Andris stood with their backs to the gaping entrance. She closed her eyes and bent her head. What she needed was to get out of here—and fast. *Answer the question and leave,* she commanded herself. She lifted her head and focused on Ethet. She brought her knees to her chest, hugging them tightly.

"It was far enough away when I noticed it, and it was just a blur of color. What is it?" she asked, her voice flat.

"A blue monkey." Everyone turned to Andris. Estos rolled his eyes. "They're rare, but occasionally show up in those woods," Andris continued in a professorial tone, ignoring Estos' grimaces.

"Oh, please." Nat released her knees, unhooked her cloak, and tossed it on the bench. The dagger clattered to the floor. She removed her boots, which landed in the opposite corner of the room. "I'm getting my things and then I'm gone." She walked over to Andris while unstrapping her belt. "Do you really think I'm that stupid?" She shoved the belt into his chest. It felt like she'd just slapped a brick wall. "There are no blue monkeys in North America, Andris. There are no forests that grow inside limestone cliffs!" she said, backing away toward the door.

"No one said you were in North America." Andris walked to the tunnel entrance and looked into the darkness. Nat stopped and watched him. She knew she should leave, but curiosity got the better of her.

"Since no one else seems willing, are you going to tell me where I went?" She meant the question to be both an accusation and a challenge, and she shot Estos a quick look before turning back to Andris.

But all she got from him was a sneer that, she decided, looked a lot like his smile.

Barba began picking up the articles of discarded clothing. "Andris, since you seem intent on goading the girl, you can explain." She gave him a disapproving look. He shrugged and rolled his eyes. "But"—Barba held up a hand as Nat began to speak—"I need you to answer a few questions first."

Nat crossed her arms. Maybe she'd get some answers of her own if she played along. "Go ahead."

"You placed the message in the tree?"

"Yes," she said through clenched teeth.

"The men that you saw—how many were there?" Estos was at Barba's side. He had an apologetic look on his face.

"Three. They were on the other side of the meadow. I know they didn't see me, because I was sitting on a branch on the opposite side of the tree."

"Why were you sitting in the tree?" Estos furrowed his brow. "I told you to put the paper in the eye and leave, not to climb the tree."

"I had a problem with reaching the tree." Nat held up her swollen hand.

"Oh," Estos said. "He must have planted them there to protect it," he said to himself, loud enough for Nat to overhear.

Nat leaned against the wall. "Whoever 'he' is, he did a good job." Her hand still hurt, but less so. Her head was beginning to pound. She suddenly remembered the envelope of money. She addressed the room. "I'll tell you what happened without interruption, then you'll give me my money and let me go home."

At first, no one spoke, then Estos said, "Of course."

Nat relayed the events. Even Annin stood still as she described her run back to the entrance. When she finished, Andris broke the silence.

"It appears you earned your money." He tossed the envelope to her. "Go change and I'll take you home. I think everyone else needs a little time to digest the implications of your successful outing." He held the door open. Nat shuddered slightly as she passed him.

"I'll go with you." Estos started to follow her.

"No, my lord. You need to be part of the conversation, since it was your idea to bring her in." Andris closed the door on him and followed Nat to the base of the stairs. "Your things are in your room," he said, pointing to the stairs as if she needed directions. "Get dressed, and I'll wait for you outside the front entrance of the shop."

He disappeared down the hall, leaving Nat alone. The more she was around Andris, the more she disliked him. She had no intention of being around him ever again after today.

When Nat pushed open the shop's door, a slightly rusted orange Power Wagon belched black smoke in front of her. She trudged toward it, squinting through the bright snow. The passenger door opened with a groan. She climbed in and used both hands to pull the door shut. She kept one hand on the door handle in case she had to make a quick escape.

A few cars moved slowly through the deep snow that covered the side streets. A city plow sat square in the middle of the road where it had broken down. Andris skirted the workers trying to coax the plow back to life and barely missed taking out a fire hydrant. She tightened her grip on the door handle and wondered where Andris had gotten his driver's license, if he even had one.

He reached the main road leading to campus. A three-foot-high bank of snow ran down the middle of the road. He gunned the engine and blasted through the bank, then turned the truck into the parking lot of the Student Center.

"Over there." Nat gestured to the entrance and pulled her bag over her shoulder. She did not want him dropping her off at her dorm. He slowed the truck to a stop, but when she pulled on the door handle, Andris quickly clamped his hand down on hers.

"A few things before you get out, Natalie." He released his grip, and she lifted her hand away from the door, knowing that arguing would be pointless. He turned off the engine.

"Go ahead." She stared out the cracked windshield at the lone snowplow making its way across the parking lot. The faster he said what he needed to, the sooner she could put this bizarre experience behind her.

"I don't trust you." The sound of the plow scraping against the asphalt filled the cab. Andris continued, "Before you get the idea of telling anyone about what you saw this morning, think carefully. No one will ever believe you. The entrance is easily hidden. Our predecessor knew there was too much at stake to leave it undefended. If anyone were ever to come poking around, they would simply find a studio for stage and theater props." His voice was cold.

He waited, and finally Nat said, "You've made your point. May I go now?"

"Not yet."

She sank back into the seat.

"As I see it, you have two choices. You can step out of this car and never see any one of us again, except Cairn or Estos in passing. What you saw and did today will become a memory of a strange dream that will slowly disappear over time. Annin will make certain of that." Andris tapped a finger to his head. "Or, as much as I hate to even suggest it, you can continue to help us since you've now proven yourself useful."

She felt her cheeks grow hot and turned toward him. "Why would I help you—any of you? You all deceived me and messed with my head to get me to do something that I never would have agreed to do. Why would I ever do anything for any of you again?" The reflection off the snow highlighted the tiny lines around Andris' green eyes as he smiled. Nat suppressed an urge to punch him.

"We have lots of money," he said, taunting her.

"I think I'd rather find another source." Nat had a feeling they knew all about her financial problems.

"Nothing will pay as well as we would. Well, I can think of a few other things, but they don't really seem your style. Then again, I could be wrong." He swatted away her slap, gripped her wrist, and leaned in close. "You learned something today that just obliterated so many of your truths. Until Annin gets into your head, you won't stop thinking about any of it. You won't stop wondering what it was you experienced." He let go, and she yanked her arm away. "The only way to find the answers is to help us. It's your decision to make, but don't wait too long. Annin has a very long reach unless you know how to block her." He gestured to the door and started the engine.

Nat flew out of the truck and up the stairs to the Student Center in a matter of seconds. From behind the safety of the thick glass doors, she watched Andris lean over, pull the door shut, and roll away. The campus plow slowly scraped over the tire tracks. Nat looked down. A scrolling green vine peeked out from under her coat sleeve.

CHAPTER THIRTEEN

Nat lapped the early morning joggers occupying the inner lanes of the indoor track. Her feet flew over the spongy surface. She lengthened her stride, pushing herself to run faster. Sweat poured from her brow and stung her eyes. She wiped it away and glanced at the vine and spear markings on her forearm before quickly looking at the massive clock hanging high on the wall. The thick black hands read 5:45. She'd been running almost an hour.

The white lane lines blurred and turned a hue of pink against the reddish color of the track. The color reminded her of the red boulder. She slowed her pace. Bright lights reflected off the bleachers set against one wall of the athletic facility. Estos sat on the lowest row and leaned over the tubular guardrail that separated the bleachers from the track. She ran by twice without lifting her eyes. On the third pass, she stopped right in the middle of the track and stared up at him.

"What do you want?" she said, her chest heaving.

"I need to talk to you, Natalie—please." His eyes looked slate gray from where she stood. She tilted her chin and let out a long, slow breath. The tip of her ponytail clung to her sweaty back. She jogged farther down the track and grabbed a dented water bottle and towel.

The metal stairs leading to the bleachers made a hollow ringing sound with each step she took. She draped the towel over her neck, unscrewed the water bottle, and walked along the narrow walkway toward Estos. He stood and rubbed his palms against his pants.

Good, he's nervous, she thought as she took a swig of water. She sat on the grooved bleacher and watched the joggers pass on the other side of the guardrail.

"May I tell you a story?"

"That's an odd way to start this conversation, but go ahead. You've got fifteen minutes." She kept looking at the track, but sensed each small movement he made when he sat next to her.

"There's a place called Fourline."

"Not Canada." She pressed the water bottle against her lips.

"No, not Canada." He laughed and Nat couldn't help herself. She turned and gave him a wry smile. Little lines formed around his eyes when he smiled in return, but dark circles lingered under his long lashes. She wiped the towel across her neck.

"About six years ago, my sister was killed right after her coronation as regent of Fourline." The laughter disappeared from his eyes.

Nat's hand froze midair. She carefully placed her bottle on the bench.

"A man my family trusted for decades secretly ordered her murder. He took over as temporary regent. He lied to the people, making them believe the Sisters—people like Barba and Ethet—had a hand in her death. Then he began systematically destroying the Sisters' Houses and everything that made our country prosperous and safe. He told my people that the Sisters had conspired with"—he paused and glanced at his clenched fists—"with an enemy that was wreaking havoc along our coastline and southern forests. He sowed so much fear that enough people started to believe him, thinking he was the only one who could protect Fourline after my sister's murder." His voice was full of bitterness, and Nat felt an overwhelming sense of loss when she examined his face. She held her questions and listened.

"I was too young to do anything, too young to rightfully assume the position of regent after her. And for a while, Mudug had me believing the Sisters had conspired against my family. But then he tried to have me killed as well." Estos rubbed the scar running from his ear down his neck. "If it hadn't been for Sister Barba and the sanctuary of your world, I'd be dead now, too. She helped us flee before Mudug could kill me."

Nat closed her eyes and tried to push the enigma of the passage momentarily from her thoughts. "This man, Mudug, wants you dead?"

Estos nodded. "If I'm dead, he can rightfully claim the regency after my coming of age passes next year. In a year, if I'm alive and claim the throne, he'll have to step down. If he doesn't, there will be war." His voice resonated with grave certainty. Nat looked at him in wonder.

"And you've been stuck here, hiding all this time?"

"For my safety, I haven't been back since I passed through." He averted his eyes from hers but not before she saw his pain. "About two years ago, Oberfisk, at great risk to himself, journeyed back. He was able to make contact with the rebels and apprise them of my well-being. Keeping me alive in the minds of the people of Fourline is critical. If the people think I'm dead, the country will support Mudug next year. He's constructed such a web of lies about the Sisters conspiring with . . ." He paused and gripped the guardrail. "If I don't return, they'll believe he's the only one who can keep them safe."

Safe from what? Nat wondered.

"We tried to send more messengers through after Oberfisk, but then little things started happening." His forehead creased. "Less than a year ago, the trips became . . . Mudug seemed to know right where we'd be. Last spring, I sent Oberfisk in to do just what you did two nights ago, and an arrow barely missed his head. We even tried sending Annin in, but Mudug was able to track her movements." He shook his head in frustration. "I doubt anyone would've believed her, anyway, even if she'd been able to deliver the message." A shadow crossed his face. Nat wondered what he meant. "Mudug is somehow able to find us when we're in Fourline."

"So you decided to send me, some random person, into a place that shouldn't even exist to see if I'd get attacked, too?" She pressed the heel of her hand to her forehead.

"No, that's not it at all." He threw his hands in the air. "I would never have sent you in if I thought you'd be in danger. And you're the furthest thing from random."

"You just said Oberfisk almost got an arrow through his head!" A jogger looked up from the track. Nat lowered her voice, thinking Andris had it right—no one would ever believe any of this. "You sent me in like some guinea pig," she said, anger seething in her voice.

"You aren't a guinea pig. You're our best hope." He sounded defiant. His blue-gray eyes searched her face. She didn't know what to believe, but the honesty in his expression kept her next to him, listening. "I know Mudug is targeting my guard and those who helped me flee," he said in a low voice. "But he has no knowledge of you. He can't even imagine that someone like you exists. Just like you wouldn't have conceived that my world exists three days ago." He spread his arms wide. "I bet on your anonymity and it worked. You did it. Those guards you saw proved you can travel freely through Fourline."

"How?" she asked, cringing slightly at the thought he'd bet on her.

"Trust me, if they'd known you were there, we wouldn't be having this conversation. None of my people have been able to move in and out of the passage without Mudug's men honing in on them within a short period of time. But you did it." He placed his hand over hers. "You did it."

Nat stared at the metal bleachers under her feet. "Why me, Estos? There are hundreds or thousands of people you could have—"

He let go of her hand and leaned against the row behind them. "Sister Barba's been assessing you since last year. You met her criteria."

"Criteria?" She gaped at him.

"She used to select candidates—women who were trained to keep a needed balance in our world."

"Sisters?" she guessed, thinking of the brief explanation Barba had given her before her journey.

"Yes, Sisters. You caught her attention when you arrived last year. She noticed something about you. We've been watching you ever since."

Nat tried to imagine anything about herself worth watching, let alone assessing. She let out a rueful laugh. "What did she notice? That I'm a stressed-out mess?"

"You have a combination of strength, intelligence, and empathy that's unusual, Natalie Barns." The sincerity in his voice made her blush. "Sister Barba and I agree that if you lived in our world, you would make an extraordinary Sister." He gently lifted her chin, sending a shiver down her spine, then dropped his hand to his side. "And we have something to offer you in return."

"Money." She arched her brow.

"It is a means to an end. But there's more than money—there's knowledge." He shrugged and gave her a sheepish look. Silence fell between them, and Estos looked at her expectantly.

"Before my journey, I would have told you to walk away and never speak to me again," she said. He nodded as if in agreement. "But I have too many questions now to do that." She looked up at the ceiling. "What you just told me and where you sent me . . . I don't understand how your world even exists."

"Natalie, if I've learned one thing since I've passed into your world, it's that the unknown far exceeds the known. With time, we can provide more answers, but unfortunately, time is not a luxury I have. Andris told you that you have a choice. I need you to help us again and go back in for me." He sounded almost pleading. "My home . . ." He cleared his throat. "But it is your decision."

She pressed her fist to her lips and regarded him.

"Will you think about it?" He brushed a stray tendril of hair from her face and stood.

She nodded, thinking she must be going crazy.

"Thank you." He gazed past her. "Looks like my fifteen minutes are up," he said and gave her one last hopeful look before clanking up the steps. He disappeared through a door high above the stands right beneath the clock. Nat sat on the bleachers for a long time, watching the hands of the clock tick by.

CHAPTER FOURTEEN

A week passed. The snow melted, creating a series of muddy quagmires on campus. Nat took her morning runs through town instead of at the indoor track. She didn't want another encounter with Estos. She needed time to think about where she'd been, what he had told her, and his request.

Her thoughts constantly drifted away during class. Her preoccupation with Estos and Fourline was all-consuming. It was a good thing the registrar's office had Nat's tuition payment. She couldn't imagine that stress on top of the crazy situation she found herself in. She'd half expected the office to reject the money when she'd made the payment. *Imaginary world, imaginary money,* she'd thought.

Paying her parents' mortgage payment and late fee had been a little trickier than simply handing over the cash. She had to get MC to send her the account information without their knowledge. Even though she was in fourth grade, MC was the most tech-savvy member of the family. She snuck the statement into the scanner at their mom's school, saved it to a flash drive, then e-mailed it to Nat. Sharing the information over the phone seemed the easiest way to Nat, but not MC. Nat called her mom after she'd made the mortgage payment.

"What do you mean you got a tuition refund?" Her mom's voice held that weary suspicion that Nat had heard anytime she'd arrived home late at night past her curfew.

"I know, crazy, isn't it?" Nat responded, hating the ridiculous sound of her voice as she told the bald-faced lie. "I guess I had the figures on one of my scholarships wrong."

"Why didn't they apply it to next semester's payment, Nat?" She could hear MC in the background, trying to distract her mom.

"No idea." Another lie. "Anyway, it was your money. I hope you don't mind that I sent it to the bank. After our last conversation, that seemed like the most pressing bill." Nat was trying to keep her voice casual.

"Strange that the overpayment was in the precise amount we needed for the mortgage payment and late fee, Nat." MC's voice grew louder in the background. "Even stranger that you had our account information." Her mom was onto her like flies on honey.

"Uh . . ."

"Marie Claire, what is your problem?" Nat heard muffled voices, then her mom came back on. "Your sister is about to bust, talk to her. You and I will finish this conversation later."

MC's voice came on instantly. "Hey, Nat, guess what, Nat, Blue had twins!" She sounded like she'd gotten into the powdered lemonade mix. "We've got twin lambs!"

Nat played along with the conversation. "Great, MC, she doing okay?"

"Yep, she's fine. She's a good mom. I've got her in the back pen where it's nice and quiet. You can't even hear Cal's boyfriend's stereo when he picks her up in the morning." MC made a deep thumping sound mimicking the stereo bass. Then silence.

"Is Mom gone?" Nat asked.

"Yeah . . . she's in the kitchen," MC whispered. "She was all over you. I couldn't think of what else to do. Sorry for being so idiotic sounding about the lambs, they are totally fine and totally cute."

"MC, I owe you. A lot. Thanks for getting me the bank information and taking care of Blue." Nat grew silent as she remembered the blue animal or thing jumping through the trees.

"Are you still there?" MC asked.

"Yeah, I was just thinking of something I saw the other day. Keep me posted on Blue. And on Mom and Dad, too, okay? If you hear them talking or stressing out, let me know." Not that she could help, but knowing never hurt anybody.

"Okay. I miss you."

"I miss you, too."

Before she hung up, Nat promised to try to visit in the next few weeks. She knew she was lying even as she made the promise. The need to work and study to keep her grades up had not magically vanished after the windfall from Estos. The semester would be over before she knew it, and she would be out of work for three weeks before the interim term started.

Nat put her phone down and returned to the chemical diagram on the screen of her computer. She stared at it a moment and then minimized the screen. The cursor in the text box of the search engine blinked. She typed "alternate universe," and her finger paused over "Enter." She pressed the backspace key. It wasn't an alternate universe. Maybe it was some kind of subterranean land? But subterranean meant no sunlight. The cursor continued to blink. Nat leaned back in her chair, stretching her arms. Her conversation with Estos left her with more questions than answers. She rubbed her hand. The puncture marks from the tree needles were fading but still visible.

"You got a tattoo and didn't tell me?" Viv entered the dorm room and slammed the door behind her. "This isn't even one of those little rebellious butterflies on the ankle, this is a serious tattoo." She held Nat's arm suspended in the air while she examined the vines.

"It's not permanent." Nat pulled her arm down. "Sis—Barba was just working on some ideas for a costume, and I was her guinea pig." She thought of Estos' face and the way he'd refuted her claim that they'd treated her like a lab experiment.

"Earth to Nat." Viv waved her hand in front of her face. "What kind of ink is it?" She touched the tip of one of the tiny spears.

"I think it's similar to henna," Nat said, scrambling for some reasonable explanation. Not even Viv would believe her if she told the truth.

"How utterly disappointing." Viv plopped into a chair and picked up a book. "What kind of costume?" She peered over her book.

"Huh?"

"What kind of costume was Barba working on? Is it for a play?"

"Some medieval-warrior-type character, I think. She was pretty tight on the details," Nat said. She pulled up the chemical diagram, knowing she needed to focus on schoolwork.

"Make sure you charge them extra for using you as a guinea pig. If your mom sees that, she's going to flip out." Viv's legs hung off the side of the circular chair.

"I did get money out of it." Still distracted, Nat examined the vines. She grabbed her phone, took a picture of her arm, and uploaded it onto the computer. "Viv, what was the site you mentioned once where you can match designs and artwork to their source?"

Viv got up and pulled out her laptop. "Your computer is medieval, send the picture to me and I'll run the search." After a few moments, she turned the screen to Nat. "Does this look familiar?" A faded illustration made from an etching showed a long-eared rabbit sitting in front of four enormous boulders. Each boulder was covered with designs carved into the surface of the stone. Viv tapped the stone on the far left and magnified the image. The vines with little spears encircled the face of the boulder.

"'*The Long-Eared Hare Loses the Race* by Thomas Gate.'" Nat read the caption aloud. "I wonder if Thomas Gate is related to Professor Gate." She typed "Thomas Gate" into the search engine while Viv studied the picture. "Here he is. 'Thomas Gate, born in Canada, died 1960. Author of children's series Long-Eared Hare. Professor at Westin College, 1940–1960.' There must be some relation." Nat turned to Viv, who was holding her laptop at a distance.

"Nat, check this out." Viv pulled the image down and enlarged it even more. A tiny figure with a smooth body crouched on top of a distant boulder. Nat couldn't make out any features or expression, but knew that it was waiting to spring on the rabbit. "A little creepy for a children's book." Viv made a face.

Nat said nothing and handed the laptop back. She'd seen that figure before, jumping through trees in a forest that shouldn't exist.

CHAPTER FIFTEEN

Nat noticed Estos first. His hair had been cut short and stood up like a scrub brush. She recognized his ripped leather jacket—it was from one of the pilot costumes at the shop. Annin wore a long, oversized trench coat. Her curly black hair was tucked into the wide collar. Her lips moved quickly as she spoke to Estos. She stopped talking and turned her head.

Nat remained in the doorway of her biochemistry classroom, watching the two warily as they watched her. Annin's surreal blue eye and eye patch still freaked her out. Sighing, she shouldered her bag and walked to the bench where they were sitting.

"Hi." Her eyes darted from Annin to Estos. "Nice hair."

Estos stood, running a hand through his short hair. "Oberfisk's idea."

She crossed her arms tightly over her chest. She felt unsteady but didn't want either Estos or Annin to know. Sleep had been a rare commodity lately, between the nightmares and the hours researching an answer that would explain where she'd been.

"How's your hand?" he asked while examining the fleshy side where the punctures were still visible.

"It's fine." She let him press his fingers into the side of her palm.

"The needles are a lot like porcupine quills." Annin lifted her chin, freeing some of her hair from under the collar. "If you don't remove them properly, they work themselves into the skin and through the muscle tissue. I've seen some embedded in bone. Avoid porc trees next time you go back through the forest."

"About going back . . ." Nat took a deep breath.

"I told you she'd say no," Annin cut in before she could continue. "Let's be done with her, Estos." She pulled a small vial from her bulky coat pocket and tossed it toward Nat, who reflexively caught it in her right hand. "We can use your classroom. It will only take a minute after you drink that"—she pointed to the vial—"for me to wipe your memory. Or, if you refuse, I'll do it while you are sleeping tonight. The here and now is easier." Annin's coat swirled around her legs as she walked toward the empty classroom across from the bench.

"What are you talking about? What is this?" Nat held the green vial between two fingers.

"Andris told you what your options are. It's one or the other." Estos' gray eyes looked weary.

"You're not making the choice very appealing for her, Estos." Nat shivered as Annin's breath warmed the back of her neck. How had she gotten behind her so quickly? "Why don't you ask her what she wants if she goes back in?" Annin pushed her wavy hair away from her covered eye. "Why don't you ask her how badly she wants to know the answers to all the questions that have been running through her mind?" She walked around Nat like she was observing a zoo animal. "Tell her that if she helps us, she will learn things that will defy her understanding of the world she knows." She paused. Nat stared straight ahead, refusing to look at her. "Or if none of that is of interest, just tell her we will pay her more." Annin leaned in even closer. "Are you in, Natalie, or are you going to make me take you back to your poverty and ignorance?"

"Shut up, Annin." Nat stepped away from her and carefully placed her backpack on the ground. She slid onto the bench and handed the vial to Estos. "I'll go back in," she said quietly. The expression on Estos' face transformed. "But I have a price." She watched him carefully. She knew she was agreeing to this for him more than anything. His scar stood out against his pale skin. She took another deep breath. "I want answers to all my questions, and I have a lot of them." He nodded in agreement. "And I need your promise I'll be safe."

"There's no risk to you, I promise." He looked grave, but Nat sensed hope in his voice. She thought she saw a flicker of surprise cross Annin's face, but when she looked closely, all she saw was the familiar stony expression.

Estos ran his hand over his bristly hair again and rose from the bench.

"What about my questions?" Nat protested and grabbed her backpack.

He held up his hand. "I left the Sisters trying to figure out a solution if you refused. We need to return with the good news. Hopefully Oberfisk and Andris haven't done anything rash in the meantime."

"Andris may not think it's such good news." Nat slung her backpack over her shoulder and fell in step with Estos and Annin. The hall began to fill with students. A rush of cold wind blew over them as they approached the thick glass doors leading to the quad. Nat shivered. They stopped near a display case by the entrance. Computerized holograms of the planets spun in dizzying circles inside the case.

"Come tomorrow afternoon." Tomorrow was Friday. Estos grabbed the handle and pushed the door open.

"I want more answers before I go back." She was not going to let him blow her off again with some other excuse. "I'm serious. Otherwise no deal." She laid her hand on the display case. The planets spun under her fingers.

"Tonight. You'll get answers tonight," Estos said over his shoulder. "Go to the place I showed you when you were sleeping." A gust of wind slammed the door shut as soon as he let go.

"I'll try," Nat said to herself as she watched the pair walk away into the wind. Estos looked back once and gave her an awkward wave. She bent down so she was eye level with the holograms. The tiny moons hurtled around Jupiter as it zipped past her nose. She wondered what tonight and tomorrow would bring.

Instead of a ladder, a vine shot up from a small leafy patch in the middle of a bright-yellow meadow. Nat grabbed a stiff leaf and hauled herself up one leaf at a time until she reached the dark rim. She flung herself over the ledge. Her dream room was empty.

"May I come in?" Annin hovered on the other side of the ledge, her face partially concealed by her dark hair. Nat scanned the whirling clouds behind Annin. No Estos.

"Come on in. You remind me of Count Dracula." Nat crossed her arms, still irritated with her.

"Count Dracula?" Annin deftly vaulted the ledge and surveyed the emptiness. A green stained-glass lamp appeared above Nat's head.

"He's a famous vampire," Nat explained. Two white circular chairs popped into place next to her. "He always asked if he could come in. Then he would drain the blood of his victims, who were usually beautiful, brainless young women stupid enough to invite him in. They run the movie during Halloween Fest at the Bellmont. It's probably not high on your list of social activities. Have a seat." She gestured to a chair.

"How do I remind you of Count Dracula?" Annin didn't sit. She instead clutched the rounded edge of the chair.

"I wasn't . . . You just . . . It's the 'May I come in' thing, that's all. It's a joke."

Annin relaxed her grip and spun the chair.

Nat looked toward the ledge. "Is Estos coming?"

"No, he can't travel as far as I can. He would need to be in the same building with you to do this." Annin plopped down into the chair with her legs dangling over the side.

"But you don't?" Nat asked, trying to hide her disappointment in not finding Estos waiting for her.

"No. I can reach you from very far away," she said so matter-of-factly that Nat ignored the possible threat and pressed on with her questions.

"But I would still have to invite you in each time, right?"

"Yes, but there are ways of getting around that. One thing you must learn to do is to send up sets of lines from your ledge and characterize them. It'll protect you from unwanted visitors."

"Tell me about the lines first, then the unwanted visitors." Nat intended on getting as many answers as she could. If she had to write an agenda to keep Annin on task, she would.

Annin spun in the chair, her long hair now brushing the floor. The upside-down eye patch flashed each time she went round. "Think of an infinite number of perfectly parallel lines." She stopped spinning and hopped off the chair. "Come here." She took Nat's arm and brought her close to the ledge. "Imagine a straight line starting here"—she pointed to a spot on the ledge—"that extends into infinity."

A white line shot up into the sky.

"Good. Make another." They walked along the ledge as one bright white line after another shot up into the darkness.

"Now, in the back of your mind, imagine them extending forever in either direction. The trick is to keep that image in your head. Depending on who or what you want to keep out, characterize the lines. Heat is always a good choice," Annin suggested.

"Imagine the lines are hot?" Nat stood a few feet from the ledge, concentrating on the lines.

"Exactly."

The lines changed in hue from yellow to light blue. Nat's face warmed as she faced them.

"You're not as hopeless as I thought," Annin said as she carefully touched a line.

"Thanks a lot." The lights began to fade.

"No, don't let them go, keep them up!" Annin's yell brought the lines crashing down. Shards of glass shattered around them as they jumped behind the chairs to avoid the flying splinters.

"You control it, Natalie!" Annin cried over the sound of breaking glass.

I control this? Nat ducked behind the chair. She imagined the game of statues she used to play with MC. Silence filled the room. She opened her eyes. Suspended bits of glass and dust hung in the air.

"Form the lines again, slowly," Annin called out as she peered over the edge of the other chair. The glass moved around and upward until the pieces coalesced into bluish lines illuminating the ledge as far as Nat could see.

"Keep that image in your head. Don't let it go," Annin said softly. The lines glowed and stayed in place. "Okay." She let out a breath. "I have a new set of directions for tomorrow's trip. Can you pull up Estos' map while maintaining the image of the lines?" She gave Nat a doubtful look.

Nat closed her eyes. When she opened them, a small forest hovered between the two chairs. Annin circled the map.

"Where did you see the Na—thing in the trees?"

Nat pointed to an area south of the cliff's entrance. Annin pulled the sides of the map, and it stretched out in all directions. The top of the cliff was visible. It crumbled into a low, long plain to the north of the forest. A small house sat at the very southern edge of the map, not very far from the message tree. Annin pointed to the house.

"That's your destination." She paused. "An old man, Benedict, lives there. He'll have a response to the message you left. You'll tell him Sister Barba sent you. But don't tell him anything else. Sister Barba, Ethet, and Estos trust him, but he is a rat." She punctuated each word.

"Wonderful."

"He won't be a problem for you. He's trustworthy enough with his own kind. No, your problem is getting to his house." Annin examined the map a moment, then traced a path up and over the cliff and straight down into the heart of the plain. "It's best you stay out of the trees this time, but we can't have you on the plain midday. Cliffs until sunset, then out on the plain at dark. You should reach his house before midevening. Get his message and return. Ready?" Annin held out her hand. Nat hesitated.

"Why can't I go through the trees this time?"

"Can't answer that, Estos made me promise." Her hand was still extended.

"He's going to answer it before I leave tomorrow. I'm done with not knowing. That's the deal." She took Annin's hand and stepped out of the cliff's entrance. The forest was on the verge of darkness. She looked up. The very top of the cliff was still covered in sunlight.

"The climbing path is over to the left." Annin sat on the same boulder Estos had occupied on Nat's first map trip. She motioned her head to the left. "It's pretty steep at the base but then it levels out. You'll need to search for the toeholds in this light."

Nat brushed her fingers over the rockface, searching for a hold until she found two indentations deep enough to ram her hands in. "This is no path." She hoisted herself up the first set of rocks. They formed a tunnel, shielding her from the forest. Pulling herself out of the rock chute, she sat back on her heels at the top of the cliff. She'd scaled the face in no time.

Cracks ran along the surface of the cliff. Her feet skimmed over the small crevices, and she jumped the wider gaps. At the very edge, the cliff crumbled away onto a plain. Scraggly shrubs poked out of the crags in the red rocks. *How am I going to get down this without breaking something?* she wondered. She eyed the loose rock and took off down the cliff face at an angle, switching back and forth until she reached the softer grasslands of the plain.

The sky was almost completely dark. No moon, no stars. She closed her eyes, visualizing the map, and began to run. A few drops of rain fell on her face, and Nat wondered if it was Annin's doing. The field was filled with tiny yellow flowers bright enough that she could see them even in the darkness. A single light came into view and illuminated a small dwelling. Nat circled the house, noting all windows and entrances. She tried the arched front door and found it opened easily into one small room containing a hearth, bed, table, cabinet, and chair.

Thump. Nat hesitated near the door when she heard the sound. No one else was in the room. Thump. The sound was emanating from the massive cabinet occupying a corner of the cottage. She grabbed a stubby candle from the hearth and lit the wick from the crackling fire. She tried the worn latch securing the cabinet door, but it wouldn't budge. The light from her candle fell on a tiny brass button above the latch. Thump. Nat swallowed and reminded herself this was only a dream. She pushed the button and heard a click, then shuffling. The cabinet door opened, and a hairy black form scrambled toward her. Nat hurried to the light of the hearth as a small, thin girl stood and pushed back a mop of tangled black hair. A much younger Annin stood before her. Nat stared at her face, mesmerized by her silvery faceted eye.

The girl looked around the room. She grabbed a glass jar from the center of the lone table and placed it under the worn blanket on the bed. She jumped on the bed, and Nat heard the crunching of glass. She was out the door in the next instant.

Nat followed her. "Wait! Annin, wait!" She chased her back down the plain and scrambled after her up the crumbling rock to the cliff top. The chase continued over the rocks and down the cliff wall. The girl was just a few steps ahead of her when Nat jumped onto the boulder where Annin sat. The girl's form disappeared into Annin's.

"What was that? Where is she?" Nat circled the boulder. Annin hopped off and reached for Nat.

"I told you he was a rat." She grabbed Nat's elbow. "Field trip's over. Time to wake up." Annin and the boulder faded into darkness. Nat stumbled in the pitch-black surroundings.

"Ouch!"

"Nat, what are you doing?" Viv's sleepy head appeared under the bunk rail.

Nat rubbed her temple and looked around her dorm room. "I hit my head, Viv. Go back to sleep." She shivered, thinking of the dream and the little girl's odd eye. She pulled her tangled covers to her chin, knowing tomorrow her journey to Benedict's house would be real.

CHAPTER SIXTEEN

Rain soaked through Nat's cloak. It hung heavily over her shoulders as she ran across the plain dotted with yellow flowers. Her feet landed with certainty. The sensation still unnerved her, but she was thankful as she made her way through the darkness and the stinging rain. Icy drops fell from her hood into her eyes. She blinked and thought of the odd send-off she'd had before passing through the membrane.

Everyone had had something to say. Estos had given her a small ruby ring and told her to show it to Benedict. He'd looked so thankful that she couldn't bring herself to refuse to go, even after he'd deftly evaded her questions. Sisters Barba and Ethet had told her not to speak too much and to act aloof. Riler and Oberfisk had cautioned her to give the woods a wide berth. All Andris had offered was a scowl. The memory of his expression lingered in her mind as she ran through the rain.

She slowed her pace and cut down a steep draw. A rutted clump sent her reeling to the side. Wet yellow flowers stuck to her chin and hands. The rain poured over her eyelids and down her cheeks. *This has to be a dream,* she thought. She opened her eyes. No, still dark and wet and somewhere that shouldn't even exist. The ground squelched under her hands. Mud covered her fingers and the side of her cloak. A dim light appeared in the distance. She took a deep breath and moved on. Rat or not, she needed to make contact with Benedict.

Nat cautiously approached the house. Water dripped from the pitched roof onto the uneven stone path encircling the house. Shivering, she rounded the back. No sign of anyone other than an old mule asleep in the tilting barn. "How about I just get this over with," she mumbled to herself. She stepped onto the slippery rock path leading toward the weathered front door. Light shone under a thin crack where a stone slab met the base of the door. Her knock was light, almost inaudible. The door creaked open and light flooded around her. A slight man stood in the doorway, his mouth twisted into a frown. He stepped back, leaving the door wide open. Droplets of rain fell on the stoop. She hesitated. He hadn't exactly invited her in.

"Well, come in, then," Benedict said, his words followed by a wheezy cough.

Nat ducked under the low opening. Benedict leaned slightly to the left with each step toward the hearth. His right pant leg hung loosely over his calf. Sparks burst from a broken log when he poked it with a long hooked rod.

"Close the door, Sister. It's hard keeping the warmth in my bones."

Nat shut the door. Water dripped from her cloak, forming little puddles around her feet. She unhooked the garment and looked around for a place to hang it.

"Over here." Benedict pointed to a weathered bench near the hearth. "I don't have much in the way of accommodations for you, Sister. Your kind rarely stops here. I haven't seen a Sister in years what with all the, well, I don't need to tell you, do I?"

Nat nodded and laid her cloak on the bench, doing her best to spread it out in front of the fire. She glanced up and recognized the massive cabinet from her dream. She nervously stepped past the cabinet and perched on the narrow end of the bench.

Benedict lifted a battered copper kettle from the edge of the hearth and hooked it to the curve of a long iron rod hanging over the fire. He limped over to a sagging rush chair next to Nat. She waited, watching him closely as he slowly lowered himself into the chair. She got a better view of his face as he settled in. His nose had an odd curve to it, and Nat wondered how long it had been broken. His hair was a deep chestnut color with a small bald spot in the back.

"I haven't seen that in a long time." He leaned forward to get a closer view of her forearm. Nat quickly covered the design Barba had drawn.

"Don't be offended." The water in the kettle began to hiss, and Benedict pushed himself out of his chair. "Can't blame me for being curious. I haven't seen a Sister from the Warrior House in years. And that"—he gestured to her arm with an empty mug—"I can't say I've ever seen that on a living Sister." He poured the steaming water into two mugs and moved slowly back to his chair. He handed her one. "Mudug got rid of your Houses and sent you north. Ha! Wouldn't he be interested to find one wandering on the Meldon Plain." He eyed her with curiosity.

Nat had to force herself to sit still and not bolt out the front door. She placed the mug on the floor and pulled the small ruby ring from an inner pocket after touching the hilt of her dagger. She remembered Barba's words to her before she left: "Treat him the way a general would treat a lowly soldier. He is nothing to a Warrior Sister."

"You have something for me," she said, her voice artificially low and cold as she held the ring between her thumb and forefinger. The red stone glowed in the firelight.

Benedict gasped. "Where did you get that?" He reached for the ring.

"You received a question in the last two weeks. Do you have an answer for me?" His thin fingers hung in the air as she tucked the ring back in her pocket.

"He's well?" Benedict watched her for a moment.

"I'm waiting." She leaned back as he scowled. She kept her face emotionless as she met his unhappy look.

"It's been a year since I've heard anything, and then Sister Barba's indecipherable handwriting makes its way into my tree. Wanting to know . . ." He stood again, limped to the hearth, and began jabbing the logs with short thrusts of the poker. Sparks flew in all directions. "I assumed it was a hoax. Some plan Mudug or the Chemist conjured up to catch me." Benedict said the name "Chemist" with vehemence. He poked the logs again and continued, "The answer is they're all marked. Tell the Sister they are all marked. Estos, Sister Barba, Andris, the lot of them, even that little half-breed. Mudug sits like a spider in Rustbrook, waiting for that Chemist of his to tell him when one of them pops up and shakes the web. He has men stationed throughout the lower valley who can be sent out as soon as the Chemist gives the word. I don't know where Estos is." His eyes narrowed. "And I don't want to know. He needs to stay away. Mudug intends to slaughter him—all of them—before next year. Don't doubt it."

Nat stared at Benedict, struggling to keep a calm demeanor. Estos hadn't exaggerated the danger Mudug posed to him. Her stomach flipped with nerves. "How does this Chemist know where they are?" Her voice trembled.

"I don't know how he did it, but I think he's got bits of each of them, and he's using a modified orb, possibly a calan orb, to signal when they appear in Fourline and where they are." Benedict made a little circle in the air. Nat listened to every word, but none of it made sense to her.

"Not knowing if the note was real or not, I only worked out two ways to counteract the orbs. Why waste the effort unless one must?" he said apologetically as he put down the poker and opened his palms like a book. He jabbed one palm with an index finger. "If he's using a calan orb, which I suspect he is, then we can erase its memory with suix stone.

Or we can simply destroy the orbs. The suix stone is the better option, because he won't know they aren't working until someone slips up and gets spotted, and by then it will be too late." Benedict rubbed his hands together. "Oh, that would twist him up like he'd eaten a rotten sausage," he said gleefully as he turned back to the fire.

"Gennes will need to know, he'll help us. He's all but given up on Estos. Given him up for dead. He never even believed me that Andris was still alive. The rebels are fighting for an uncertain future without Estos." His eyes brightened. "But when he sees that ring, he'll come around. That ring might be just the thing to get Gennes to help us. He has a small illegal suix mine far north of Rustbrook, you know."

Nat didn't know but nodded slowly, hoping she appeared wise and knowledgeable. A log fell from the hearth stand.

"Three or four weeks. Get word to Sister Barba, I'll have a plan worked out in three or four weeks. I'll expect you back here by then."

"Me?" she squeaked. Wise and knowledgeable went by the wayside.

"You, of course. Didn't you hear me telling you they'll be killed if they come out of hiding now? Destroying the tracking orbs is the only chance for Estos to safely join the rebellion. Now is the time for him to reappear, to prepare for next year. There's much work to be done to expose Mudug and undercut his operations before it's too late." He frowned.

She glared at Benedict, hoping she looked offended. Silence and angry looks seemed a better path than apparent ignorance. Her head spun with concern for Estos and everything that didn't make sense. Her glare must have worked, because Benedict's expression softened.

She stood and draped her surprisingly dry cloak around her shoulders.

"My apologies, Sister. I didn't mean to offend you. Three or four weeks, then?" Benedict's voice held a conciliatory tone as he limped behind her toward the door.

She placed her hand on the iron latch. Would she come back and go through this insanity again?

"I can't do this on my own, Sister. You know as well as I what Estos' return means," he said with a quiet intensity.

"Four weeks." She pushed down on the worn latch. The memory of young Annin fleeing through the door flashed through her mind. She glanced quickly toward the cabinet, wondering if someone—something—was in there.

"Stay clear of the forest. The Nala have worked their way far out of their territory since your kind left. The rain may keep them down tonight, but I wouldn't chance it. But why am I telling you this? No one speaks of the Rim Accord these days, but I can't imagine a Nala would take on a Warrior Sister, especially one from your House. Travel free, Sister, travel free." He wheezed as he pushed the door shut, leaving her in the darkness with the rain pouring over her.

Nat wasted little time. She ran across the meadow into the night. Replaying the conversation in her mind, she tried to make heads or tails of what he'd said. The forest loomed like a dark sentinel off to the right. She veered away from the trees and cut through the meadow toward the cliff. Her feet sloshed against the wet ground. The map was still in her head, but her body was tired and wasn't moving as fast and as sure as before.

After what seemed like hours of running, the ground transformed from a soggy mess to a slick, rocky nightmare. Chunks of rock replaced the tall grass. Her thighs burned as she climbed the hill. The dark outline of the cliff loomed in front of her. The rain had not let up and was now pouring down as she tried to scramble up the slag. One foot caught on a rock, bringing her hand down hard on a jagged edge as she tried to break her fall. She bit her lip to keep from crying out. *Just get to the top,* she thought. The black gaping mouth of a small cave materialized above her. Standing, she slowly crisscrossed up the slag toward it. The rain and wind whipped her cloak back when she reached the top. She stumbled forward and crawled into an oval-shaped space not more than a few feet deep. The water came down off the rock in sheets, but the small cave was dry and offered a little protection from the wind. She wrapped her throbbing hand in a loose tie from her cloak and closed her eyes. *I'll just rest for a few minutes,* she thought. Annin's parting words echoed in her mind: "If you sleep, set up your barrier."

Every inch of her skin was cold when she awoke. Her muscles protested each movement as she slowly uncurled her body and stretched. She peered out the entrance of the small cave. Water droplets glistened on treetops clustered to the left. She squinted at the sun and wondered how long she'd slept. She carefully crawled out of the entrance, protecting her still-aching hand as much as possible.

A beautiful field covered in yellow flowers spread out below the base of the cliff and to the right of the forest edge. Wrapping her hand again tightly, she took one last look at the blanket of flowers below her and scrambled up the next level of rocks. They would be wondering where she was. She methodically moved her hands and feet over the cliff's uneven surface. Would Estos be worried about her? Benedict had warned her about something called the Nala. Why hadn't Estos mentioned them? Were they Mudug's soldiers? She jumped awkwardly down a boulder and jogged a few steps to warm up her stiff muscles.

A yellow-throated bird let out a warble that sounded like jumping octaves on a piano. A reply came from the distance. Nat paused a moment and watched the bird tilt its head and fly in the direction of the reply. She looked over the treetops. A faint memory of them shaking tickled the back of her mind. Tree branches brushed against the cliff. She picked up her pace and saw where she would start to descend the cliff face in the distance. She played Benedict's warning over in her mind: "They'll be killed if they come out of hiding now. Destroying the tracking orbs is the only chance . . ." Was she really Estos' only option for a safe return? Estos, and now Benedict, were both clear about Mudug's deadly intentions. She shuddered.

The bird sent another octave call. The memory of the shaking tree-top nagged at her. Had it been in a dream? She pushed the thought aside and tried to focus on what to tell the others. If she told them everything, they would want her to come back. It was one thing to come to this crazy place for a few hours or a day, but what Benedict had described last night was more like days or even weeks. What was the point of doing this for Estos or even money to pay for school if something happened to her?

Nat jumped over a few more rocks. In three weeks it would be the middle of Christmas break. What if she did agree to come back? Other than a few scrapes and a swollen hand, nothing bad had happened to her here. She looked out from her vantage point on the cliff. The forest and distant fields of the foreign world spread out before her with vibrant colors warming in the morning sun. What amazing species and plants could she discover in this world? She carefully slid over the jutting rock and began working her way from toehold to handhold down the face of the cliff.

She tightened her grip, leaned back, and looked down until she could see the top of the boulder where Annin and Estos had waited for her. *Not too far away,* she thought. Her feet slid down the rock chute, and she jammed her fingers into the shallow crevices. Her breath made a little puff of steam in the cold air. She pulled her cloak to the side so she could see below herself as she descended. A loose rock skittered down the chute when the hilt of her dagger scraped against the side. She dropped the remaining few feet to the forest floor.

The forest was quiet. Nat looked toward the tops of the trees for the birds. Instead of them, she saw three treetops swaying like someone had pulled back their tips and let go. The rest of the trees stood motionless. The swaying trees reminded her of something, something she couldn't remember. The movement made her skittish. She turned and looked around the forest. The sunlight reached the forest floor, but it illuminated only the lush ferns and rotted logs scattered around the massive trunks. Nat jogged toward the hidden entrance and glanced back at the trees.

"You are in the wrong place, Sister," a voice hissed from above. Nat's eyes widened as she took in a figure crouching over the top of the rock chute she'd just climbed down. Its skin was smooth and rippled with a swirling bluish color. It had two silvery-blue faceted discs for eyes. *Annin has the same eye.*

A memory hurtled back to Nat of a blue figure jumping from tree to tree on the other side of the dream barrier she'd set up last night. She held her breath and stepped farther away from the strange creature. Her hand clutched the hilt of her dagger. The figure lifted an arm that ended in a sharp point.

"Why are you going from there to here?" It extended its pointed arm in the direction she'd come from.

The entrance wasn't far—just around the boulder. The creature stood. Its pointed feet curled around the edge of the rock chute.

"The Nala control this forest, Sister. Your place is north, at least for now," it hissed as it leaned forward, clinging to the rocks with its feet.

Was this thing the Nala that Benedict had warned her about? He'd said they'd leave her alone, but this one didn't look like it intended to let her go peacefully. It looked like it was ready to toss her around with its pointed hands. Nat drew out her dagger and pushed away her cloak, exposing the pattern on her arm.

It leaned farther forward. Glimpsing the markings on Nat's arm, the creature hissed and twisted its head to the side. "Can't be! Your House was destroyed!" the Nala screamed, its body elongating, then compressing in fury. "He lied! He lied!" The creature sprang from the rock to the treetop, screeching and hissing. It threw itself into the next tree, then another, until Nat could no longer see it, but its hissing screams echoed through the forest. Nat raced around the boulder to the entrance, keeping her dagger out and ready. She quickly glanced up to make sure the beast was gone, then pushed at the membrane. If the creature followed her, what would happen to Estos and the others, let alone her?

The strange orb was waiting on the other side of the membrane and zoomed off down the tunnel as Nat fell, panting, on the dirt floor. Her dagger dropped with a thud. The Nala's screams echoed in her head, but no sound came from the other side of the membrane. Nat retrieved her dagger, pulled herself up, and ran down the tunnel to warn Estos.

CHAPTER SEVENTEEN

Ethet cut the strip of gauze and moved between Riler and Andris toward Nat. She wrapped the wet gauze around Nat's wrist, and a tingling sensation spread through Nat's injured hand up her arm. Annin forced an enormous mug into her good hand. Nat grimaced as she sipped—it tasted like dirt. She looked over the rim. Everyone was in busy little clusters, discussing her jumbled description of the encounter with Benedict. She heard Estos whispering to Barba about sending her back in to help the odd old man. He quickly glanced her way, then bent his head closer to Barba. No one said a word about her warning. She trembled with frustration.

"Didn't you hear me? There's a crazy-looking blue creature on the other side," she said again. If that thing had seen her come through the membrane, it could be scrambling its way down the tunnel right now. Instead of grabbing one of the fifty swords she'd seen stacked in the warehouse, Oberfisk and Riler were busy crushing herbs for Ethet.

"The Nala can't come through, Natalie," Annin said. She was dressed in a deep-red shift with long bell-shaped sleeves. A thick black band held back her wild hair. She motioned to Nat to take another sip. "Nothing organic can come through if it doesn't already exist on the other side. The Nala don't exist here." Annin's sleeve flopped to the side. Nat stared at the blue-tinted skin that she'd always assumed was some type of tattoo. Annin quickly pushed her sleeve down and grabbed the mug. The look on Annin's face made Nat shiver.

"What are the Nala? Are they some kind of predator?" She caught Oberfisk's eye, but he coughed and turned toward Riler. She scanned the room, searching for someone who would answer her question. Andris stood near the tunnel entrance, legs askance. His arms were crossed tightly over his broad chest.

"What makes you think they are predators?" This was the first time his steely eyes weren't filled with disdain when he looked at her. He had a genuine look of curiosity.

"The forest was full of birds before I saw it. Right before it appeared, the woods went silent," she explained.

Sister Barba broke in before Andris could reply. "It is a type of predator, Natalie. A complicated predator. The Nala are highly intelligent. They live in areas near the coast. Once they were satisfied with preying on aquatic life, but that was long ago." She glanced down the tunnel. Her orb hovered near her face, casting light on her pale skin. The orb was another thing that confounded Nat, but an explanation could wait. Barba was finally providing useful information, and Nat wasn't about to let her stray from the topic at hand. "The Sisters and the Nala reached an agreement many generations back. But I fear the Nala are no longing abiding by all the terms." Barba shook her head and gave Ethet a knowing look.

"You should've told me about them before I went in." Nat glanced at Estos. Out of the corner of her eye, she caught Oberfisk nodding slightly.

Andris laughed as he unsheathed his dagger and began picking at the blade. "Would you have gone in? Would you have believed us if we'd told you about them?" Nat said nothing. "See our point? Too much information doesn't serve our end. Estos was right not to tell you," he said.

Estos shot a warning look at Andris.

"What? It was your decision not to tell me?" Nat lifted herself carefully from the bench and walked gingerly to Estos, who stood a few steps from Andris. He wore a chocolate-colored vest with tiny silver leaves embroidered along the edges. "He gets a look for telling me you lied?" She pointed to Andris, whose mouth curved into a smirk. "But it's okay for you to send me in there with no idea of what was waiting for me?"

"Has the notion that our world exists been easy for you to accept?" Estos' voice held an edge. A flush covered his pale cheeks. She frowned and shook her head. "It was difficult for all of us to understand your world when we came here. You have to trust that I gave you the information I thought you needed for the trip."

"You thought wrong, Estos." A hush settled over the room. Nat continued, trying to keep her anger under control. Estos shifted, but kept his gray eyes locked on hers. "My world doesn't have threatening blue creatures with spikes for hands."

"No, it has nuclear weapons, satellites that track your every movement, and drones and missiles that can evaporate you during a walk in the park. It has so much more than our world—so much more, Natalie," Andris said bitterly.

"Andris, enough," Estos ordered.

"None of us wanted to discourage you from helping us by informing you about our country's unique inhabitants." Barba was at her side, her arm extended. Nat suddenly realized she was exhausted and shaking. She cautiously took Barba's arm, and they returned to the bench. "You were never in any danger from the Nala. I promise," Barba reassured her. "Those markings on your arm." She pushed up Nat's sleeve as she knelt beside her. "They're special. No Nala would harm you." Barba's voice reminded Nat of her mother's, soft and comforting.

"How does a drawing on my arm protect me from that thing back there?" She gestured to the tunnel.

"The Nala would never accost a Sister from the Warrior House. Your markings"—she traced the pattern on Nat's arm—"and your dagger are from the oldest Warrior House. A Nala would never attack if it saw those markings."

"Why? You said they'd broken their agreement." She tried to stifle a yawn but failed.

Barba's wide green eyes were filled with kindness. She patted Nat's hand as she explained, "Because the Sisters of the Warrior House are trained to protect others from the Nala. The markings on your arm are from a very old, very special Warrior House. The Sisters from that House were trained from an early age to not only protect our population but also actively seek out the Nala and destroy them. When the Nala saw your markings back in the forest, it knew better than to remain anywhere near you."

Nat closed her eyes a moment. "But I'm not a Sister, and I haven't trained since childhood in the extermination of blue creatures."

"It worked, didn't it? You made it work, Natalie." Barba curled her small fingers around Nat's hands. "Your intelligence is a more effective weapon than brute force." Andris shook his head and turned to face the tunnel entrance. Silence settled over the room.

Estos paced in front of her, looking worried. "Natalie, I think you understand what's at stake for me, for us." He folded his hands in front of him. "There's no point in postponing the question: What will it take for you to go back and help Benedict?"

She looked around the room. Every set of eyes was on her. She could almost feel their anxiety and fear. Her anger seeped away. If she said no and walked out the door, what would happen to them? Could they find someone else or figure out another plan in three or four weeks? She doubted she was as special as Barba made out, but if it had taken Barba more than a year to assess her fitness to travel to Fourline, the likelihood of finding someone else who would willingly travel there so soon was slim. She'd heard Estos' and Benedict's grim thoughts on what would happen to the people of Fourline if Estos didn't return. The daily news from her world was filled with examples of how dictatorial regimes manipulated and killed people. Would the same fate befall the people of Fourline?

She thought back to all the conversations she'd had with Estos and Barba and realized they hadn't lied to her. They just hadn't told her everything. As much as the Nala freaked her out, it had run away from her after it had seen her markings. She looked up at Estos. His lips were set in a thin line and dark circles hung under his eyes. What would happen to him if she didn't go back? She swallowed. *I must be insane,* she thought. She opened her mouth to agree to help, but Estos broke in before she could say anything.

"We'll pay your entire tuition for next year if you help Benedict."

Nat's eyes widened, and tea dribbled into her lap from the mug that dangled in her hand. Andris scoffed.

"Leave her be, Andris. She's had enough, and she's already done us a great service. We can't expect her to return for nothing." Estos turned away from the soldier. "Would you agree to return in exchange for the money?"

Nat looked at her bandaged wrist. His words stung. Did he truly think she was solely motivated by money? "Estos, that's twenty thousand dollars if I keep my scholarships."

"Extortion!" Andris spat on the floor and took two long strides toward the bench. "We don't need her. We know what the problem is. I'll go in," he said to Estos. "Gennes will do anything I ask once he sees me. He's not going to lift a finger to help Benedict or this imposter." He thrust a finger at Nat.

"You heard her, you'd be dead before you got to Benedict's." Annin hopped off the counter and moved quickly between Andris and Estos. "Or worse, they'd take you to Mudug and force you to talk."

"I'd die before I talked." Andris' voice was cold as he glared at Annin.

"Are you certain, Andris?" Ethet nervously touched her short gray hair. "I know the Chemist. If Mudug's men captured you, he'd see you stayed alive until you told him everything. Your strength and training are no match for him." Andris scowled at Ethet. Her long, lithe figure leaned over the work table as she addressed Andris. "If you were captured, if any one of us were captured, everything we've worked for and everything and everyone we've lost would be for nothing."

"Don't speak to me of the dead, Sister." Andris' voice was cold. "All you've lost is your precious power and your precious House. I lost much more."

"No more than I did, Andris." Estos spoke in a low voice. "I'll not add you to their names."

The room was silent. Nat looked from face to face. Riler, Kroner, and Oberfisk looked very much like they wanted to be anywhere but in this room. Barba's knuckles were white as she held Cairn's hand. Annin turned away. Ethet's face was flushed.

Estos broke the silence. "Cairn, can we pay her what I've offered in advance?"

Cairn nodded.

"Annin, can you pathway the Sisters to Natalie's dream space to train and teach her before she returns?"

"Of course," Annin said.

"It's up to you, Natalie. Will you help us?" Estos' pale eyes settled on her.

She nodded before she could think.

"It's settled, then." Estos stood.

Everyone but Nat began talking. She slumped against the wall, feeling slightly ill.

Estos approached Andris. The soldier looked past Estos' shoulder, refusing to meet his eyes. "She will squeal the minute they catch her." Andris' voice was hard but pleading.

"No one will catch her, and unlike you, she has nothing to tell them," Estos responded so only Andris could hear.

"If you send her in, she is as good as dead." Andris spoke softly. He studied the young king intently.

"I wouldn't send her in if I didn't think she had a good chance of coming back."

"A chance?" Andris scoffed. "She has as much a chance as a long-eared rabbit in a Rustbrook stew kitchen."

Estos looked over at Nat, who was now deep in conversation with Sister Barba and Ethet. "Barba is no fool. She's confident in her choice."

"Intelligence over strength, I heard her. But where does complex thinking get you if a Nala's about to jump on your back?" Andris wore a troubled expression.

"She can run. You just need to teach her how to fight and get away." He patted his friend on the shoulder. "We picked her for a reason, Andris. If you train her, she'll have more than a chance. She's up to the task."

Andris raised his eyebrows. "You won't interfere with my training?"

Estos held up his hands. "No. I promise. I'll have Annin pathway you."

"I wouldn't tell her ahead of time." Andris watched as Nat listened tiredly to Barba. The girl glanced up and found him observing her and looked away quickly. "She doesn't like me much."

Estos laughed. "Can you blame her?"

CHAPTER EIGHTEEN

Eric, who lived on a nearby farm and attended school with Nat, maneuvered his beige Toyota truck down the slick road leading to Nat's house. The bare cottonwood trees surrounding the small house were covered in snow. A brown-and-white collie barked as the truck approached.

Nat grabbed her bag from the narrow space behind the bucket seats. "Thanks for the ride, Eric."

"No problem. Tell your folks hi. Let your dad know I'll be going out of my mind at home and to call if he needs any help." His thick arm tugged the strap of her bag free. She nodded. He was trying to be nice. Nat knew he had more than enough work at his family's place to keep him insanely busy through their break.

"Mom says he's doing better. Almost back to normal."

"Uh-huh. Tell him anyway."

Nat jumped out of the truck and unhooked the latch on the white gate.

"Do you need a ride back up after break?" Eric called out as Nat stepped through the gate and began ruffling the fuzzy head of her bouncing dog.

"No, I'm taking the bus the day after Christmas. I've got a weird interim-term class that starts early in January."

"You getting more credit for that?" He put the truck in gear.

"Kind of." Nat smiled.

"That's what I thought. Take an hour off, Nat Barns." He waved and pulled around the drive that circled the house and barn. Nat watched as the tail end of the truck disappeared up the hill. She still wondered if the college and her parents would buy Barba's and Cairn's crazy scheme for her January-term class. The Gates assured her they would take care of getting the fake course authorized by whoever authorized January-term classes. Her parents were her problem.

She gently shoved her dog away and rubbed the nose of a bay horse that appeared expectantly, pushing against the fence opposite the house. "Sorry, no treats." She held up her empty hands. The horse snorted. Nat opened the back door of her house and walked into the mudroom. A cluster of heavy work coats and caps hung on pegs above a neat line of boots. She sat on a red-vinyl padded bench and pulled off her shoes. Opening a small cabinet next to the bench, Nat retrieved a pair of dusty house shoes from the far corner. She remembered the cabinet in Benedict's house and shuddered. How could she trust someone who locked children away?

"Nat?" Her father's voice came from around the corner.

"Hi, Dad." His leg was propped up on a worn green cushion. Purplish toes stuck out from the graying cast. He held a fist-sized chunk of wood in one hand and a small carving knife in the other. She kissed him on his bearded cheek, and he gave her an awkward hug. The kitchen-table chair scraped the linoleum as she pulled it out and sat down.

"How's the leg?" She pushed little wood shavings into a pile.

"Fine. I need to find the right kind of prop for my leg to use in the shop. Your mom brought me some pieces to work with in here until I get that figured out." He held up the chunk of wood, and Nat could see the shape of a broad wing. Two boxes of carving tools cluttered the counter behind the kitchen table. *He must not be able to get out to the shop much at all if Mom is letting him take over part of her kitchen,* Nat thought.

"I'll figure out something for you."

"I thought you might say that." He smiled. The lines around his eyes were deeper than she remembered.

"I need a cup of something hot. How about you?" He nodded, and Nat brushed his flannel-covered arm as she passed by him to the sink, filled a kettle, and placed it on the stove. She opened the pantry door and rummaged around for the hot cocoa. The shelves seemed a little emptier than usual.

"Where's Mom?" She pulled two chipped coffee cups from the cabinet. She wanted to tell them at the same time about returning to school right after Christmas.

"She was going to take Marie Claire Christmas shopping after work. Cal is helping Marjorie Evans get the greenery up at church. She said she'd be late." Her father pulled the knife in a swift movement across the wood.

"Well, that's not new." Steam rose from the mugs. Nat crumpled the cocoa wrappers and tossed them into the garbage. "Are you sure Cal's at church?"

He took a sip, and a bit of foam clung to his brown mustache. "Your mom called Marjorie to check." He chuckled.

"Do you know if Mom had plans for dinner? I could start something." She scanned the kitchen and spotted an empty stew pot on the stove.

He pulled his leg gently from the chair. "I was supposed to start the stew an hour ago so it can 'simmer properly,' whatever that means." He hopped over to the refrigerator and grabbed a package wrapped in white butcher paper. Nat took the package and let him balance on her shoulder.

"Sit down, I'll do it."

"I'm not an invalid, Nat." The look in her father's eyes told her not to push the offer.

"I know." She swallowed the sudden urge to tell him everything that had happened to her. She looked down at the floor and pushed a clump of dog hair with her slipper. "Let me start this. Then we can go to the barn and look at your shop. All you need to do is tell me what you want done and I'll do it." She ripped the paper and turned when her father didn't answer. She knew immediately she'd said something wrong.

"I'm tired of people doing everything for me, Nat. This thing should've been off by now." He slapped the cast, making a dull thud as his fingers hit the hard surface. He slumped in his chair, looking up at the ceiling.

Nat cut some butter into the pot. "Could be worse, Dad." She stirred in a little flour. White streaks covered her purple flannel shirt as she added another tablespoon of flour. "You could've broken both legs. Then I'd have to build you a body sling out of that nasty leftover stretchy fabric Mom used for Cal's coed dress last year." Nat poured in broth and watched as the roux bubbled. "To quote someone who happens to be my parent, 'Think of how lucky you are.'" She added the meat, wiped a splatter of roux from her hand, and glanced at him. "I'm taking a theater class in January." She turned. Her father's nose crinkled like he smelled something rank.

"More theater?"

"Yeah, it's just for J-term. But get this." She slid into the seat next to him, keeping her voice upbeat and excited. "The shop I started working for this fall wants me to help with a show they're costuming up in Canada. I'll fill my last fine-arts credit and get paid. And . . . drumroll, please." Her dad tapped his hands on the table. "I got another scholarship, and not just any scholarship. It covers full tuition for the next two semesters! No loans for next year." Nat smiled so wide it made her cheeks hurt.

"Wow." Her dad's expression morphed from surprise to confusion. "How did . . . ? That's great, Nat. I wasn't sure how we were going to . . . That's great."

"I'll have money from work now that won't have to go to tuition payments." She let the information hang in the silence. She would send it home, but she wasn't going to say that right now. Nat hopped up, put the lid on the pot, and grabbed the single crutch leaning against the corner. "Come on. Let's go to the barn."

When they returned from the barn and shop, her dad was in a much better mood. They'd modified an old sawhorse by lowering the legs, adding little wheels, and strapping a ripped horse blanket around the body. He could scoot it easily from place to place and rest his leg while he worked. Nat was not so upbeat. Materials, buckets, feed, and empty pellet bags were strewn around the barn and shop. She'd nearly twisted her ankle on a degreasing gun by the tractor. She knew he'd trip on something before he made it to any of his machines if the shop stayed the same disaster. *Cal should have the place in order,* she thought. MC was taking care of the sheep, and she was only nine. Her mom was working and trying to keep the place running. What was Cal doing?

Piano scales greeted them as they entered the house. MC hunched over the old Acrosonic piano, playing scales. Nat's mom was putting away a few groceries.

"Nat!" The piano bench fell backward as MC leapt up and hugged her. Her mom gave her a quick hug as well.

"Were the roads okay coming down?" Her mom's thick hair was clipped back with a long silver hair clip. A few strands hung in her face, which reminded Nat of Barba's wispy red tendrils. She handed Nat a half dozen potatoes and a peeler and continued to whiz around the kitchen without pausing.

"Pretty good," Nat replied. "Dad, that reminds me." She turned to her father, who had resumed his position at the kitchen table, wood in hand. "Eric wanted to come over if it was okay with you. He can't get his dad's lathe working and thought you might let him borrow yours in exchange for whatever you might need him to do around here." She'd need to remember to tell Eric his dad's lathe wasn't working. She wasn't even sure if his dad had a lathe. She watched her father, looking for the suspicion in his face. He bought the lie.

"I'll give him a call after Christmas. He can help me move that panel I'm working on if I get done with it." He continued working on the wooden wing. Nat's mom looked over her shoulder at her husband.

"You think you can finish the panel now?" Deep lines formed on her forehead above her dark eyebrows.

A car door slammed. The sound of boots hitting the wall came from the mudroom.

"What's for dinner, Mom? Hi, Nat." Cal, blonde hair whipping around as she barely acknowledged Nat, brushed past her and lifted the lid on the pot. "Yuck. I'll pass."

"No, you won't. Set the table." Her mom pointed to the utensil drawer.

"My fingers are all cut up from hanging the pine boughs, and now you want me to set the table?" Nat had forgotten how ugly her sister's face became when she whined.

"I'll do it." MC's ponytail flipped from side to side as she scurried to the cutlery drawer. Nat waited for her parents to say something, but neither of them did. Cal flopped into a chair and stretched out her long legs. Nat walked to the mudroom and grabbed a pair of worn leather work gloves. She tossed them into her sister's lap.

"Mom, dinner in about an hour?" Nat asked, and her mom nodded. "Since you're not doing anything, put those on and come with me. They'll protect all that tender flesh."

Cal snatched the gloves and followed her sister into the mudroom and out the back door. "I'm home five minutes, and you're already telling me what to do." She pulled up the zipper on a ripped work coat.

"Somebody needs to. Been in the barn recently?" Nat said. Cal shrugged. "Didn't think so." Nat pushed open the dented main door to the barn. She gestured to the shop strewn with equipment at the back of the barn. "How do you expect Dad to get better and get any work done when he can't even walk a straight line to his shop? Mom has enough on her plate, and MC is picking up more than her share."

"What do you know, Nat?" Cal kicked a bright-orange bucket, which ricocheted off a spool of sheep wire. "You haven't been here, you have no idea what's going on. You're off at your expensive college, stressing Mom and Dad out about how they are going to pay for it when they don't have enough to pay for my dance lessons."

"They don't have to worry about that anymore, Cal."

Cal got quiet. "Did you drop out?" Her voice sounded expectant, almost hopeful.

"Of course not, you idiot. I just figured out a way to cover my tuition." Before Cal could ask more questions, she quickly continued, "Now start with the mess by the tractor. Dad's never going to be able to pay for your stupid dance lessons if he can't get down here."

Cal sulked throughout dinner but brightened when Nat told her parents she was leaving right after Christmas.

"Where in Canada is all of this again?" her mom asked while pushing a clump of potato around her plate.

"North of Quebec somewhere, which is another reason I have to go back early. It will take a few days to get there. They have to haul a bunch of stuff up." She turned the subject to MC's part in the Christmas pageant and hoped they wouldn't ask any more questions.

CHAPTER NINETEEN

Nat tucked the fleece blanket around her legs and listened to the sounds of the sleeping house. Little squeaks emanated from the mudroom where her dog slept. *He's probably dreaming of chasing sheep,* she thought and wondered where her dreams would take her tonight. The furnace kicked on, spewing hot air out of the old green grate with a low-pitched whine. She heard her little sister's steps padding across the wood floor of the living room.

"It's ten o'clock, MC." She placed her book on the floor next to the couch.

"I can't sleep." A line formed across MC's forehead.

"Why not?" She lifted the blanket, and her sister snuggled under the covers. Nat had to shift her hips to make room. At nine, MC was almost up to Nat's chin.

"I'm worried." She nestled next to her.

"About what?" Her sister's silence spoke volumes. "Hey," Nat said as she brushed her hand over MC's hair. MC lifted her chin. "Too many worriers just make more worries. Dad's going to be okay."

MC pushed her tousled hair away from her splotchy cheeks. "I'm not just worried about Dad, I'm worried about you, too. You don't come home like you used to or call like you used to or write back to me. I've only talked to you three times since you left for school and that was about Mom and Dad and the bank, and now you're leaving right after Christmas."

The words tumbled out and crashed into Nat like a waterfall. She wrapped her arms tightly around MC and tucked her head under her chin so she wouldn't see the tears forming in her eyes. "I'm sorry, MC." Nat's heart ached. "You know I love you, and I can't imagine my life without you in it." She suddenly thought of Estos and his sister. She couldn't imagine what it would feel like to lose her sister. "I'll make it up to you, I promise." She kissed MC's forehead.

"Soon, make it up to me soon," MC demanded in a sleepy voice.

"As soon as I can." Nat laid her chin on MC's head and tucked the blanket around her shoulders. The clock ticked loudly on the mantel. MC's gentle snores joined the ticking sound. She looked down at her sister. If Nat had any idea what was waiting for her after she fell asleep, her worrying would never end.

A small funnel of air began spinning from the green grate. Nat leaned closer. The funnel grew faster and wider. She reached for the edge of the couch and clutched MC as the funnel ripped away the tile floor and pulled her to its center. MC spun into the darkness. A gag of dust filled Nat's mouth when she tried to scream her sister's name. The funnel pulled Nat higher and higher into the air until she hung suspended in the night, looking down at the roof of her house. She cartwheeled through the spinning air, grasped the ledge to her dream room, and hurtled over. The other side was dark and quiet. Nat visualized the protective bars of light.

"You're getting better at finding your access points." Annin's face glowed behind the light of the white bars shooting up along the ledge. Two faint figures appeared behind her.

"Come in." Nat motioned to Annin. The lights slowly disappeared, and Annin hopped over with her usual agility. "Would have been nice if you'd found it a few hours ago, though," she said in a deadpan voice. "I don't like waiting, especially when I have to wait with him." She jerked her thumb toward the ledge. Andris hovered in the funnel on the other side with Estos next to him.

"Wait a minute, nobody said anything about lessons with Andris." Nat took a step back from the barrier and the light bars shot up from the ledge.

"You like him about as much as I do." Annin had an amused smile on her face. "Doesn't matter, though, you have to let him in. Take it up with Estos. But can we get this over with so I can get some sleep?" She looked longingly at the other side of the ledge.

He wasn't a Sister. Nat wondered what Andris was going to teach her. How to make other people feel like garbage?

"Fine." Nat let out a long breath. "You can come in." The bars receded. Andris' feet landed on the ground. Estos followed and gave her an apologetic look. Annin sat down near the ledge, still wearing an amused smile.

"What's this about?" Nat asked Estos.

"Your training, of course," Andris answered. His eyes reminded her of the green scum that grew around the edges of the water troughs in the heat of August.

"Andris and his brothers have trained me in combat since I was ten." Estos dipped his head. "I don't have a Warrior Sister to teach you how to get away from a fight, so Andris agreed to train you. This is all precautionary, Natalie, as I'm certain you won't need—"

"Remember our agreement," Andris said with a slight warning edge to his voice. Estos frowned but closed his mouth.

What agreement? Nat wondered, growing uneasy as Andris approached her. "You and I are fighting?" Her voice trembled slightly when she asked him.

He laughed. "No, you and Estos will spar." He looked almost pleased as her jaw dropped. "I need to observe you first to see just how bad you are. Estos volunteered to attack you." His lips twisted into a smile. "Let's get started."

Estos moved slightly to the left. Nat opened her mouth but thought better of it. Estos stepped to the side and turned his head, looking into the void past Nat's light barrier. Nat followed his gaze and felt a brush of air against the side of her head.

"Make contact!" Andris cried as Estos' foot landed on the ground. His kick had missed her head by an inch. "I agreed to do this, now you uphold your part," Andris barked at him. Nat looked around, confused.

"Try to block me, Natalie," Estos whispered.

"I heard that!" Andris yelled. "Start again!"

Annin's tittering laughter filled the air. Estos took a deep breath and circled Nat with a grim look on his face. She followed his lead and tried to watch his hands and feet, but his kick to her midsection was too swift. Nat fell to her knees and clutched her stomach. Estos blurred in and out in front of her. He had a horrified look on his face.

"If your plan is to wallow on the ground the first time you get knocked down in Fourline, you might as well give up now. You're supposed to be a Warrior Sister. Get up." Andris nudged her leg with his worn leather boot.

She imagined the pain floating from the side of her stomach. The throbbing disappeared. She looked up at Andris. His face bore an expression that was both smug and bored.

"Couldn't be in a worse position than the one you're in now," Andris said, smiling in response to her look of hatred. He held up a finger. "I take that back. A Nala clinging to your back would be worse."

Estos extended his hand. She ignored it and pushed herself off the ground.

"Well, well, at least you can pull yourself up." Andris clapped one hand lightly against the other. Nat brushed nonexistent dust off her pants, trying to rein in her anger. "Let's try this again."

"Not with Estos—with you." She pointed to Andris.

His eyes narrowed. "Very well, he'll be too soft on you, anyway. Take him back, Annin."

"No," Estos protested.

"She'll be fine, it's her dream space," Andris said in a slightly patronizing voice.

Nat glanced toward the ledge. Annin and Estos had vanished.

"Estos and Barba seem to think my training you will result in something other than a colossal waste of my time." She stiffened as he circled her. Her anger grew to a point that all she wanted to do was humiliate him and prove him wrong. He droned on in a condescending tone. "How am I supposed to train a fraud, an opportunist, to be a Warrior Sister?" He shook his head and laughed harshly. "I doubt you'll even go." He spat on her floor. "If you do, you'll fail."

This is my dream space, you jerk, she thought. His eyes narrowed and his left hand jabbed toward her face. She ducked and punched him in the stomach. A track spread before her, and Nat burst onto the brick-colored field, running away from Andris before his next strike. Bright halogen field lights popped up like flowers in front of her, lighting the way. Her feet flew, taking her farther and farther from Andris. She stopped suddenly and whirled around. He stood in a small globe of light at the start of the track.

"I don't get you!" she yelled. "It's your home, it's your ticket back if I go in and—"

"And do what? Pull off whatever scheme Benedict pulls out of his arse?" he shot back. "Don't delude yourself. You managed to get in and out the last two times, but you were never in any real danger of being discovered. You're going into the heart of Rustbrook this time." He pointed a finger at her. "Mudug will smell you out for the fraud that you are. He'll catch you and we'll be worse off than before."

A balled-up sock appeared in the air between them and hurtled down the field. Andris opened his mouth in surprise, and the sock slammed between his teeth. He yanked at the edge of the sock, but it held fast. Nat tried to keep the image of the sock and the running field in her head while she spoke. Now would not be the time to lose the images. Her words came out slow and halting.

"If Estos, Barba, Annin, or any of the others thought I couldn't do this, they wouldn't send me in. You're the only one. Why is that?" Her voice grew louder. She was beginning to enjoy herself as she watched him struggle. "I may not know how to fight, but I can run. If you'll shut up long enough to teach me how to get away, I'll be fine." Even from a distance, Nat could see Andris' face was crimson. He let out a guttural growl.

"No? Okay, how about this. Race me," she challenged. "If you catch me, I'll lie and tell Estos that you've been training me. I'll even give you a chair to sit in while you waste your time in my space up here." She gestured to her head. "But if I win, no more insults. Just teach me what I need to know to get in and get away. Agreed?"

She knew he was too mad to even consider agreeing. He was going to come after her the second she removed the gag. She carefully let the image of the sock fade from her mind. Andris' mouth snapped shut as the sock disappeared. He hurtled down the track toward her. When he hit the halfway point, she turned and took off. His cursing echoed behind her. Nat sprinted for a few minutes, then slowed her pace. He sounded like an elephant on a rampage, his feet landing heavily with each step.

"You can't imagine your way out of this!" he yelled while running.

You don't think so? What was it Barba had said, intelligence over brute force? Nat imagined the breath and muscle a real race required. She focused and felt the sweat begin to trickle down her brow. The track veered to the left. Andris' slapping feet sounded close. In a moment, he'd try to lunge and grab her. She glimpsed back. He was within a few yards, but his face was bright red. She smiled and quickened her pace. They rounded the turn and hit the second straight leg. It wouldn't do to just beat him on a track field. She had to disappear to show him.

The track melted away, and the meadow near the crooked message tree appeared. Nat took a second to enjoy how simply the images were coming now that she'd had some practice, and then she bolted to the right toward the overgrown path in the forest. The branches whipped around in the wind. She jumped over rotted logs and ferns that brushed the thick tree trunks. Andris' crashing noises became more and more distant as she wove her way to the hiding place she remembered. Skipping over a fallen log, she paused, stepped on its elevated trunk, and jumped onto the lower branch of the neighboring tree. She scaled the tree, grabbing three more thick branches until she was at least twelve feet off the ground. Two more branches up and a leap would get her to a cliff overhang. She tucked her body as close to the trunk as she could and slowed her breathing.

Andris wasn't as far behind as she expected. He rounded the fallen log within a minute. She watched as he spun around and followed the line of the cliff wall. She settled back into the tree and waited. Five minutes passed, then ten. Nat climbed the next two limbs and jumped toward the cliff. She started a slow jog toward the rock chute leading to the red boulder.

When Andris finally showed up at the boulder, Nat had a collection of odd pinecones and leaves laid out on its crooked top. She looked up. The chase had sapped some of his anger, but not much.

She tossed one of the smooth cones into the air. "Do you know for certain I'll fail if I go back in, Andris?" Her voice was quiet as she curled her fingers around the cone.

Andris lifted his chin and looked at her.

"You don't, do you?" She stared at him from atop the boulder, chin resting on a raised knee.

Andris wiped his brow. "No," he said finally.

The forest disappeared. A thick red mat and a single floating halogen bulb took its place.

"I'm going back." She looked into the blackness surrounding them. "Estos has too much to lose, and now so do I." She took a step closer and pressed her arms tight to her side to keep him from seeing her shaking. "I'll take whatever training, whatever advice you want to give, but I just beat your sorry butt in a fair race, so don't tell me I'm a fraud or that I'm going to fail. Especially when you don't know."

Andris nodded slowly. "All right," he agreed. He took a step toward her, shaking his head, his expression more curious now than angry. "Do you know how to do anything besides run?" he asked, rubbing his short beard.

CHAPTER TWENTY

"Always use direct eye contact," Barba said for the hundredth time. "Don't look above, below, or to the side."

Nat glanced at the lab classroom's door.

"No, no, you're looking to the side. Your job is to observe emotions and anticipate movement. And for the love of all things, do not speak more than absolutely necessary. Warrior Sisters are not loquacious, they are—"

"I know, Sister. They are aloof, fierce, and aware." Nat recited the oft-spoken descriptions she'd heard over and over during her training the last few weeks. "They're everything I'm not," she said in a tired voice and slumped over the stainless-steel counter.

"You have more Sister in you than you know, Natalie," Barba said with a hint of impatience in her voice.

Ethet held up her hand, silencing Barba. The classroom in the Science Center became eerily quiet. As far as Nat knew, she, Barba, and Ethet were the only people in the entire building, since everyone was still on break. Cairn had given Ethet a set of keys to the building so she could use a centrifuge to extract plant oil. The location was convenient for Nat's final training lesson.

"I believe we are almost done, Natalie," Ethet said and placed a stoppered vial full of a balm made from the plant oil next to Nat. *I hope so,* Nat thought. Her brain felt ready to explode from all the last-minute information they were cramming into her. *So much information, but so few answers.* She stifled a yawn and rubbed her sore arm. Her body ached from the hours of self-defense drills Andris had run her through with Estos the night before.

Ethet poured a brown liquid from a thermos into a battered cup and handed it to Nat. She eyed the herbal tea with suspicion, wondering if it was the same foul brew Ethet had been forcing her to drink since she'd arrived back on campus the day after Christmas.

"The balm fights infections." Ethet gestured to the vial and crumbled a dried herb over a fine linen cloth with her other hand.

Nat sipped the sludge-like tea and made a face.

"Pay attention, Natalie." Ethet frowned. "This wrap and the dennox are useful for both open wounds and bites. You may find need for it during your journey." Her authoritative voice forced Nat to focus on the strip of linen. Ethet folded the fabric over several times and tucked it into a cloth case that held a small collection of herbs. "Fortunately these herbs grow on both sides of the membrane," she said as she tied a knot in the leather string binding the case. "There are more herbs I wish I could give you . . ." She regarded Nat for a moment and pressed the case into her hand. "Don't forget to bring this tonight."

Nat stared wearily at her. "I won't. Are we done now?" she asked, glancing at both Sisters. The aching pressure in her head was almost unbearable.

"Yes, we're done," Ethet said gently. Barba nodded in agreement.

Nat sighed, slid off the stool, and walked out of the classroom. She wandered through the deserted halls of the Science Center and out the entrance. The December day was bright and pleasantly warm for winter. Little pools of melted snow covered the walkways crisscrossing the quad. She picked a walkway at random, wondering where to go. She could return to her room, but the idea of spending her last few hours in the dorm was not appealing.

Strains of piano music spilled out from an open window in the college's chapel. Nat paused and listened to the swell of the music, then pushed open the chapel door. She sat in a pew at the back of the church next to a stained-glass window. A woman played on a grand piano near the altar, utterly lost in the music. Other than the pianist, the chapel was empty. Nat stared at the woman as she played, awed by her focus and intensity. The music soared through the open space of the church. Nat closed her eyes, frustrated with how all of them had evaded so many of her questions over the past few weeks.

She didn't realize Cairn was sitting next to her until she opened her eyes minutes later. She glanced his way and then focused on the rust-colored tiles. A small puddle was smeared between her boots.

"Barba asked me to find you," he said.

The music stopped. The pianist looked up and saw them sitting at the back of the chapel. She gathered her music as if embarrassed and exited through a door near the altar. Nat shot a perturbed look at him.

"I just saw her. Isn't it a little late for more lessons? I'm leaving in a few hours," she responded, wanting nothing more than to be left alone to clear her mind.

"No more lessons. She was just a little concerned about how you were holding up." He leaned forward and laid his hands on the pew in front of them.

She turned to him. The bright lights hanging from the ceiling reflected off his glasses. "I've been training with and listening to your family and your friends for weeks, and I still have no idea how Fourline can be . . . how it's even there," Nat said.

He looked away from her and cleared his throat.

"Vow of silence for you, too, huh?"

"Natalie . . ."

"I don't mean to be rude, but would you just go?" Nat rubbed her forehead. "Tell Barba and Estos not to worry, I'll be there." She wouldn't break her promise to help Estos. It was too late for her to change her mind, anyway—that opportunity was lost weeks ago when she'd told her parents about the fake scholarship money.

"Natalie," he said again, "not telling you everything is only to protect you. I promise you that."

"You can't fault me for wanting to know what I need protection from," she snapped.

Cairn stood, his hands still resting on the back of the pew. He hesitated, then leaned down and whispered into Nat's ear, "Years ago I was wondering the same things you're wondering right now."

Nat looked at him with surprise.

"It was my father who first came through from Fourline. He found the entrance, Natalie, but from the other side." He stopped and looked around the open expanse of the chapel. He gave her a comforting pat on the shoulder. "Some of your questions simply cannot be answered. But know this." His expression turned serious and Nat gave him her full attention. "There is no way Estos or any of us can ever adequately express our gratitude for what you've agreed to do." His voice trailed off and he straightened his long body. "See you in a few hours, then," he said as he slipped on his coat and sidestepped out of the pew.

Nat watched him leave and then stared at the shafts of colored light streaming in through the stained glass.

CHAPTER TWENTY-ONE

For a hermit, Benedict liked to talk. Now that the rain had stopped, he was chattering like a bird. Fortunately, he didn't expect much in the way of a reply. Nat pulled off the damp hood of her cloak so she could hear him better. Her bandaged hands came away covered with donkey hair.

The two were dressed as Yarkow pine merchants doing a little business off the beaten path to avoid a run-in with Rustbrook soldiers. From listening to Benedict, Nat had learned that Lord Mudug had a transportation syndicate. Merchants paid a "security fee," and Mudug's men would accompany the merchants through Nala-infested territory. According to Benedict, Mudug had proclaimed the entire southern territory infested, so even when there was no risk of Nala anywhere in the area, merchants still had to pay. It wasn't uncommon for merchants to use the path less traveled to avoid paying the fee.

"We'll stop to do a little trading in Yarsburg. There's usually a group or two that travel without protection, quietly trading there. We can sell the donkeys and drop a hint that we're joining a wagon of free traders heading west."

Nat rubbed her back. Two days on a donkey was more than enough for her. The coarse double-burlap cloak that covered her Warrior cloak was matted with donkey hair. She'd been looking at the back of Benedict's donkey for so long now that she was an expert at dodging the piles it dropped.

"If word got to Gennes, one of his men will meet us a day's walk from Yarsburg. We'll need to get through the slag hills in the dark to meet him on time. Gennes' man won't wait for us." Benedict glanced back with a nervous expression. "You have an orb, don't you?"

"Of course." Nat tapped into the condescending voice she'd worked on with Barba and Cairn before leaving. A mini–acting class in playing the part of a Sister was just one of the crash courses she'd had in the days leading to her departure. How to use Barba's orb was another. She felt inside the special pocket that held the orb. It warmed slightly at her touch.

"No offense meant, Sister." Benedict wiped the back of his hand across his nose. "So many orbs were destroyed or confiscated when Mudug burned the Houses. It wouldn't be a shameful thing if you didn't have one or if you couldn't make one during your apprenticeship."

"I have one," Nat said firmly. He'd been poking and asking about her apprenticeship since they'd started this interminable ride. Nat had let it slip that she was from a northern fringe house like Ethet suggested, but she wasn't sure he was buying it.

Benedict rubbed his thin leg and continued. "Good. We'll need light to get through those fields, and a torch would draw too much attention."

Nat felt her inner pocket a second time, touching the orb and remembering the moment Barba had turned the confounding thing over to her. Based on Barba's expression, she knew the orb had better come back with her. "The orb has a part of its Sister in it," Barba had explained. "That's why it responds to only the Sister." She had pressed her orb to her lips and whispered to it before placing it gently in Nat's palm. She'd continued, slightly misty-eyed. "Speak to it and it will listen to you now," she'd said. The orb had felt cold when Nat had touched it to her lips. Feeling slightly stupid, she'd whispered, "Hi, orb." The orb had warmed instantly.

Benedict's voice broke her away from the memory. "It's coming up here after the bend. You'll be wanting to stop, I suppose, but just for a few moments. We can't waste our time, especially on things that can't be undone."

Nat glanced around. The donkeys crossed over a little creek and up the side of the gulley. She leaned forward as they emerged from the gorge. Tall, wet grass brushed the soles of her boots. A fine mist was coming down. She gazed into the distance. Ahead of them stood a gently sloping hill. The blackened ruins of a series of buildings stood in contrast to the lush green crowning the hill. Nat pulled back on the thin leather rein. Her donkey brayed in protest.

"What . . . ?"

"I know, I know. It's still a shocking sight to me as well. I used to come here to get the herbs from the Sisters and consult with the Head of the House." Benedict directed his donkey to the road. "Might as well use the road a bit. Hardly anyone ever travels this way anymore."

Nat followed. So this was one of the Houses, or at least what was left of it. None of the maps Barba or Estos had provided her included any images of them. After discovering that they were places of learning, she had imagined small brick school buildings. But her imagination and Barba's limited descriptions had been far from the truth. This House had been made up of many buildings, all massive in size.

The road curved gracefully up the hill and ended at the remains of an old brickwork archway. As they rode under the remains, three jackrabbits scampered from beneath an enormous scorched door. What remained of an intricate carving of a sun covered its entire central panel. Nat thought she recognized smaller carvings of a vine, a bird, and a sword as they passed by.

Benedict stopped his donkey, dismounted with a slight wobble, and tied the reins to the remnants of a stone post. "I'll do a little scavenging while you pay your respects, Sister. I found a crop remaining from the Head's private garden last time I was this way. She'd want them to go to good use, and we may have need of the herbs where we're going." Benedict hobbled off around the charred remains.

Nat slowly dismounted, unable to take her eyes off the three massive stone staircases leading to the sky. Their wooden destinations had been burnt to oblivion. She picked her way over piles of crumbled brickwork to a set of stone stairs leading to what must have been the entrance to the House. The charred remains of another door slanted on its side near the entrance. She thought how her father would admire the engraving and the thickness of the wood that had clearly withstood such intense heat. With an awkward step, she slipped on a wet, glassy stone and landed on her side. Her arm shot out instinctively as she landed. When Andris had taught her how to fall without cracking her head, the floor had been much softer than this.

Rubbing her arm, Nat sat up and examined the slippery stone. Words were etched into the surface. She wiped away a clump of desiccated leaves and dirt. A row of stones encircled the entrance. Each had a name carved into the greenish surface. "Head Sister Ethea Matris, Head Sister Etheb Zornob, Head Sister Ethec Sallin." She read name after name until she came to the last stone: "Head Sister Ethet Nightswain."

"Ah, Sister Ethet."

Startled by the voice, Nat rolled to the side and unsheathed her dagger.

Benedict dropped his bundle of herbs and stumbled backward. "Now don't get all cackled!" he cried.

"I don't like people sneaking up on me." She sheathed her dagger.

"Then you picked the wrong House to belong to, didn't you?" he said angrily. "Mind me, would you look at this jumble." Benedict clutched his ears. "The dennox is mixed in with the camroot. Can't have that now. Take one for a Nala bite and find out you've lost all use of your limbs." Benedict knelt with care and picked through the pile with worn hands.

"You've got dennox?" Nat knelt and helped Benedict sort the fallen roots and herbs. Ethet had grilled the roots' names and purposes into her over and over again. When dennox was dried, it could be made into a paste to cover any type of bite, particularly a Nala bite.

"I found a little bounty back there." He pointed to an open patch near a thicket of trees. "That, and some camroot."

Nat pulled out the small fabric case Ethet had given her. "I've got a bit of dennox, but my supplies are down."

"Since when does a Warrior Sister carry an apothecary?" Benedict eyed the case.

"Since this." She waved her arm in the direction of the ruins. Benedict sighed. He pulled the long, thin strands of dennox from the rounded leaves of the camroot. Nat put judgment aside and asked, "You knew Sister Ethet?"

"What a silly question. Of course I knew the Head Sister. Any healer of worth knew Ethet Nightswain." He sat back, raised his tunic above the boot line, and began rubbing his leg. Even under the breeches, Nat could see how thin it was. "She was an apprentice when my father brought me here with limb sickness."

"Polio," Nat said softly to herself.

"She was a good friend." Benedict rolled slightly and stood. "We had a few disagreements about the duozi." He spat on the ground. "I never understood how she could tolerate them. If you can't heal them, then the best place for them is with their own kind or dead," he said bitterly. "She never listened to sense. She'd keep them around and try to heal them, even when they were too far gone." He walked slowly and carefully over the rubble toward the donkeys. Nat followed, listening.

"Word was she sent Sisters sympathetic to duozi into Nala territory to study under that crazy predecessor of hers," he grumbled as he approached the donkeys. "Her love of the duozi was her House's downfall. Mudug justified his destruction of this place because she helped them. Called her a sympathizer. Where were her little duozi then?" He looked back at the ruins.

Nat wondered what he meant as they untied the tethered donkeys. She helped boost Benedict onto the unwilling animal. The frustration of pretending to know and understand everything he said was beginning to wear on her. The sleeve on Nat's tunic rolled up as she helped Benedict. His gaze lingered on her markings.

"You'll want to cover up before we get to Yarsburg. Most people this far from Rustbrook secretly support the Sisters, but enough believe Mudug's rumors about the Sisters conspiring with the Nala. You'll be turned in if you let anyone see that."

"I can take care of myself," Nat said, tucking a loose strand of hair behind her ear.

"Ho-ho. I think I hit a bit of a nerve." He leaned crookedly in the saddle. "You may be up for a challenge, Sister. Living on the fringe as your like's been doing these past years leaves you missing out on one important thing."

Nat climbed onto her donkey, wincing slightly as her sore bottom hit the saddle. "And what's that?"

"Information." He touched a skinny finger to his temple. "What you don't know can kill you." He smiled.

"Then humor me and treat me like an imbecile. Tell me everything that's happened while I've been living on the fringe." She coaxed her donkey to move and glanced back. "You talk enough that you should be able to tell the story of the world before we reach Yarsburg."

Benedict snorted and turned his donkey. "First thing I'll tell you, Sister, is you're going the wrong way." He pointed to the distant mountains. "Yarsburg is that way."

Her cheeks grew hot with embarrassment. The donkey brayed and turned as she pulled gently at the reins. *He doesn't need to treat me like an imbecile—I am one,* Nat thought.

CHAPTER TWENTY-TWO

Nat leaned against the corner of the stall. The stable was dark except for two lanterns hanging from iron loops at the entrance. One good knock, and the whole place would be up in flames. She yawned. A fat mare from the neighboring stall leaned down and nibbled on her hood. The smell of her cloak made her wince as she brushed the horse away. It still had the cheesy smell of a goat bladder.

The boy had not meant to do what he did. If she had been in his shoes, she would have done the same to get away from Benedict. The rough wood caught her outer cloak as she slid a little lower. Benedict lay across from her. His sleeping form rose slightly with each breath. She marveled at how he could sleep as she replayed the events of the afternoon in her mind.

When they had arrived in Yarsburg, the town was packed with traders, carts, horses, goods, and stalls that appeared the moment a trader caught the scent of a trade or sale. With her earlier slip fresh in her memory, Nat followed obediently behind Benedict. If anyone noticed them in the throng, they would glimpse a withered old apothecary and his apprentice. She hoped he would interpret her actions as part of their master plan as opposed to her fear of stepping the wrong way.

After trading a bit of the strong, fine threads of harmsweedle for some brown bread and a fat sausage, Benedict turned up a cobbled street that stank of vinegar. Clusters of long intestinal casings hung from wooden rods behind stall fronts. He stopped and interrupted a gangly man pulling a milky casing from a cylindrical vat. She listened as they bantered about what time the guarded convoys were leaving town and recent sightings of the Nala. Her ears perked up when the man mentioned the recent capture of a Warrior Sister near Daub Town.

"Word is she helped the Nala attack another convoy, then made off with their goods to sell on the black market in the fringe," the man explained. Benedict made disgusted tsking noises.

Nat held the donkeys and hid her forearm under her cloak. The man flipped a casing onto a drying rod as they finished their conversation. Flecks of foam landed on her cloak and boots. She stepped aside and noticed a boy about MC's age who sat on the ground near a bowed wooden barrel. Loose, dark curls covered his face as he bent over what looked like a deflated balloon. He quickly dipped his hand into a small earthen pot and rubbed the object before tossing it into a pile. Every part of him, except his hair and wet hand, was covered in a fine brown powder. A bulbous woman, occupying the stall seat, selected one balloon from the pile and jammed the opening over a small cup connected to a billow by a tube. As she pressed down on the billow, the balloon object expanded, revealing a series of spidery marks. She pulled the cup off the tube and the pale, veined object remained inflated. Above her hung a jumbled row of the bulbs capped with leather tops. They looked like odd canteens. She watched the boy as Benedict approached the woman.

"Fellow over there says you may know someone who buys donkeys." Benedict looked at a string of gourds. "I'm not looking to sell them for slaughter price. They are right good beasts."

The woman scratched her chin. "Neas." She turned to the boy. "Take him and the animals to Yester." She turned back to Benedict.

"Yester'll give you a fair price. Donkeys are fetching a good coin. They don't get all jackamahoo in the head like the horses when the Nala are around." She handed a soiled cloth bag to the boy. "Take these to Yester, too. Don't leave until he pays."

The boy nodded. "Yes, Mam."

"And come right back," she called out, but Neas was already darting quickly through the crowd. Benedict and Nat hurried to keep up with him. People stepped to the side when they saw him coming. Traders brushed their arms as Neas ran past. After a series of turns, the boy waited under a crude rock archway until Benedict and Nat caught up. He darted under the archway and down a dirt lane toward a long line of stables. When he reached the dusty entrance to one of the stables, he cupped his hands and let out a small yell, then stepped away. A dark-haired man with three-pointed beard tips and manure-encrusted boots began conversing with the boy from a distance.

"Yester?" Benedict interrupted.

"That is me." Yester stared past him and surveyed the donkeys. Benedict took the reins from Nat and limped closer. They began bartering over the animals.

Neas jumped slightly from foot to foot as Nat walked toward him. His speed reminded her of racing along the dirt road to her house when she was younger, and his hair reminded her of someone.

"I wouldn't go too near the boy," Yester called out as he shook hands with Benedict. "Neas has a perpetual case of lice. His mother swears by that dust she covers him with, but it never seems to do him any good. He's been covered in brown pulops powder for six months now. Neas, put them bladders by the tie post. I'll give you your mam's money after I settle up with this man." Yester disappeared into the stable, pulling the two donkeys.

"Pulops powder?" Benedict reached into his satchel. "What you need is a head shaving and a bit of yarax ointment." He twisted the root in his finger as he drew near the boy. The root grew to strange dimensions in the shadow of the setting sun. "Here, take it. Consider it payment for leading us here." The boy stepped back. "Take it, your mam should know what to do with it. Pulops powder, what is this world coming too?" Benedict let out a wheezy laugh.

Nat caught a strange glimmer in Neas' eye as he reached tentatively for the root. Benedict's hand grasped his wrist with surprising strength. He pulled the boy closer and pushed the mass of hair away from his face. One eye was silver surrounded by a brilliant blue web. "I thought I smelled a duozi," Benedict growled and twisted the boy's wrist while rubbing off some powder. A bluish tint appeared on the boy's forearm.

"What are you doing?" Nat cried. Neas yanked repeatedly, trying to free his arm, but Benedict held tight.

"No lice, just stinking Nala running through you. How do you think Yester will act when he finds out your mam's been harboring a duozi?"

"Let him go!" Nat pulled Benedict by the shoulder just as Neas flung his bag of bladders at Benedict's leg. The bag crashed into him and bounced off Nat's cloak. Benedict released the boy and crumpled to the ground. Neas took off running into the hills behind the town, glancing back once to see Nat waving him on.

"What the blast was that all about?" Benedict rocked on his side, cradling his shin. His face was bright red and angry. Nat thought he looked like a fish flopping on a riverbank. "Didn't you see what the boy was?"

"He's a boy," Nat hissed. "And if you say a word to Yester, I'll tell him you just sold him two worm-infested beasts."

"You—you're trained to kill the Nala, and you just let one slip away."

"He wasn't a Nala." She pulled him roughly to his feet.

"He's a duozi, there's no difference."

"There's plenty of difference," she said, not really understanding what he meant by duozi, but she didn't care. She was so mad that it took everything not to push Benedict back down and walk away.

"Is everything all right?" Yester stood in the stable entrance, shielding his eyes against the setting sun.

"It's fine. He just took a wrong step." Nat tightened her grip on Benedict's wrist under his cloak and smiled broadly. "The boy left, said you can pay his mam later." She adapted her tone to sound like Yester's. Benedict grunted slightly as Nat pulled up on his arm. From Yester's perspective, it looked like she was helping him steady his legs.

"We'll need a place to stay for the night," Benedict said gruffly, looking at the ground. Nat eased up a bit on his wrist.

"I've an empty stall in the back where you can rest the night. But mind you, if I find a horse missing in the morning, I'll hunt you down myself," Yester said.

"Not to worry. We will be off before morning to join a caravan leading to Rustbrook. That is if you have my money so we can pay our way?" Nat loosened her grip on Benedict, allowing him to extend his hand for payment.

They ate a small dinner of bread and sausage in silence on a cluster of rocks outside the stable. Benedict scowled and sulked as he cleaned up in a trough before flopping on a pile of straw. "We leave in two hours," he said, then turned and fell asleep.

Nat fought back another yawn and glanced at Benedict. Her body cried for sleep, but she didn't want to be anywhere near him. The horses nickered when she walked past their stalls. The sky was bright with stars and a half-moon. She settled into a nook by the rocks. She blinked once and her eyes shut fast.

"How did you get here?" The protective lights shot up along the ledge of Nat's dream space.

"I came into Fourline after you. Aren't you glad to see me?" Annin spun, arms extended, crazy curly hair flying.

"Yes, I'm glad to see you." Nat's voice was tinged with frustration. "I feel like I've started reading a three-thousand-page book halfway through. I have no idea what's going on here, what to say or what not to say."

"Maybe you should have paid more attention during your lessons."

"Maybe you should have spent a few minutes explaining some of the finer details of this place. I've stuck my foot in my mouth so many times today. If Benedict doesn't know I'm a fraud, it's because he's a dimwit."

Annin chuckled, then grew serious. "As I recall, your first lesson was not to say anything, or as little as possible." She plopped into the circular chair and began pushing it around with her foot.

"Easier said than done. Why am I even here if you can come in safely?" Nat sat in another chair and leaned toward her.

Annin laughed. "I'm the furthest thing from safe, Natalie. Barba, Ethet, and I agreed that my presence might serve as a distraction for Mudug while you are here. I'm here for as long as I can stay ahead of Mudug's trackers."

"You, Ethet, and Barba agreed? What about the rest? What about Estos?"

Annin glanced toward the ledge when Nat said his name. "Sometimes decisions are best made without the full committee," she shot back.

"I never got the sense Estos was just part of a committee."

Annin glared at Nat a moment and jumped out of the chair. "You need to use the distraction my presence brings to your advantage and get your job done. Where are you headed?"

Nat watched as Annin paced back and forth in front of the ledge. She couldn't be aggravated with her; just seeing her in this dream space was like a lifeline to home. Nat sighed. "We're meeting Gennes or one of his men tonight. Benedict said Gennes can get the suix stone."

"Make an opportunity to speak to Gennes without Benedict," Annin said as she continued to pace. "Do it early and get to your point. You need to be the one to tell him Estos is still alive. Gennes has little reason to believe Benedict. If he doesn't flat out refuse Benedict's request for help, he'll waste what precious time you have toying with Benedict. If I were you, I would rid myself of Benedict as soon as you get to Gennes. At the very least, appear not to get along with him."

"That won't be a problem after today." Nat rubbed the back of her neck and was thankful that the goat-bladder smell didn't travel into her dream space.

Annin's fingers caught in her tangled curls. Both eyes were visible with her hair pulled away from her face. Her faceted eye drew Nat like a magnet. Nat forced herself to focus on her normal eye.

"If Gennes doesn't believe that Estos is alive, try telling him something about one of us." Annin tapped a finger to her lips. "Something about Andris."

"What do I know about Andris? He's crass, rude . . ."

"That won't work. Everyone knows Andris' reputation."

Nat thought a moment. "He's got a tiny scar under his left eye. I noticed it while we were training. He told me he got it from a thorn bush. That is the only remotely unique thing I know about him."

"That might work." Annin looked between the lights beyond the ledge. "I'll try to contact you in a few days. I have a little errand for Ethet to attend to that may put me too far away, but I'll try." Suddenly she was still. "I need to go."

"Annin, wait! The boy, there was a boy today. He had the same eye like you. Benedict went crazy when he saw him." Nat quickly relayed the rest of the story.

"I told you Benedict was a rat," Annin said angrily.

"What made the boy's eye like that?"

"The Nala." She tilted her head back. "They chose him and bit him."

"Chose him?" Nat asked.

"Yes." Her voice seemed very far away. "Barba told you the Nala were predators."

"They choose people to bite?"

"Don't worry, they don't choose to bite all people they encounter, mostly they just impale or rip them to shreds. They just bite the people they want to make into duozi."

"You're not really helping my nerves here, Annin. What do you mean 'make into duozi'? As in, make into them? Are you . . . ?" Benedict's harsh words about Ethet helping the bitten rushed back as she asked the question.

"No, not a full Nala, just part. Someone helped me before . . ." Her voice trailed off. "It has its benefits. I'm quick, I can get into people's heads, I have some unexpected friends." She watched Nat for a reaction. "It's all complicated, and none of it matters to you right now. But you can't trust Benedict, Natalie. Especially not now, not after you interfered with him today." She approached the ledge and Nat brought the lights down. "And don't worry about the Nala, they don't bite Sisters." She laughed. "But I'd keep these lights up if I were you." Then she was gone.

"But I'm not really a Sister," Nat said to the darkness.

CHAPTER TWENTY-THREE

A few hours after they left the stables, Nat was certain either she or Benedict would end up with a twisted ankle from trying to maneuver in the darkness. Even with gradually sloping hills and few rocks or other obstructions, the going was slow and uneasy. Benedict's strides were short, but he made fair progress until they reached the slag.

"Orb," he whispered.

They'd said fewer than five words to each other since their departure, so his sudden command startled Nat. She felt in her pocket and brought the glassy ball to her lips.

"Small light," she whispered. The orb began to glow, dimly casting light on the thin slabs of rock surrounding them. The light was hardly enough to see by, so she whispered, "Grow." The orb grew brighter, revealing a massive hill covered in slippery gray rock.

"Turn that down!" Benedict hissed.

"Softer." The light dimmed.

"Do you want the whole world to know we're here?" He began progressing up the hill by taking an angled path up the slag heap and using two walking sticks for balance. "What I wouldn't give for a Sister trained in a proper House instead of a fringer." *You and me both,* Nat thought.

Benedict slipped on a pile of slag and righted himself. "Sending the light up here would be helpful, Sister," he said, his tone low but nasty. She paused. In fifteen seconds, she could be past him. She figured a minute, maybe two, and she would be completely out of sight. Then what? She was stuck with him until they found this Gennes person. But when they did, she was going to do exactly what Annin had suggested.

Nat made a show of slowly tightening the smelly burlap cloak so it wouldn't snag on the rocks. He watched her impatiently until she finally ordered the orb in front. The two made slow progress up the massive hill. Nat pulled up the collar of her tunic. Little puffs appeared in front of her face as she breathed. Benedict grumbled and swore as he moved forward. She had little sympathy for the man after what she'd seen him do to Neas, but she knew his legs couldn't take much more of this. About three-quarters of the way up the hill, Benedict collapsed and slid down several feet of loose slag. A small avalanche of rock followed Nat as she clambered toward him. The orb hovered above Benedict. A bloody gash appeared below his knee.

"Help me." He clutched her forearm and she pulled him up. He took two wobbly steps, then fell back onto the rocks. "Here I am, prime Nala bait with a Sister from the Warrior House to protect me," he scoffed. "I should be fine, right? Oh, I forgot, you like the Nala. Why don't you start yelling to let the malicious vermin know I'm here, ripe for the picking?"

Nat bit her lip. She pulled a bandage from the cloth case Ethet had given her and wrapped the gash. But Benedict wasn't done. "Maybe we can invite them for a little tea? I'm lucky, I'm too old to be made, so they'll toy with me and then rip me to shreds while you watch."

"Shut it." Nat stood and yanked Benedict to his feet. He let out a grunt. She pulled his arm around her shoulder and started dragging him up the hill. "There are fifty million places I would rather be right now than on this rock heap with you. If you don't want to end up as a busted pile at the base of this hill, keep quiet."

"Why did Estos send me a fringe Sister? What could he possibly have been thinking?" Benedict said, ignoring her threat.

Nat focused on each step, trying to keep balance under Benedict's weight. She stopped for a minute, readjusted her grasp, and scanned the darkness above her for the top of the hill.

"This isn't some fool's errand we're on," Benedict continued right in her ear. "If Estos doesn't show himself, prove himself, the whole rebellion will collapse." His breath was hot against Nat's face. "Maybe that's what you want, Sister? Mudug and the Nala running everything?"

"Orb, knock him out." The orb moved swiftly and struck Benedict's temple with a quick crack. He went limp, and Nat caught his unconscious body before he hit the rocks again. "Thanks," she said to the orb as she struggled forward with the now-silent Benedict. The orb bobbed slightly and moved slowly in front of her feet. Her shoulder ached and her feet slipped with each step. It felt like an elephant was sitting on her shoulder. She stumbled forward, grabbing large boulders with her free hand. Her eyes focused on the orb as it lit her way toward the top, one agonizing step at a time. When she reached the ridge, she dropped Benedict against a scraggly tree. She turned a slow circle in the darkness, unable to see beyond the light cast by the hovering orb. Maybe knocking out Benedict hadn't been the best of ideas.

Nat closed her eyes and focused her memory on the maps Estos and Annin had given her. She placed a hand on the rough bark of the tree. Nothing. None of the places they had led her in her dreams were remotely near this rock nightmare. She heard a scraping sound and opened her eyes.

"Orb out." The light vanished. Nat retreated from the tree and tucked her body tightly near a bush. Her eyes adjusted to the darkness. She could see the shape of the tree and Benedict slumped at its base. A figure moved near the tree and bent over Benedict. Nat swallowed and reached for her dagger. If she could frighten the Nala away . . .

"Orb, blaze," she whispered. The figure spun in her direction and then threw up its arms against the blinding brightness of the sphere. The plan worked, except now Nat could hardly see, either.

"Will you turn that blasted thing off! If I wanted to harm you, I'd have done it by now. You made more noise coming up that slope than a pack of hounds chasing a fox." The figure swiped a hand at the orb, which zipped easily away.

"Sorry. Orb, dim. I thought you were a Nala." Nat remained rooted in her position as the brightness diminished.

"Do I look blue to you?" A man with reddish-brown hair stepped toward her. His long beard was parted in the middle and pulled tightly under his ears, where it was bound by black cords to his hair, making two bizarre ponytails.

"No, not blue." Nat stifled a nervous laugh as she took in his six feet of height. He wore a black leather coat with long slits that commenced at his thick belt and ended at his knees, and he held the broadest sword Nat had ever seen. His brownish-green eyes looked familiar.

"A hysterical Sister and an unconscious oath breaker. I should have known better." He bent over Benedict's stiff form and roughly pushed up his chin. "I thought if the old cheat was willing to scale the slope with that shriveled leg of his, there would be some good reason to meet him. I should have known better," he repeated. Benedict's chin dropped like a rock as the man let go. "Have a delightful midnight walk, Sister." He sheathed his long sword and turned.

"Don't go!" Nat blurted. "I need to speak to Gennes. Can you take me to him?" The idea of sitting alone on this hill until Benedict regained consciousness and chewed her out for messing up their meeting was unfathomable.

The man twisted slightly so he faced the tree instead of her. "Why would I take you two to Gennes?"

"I have important news for him, and a request."

"What news?" the man demanded. "Are the Sisters finally coming out of their holes to save us? You've wasted my time, and I'll not waste Gennes' by bringing you to him."

"But I have a message for him from . . . people." Nat fumbled with the words. She smacked her forehead as he turned away. She had to say something to get him to stay and listen. "Andris! He knows Andris, right?"

"Andris is dead!" The man unsheathed his sword. "Anyone claiming he's alive is a liar." He lunged toward her. She quickly stepped to the side and tripped him, sending a shock wave up her leg. He rolled easily and sprang up.

"Andris is alive." She ducked and spun. The sword whistled past her head. "I saw him a few days ago," she said as she scurried behind him. The orb whizzed around his head, and Nat quickly stepped out of range as he batted it away. "He has a tiny scar below his eye. It's from a thorn bush." Her voice was pleading now. "He told me it was from a thorn bush."

The sword clattered to the ground. He lunged and grabbed her shoulders. Nat screwed her eyes closed, waiting for a blow.

"Andris is alive! My brother is alive!" the man yelled at the top of his lungs.

Gennes traced the shape of Estos' ring as it lay in the palm of his hand. The dark-red stone looked like a drop of frozen blood in the dim light of Barba's orb.

"You can't tell me where they are, or you won't tell me?" he asked in a low voice. Nat studied the man she now knew was Gennes. What would he believe or understand?

"They're in a place they can't leave without Mudug's men attacking them. They're safe but trapped. If I told you where they were, it wouldn't change anything. There would just be the added risk of one more person knowing their location." She pointed to Benedict. "He doesn't even know where they are. But he has an idea how to sneak them out undetected. We need suix stone and a few of your men. Benedict thought you could help."

Gennes waved dismissively. "I don't put credence in any plan of his involving alchemy." He tightened his fist around the ring.

"Estos believed in him enough to send me to help him," Nat countered. She wanted to add Ethet's stamp of approval, but something held her back.

"And Andris? What did he think of the fool's plan?"

"Andris wanted to come instead of me, but Estos wouldn't let him risk it. Any problems he had with the plan had to do with me being the one accompanying Benedict." A truth in a lie.

Gennes nodded. "The boy always had a hot head to lead a charge. I expect he's none too happy with staying put."

"You have no idea," Nat said.

He handed her the ring. "Sister, my better judgment says to leave you and the hermit over there to your own devices unless you tell me where Estos and my brother are."

Nat lowered her head. "I can't," she said. "But if you refuse to help us, you're blowing the best chance for both of them."

"Blowing?"

"Giving up, destroying. Besides"—she coughed, trying to cover up the gaff—"what do you have to lose by helping us? It's just a little suix stone."

Gennes' laugh boomed and Benedict groaned. "Just a little suix stone! You're an odd one for a Sister. Odd words and a little funniness about you." He scooped Benedict up like a rag doll. "Come on, Sister. The farther we travel before he wakes up, the less I have to listen to his tongue wagging like the mutt he is."

Nat let out a long breath and followed Gennes. "That makes two of us."

When Benedict regained consciousness, he discovered he was bound hand and foot to a fat packhorse. He was jostled back and forth as the horse rode over the uneven trail. The bickering that commenced between the giant Gennes and the diminutive Benedict was incessant. Despite knowing she needed to listen to every conversation, Nat couldn't stand it and focused instead on the little plants that grew in the pinkish-red rock cliffs surrounding them. She watched as tiny petals popped out when touched by the morning sun.

When they reached the base of a large rockslide, Gennes halted his horse and dismounted. "You can tell me your plans now, and I'll untie you after I hood you." He pulled a gnarled-looking cloth sack from a worn leather pouch behind his saddle. "Or I'll slide it over your head, and you can ride the rest of the way like a bound goat."

"You're a cursed duozi breeder, Gennes. Untie me!" The slight muscles on Benedict's neck strained as he lifted his head.

"Decision made then. Tied up for the rest of the trip." Gennes began pulling the sack over Benedict's disheveled hair.

"Stop!" Benedict thrashed ineffectually against his bonds.

"Gennes, he'll asphyxiate if you hood him while he's hunched over like that," Nat said. "Listen to his breathing now." It was ragged. She suspected the polio had weakened his lungs as well as his leg. There was no way he would make it under the heavy cloth hood.

"I don't need the help of a duozi devotee." Benedict's muffled voice sounded under the hood.

"Oh, don't be so quick with your tongue." Gennes pulled it off. "A little Nala bite would do you good. Might help that walk of yours, eh?"

"You blasted duozi wreck—"

"Enough with the duozi stuff!" Nat yelled. The men grew quiet. She squared her shoulders. "He was a boy, Benedict, a boy! I wasn't going to let you harm a little boy!" Gennes stared in confusion as Nat yelled at Benedict. The words tumbled from her mouth. "You're just as bad as the Nala. No, you're worse—you punish helpless children who've already been victimized!" she cried, thinking of Annin. Her voice grew louder and reverberated against the rocks. She held the image of Annin bolting from Benedict's cabinet in her mind as she pulled up her sleeve and shoved the markings under his nose.

"This applies to the Nala, not duozi. I won't harm someone who's been bitten. The sooner you get that through your head, the sooner we can move on and help Estos. And you"—she turned on Gennes, anger flowing through her—"you are as bad as your brother." She pulled down her sleeve and unsheathed her dagger. "I'm untying him before he passes out. You can stop me or you can help me." Nat thrust her dagger blade against the thick rope. She began cutting carefully, waiting for Gennes' enormous hand to clamp down on her shoulder. Instead he rounded the horse and began cutting the bonds on the opposite side. He finished before Nat was done with her first. Benedict slid off and crawled to his feet before he collapsed against a rock. Nat forced the lip of her canteen to his mouth. He wiped away a dribble of water from his chin and looked up at Gennes, who stood scowling.

"Tell Gennes the plan, Benedict," Nat urged.

Benedict kept his eye on him, not looking at Nat. Finally he dropped his head. "We need to put the past behind us, Gennes," he said. "Getting Estos back is more important than . . . hating me forever." Keeping his head down, he continued, "I never meant for her to disappear. I did everything . . ." He was gulping out an apology. Now it was Nat's turn to look back and forth between the two men. To her astonishment giant tears were flowing into the tight strands of Gennes' beard. Nat stepped away. She glanced at the rocks, avoiding the look of pain on his face.

Gennes closed his eyes. "I will never forgive what happened, Benedict. You broke your promise to aid her. You broke your promise to my brothers."

"I know." Benedict's face held a look of defeat.

Who were they talking about? Nat stepped back, feeling more out of place than usual.

Gennes wiped his cheek and plopped down next to Benedict. The two men sat side by side, gazing at the pink cliffs.

"I'll put the past aside for Estos. Tell me your plan, old man."

Benedict nodded. "It all hinges on getting the suix stone to the right place."

CHAPTER TWENTY-FOUR

Gennes' "camp," as he called it, was a thriving community nestled in a series of rock terraces surrounding a natural amphitheater. The floor of the amphitheater contained a gaping hole that resembled a toothless mouth. Nat halted her horse as they exited the narrow canyon leading to the camp. From her vantage point she could see tiny figures moving around and into the mouth. The surrounding terraces rose far above the ground. Spots of green dotted the roofs of buildings and climbed along the terrace walls.

"Where does the water come from?" She brought her horse as close to Gennes as she dared. The pathway to the first terrace was barely wide enough to accommodate both horses riding abreast.

Gennes lifted a hand from his saddle horn and pointed to a crevice high above. "We found the spring shortly after discovering the ruins. It's far enough away from the suix lode to avoid some of its nastier properties. The spring is sweet as wine, it is, Sister—sweet as wine." Nat wondered what the nastier properties of suix stone were as Gennes pointed to the green falling from the terraces. "We've been able to grow and harvest enough to feed our band and then some. It's helped us remain undetected all this time. No need for provision raids and that sort. Although I do miss having a slab of beef," he said wistfully. "Can't really keep too many grazing animals here. But the Nala have yet to make an appearance, which is to our benefit."

"Gennes?"

"Hmm?" he responded as he surveyed the camp.

"You haven't said anything about the plan," Nat ventured. The horses' hooves sounded hollow on the wooden bridge leading to the first terrace. "Do you think it will work?"

"No," Gennes said. Nat's heart sank as they passed a set of guards holding crossbows made from an ebony-colored wood. "It needs some refinement to work, Sister, and refine it I shall." They passed a row of chicken coops surrounded by a wall of matted stalks with crested wheat buds. Nat looked up. The wheat stalks grew perpendicular to the wall the entire way to its summit.

"Sister, did you have a House?" Gennes asked as she looked up at the wheat.

"A house. My family has a house in—" She caught herself. "My other . . . the other Sisters, I mean, had a House until it was destroyed. So, no." She scrambled to cover up her slip. "No, I do not have or I don't come from a House. I'm a fringer."

"I wondered." What? What was he wondering? "You just seem a little different than the other Warrior Sisters, and those markings of yours are very old." Gennes, motionless, waited for a response.

Why is everyone so fixated on my markings? Nat thought. "My training was a little unorthodox, Gennes. The Sisters I know had to adapt to strange circumstances." She tried to make her voice sound as authoritative and confident as possible, but she quickly conceded failure and nervously grinned at him.

"Haven't we all, Sister." He dismounted and handed his reins to another soldier with a jagged beard. "Off the horse, old man." He extended his arm to Benedict for support as he awkwardly got off his horse. "We'll work on the plan, Sister. Have no worries. Perhaps after

Estos returns, those strange circumstances will become just a distant memory."

A memory none of you would ever believe, Nat thought. She slid off her horse and stretched her aching legs.

"We rarely have Sisters here, but I do have accommodations. Blanken will show you the way." A soldier with a jagged beard stepped forward. "It may seem traditional to an unorthodox Sister such as yourself." Nat knew Gennes was teasing her now. "But please accept my hospitality under the Rim Accord." He bowed slightly, and she bobbed her head far below his massive figure.

Nat followed Blanken up a series of uneven steps roughly carved out of the stone wall. She watched Gennes and Benedict from above as they slowly made their way through a crowded market and then disappeared into a long tent.

"Here you are, Sister." Blanken stood next to a wooden door set directly into the cliff wall. The now-familiar vine, sword, bird, and sun images appeared faintly on the worn wood. To avoid falling off the narrow ledge, Nat stepped to the side as Blanken opened the door. She walked into a dimly lit room.

"It's a bit dark in here." Nat hesitated.

"Are you missing your orb?" His voice held a touch of sympathy. "There is a taper on the wall if you need more light."

"I have my orb, it's just dark."

"All right, then, I'll see that some food is brought to you," Blanken said, sounding relieved.

"Thank you."

"Could you move in a little, Sister, so I can shut the door?" He stood near the ledge with one hand on the door handle.

"Oh, right." Nat hurried in and he closed the door behind her. Dust moats floated in the ray of light coming from the small circular window carved above the door. The beam illuminated one wooden leg of a tiny bed made of woven rope. Nat cautiously moved toward the bed, unhooked her travel cloak, and lay down.

The breeze bent the slender top of the tree. Nat swayed back and forth, clinging to the uppermost branch. An ocean of leaves and pine needles spread below her. A jagged peak erupted from the forest floor. She watched, fascinated, as one sharp, rocky point after another formed a half circle in the middle of the trees. She brought her attention back to the trees. Their movement had a certain rhythm. She closed her eyes, lulled by it. When she opened them, the trees were still, but the wind blew past the tops. It grew in strength, but the trees remained motionless. She pushed her hair away as it whipped her face.

"Nat, run!" A panicked voice rose from the forest floor. She looked down. The dense foliage obscured anything beyond a few feet. "Get away from here!" The voice sounded closer, louder. Nat let go of the branch and began running over the tops of the trees, her feet skimming the leafy crowns. She jumped onto one of the jagged peaks and shoved her hand into a sharp crevice. She held on as she searched for a foothold. She began to scramble up the peak and glanced down. Tiny blue creatures rushed up, clambering over each other. She froze, unable to move as she watched them fly up the rock.

"Move!" the voice demanded. Nat whipped her head around. A wisp of cloud floated just out of reach. She looked down once more and pulled her leg up just as a Nala reached for her ankle. She got to the top of the peak and pulled herself over the ledge. "Lights!" she yelled. A thousand straight lines shot up into the air along the ledge. Howls erupted as the blue figures flung themselves against her barrier. Nat shook uncontrollably and tucked her head between her knees as dozens of Nala screamed.

CHAPTER TWENTY-FIVE

When Nat awoke, a tiny, flickering flame emanated from within an amber-colored glass secured to the rock wall. Her stomach grumbled loudly. She sat up and sniffed. A grainy smell filled the small area. Someone had been in the room while she'd slept. She rubbed her eyes and tried to remember the edges of the dream as she rose to search for the source of the delicious smell.

"Ouch!" The low beam above the bed was a few inches from her, barely visible in the light. The bump on the top of her head was tender to her touch. She ducked and shuffled carefully toward the smell. A tiny pot sat on a three-legged table. Nat knocked over a stool, righted it, and sat. She inched her chair closer to the table until her knees bumped the edge. Warm steam enveloped her hand when she lifted the lid. She felt around the pot for a spoon or some utensil but found nothing. Her stomach complained again. She was just about to lift the pot to her lips when she remembered the orb.

"Orb, light." A little ray of light shot through her cloak. She dug the orb out and let it hang above the table. The light slowly grew and the room took shape. *First things first,* she thought, digging the now-visible spoon out of the pot. The porridge burned the inside of her mouth. Prime rib it wasn't, but the warm honey flavor was delicious. She scraped the pot until there wasn't a trace left.

With her belly full, Nat turned her attention to the details of the room. Other than the bed and table, the only piece of furniture was an empty wooden bookstand at the very back near the rock wall. A heavy tapestry hung behind the stand. "Orb, shine brighter." The brilliant hues of the tapestry shone in the light. A series of vibrant images jumped to life. In the upper corner, four young girls, their hair strung with tiny yellow flowers, wept on a shore by the remnants of a wrecked ship. In the distance, a blue figure clung to a rock, waves crashing over its body. In the second image, the girls encircled a blue figure tangled in a fishing net. Nat recognized the Nala clawing at the net. She touched the blue embroidered threads and shuddered.

In the next scene, one girl knelt by the Nala, her knife pointed at its throat. Her other hand lay cradled next to her body. Bright red threads formed the blood droplets falling from her injured hand, and blue threads colored her arm. In the next image, a second girl applied a poultice to the injured girl's hand and held a yellow vial above her mouth. A third girl looked through a long scope at more blue figures crawling over a distant cliff, and a fourth girl bent over the captured Nala with her mouth open in conversation. In the final image, the four girls, now older, stood on the cliff facing a pack of Nala. The arm of the girl who was bitten was no longer blue. She wore a cape embroidered with a silver spear and held a dagger to the neck of a Nala. The second girl stood slightly apart, observing, while holding a parchment in one hand. Her cape was embroidered with a thick vine. The third girl wore a cape emblazoned with the image of the sun and held a vial filled with a bright-yellow liquid. The fourth girl's cloak held the image of a bird. She spoke to the Nala and pointed to the dense forest and the sea. In the background behind the girls, hidden among the rocks and trees, were dozens of other girls' faces. Nat leaned in closer, inspecting the final image. She held her forearm near the first girl's cloak. The embroidered spear was the same as the spear on Nat's arm.

She jumped when someone knocked on the door. "Sister?"

Nat grabbed the orb and stuffed it in her cloak. Clasping the door handle, she pushed the door open. Blanken deftly moved out of the way. A curved shadow covered the rock terraces. The last rays of the sun shone on a thin band of rock directly across from her.

"Gennes would like to see you now. Please gather all your things—I don't believe you will be coming back here."

Nat looked around the room. Other than her small satchel, she had nothing to gather. She stepped onto the terrace.

When they reached the first village, they took a path leading away from the cliff settlements.

"I thought you said we were meeting Gennes?"

"You are," Blanken said. "Down there." He pointed to the pit.

They followed a series of switchbacks carved into the rock. Unlike the old, worn rock dwellings and paths above, this path looked recently made. When they reached the basin, a line of fifteen people, covered from head to toe in thick gray bodysuits, waited to begin the hike up the path. Nat looked around and realized that they had just come down the only route leading to or from the basin. She followed Blanken as they approached a sun-bleached tent about half the size of a football field. The interior of the tent was divided into a kitchen and dining area and a first-aid station. A small wooden shed stood in the far back corner. Gennes and Benedict, bent over tankards, sat across from each other at a rough wooden table adjacent to the shed. Gennes gestured to the bench, and Nat slid in next to Benedict, keeping a little distance. A gray-suited worker with thick blond hair swept around the table. He looked up and smiled. He had an open, pleasant face and greenish-brown eyes. Nat stared, thinking he looked familiar.

"Sister, I believe Benedict and I have come up with a workable plan. We are the fortunate locators of not only suix stone but also the fairly rare element riven. Mudug has been hoarding it—and not for treatment of Swelling's disease. My spies tell me he is under the belief that it acts as a cure to the Nala's venom." Gennes curled one of his pointed beard tips around his finger.

Swelling's disease? Nat gave Gennes a curious look.

"Riven is no cure for Nala venom, any Sister can tell you that," Benedict interrupted and grudgingly acknowledged Nat. "But Mudug's never been one to put much faith in the Sisters' teachings. He relies on the Chemist for direction."

Gennes nodded and took a long drink. Foam clung to his mustache. "Mudug's monthly hearing day with the people is in a few days." He wiped away the foam and slammed down the tankard. "Hearing day, what a ruse. He sits next to the throne and pretends to listen as people plead for help to find missing loved ones or beg for forgiveness of a tax debt so they're not sent to the Rewall. All the while, he's the one ordering the death of any who dare criticize him. He's the one filling his coffers with taxes and taking the freedom of those who can't pay. When Emilia was regent and the Sisters controlled the Nala, there was peace, now there's nothing but his murderous ambition and greed." He paused, calming himself and focused on Nat. The rage faded from his eyes. "You will go to the hearing chambers and make a request." He pulled a rough parchment from his tunic and began smoothing it out on the table.

"What's the request?" Nat asked, eyes fixed on Gennes.

"You'll offer to exchange the riven for the services of his Chemist to heal your brother."

"What? What brother? You don't mean him?" Nat pointed to Benedict. The hermit took a long swig from his tankard. His head tipped forward. She wondered how long they'd been drinking.

"No, of course not. He's the last person I'd send into Rustbrook." Gennes gave her a funny look. "Soris, join us," he said. The gray-suited man leaned his broom against the shed and took a seat next to Gennes. Two pairs of matching green eyes stared at her.

"You two are—"

"Brothers," the men replied in unison.

"How many of you are there?" she asked in wonder.

"There were four. We thought we were the only two left until you brought the good news." Soris extended his hand and Nat awkwardly grasped it. It felt rough. "Thank you," he said, letting go of her hand. She had a sudden urge to grasp his hand again until she remembered he was Andris' brother. "It's been some time since we've had any good news." His expression was soft and kind. "He's well, then?" he asked. The others waited for a response.

Nat blushed when she realized she was staring. "You mean Andris?" She glanced at the tabletop. "He's well. I mean, he's argumentative and utterly unpleasant to be around, but he's well." Soris smiled, and he beamed with happiness. Nat wondered if the three men really were related. His smile reminded her of Marie Claire, and she closed her eyes for a moment, thinking of home.

"Soris here is your brother, recently bitten by a pory snake. The pory snake has exceptionally slow but deadly poison. Its bite marks are conveniently similar to those of a puncture by a porc-tree needle," Benedict explained. "I'll administer the punctures before you go." Nat rubbed her palm, remembering the sting of the needles. "With the Healing Houses closed and their remedies unavailable to purge the pory snake's nasty toxin, you'll have no choice but to seek out the help of the Chemist." He leaned over the table. Light reflected off the bald spot on top of his head. "Mudug wants riven. He should offer up the services of the Chemist in exchange for the riven—assuming you're smart enough not to let him take it off you."

"I'm sure the Sister can manage to avoid that," Soris responded. She glanced at Soris, thankful to have someone defend her.

"I've confirmed the Chemist is using a map with orbs as locators, as I suspected. If he's keeping to his ways, the map will be in his private chambers, well guarded and away from the rest of the castle." Nat got a good look at Benedict now that he was sitting straight instead of hunched over his drink. Dark circles shaded his eyes, and a crust of dried blood covered his tonsure.

"Once you get to the Chemist, you have to find a way into the room with the map. The room will have a guard in front. He never likes his work disturbed." Benedict pointed to the parchment that lay between Gennes' broad hands. He slid it across the table. Soris' hand brushed Nat's as they reached for the parchment at the same time. She studied the sketch of a long outbuilding with three doors. "Here." Benedict pointed to the second door. "That's where his guard's been spotted."

"How are we supposed to get around the guard?" Nat asked. She was beginning to feel like she was trapped in a Ferris wheel, spinning faster and faster, with no way to get off.

Benedict withdrew a small packet wrapped in waxy paper. "Instant sleep. A favorite of Sister Ethet's. Direct contact with the skin, and a grown man will pass out." He chuckled. "Just make sure he falls quietly. You'll sneak in, find the locator, and sprinkle the suix stone around the edges. After you collect your brother, go to the safe house in the city, remove your disguises, and leave."

"What disguise?" Any more disguises and Nat wasn't sure she would remember who she really was.

"Bastle herders!" Benedict beamed.

"Brilliant, isn't it?" Spittle flew from Gennes' mouth as he laughed. "You'll be all trussed up and he's beardless. No one will see or dare look at your arm. I grant that the Chemist will want you out of his laboratory quicker than a whip, so you'll need to work fast." Gennes wiped his eyes. "Sometimes, I am so clever. I wish I could see this plan play out." He stood and his laughter died. "Unfortunately for me, I've got a little ambush in the works near Mudug's mine. I have to ride tonight. I leave you to your preparation. Speed and luck go with you, Sister. Travel free." Gennes clapped Soris on the shoulder. "Be careful, brother."

"I will," Soris answered. "Expect to see me in a week, with nothing but stories of how we hoodwinked Mudug." His eyes twinkled mischievously, but his mirthful expression melted away as his older brother looked him squarely in the eye.

"Nothing foolish. In and out, you hear? I've my mind on enough now to worry about you."

Soris nodded. "Nothing foolish. And why would you worry when I have a Sister with me?" He bowed his head respectfully toward Nat. Her stomach clenched.

"She'll keep you safe from the Nala, but not a legion of Mudug's guards." Gennes tapped his head. "This mission is more about brains than strength. Use yours and I'll see you soon." He embraced Soris in a bear hug. A trio of rebel soldiers fell into step behind his massive figure as he strode out of the tent.

"Gennes supplied enough suix stone for the ruse." Benedict nodded at a square box on the table. "While I create some unpleasantness for Soris, go collect the riven," he told Nat. "The guard is waiting to take you." He lifted a shaky hand and pointed to Blanken, who stood near the tent's entrance.

Nat scrunched up her face. "Me?" Did he seriously want her to go into that pit and dig out some substance she'd never seen, let alone heard of?

He looked at her as if she were a child who refused to do a chore. "Do you have a volunteer in mind? No? Hurry up, there's no time to waste." He extracted a long porc needle from the folds of his tunic. Soris held out his right hand. "He's not complaining about his duty," Benedict grumbled. He rummaged through a small box of vials.

Nat stepped over the bench. She placed a hand on Soris' shoulder and whispered in his ear, "Don't let him do anything but poke you with the needles." His brow furrowed. She brushed a stray strand of hair behind her ear. "A friend of mine said not to trust him, and I'm beginning to believe her."

"Sister." Blanken stood at her side. "We should go."

Nat widened her eyes and nodded toward Benedict, who was in the middle of mixing the contents of two vials. Soris shrugged. She hoped he took her warning seriously, but there was nothing else she could do.

"Give my regards to that old worm in the hole," Benedict called out as she followed Blanken. "Hold your hand still," he said to Soris. "Mine are a bit shaky."

Nat heard Soris cry out as the tent flap closed behind them.

CHAPTER TWENTY-SIX

The pit was a gaping mouth that grew wider in dimension as Nat and Blanken approached. It seemed to be sucking in the last of the twilight. Blanken led her around the edge and handed her a flaming torch. He pointed to a small wooden platform with ropes and a pulley hanging near the lip.

"Mind your head when you go down. I'll do my best to keep you steady, but the platform sways a bit." He grasped the edge to hold it still. She eyed the rusty pulley and ropes when she walked onto the middle of the platform. It dropped a foot, then descended rapidly. Blanken grasped the rope and slowed its descent. With nothing to hold on to, Nat sat on her heels, but the flames from her torch licked the rope. She scrambled to stand before the rope caught fire.

"You'll meet a pit guard about halfway down. Pull on the rope when you're ready to come up," Blanken called out from above.

"How about now," she said to herself.

"What?"

"Nothing, let me down." The platform descended. The torch flame cast shadows against the rocky walls. Switchbacks were cut into the side of the pit. Flaming torches broke the darkness at every turn. A crude series of pulleys and platforms extended throughout the cavern, beginning and ending at different levels. Other than the flames, there was no movement or sign of life.

She inched closer to the edge of the platform, hoping to glimpse the bottom of the pit, but the platform began to sway. She didn't dare move again for fear she would send it swinging into the wall. She calmed her nerves by looking at the bright crystals and milky-looking stratum in the rocks as she descended. When the platform landed on a wide rock ledge, she quickly stepped off and peeked over the precipice.

The sharp point of a dagger dug into Nat's cheek, and an arm slithered tightly around her neck. Nat froze. The hand holding the dagger moved from her cheek to her arm. A thin hand yanked Nat's sleeve up to her elbow.

"That's pathetic," a hoarse voice said. The arm released Nat and she fell to the ground, clutching her throat. "You have that on your arm, and you froze like a little rabbit before the eagle swoops in for lunch." Nat watched in alarm as the emaciated woman in front of her gobbled an imaginary feast. The woman's red dreadlocks swung wildly from side to side with each erratic bite.

"No wonder Sisters are dropping like flies," the woman said as she smoothed a handful of greasy locks behind her ear. Her ragged split sleeves fell away, revealing dull green markings of vines and swords on her arm. "This used to mean something!" she shouted, pointing to them. Nat scooted to the side, closer to her fallen torch. "Uh-uh." The woman wagged a bony finger in warning. "Try and attack me," she challenged and thrust her face in front of Nat's. She smelled like a dead animal. Nat coughed. A flaming scar ran from the woman's temple down the left side of her face.

"I'm not here to attack you," Nat said, struggling to speak through her coughing. The woman reeked. "We're both Sisters."

The woman immediately sat back on her heels and folded her arms. "All my Sisters are dead," she said flatly. She turned onto her knees and crawled slowly toward an opening in the cavern wall. Nat let out a long breath and stood up. She shook uncontrollably. The woman's lingering rank smell was the last straw for her frayed nerves. Her stomach flipped and she retched off the side of the cliff. Wiping her mouth, she looked at the platform and shook her head, knowing if she went up now without the riven, Benedict would send her right back down. She turned and followed the woman.

Little pockets of light dotted the dark tunnel. Nat examined one of them and found a small orb about a quarter the size of hers.

"They shrink, you know. When a Sister dies, her orb shrinks." The woman appeared at her side.

Nat's shoulders tensed. "I didn't know," she said, trying not to let the woman see her shake. "Why is it still shining if its owner is dead?" Barba had taught her little about orbs.

"Good question, my little apprentice." Her arm slid through Nat's. The torn sleeve of her tunic caught on Nat's belt. A spider sped up a tangled clump of the woman's hair. She led Nat farther into the dim tunnel. "When you are with a Sister and she—well, when she is in the throes of death, she may bestow her orb upon you. It's like giving a memory. And the memory is the light." Her voice was calm as they paused before a crevice containing two more small orbs. "I have lots of memories." The woman gave Nat a knowing smile, complete with missing teeth. Nat smiled in return, and the woman's dark eyes bore into her. "What are you smiling for, you fool? They're dead!" She gripped Nat's arm like a vise and gestured to the orbs.

"S-sorry. I didn't mean . . . Gennes sent me down here to collect some riven," Nat said, stuttering with nerves.

"Gennes? Has Sisters doing all his dirty work now, does he?" The woman released Nat's arm, and Nat took a defensive step back. The woman stared at the rough ceiling of the tunnel and rubbed her chin. "Been a while since I was above ground. Maybe you can switch with me? I'll take Gennes the riven and you can guard the rubbish." She winked at Nat and spun around. "Rubbish! Wake up, my sweet little murdering rubbish!" she bellowed as she stormed from the tunnel into a small room carved out of the rock. "We have a special visitor with a special job for you!" Nat scanned the cavern. No one else was in the dismal place. A heap of worn blankets surrounded by stacks of aging books lay across from the entrance. A beaten cup and shallow bowl teetered on the edge of a tiny table. The woman continued to yell. All at once, she stopped and faced the opposite wall. "Did you finally die?" She spat a black glob on the floor in front of a barred door set into the rock. A slight shuffling sound came from behind the door. Nat heard a coughing fit, then a male voice.

"Cassandra, you've been ingesting the mercury again, haven't you?"

Cassandra jangled a set of keys in front of a wide lock and said in a reasonable voice, "Rusrel, I'm going to let you out. You are going to dig up a little riven for me." She flung her head to the side to face Nat. "How much do you need?"

Not knowing what to say, Nat cupped her hands together.

"You will bring back that much." Cassandra thrust her hand with the key toward Nat. "And then I'll lock you up again. Any questions? No?" She jammed the key into the lock and bent toward the iron door. "Just remember, Rusrel, I am always looking for an opportunity to kill you," she said cheerfully as she turned the key. The lock clicked and the door squeaked open.

Rusrel's gangly legs unfolded like a crawling spider. Two arms crusted over with scabs and sores appeared next. Nat covered her nose as a foul stench rolled over her. She swallowed her vomit.

Cassandra rocked back and forth on her toes with eyes locked on the opening. "It's been ages since I let him out," she said in a conspiratorial whisper to Nat.

When Rusrel emerged from his cell, all Nat could think of were pictures she'd seen of concentration-camp victims. The filthy sleeveless tunic swallowed his sunken chest. The remaining bits of stringy hair matted to his head were interspersed with weeping sores. He shuffled on stick-like legs toward the tunnel entrance. Nat pressed against the wall as he moved past her and gave her a black smile.

"Your orbs are getting smaller, Cassandra." His voice was weak but spiteful. He turned his head and grinned again.

Cassandra halted and fidgeted with the hem of her tattered tunic. She then quickly kicked Rusrel, who crumpled to the ground. She jumped on top of him.

"Stop!" Nat yelled. "We need the riven." She couldn't think of anything else to say to keep Cassandra from pummeling his face into the ground. "We need him to get the riven," she repeated.

"Yes, we do." The fire vanished from Cassandra's eyes. She pulled Rusrel to his feet and pushed him toward the opening. Nat leaned against the tunnel wall, catching her breath. "Coming?" Cassandra called from the entrance.

Nat swallowed again and forced her legs to move. She emerged from the mouth of the tunnel just as Rusrel disappeared over the ledge on a long knotted rope. Cassandra crouched near the ground where the rope was staked. It shifted from side to side, pressing against the stone.

"Who is he?" Nat asked as she sat down next to her.

"Him?" Cassandra pointed at the rope, then leveled her eyes on Nat. "Rusrel," she said slowly, "is the killer of the queen." She leaned precariously close to the edge. "A little farther, you murdering scum!" she screamed. Her voice echoed through the pit. Nat listened to the stream of curses as she yelled at Rusrel. *This woman is insane,* she thought. She couldn't believe Benedict had sent her down here without warning. Cassandra's voice died away, and the only sound was the rope rubbing against the ledge. The rope grew slack and she loosened her grip.

"Where are you from?" Cassandra asked as her eyes darted to Nat, then back over the ledge.

"Far away," Nat replied cautiously.

"Do you remember what your House was like?" Cassandra asked.

"Yes. Do you remember where you're from?" She regretted the question the moment it slipped from her lips. Cassandra shuddered but remained silent.

After a few minutes a weak voice called out from the depths. Cassandra stuck her hand under the rope. "Help me pull him. The offal's too weak to climb up on his own." She heaved a meter of rope up and Nat grabbed the slack. The two women pulled hand over hand until Rusrel's head and shoulders appeared. Cassandra hooked her arm under his armpit and yanked him up. A little silver bucket rolled onto the ledge, spilling purple-tinted crystals.

"Don't tell me we've wasted our time here, Rusrel!" Cassandra pushed the crystals with her bare toe.

"It's in the bottom of the bucket, Cassandra." Rusrel lay on his back, chest heaving. "Would you look at the sky," he said to himself while she examined the contents of the bucket. She twisted around and glared at him.

Nat grasped the bucket's handle. "I'll go now," she said. Cassandra took no notice. Nat stepped onto the platform and pulled on the rope to signal Blanken.

"So dark, so thick and dark," Rusrel said, still looking at the night sky. He closed his eyes. "Just like her hair."

Cassandra's left eye twitched slightly. The platform rose slowly above the ledge. Nat clutched the bucket with one hand and the rope with the other.

"She was so beautiful." Rusrel's voice grew stronger. Cassandra loomed over him. The top of her head disappeared from view as Nat rose higher and higher. For a moment, the only sound was the creak of the pulley. Nat shut her eyes and clung to the rope as a piercing wail erupted from below.

CHAPTER TWENTY-SEVEN

It wasn't Soris' fault, but that didn't matter. He asked another question from astride his horse, and Nat ignored him, again. She didn't want to talk to him, not with Rusrel's scream and Benedict's bitter laugh still echoing in her head.

Soris lifted his wet glove and brushed drops of rain from his cheek. He winced slightly, and Nat wondered how badly Benedict had hurt him with the porc needles.

"You've known Benedict awhile, then?" he repeated.

Nat sighed and brushed rivulets of rain off her horse's long neck. Water splattered against her face when the horse flicked its head to the side. "No."

"When you came back from the pit last night, you lit into him like you knew him well enough. Can't say I've ever seen a Sister do that before."

"What, get angry? Can't Sisters get angry, especially when someone lies to them and tricks them?" she said more defensively than she meant. She didn't want him to think she was irrational.

Soris looked through the rain and down the muddy road. "Yes, of course they can. You're just different. Most Sisters I've met are pretty controlled." He glanced back. She was hunched over the saddle horn, wet cloak plastered to her back.

"I must've been trained differently than the ones you knew," she said, thinking of Andris' constant criticism and berating, Barba's and Estos' nonstop torrent of information, and the concoctions Ethet made her drink.

"It makes no difference to me how you were trained, Sister." He shrugged. Black clouds rolled above the valley, blotting out the remaining light. "We need to find cover." He pointed to the clouds. Droplets of water hit his face. The clouds spun and rolled through the sky. She nodded and urged her horse to follow his off the road onto an overgrown path.

The rain fell harder. Their horses raced over the slippery grass. Clumps of mud splattered against Nat's arms as she trailed Soris. The wind ripped the hood off her head. They rounded the base of a low hill. The crumbling remains of a stone wall stood amidst tall grass and weeds. The gray stone was slick with rain. On the other side of the wall, lonely columns stretched to the sky. She slowed her horse and examined the ruins. *Another House,* she thought and wondered which one.

"This way!" Soris called from ahead, gesturing to a grassy path under a stretch of trees. They made their way under the leafy canopy until they reached a large meadow. Nat pulled on the reins and looked up in awe. Branches and tendrils stretched across the sky, forming a verdant cover over the open meadow. Shafts of gray light and streams of rain penetrated the cover, but the meadow was peaceful compared to the storm raging beyond. Nat urged her horse on. Tattered old ropes hung from the canopy, their frayed ends swaying eerily in the wind. She passed a jagged wooden post just as Soris skirted the edge of the meadow and disappeared behind a long building opposite Nat.

The first level of the building was made of the same gray stone as the wall. The second level was a covered deck looking out on the meadow. Thick wooden posts supported the roof. As she drew near, she noticed each post was carved from bottom to top with images of the vine, sword, bird, and sun. The middle post was covered with carvings of weapons, swords, spears, and arrows. The building, she discovered, was anything but intact. The side wall was partially caved in, exposing a dark interior through an opening big enough for Nat and her horse to pass through. They entered a long room segmented by three wooden stairways in various stages of rot. Soris reappeared from behind the second stairway. Nat dismounted, took the reins, and gently pulled her horse forward while kicking rocks out of the way.

"I hope you won't take offense that we're using this as a stable, Sister." He unhooked a saddlebag and dropped it on the floor. A mouse scampered from under the leather.

"I don't mind," Nat said. She unbuckled the strap holding her bag.

"Cassandra would've—" He paused a moment. "She would've had a problem coming here. But I figured you'd be fine, given it wasn't your House and we didn't have any other available options."

Nat studied Soris. Why did he bring that crazy Sister into the conversation?

He glanced at her nervously and busied himself removing the saddle. He sat the saddle on its end and began wiping down his horse. "I didn't think it was right what Benedict did, Sister. Sending you down into the pit." He spoke more to his horse than Nat. "I've heard she has walls of orbs. Benedict shouldn't have done that to you."

"Thank you," she said quietly. The kindness and concern in his voice struck her. She slid her saddle off her horse and stood it upright in a dry, rubble-free corner by the stairs. She watched Soris as he worked on his horse, rubbing its limbs. His wet hair lay at a funny angle against his forehead.

"I wasn't mad at Benedict because of the orbs," she said as she approached her horse. "Benedict was trying to get back at me for something by sending me down there."

"Get back at you for doing what? Bringing him to Gennes? Protecting him? Gennes said he had to fend you off when he threatened Benedict." Soris picked up a scattered array of broken branches with his good hand and tossed them into a pile.

"It's complicated." She pulled the thick saddle blanket off her horse and shook it. Puffs of horsehair filled the air.

"Benedict and my brother planned our mission. If you have a problem with Benedict, I should know about it." Soris stood directly across from her, arms crossed. His expression was agitated, and he looked like a younger version of Andris.

"It's nothing to do with the mission. We don't agree on how to treat a . . . duozi." She hoped he'd let it rest at that, because she couldn't very well explain how she knew he locked duozi children in cabinets.

"A duozi?" he replied, looking confused.

"Yep, a duozi." *Did he not care for them as well?* she wondered and turned her back on him, ending the conversation. Soris waited a moment, shrugged, and moved to the far end of the building. A piece of broken tile lay on the floor next to a clump of thick grass that her horse was consuming. The tile threw off an opalescent color. Nat picked it up and examined its bulging surface in the gray light. The curved tile was a piece of broken orb. The tip pricked her finger and a small droplet of blood welled up. She sucked her finger and pocketed the piece. She looked around at the ruins and shuddered.

Soris kicked bits of rubble from the corner, then sprang lightly up a set of stairs. The wood creaked under his weight. He came bounding quickly down and jumped off the side instead of using the last few stairs. He shook his right hand and stuck it under his opposite arm.

"This should do for tonight. I doubt we'll have company." He nodded at the thick line of trees visible through the shattered window. Nat had the feeling he wasn't talking about people. He pulled out a compact crossbow made of dark wood and set it next to his bedroll. His mouth tightened when he bumped his hand.

"How's your hand?" She dropped her bedroll near his and pulled her orb from her robe. It began to emit a gentle glow and heat as it hovered near them.

Soris slid down to the ground and smiled wanly. "Starting to hurt a bit."

She flicked a spider off her bedroll and knelt next to him. Carefully pulling his hand into her lap, she examined the two punctures. The wounds themselves were hardly visible. The skin around them, however, was a swollen red ridge covered by a weepy ooze. She considered using some of Ethet's herbs to relieve the swelling but hesitated. The punctures had to look bad for Mudug to believe their lie. She handed him a water gourd. He took a sip and handed it back.

"He didn't do anything other than puncture your hand?" she asked as she gently examined the palm.

Soris shook his head and winced. "Well, he outdid himself, didn't he?"

She took a drink and gestured to the crossbow. "Are you planning on using that one-handed?"

Soris laughed. "Won't need to with you around, at least not here. The Nala won't bother us if they see that." He pointed to the design on her arm. She choked as she swallowed another gulp of water. Soris lightly patted her back.

"I'm fine," she coughed. She hoped he and Barba were right about the markings. She took another drink.

"The Nala are the least of our worries," Soris continued. "It's the guards in Rustbrook we need to think about. I'm leaving the bow here along with our clothes."

"Our clothes?" She glanced at her tunic.

Soris smiled again. "Our real clothes. We're bastle herders, remember?"

"Must have slipped my mind." She corked the gourd and leaned against the rough wall.

"The guards in Rustbrook will paw through everything. We're going to have a hard enough time hiding the suix stone, riven, and the sleeping tar Benedict gave you. If I walked into Rustbrook with that bow, or if they found your orb or cloak, we'd be finished before Mudug could spit in our direction. We'll stash our things here and then come back afterward."

Nat looked at the orb. Barba wouldn't be happy with her leaving it. But she wasn't very happy with Barba. She let out a rueful laugh.

"What's funny?" Soris chewed a bit of jerky.

"I just promised my . . . my Head Sister something about my orb. She'd have my hide if she knew I was leaving it."

"Doesn't need to know, does she?" Soris said through a mouthful of meat.

"No, she doesn't. She was less than upfront with me about a few things. This would be a minor payback in comparison."

Soris chewed a little more, and Nat began to wonder what kind of meat he was eating. She examined the stringy jerky and took a small bite.

"Is my brother with your Head Sister?" Soris asked.

Nat chewed slowly and swallowed. She took another drink before answering. "He is," she said, feeling the need to be vague.

"He really is well, then?"

Nat nodded. "Yes." She looked closely at his face and messy blond hair. "You two aren't much alike. Your brother's got a pretty hard edge to him."

Soris glanced at her and smiled. "He's not so bad," he said. "Just always felt like he had something to prove with Gennes and Gordon as his older brothers."

"Gordon?" she asked before remembering Gennes' comment about the remaining brothers.

His smile faded and his full lips pinched together. "Gordon was the oldest."

"What was he like?"

"Calm. Nothing unnerved him. His men loved him. I guess that's why Emilia took a liking to him." He shrugged as if brushing off a sad memory. "We all looked up to him."

Nat wanted to ask about Emilia, but a cloudy look settled over his face. "How about you?" she asked instead.

"What about me?"

"Did you feel like you had something to prove?"

"No, never," he said honestly. "Now I just want my brothers back together, to have everything the way it was before all this happened." He gestured to the ruins. The two chewed their food in silence. "Do you have any brothers?" he asked.

"No, I have two sisters. Both younger than me." She broke off a clump of cheese and handed it to him.

"Fortunate family," he said with a mouthful. "My mom and dad would have given a leg for a daughter. Instead they got four boys. My mom was always saying that she'd had one for each House, the only problem was we couldn't get in."

"Boys can't study in the Houses? I mean, of course boys can't study in the Houses." Flustered by her slip, Nat jumped up and began to busy herself by preparing a fire with the sticks Soris had collected. When she had a small flame going, she sat back on her heels. "So, where did you and your brothers study?" she asked, keeping her head down and her eyes on the flame.

"Since the Rim Accord was between the Sisters and the Nala . . ." Soris paused, and Nat finally looked up. He was waiting for her to agree, so she nodded. "Our family did what all respectable families do with their boys. Gordon and Gennes lived with our dad in Rustbrook and trained. Andris and I stayed on the farm with my mom and learned how to run the business. My father and brothers would come back each spring for the plantings and in the fall for the harvest. Then they'd be on their way again." The flame was full now, and Soris spread his wet cloak to dry on a large stone. Nat retrieved her cloak and did the same.

"I don't see Andris as a farmer," she said as she smoothed the cloak.

"Neither did he." Soris laughed. "Hated every bit of it. He wanted to be with Gennes and Gordon." He lowered his voice and squinted. "He always said, 'It's like being on a slow pony ride in the round pen. My arse always hurts and I'm getting nowhere.'"

Nat smiled at the impersonation. "Pretty good. You've got his growl down." She stood and crossed her arms, her mouth set. "'As I see it, you have two choices, Sister: do exactly what I say, or do exactly what I say. What's it going to be?'"

"Any doubt I had about you knowing my brother just vanished," Soris said, clapping.

"Your brother and I spent more time together than either of us wanted," she said as she looked through the thick, splintered glass of the nearest window. "I know that he would give anything to be here instead of where he is."

"He never was one for staying in one place or being patient. He was always getting me into trouble going on Nala hunts in the forest or preparing an ambush along the road to the farm. He drove my mom to the edge, which was no small feat. She was an Emissary Sister. I could never win an argument with her or get her goat. But Andris always could."

Little puffs appeared as Nat exhaled. She studied Soris' face as he stoked the fire. He looked lost in his memories. She wished she could share something about her life as openly as he'd just shared with her. She warmed her hands over the low flames before returning to her bedroll. "How did he end up in Estos' guard?" she asked. She wanted to keep the focus on him, knowing vagaries and lies were all she could offer in return.

"He locked the foreman in the icehouse with the season's butchering after Gordon and Gennes returned to Rustbrook. Mom handed him a bag with some rations and her training dagger and kissed him good-bye. I can still hear his whooping as he raced off down the road."

"You were the last one left." She thought of MC and felt the now-familiar ache of missing her family.

"Yes, but I never wanted to go to Rustbrook. I loved the farm, still do. One day, maybe after all this is over, I can go back. Start things up again."

"What about your parents?"

"They disappeared around the same time Andris did. The last time all of us were together was in Rustbrook before Emilia's wedding. Gordon sent for us a day before, but my mom and I had no idea what was in the works. I'll never forget watching Estos introduce my brother as Queen Emilia's husband. Even from where I stood in the crowd, you could see Mudug turn red like a beet. Rusrel passed out." Soris leaned his head against the wall, lost in the memory.

The names and information swirled through Nat's head. "The man in the pit was named Rusrel."

"Same man." Soris looked into the fire. "What House were you in when it happened, Sister, when everything began to fall apart?"

"I . . . I was trained in a fringe House."

"That explains those markings." He pointed to her bare arm. "I've never seen those on a Sister, except in books."

They sat quietly. The muted rain continued to fall.

"Soris, how did Rusrel end up in the pit in your brother's camp?"

"It's a long story."

"Are we in a rush to get somewhere tonight?"

"No." His forehead creased. "After Gordon was killed, Estos disappeared. My dad and Gennes went north with a few men looking for him. I know they were looking for Gordon's killer, too. Andris wanted to go, but Gennes made him promise to stay and guard Emilia. After they left, Andris came to me and said Emilia didn't need guarding, that she wanted him to go find Estos."

"So he left?"

"He left."

"And you were supposed to watch Emilia for him?"

"Yes. Can you guess what happened after he left?" he asked bitterly.

"As I was leaving the pit, Cassandra was screaming at Rusrel, calling him a murderer over and over again while she . . ." Nat closed her eyes. "He killed Emilia, didn't he?"

"Yes, killed her while I was supposed to be watching her."

"It wasn't your fault, Soris," she said, placing her hand on his arm and remembering what Estos had told her about his sister's death.

His eyes had a hollow look to them. "You're probably right. She wouldn't listen to me, anyway. I was just a kid." He tossed a stick into the fire. "We both made it easy for Rusrel."

Nat laid her head on her knees, resisting the urge to say something.

Soris gave her a quick, sad smile and continued, "Mudug then sent Rusrel with the guards to destroy the Healing House west of Rustbrook, claiming they were harboring duozi. Cassandra and a small group of Warrior Sisters ambushed them. The Sisters were outnumbered, but she managed to get away with Rusrel. It would have been better if they'd both died, if you ask me. Cassandra was pretty far off the cliff when she stumbled into Gennes' camp. She'd been dragging Rusrel around for months as her captive." Soris stood slowly, shaking his puffy hand. "I'll take the first watch, Sister. This hand will be useless in a few hours. I'd rather watch while I can."

Nat nodded and offered him some more dried meat.

"No, I'm good." He held his hand up in protest. "Never liked dried bastle. Disgusting animals, even if their wool is worth a precious sum." He shivered. "But we're bastle herders now, aren't we?" He grabbed his dagger and headed up the stairs, leaving Nat alone.

CHAPTER TWENTY-EIGHT

She lay with her eyes open, staring at the rotting wooden beams that stretched across the ceiling. Like everything else she'd come across in this place, the beams were barely holding.

The faces of the people she'd met filled her mind. Everyone was suffering in some way. Benedict was so full of anger and suspicion that he attacked innocent children. Cassandra bore the memory of death and was just barely clinging to her sanity. People like Annin were hunted down and treated as parasites, even though they had done nothing but fall victim to some monster. The Houses, which even in their rubble told of past grandeur, were in ruins. She thought about Soris and her family. How would she feel if her parents disappeared, or if Cal up and left one day? What if this place were her home?

One of the horses snorted. Another let out a low whinny and stomped on the broken tile. Nat sat up and grabbed the crossbow. "What's wrong, boys?" she whispered. The horses tugged at their tethers with their ears flat against their heads. Their eyes were wide and their skin danced as if it were fly season. Nat looked at the patch of open night sky through the stairwell and saw nothing.

The stairs groaned as she climbed onto the second viewing level. "Soris?" she whispered. A crumbling half wall obstructed her view of the landing. "Soris?" she said louder. She pulled out the orb. The sphere traveled toward the end of the viewing stand. In the soft light, she saw him, his head slumped over, snoring loudly. She jumped carefully over the exposed holes in the floor. "Soris, wake up. I'll take watch since you are doing such a good job."

"Watching for what?" the voice hissed from above. The orb blasted with light. Nat spun around, pressing her back against the wall, and swung the crossbow toward the ceiling. The slick blue figure balanced on a beam. One pointed arm lay on the rough wood while the other hung casually down like a blue ice pick. "I've made no aggression, Sister. Put down your weapon," it said.

She didn't move. She didn't think she could. Soris snored on. Inching her foot slowly toward him, she nudged his leg with her toes. The Nala remained in its relaxed position. "What do you want?" Nat asked, trying to keep the fear out of her voice.

The Nala blinked, and a thin blue membrane covered its webbed eyes. "Information, Sister. What are you? Wisdom or Emissary?" The orb moved closer to it, illuminating its bright, pointed teeth as it spoke. It pulled away from the orb as if repulsed by the light. She glanced at her forearm, realizing her markings were covered.

"What does it matter to you?" she said. The Nala batted at the orb. "You need to leave—now." She nudged Soris with her toe again as she spoke. He jerked awake. The Nala let out a long hiss.

"Sisters of the Rim!" Soris exclaimed, dislodging chunks of mortar with his hands as he scrambled up.

"Leave now, Nala." Nat raised the crossbow. It leapt to the next beam, and she swung the weapon, tracking its moves.

"Sisters no longer control the Nala." Its voice seethed with anger. The orb whirled around its head, causing it to thrash from side to side. It jumped and scrambled along the edge of the roofline. Nat kept the crossbow trained on its disappearing figure. The orb chased it down the roof onto the treetops beyond the canopy.

"Do you think there's more than one?" Nat asked Soris. Her arms were shaking, but she still held the crossbow.

"Maybe," he croaked. The orb reappeared, zipping through the dark leaves.

"If it's okay with you, let's get away from these trees," she said as the orb returned. The sphere hovered protectively over her shoulder. Soris nodded in agreement and they ran for the stairs.

"I don't understand why it didn't leave the minute it saw you. The Nala always leave Warrior Sisters alone. They have since the Rim Accord. Have you ever seen one act like that? I thought it was going to attack you." Soris pulled the floppy hood of his bastle-herder cloak off his head with his good hand. Nat slowed her horse and turned as much as the tightly wrapped fabric of her clothes would comfortably allow. Every inch of her body, with the exception of her hands and a small square for her face, was wrapped in layers of a dingy cream-colored cloth. The riven and suix stone were tied to her inner thigh and the sleeping tar to her hip. She felt like a mummy. She looked at Soris and realized she could have it worse.

His freshly shaven face was the color of paste. He leaned slightly to the right while his left hand held the reins. His horse kept veering left. Nat couldn't see his right arm, but his hand had been swollen and dripping with pus when they'd stopped in the morning to hide their gear and change. The orb, tunics, and weapons were stashed in a narrow fissure in the roots of a tree along the upper banks of the Rust River. The location was less than perfect, but it was away from the ruins. After last night, the farther they got from the ruins, the easier Nat found it to breathe.

"It never saw my arm. I didn't tell it what I was," she finally replied, feeling foolish.

"Why not? Did you want to antagonize it, get it to try to bite you? What in the Rim were you thinking?" Soris asked.

Nat wanted to tell him she hadn't been thinking, because a blue creature with giant stick pins for arms and razors for teeth had been perched right above her head. "I . . . I just wanted to see what it wanted. I mean, what was it doing? It shouldn't have been there in the first place, right?" Soris nodded wearily. "You said it yourself, the Nala aren't supposed to be anywhere near the Houses even if they are in ruins."

"I understand your indignation, but it was an odd time to hide the Warrior Sister markings. Next time, will you just send it on its way? I thought I was going to end up a duozi or worse." He grimaced as he spoke.

"It won't happen again, I promise." Nat chewed on her lower lip as she glanced down at the dirt road strewn with rocks.

Soris' horse veered left. He jerked on the reins and the horse stumbled. His right arm slammed into the saddle horn. He cried out, sending an echo down the valley. Nat pulled back on her reins and slid quickly off her horse. Soris' face was covered with a sheen of sweat and his arms were crossed close to his torso. "Can you lead him for a while?" he panted, nodding to the horse.

"Let me see your arm first," Nat demanded as she carefully pulled the edge of his cloak away. His hand looked like someone had blown up a surgical glove and stuck it in his tight sleeve. "This is never going to work. We've got to make a sling or you're going to keep hitting your hand while we ride. Can you get down?"

Soris nodded. He grasped the saddle horn with his left hand and kept his right arm slightly raised while he awkwardly dismounted. Nat rooted around in the saddlebag and brought out what looked like wide white gauze. She unrolled it and felt the sticky underside. *It'll work if I double it over on the sticky side,* she thought. She made three loops and pressed one sticky end to secure it.

"This should do," she said as she pulled Soris' cloak free and draped the bands over his neck before adjusting a band under his elbow, forearm, and wrist. His other arm draped over her shoulder.

"You have pretty eyes." His face was a few inches from hers.

"You're hallucinating," she said but felt heat rise in her cheeks. "How does your hand feel in the sling?"

"Good as new." He gave her a lopsided grin.

"Liar." Nat linked her hands together and helped boost him back into the saddle. She took his reins and walked to her horse. The river running near the road curved, and a wide boat loaded with packed bales of wool sailed by on the rusty water. She waved in response to the salutation from the sparse crew. "How much longer till we get there?" she asked.

Soris lifted his head. "Shouldn't be more than an hour." His head dropped. The road veered away from the river and merged with a wider packed-dirt road. Caravans of people and animals clumped together, clogging the passage. Nat and Soris fell behind two narrow wagons laden with wooden barrels. A lanky teenager lay across a row of three barrels. He opened one eye a slit when Nat's horse snorted. When he saw Nat, his eyes popped open and he scrambled across the barrels to the driver's wooden bench. The boy whispered into the driver's ear and the wagon began to move to the right, giving Nat and Soris a way round. The driver, dressed in a thick, faded blue tunic, leaned away from Nat as she passed. His felted hat crushed into the boy's face.

Nat pulled the reins on Soris' horse tight, bringing him alongside her. "What's his problem?" she asked in a whisper.

"Probably doesn't want your bastle fleas." Soris slowly turned and watched the wagons as they almost ground to a halt behind them. "Let's have a little fun," he said with a weak smile. "If I try to scratch myself,

I'll fall off. But you can go at it like you've got the mother bastle flea. I guarantee it will clear a path for us."

"Bastle fleas, okay." Nat transferred both sets of reins into one hand and began scratching at the tight wrapping around her hair, then moved to her shoulders and arms. A wide path appeared the moment the travelers saw her digging into her wrappings. Nat greeted their scowls with a grin and kept scratching. She leaned over and dug into her leather boot like she had a colony of little bloodsuckers tucked beneath the tight wrappings around her legs. She pulled her hand out and flicked an imaginary flea at a man wearing a monstrously broad-brimmed purple hat and a beard that formed a single point and tufted at the end like a broomstick.

"Watch it there," he groused and moved quickly out of their way.

"Sorry." Nat giggled, feeling slightly giddy from lack of sleep and amused at how repulsed her fellow travelers were. They found themselves at the front of the caravans in no time. When Nat looked back, the wagons, livestock, and travelers were scattered on opposite sides of the road. "I feel like Moses," she said.

"Moses?"

"A man . . . good at parting things." Nat bit her lip. She was developing a sore from chomping down when she said the wrong thing. Her tongue ran across the tender area on her lip. *Maybe it will remind me to stop talking so much,* she thought.

"I think I see the city now." Soris raised his head as they rounded a bend. An undulating stone wall curved along a hill in the distance. The taupe-colored stones ended abruptly near the riverbank. Tents of every shape and size dotted the sloping landscape around the wall and up and down the hill. "Take the route near the river," he said, his voice ragged. "We'll cause a riot if we try to make our way through the crowds around the main gate. It'll be to our advantage when we leave, but right now . . ." His voice trailed off.

"Soris?" Nat brought his horse to her side and gently pulled off his hood. His eyes were slits and his mouth hung open. She uncorked the water skin and squirted some on his face. "Get it together, Soris. I can't do this by myself." She gently slapped his cheek. He shook his head and opened his eyes wider.

"What was that for?" He tried to raise his right arm and contorted his face.

"You were about to slide out of your saddle." She wiped a few drops of water from his face. "If something happens to you between now and the Chemist, what should I do?" She pulled the horses onto the side path following the river and noticed the hostile faces of those in the caravans as they lumbered past on the main road.

"Get us to the bookshop on Wesdrono Street." He tried to swallow a little more water from the skin, but most of it trickled down his cheek. Nat retrieved the skin from his shaking hand and urged the horses forward, away from the main road. "Ask for Mervin," he said just loud enough for her to hear.

A narrow archway interrupted the stone wall right before it ended by the river. "Through there?" Nat asked as she noticed the lone guard standing near the open archway. Soris nodded and carefully pulled his hood back over his hair slicked with sweat.

"After we get through, pull your travel cloak shut so people can't see your wrappings. We don't want to draw any attention to ourselves in the crowds." He grimaced and slowly righted himself. Nat tightened the reins and proceeded forward along the uneven path.

CHAPTER TWENTY-NINE

The guard, wearing a sun-baked blue tunic emblazoned with a white circle, blocked the archway to the waterfront. He took one look at Nat and quickly stepped out of the way.

"Mind yourself now," the guard said nervously. "What's your business?"

"The same as theirs," Nat said as she pointed to the massive crowd near the front gates.

"Why aren't you with them?" the guard retorted, still keeping space between Nat and himself.

"We don't want to cause a problem," she said sweetly as she leaned down to scratch her knee.

"Go on through." The guard took another step back. "You're lucky you arrived today, otherwise I would have turned you away," he said as he scratched his arm. "Nastiness! Make sure you keep to the side roads," he bellowed as he dropped his sword and began frantically brushing his arms up and down.

Nat nodded dutifully and hurried through the archway with Soris trailing behind. She secured her travel cloak, hiding the bastle-herder wrappings, and pulled her hood over her brow. "Now what?" she asked as she scanned the harbor. A flock of seagulls ripped through a pile of discarded fish on the uneven ballast stones that popped out of the road like enormous pebbles. Scores of men crossed the wobbly way in front of them, loading and unloading the boats that neatly lined the dock.

Soris gestured to an intersection of three sets of steep, narrow stairs with a wide walkway underneath them. As they made their way through the shadowy walkway, Nat pressed her horse close to the bumpy stone side, away from the stream of traffic moving to and from the boats. She paused. High on a hillside, past the tiered rows of houses, shops, markets, and gardens, stood a castle that looked like three consecutively smaller squares stacked on top of each other. Tiny blue flags flapped in the breeze, prevented from flying away by four spires adorning the top square. Two squat rectangular buildings flanked the castle. South of the hill, grand residences and large gardens flowed toward the river.

"Head toward that square." Soris' hood hung down to his nose. He was hunched into a crooked *c*.

Nat tightened her grip on the reins of his horse. "Don't you dare fall off on me, Soris," she hissed as they edged into the crowd.

"I won't, at least not on purpose." He started to cough. That was new. What had Benedict really done to him? She cursed the shriveled man under her breath and ignored the hostile looks from some of the crowd.

They crossed a wide wooden bridge, the rail at the end marred by a burn mark. The scorched emblem of a bird and vine was barely visible. Ahead, in a small square, the tip of a black obelisk poked out of a crowd thronging around its base. She brought the horses around the side, behind the crowd. A parchment was affixed to the black stone. Nat leaned forward in her saddle to read the writing:

By Order of Lord Mudug
Upon determination by the Special Investigation
Section of the Merchant Division, authorized by the

acting Temporary Regent, Lord Andrew Mudug, that one Sister of the now-defunct Western Warrior House has, in violation of the Rim Accord, conspired and plotted with the Nala to disrupt the sole southern shipping route of our great territories, the Temporary Regent orders the following:

The rest of the words were lost in a sea of unwashed hair and head scarves. Forgetting herself, she leaned down and tapped the shoulder of a man with a basket of smelly fish strapped to his back. "Can you tell me what the Temporary Regent's orders are? I can't see."

"Mudug's orders, eh?" the man responded, his four-point beard sticking straight out above his ample neck. "He's set the Sister's hanging for this afternoon in Rustbrook Square."

"All for show," a teenage boy burdened with a similar basket said bitterly.

"Hush," the elder fishmonger said and walloped the back of the boy's head.

The boy rubbed his matted hair. "Just speaking the truth. He thinks a hanging will make us forget that he raised the transport tax. You said the same last night."

"Watch it." The fishmonger gripped the boy's arm tightly and looked nervously around at the faces in the crowd. "Take your basket to the stall," he said and pushed the boy away. "He's a bit confused in the head." He let out a tense laugh. "Where would we be without Mudug's guards protecting our merchant convoys and transports? The Nala would rip us to shreds."

Nat clutched the neck of her cloak and nodded in feigned agreement at the man's cover story. *So not all the people are buying Mudug's lies,* she thought. She looked at Soris, who appeared to be asleep. "Sir, could you tell me where Wesdrono Street is?" She tried to pronounce the name correctly, but it ended up jumbled on her tongue.

The man stuck his chin out and replied, "Right straight through that lane." He pointed beyond the obelisk.

"Thank you." She urged their horses through the throng of people, apologizing as they bumped, stepped on, and knocked over people. She considered getting rid of the horses but dismissed the idea when she glanced at Soris. Lugging him and their supplies through town would be impossible.

The geometric castle disappeared behind the gray stone walls bordering the lane. There was no way she could get him up there by foot. After every step the horses took, she glanced back to make sure Soris was still upright and not rolling down the lane. Benedict had to have done something other than stick him with porc needles. Her hand had hurt when she'd been pricked, but nothing like what Soris was going through. *Does he have an infection?* she worried.

The lane led to another intersection. To the left, beyond a row of small, neat shops, the road opened onto a square. A two-story tower stood in the middle of the square. The sound of hammering echoed down the road to the intersection. She scanned the street for signs and caught sight of a familiar glow in the doorway of one shop.

"An orb!" She pulled Soris close. "I just saw an orb in that doorway."

Soris, raising his head just enough to peer under the edge of his hood, said in a slurred voice, "I don't see anything."

"It was there . . ." The glow was gone, but Nat spied the edge of a cloak whipping past the darkened entrance.

"Can you get to the bookstore?" he asked, his tone pleading.

"I need to figure out where we are," Nat said, more to herself. People milled past, pushing against the horses. She dismounted and waded through the throng across the intersection, one hand on the reins and one hand tightly clutching the neck of her cloak.

The painted "Wesdrono Street" sign was stenciled onto the bricks of a two-story building at the corner of a narrow lane. She peered down the shadowy street and pulled their horses over its broken cobblestones.

A sense of calm came over her when they entered the quiet lane. The tall, narrow buildings that lined the street created a buffer from the bright light and noise behind them. At the end of the street to her right, a book-shaped sign hung below a weathered wooden post. Dark material lined the glass of one of the shop windows. She wiped away a small circle of grime from the other window and peered inside. Rows and rows of bookshelves, many of which sat empty, were angled toward the back of the shop.

Nat tied her horse to a set of copper rings affixed to the sidewalk. She unbuckled her saddlebag and slid it over her shoulder before helping an incoherent Soris from his saddle.

"I already pulled the ditch, Mom," Soris mumbled as Nat propped him against the wall before tying up his horse and removing his bag.

"It's going to be okay." She felt his forehead. It was burning hot. "And you did a good job." He whispered a rambling response. She pulled his good arm over her shoulder and gently guided him up the stairs to the entrance. He babbled the entire way. Whoever was inside was going to help them up to the castle, or she'd threaten to release a torrent of fleas on them.

CHAPTER THIRTY

Nat opened the red door. A rolling ladder leaned against a tall shelf. Weak light shone from the high arched window above a tiny counter at the back of the store. The shop appeared empty. After shutting the door tightly, she called out, "Hello! Is anyone here?"

Two heads appeared from either side of the counter.

She stumbled forward with Soris. A woman with chin-length hair and a sharp nose emerged from behind the counter. She took one look at Soris and reached for his other arm. "Mervin, it's Gennes' brother, get—"

"Watch his arm!" Nat cried out protectively.

The woman let go. "Bring him over here," she ordered. "Mervin, get the door."

Mervin nodded, and a lock of black hair fell over his eyes. He took a few long strides to the front door, turned the sign to "Closed," pulled down the blind, and slid the lock in place. "I'll take him. Right hand's the problem?" he asked as he extended his long arms toward Soris. Nat nodded. He scooped him up like a leaf. Soris let out a moan.

"Come then." The woman slipped her long hand into Nat's and pulled her gently around the counter to a concealed stairwell. Mervin's head disappeared down the stairs. They passed crates of books and boxes and walked into a cramped office. The woman cleared papers off a tiny wooden chair and motioned for Nat to sit. Mervin set Soris on a wide bench and began inspecting his arm.

"What happened to him?" the woman asked.

"Pory snake," Nat said, uncertain about telling two strangers the truth.

The woman pursed her lips.

"What do you think, Matilda?" Mervin gently let go of Soris' arm. Matilda rummaged through a small wooden box. She removed a vial containing an amber-colored liquid and waved it under Soris' nose. His head shot back and banged against the wall.

"Always works." Matilda chuckled. "How are you, dear?" she asked loudly. "Seems you're in a bit of a pickle. Bitten by a pory snake while out herding your, uh, bastles, is it?" She dropped Soris' robe and gently pinched his bare chin.

"Matilda?" Soris rubbed his head with his good arm.

"What was that stuff?" Nat asked as she reached for the vial.

Matilda stoppered it. "It'll rip those wrappings off you if you breathe in too much." She turned her attention to Soris. "Is she trustworthy?" she asked Soris as she eyed Nat. He nodded, then shook his head as if to clear his thoughts. She handed the vial to Nat. "Use it sparingly," she warned.

"Is it still hearing day?" Soris asked as he looked around the room.

"It is, and should be one for the record. Mudug's executing a Sister this afternoon." Matilda leaned toward Soris. "You're not here to do something illegal for your brother, are you?" she asked.

"That depends on who you ask." Soris smiled weakly. "My sister here"—he pointed to Nat—"is bringing me to Lord Mudug in hopes that his Chemist will provide me with the antidote to the pory bite."

"Oh, really?" Mervin said.

"Why would he do that?" Matilda asked.

"The details aren't important," Nat broke in. Soris gave her a reassuring look. "Okay," she conceded. "The details are important, but it's best that you don't know."

Matilda crossed the small room and loomed over Nat. "Who is she, Soris?"

"It doesn't matter who I am," Nat said. "With Soris the way he is, I can't get him to the castle by myself. I need your help. If you won't help, we'll be on our way." She stood and adjusted the straps of the saddlebags. As she turned toward Soris, her bags struck a stack of books. The room filled with dust as they hit the floor, which set off a spasm of coughing. When the air cleared, Nat muttered, "I'm sorry," and bent to pick up the books.

"Hold on," Mervin said. "You're an odd one, bent to get out of here, then bent to pick up books." He chuckled. "Did I see you had two horses out front?"

"Yes," Nat replied.

"Stay here and try not to knock over anything else." He nodded to Matilda and the two quickly disappeared up the narrow stairs. Nat slid next to Soris.

"They'll get us there, Sister, don't worry," Soris said. "They've known my family for a long time. We can trust them."

"I'll stop worrying when this is all over and I'm home." She stood, unable to get over the feeling of dread that was quickly overtaking each thought. "Maybe Andris was right."

"Right about what?"

"He said I'd fail."

"He said that about me plenty of times and look at me today." He held up his swollen hand and gestured to the dark room with the other. "On the verge of passing out on the way to meet my enemy, relying on the most irregular Sister any House has ever known. Proved him wrong, haven't I, Sister?"

"He'd be impressed with you, Soris," Nat said.

"He'll be impressed with both of us when this is over, and it will be over soon." He reached for her hand and gave it a small squeeze. "We won't fail. Have a little faith." His words lifted her spirits.

Footsteps echoed down the stairwell and Mervin appeared. "All set to go, you two?" he asked. Nat and Soris nodded. He helped Soris off the bench and up the stairs. Nat followed, thinking more than faith, what she needed now was a small miracle and more than a share of luck.

CHAPTER THIRTY-ONE

"Now! Jump now!" Mervin called out from the front of the wagon. Nat jumped, and Soris fell off the back of Mervin's hide-covered wagon. They hid behind a pale brick enclosure that served as the castle's main garbage receptacle. Mervin flicked his horses to increase their speed. The wagon disappeared down a side street. He never looked back.

Nat peeked around the side of the enclosure. A few people wandered down the lane toward the crowded castle entrance. No one walked near the garbage. *Little wonder,* she thought, brushing away two flies and breathing a sigh of relief. No one had seen them get off the wagon. "Soris?" She stuck her head over the low brick wall. The smell of rotten garbage assaulted her nose and she gagged.

Soris was bent over, puking into a pile of moldy bread. "Get me out of here. I can't handle this smell," he gasped. Flies congregated around his mouth and hand. He flopped his arm over her shoulder, and they slowly walked up the garbage-strewn alley leading to the castle's kitchen.

"I don't know that this is going to be much better," she said as she crinkled her nose against the smell. "Do me a favor—if you have to throw up again, aim for the wall."

"I'll do my best to get your shoes," he said, then slipped on a smear of green gunk.

"Careful, we're almost there." She pulled him closer and wrapped her arm around his waist. Heat radiated from his body. She paused at the top of the alley. They were in a tiny courtyard that smelled like rotten fish. A crumbling brick wall surrounded the courtyard on three sides. Nat heard the sound of wheels crunching against gravel. The tops of the carriage compartments were barely visible over the wall. To their left, muck-covered steps led to a worn wooden door.

"This must be it," she said, remembering Mervin's instructions on how to get into the castle's kitchen. They walked up the steps and listened. Hearing nothing, Nat pushed open the door and tripped over a huge woven basket of rotting food. "Yuck." She brushed what looked like a clump of mashed potatoes and rotten spinach off her leg. Soris wiped his hand on the side of one of the baskets, leaving a smear of beet juice. After going up two more steps and passing a set of rat traps, they entered a large scullery filled with brooms, mops, and wooden buckets. Soris stopped a moment to dip his hand into a bucket containing gray water, then wiped his hand on the thick ropes of a mop. Nat cringed.

"I don't want them to think I'm bleeding," Soris whispered when he saw her face. "It's a pory bite, not a Nala bite."

Nat held a finger to her lips. Mervin had said the kitchen should be deserted by now, since castle staff was light on a hearing day—and especially light on a hanging day. They peered around the archway into the enormous kitchen. A thickset woman pulled a flat wooden paddle laden with loaves from a hearth and expertly slid the bread onto a long table. Nat's mouth watered as the smell of the bread filled the air. Soris pointed to a set of stairs to the left of the kitchen that led to a landing and a trio of doors. Nat shook her head, wondering how she was going to get him up the stairs without the baker noticing.

The woman set the paddle between two of the hearths. She returned to the opposite end of the table and lifted a white towel.

"Bang! Bang! Bang!"

The woman jumped and clutched her chest at the loud knocks on the door. A scowl formed on her face. She stomped away toward the sound.

"Come on," Nat said, and they crept cautiously out of the scullery and into the kitchen. They passed a line of washbasins, then froze at the sound of the woman's voice.

"Now why would I have ordered a tub of binding glue?" she asked.

"No idea, but the message we received said the kitchen needed delivery today." Mervin's voice rose above her complaints. "Put me out a bit, it did. Having to drop everything on such a day and manage to get through the crowds." Nat and Soris slowly climbed the stairs. Nat looked toward the door where Mervin and the woman stood. Mervin gave her a quick wink. "You're not telling me this was a joke, now, are you?" he said to the woman.

"I would never," she replied. "Who did you say delivered the message? Maybe they meant another part of the castle? Aren't you always bringing bits in for the Chemist?"

Nat stiffened. The Chemist? Soris, seeming to have regained some strength, tugged at her sleeve. They reached the top of the stairs just as a kitchen maid entered from a door below, carrying an enormous empty tray.

"Beatty, do you know anything about a glue delivery?" A clump of dough flew off the baker's thick fingers as she pointed at the kitchen maid.

"Glue delivery? Maybe it's for the rats." Beatty gestured to the scullery with her free hand. "One jumped out at me yesterday like a nasty little Nala. All claws and sharp teeth. Frightened me to death, it did." Her voice faded as Nat slowly eased the first door closed. She silently thanked Mervin for creating the diversion.

"Which way, Soris?" They were in a long, dim hallway with stairs leading up one end and down the other.

"Mudug will be in the great hall today, it's not far." Soris nodded to the stairs going up. His face was the color of the mop water.

"Do you need to rest?" she asked.

"No time, Sister." He swallowed. "I'll be fine." He started for the stairs and collapsed against the wall.

"Soris!"

"Stop! Both of you, stop!" Two guards emerged from the lower staircase. They carried a large beaten-copper bowl set into an ornate wooden stool with carved armrests. They dropped the stool, which toppled over.

"Please, can you help me? He's so sick. He was bitten by a pory snake." Nat spoke quickly as a guard with thick hands and a reddish beard began to examine Soris. He dropped Soris' cloak like it was on fire as soon as he saw his bare chin.

"Bastle herder," he muttered. Both guards took a step back.

"I need to get him to Lord Mudug's Chemist," Nat pleaded. Tears sprang from her eyes.

"Now, miss, I don't know how you got back here, but you need to leave." The other guard motioned to the door leading to the kitchen stairs with his thick, hairy arm, then addressed the red-bearded guard. "Lift him up, Darrin."

"I'm not touching him. You lift him up, Cecil," Darrin said.

Nat watched in amazement as the guards argued back and forth.

"First you make me haul that blasted toilet around, and now you want me to take a flea bath. I'm not doing it." Darrin crossed his arms and stuck out his chin.

"Neither of you has to lift him. I'll do it." Nat once again draped Soris' arm over her shoulder. "Just take me to the Chemist."

The guards began laughing. "You can't seriously think we'd take you to the Chemist or that he'd even see you," Cecil said.

"I have something valuable to trade for his services," Nat replied.

"Turn it over to us and we'll see what Lord Mudug has to say," Cecil said.

"I don't think so." Nat adjusted Soris and he let out a groan.

"Search them," Cecil told Darrin.

"You search them! Have you ever been bitten by a bastle flea? Worst experience of my life." Darrin rubbed his enormous thigh. "It felt like a stinging needle in my leg that would never go away." He eyed them nervously and took another step back. "I told you I'm not getting near them. Let them go to the hearing chambers. If she wants to take her chances with Lord Mudug, so be it. If she's lying, someone else can deal with them. If she's telling the truth, maybe we won't have to haul His Lordship's privy around the castle anymore."

Cecil rolled his eyes. "Fine, get a move on, then," he said to Nat as he pointed to the stairs. "We'll follow you to make sure you're not up to trouble."

"Trust me, the last thing I mean to do is cause trouble," Nat lied.

"Just don't," Cecil said firmly, taking a cautious step, eyes darting over the stone floor and walls.

Darrin remained behind. "I'll just see to His Lordship's toilet."

"No, you won't. Get up here, you coward." Cecil pushed Darrin in front of him, and the quartet began a sluggish ascent up the stairs.

The hearing chamber was shaped like an hourglass. Nat scanned the room and the straggly-looking crowd as they waited off to the side. A thick blue tapestry obscured them from the crowd. Columns covered in etchings of vines stretched to the soaring, curved ceiling. A granite platform with an empty, ornate throne and a chair were at the front of the hall. Nat watched intently as Cecil and Darrin approached the figure occupying the chair.

Lord Mudug leaned forward, spreading his legs to accommodate his girth. Cecil clasped his hands as he whispered into Mudug's ear. Mudug's long gray mustache swept past his chin and dangled at the base of his throat. His black eyes darted around the room, then settled on

Nat and Soris. His eyebrows curled over his eyelids like pepper-colored caterpillars. A dismissive smugness colored his expression.

Nat felt nothing but distrust when she looked at the man. "Don't suppose anyone here is going to recognize you?" she whispered to Soris while keeping her eyes on Mudug.

"I never met him," Soris responded, clinging to Nat. "But I'll keep my head down until this is over." He leaned into her, tucking his head into her neck. "Good acting back there," he whispered.

She let out a nervous laugh, thinking back to Cairn's improvisation exercises. "I had a good teacher." She looked at Mudug again. He tilted his chin, and the tips of his mustache brushed his chest. "Looks like we've been granted an audience," Nat said when Mudug nodded in her direction, and Cecil gestured for her to come forward. She lugged Soris toward the platform and heard a few people murmur "bastle herders." Nat struggled to look behind her and saw the path they cleared through the crowd. Had everyone moved because of them? She stopped right in front of the platform. Soris' breath hit her face in short, shallow bursts.

Mudug glared at her for a moment, then spoke to Cecil. Cecil's face drained of color, and he tugged at Darrin. The pair quickly disappeared into the crowd. Mudug rose from the chair and towered over a rail-thin scribe next to him. The scribe's lips moved furiously as he read to him from a parchment. The two walked toward the rear of the platform. Mudug bent his ear toward the wispy scribe, apparently already forgetting that he'd beckoned Nat. Nat's stomach twisted as she watched him depart. She grabbed Soris and pushed her way to the front.

"Lord Mudug, my brother needs the help of your Chemist. He was bitten by a pory snake." Her voice caught slightly, and she spoke louder. "Please, there is no one else who can heal him."

Someone in the crowd muttered, "A Healing Sister could mend him." Nat turned to find a squad of guards moving in on a woman wearing a bright-red scarf tied around her head and clutching a sickly child to her breast. The guards circled the woman and pushed everyone through the high, narrow doors. A guard approached Nat and Soris.

"My brother needs your help," Nat repeated earnestly. It didn't matter—Mudug hadn't heard a word. His broad back faced the crowd. He made his way around the smaller chair while giving directions to the scribe. A trio of older men in poufy red hats shook their heads at Nat. *This isn't happening,* she thought. She hadn't come all this way to be ignored.

"Stay here," she said to Soris and leapt up onto the platform. Her hand was on Mudug's thick shoulder before the guard reached her.

"I have riven," she whispered quickly. Mudug's black eyes focused on her. Two towering guards grabbed her arms. Mudug held up his free hand.

"What did you say?" His voice was like gravel.

Nat said nothing but didn't break eye contact with him even as she struggled against the guards' vise-like grip.

"Let her go." The guards released her and stepped away a little farther than Nat expected. She flipped the edge of her cloak, revealing her wrappings, and they inched back even farther.

Nat clasped her hands at her waist and met Mudug's eyes. "I have riven," she repeated, her voice barely a whisper.

His eyes darted to the guards behind her. Leaning in, he asked, "On your person?"

Nat thought quickly. If she said yes, would he just order the guards to take it from her? Bastle fleas might keep everyone else away, but she doubted the guards would disobey a direct order from Mudug. "I have it nearby. I'll give it to you after your Chemist heals my brother." She met his dark stare with what she hoped was a believable expression.

The scribe interrupted. "Lord Mudug," he said as he clutched his parchment tightly to his chest. "The Sister's transport is ready. The guards are awaiting your final orders."

"Yes, yes, I'll be there." He waved the scribe away, then called out, "Wait, hand me parchment and pen." Mudug snatched the items, scribbled across the parchment, folded it in quarters, and handed it to the guard nearest Nat. "Take them to the Chemist. See he gets the note." He turned to Nat. "It may be a fortunate day for you and your brother." He leaned in slightly. "But if you are lying to me about what you are offering, we may be hanging more than just a Sister today." He smiled broadly. Nat stumbled off the platform.

CHAPTER THIRTY-TWO

The guard kept a fair distance, but prodded them forward with his spear. Nat would pause and scratch her knee, neck, or belly, and the guard would back up a few steps. *The farther away the guard's spear, the better,* she thought as she helped Soris down the spiral staircase. Soris' head rolled to the side and banged against the stone wall. "Ouch!" The pain brought him to his senses, and he paused a moment, trying to right himself.

"Keep moving," the guard growled. He knocked his spear just above Soris' head.

"He's doing his best," Nat retorted, glaring at him. She scratched the side of her nose.

The guard raised his spear. Not wanting to turn into a human shish kebab, Nat moved as rapidly as she could while managing Soris' weight. The stone steps were narrow and high. She slid along the curved wall as they descended. They passed through shafts of light from the arrow slits. Nat wiped a trickle of sweat from her brow when they stopped at a small landing. She leaned against a low door, hoping the guard would let them rest a few moments before moving on again. The sleeping resin Benedict had given her was wrapped in a water-resistant cover tucked in the tight folds of her clothing. She hoped it really was water resistant, or she might drop before they even made it to the Chemist. Taking a deep breath, she adjusted Soris' arm and stepped down onto the next flight of winding stairs.

"No," the guard said gruffly. "Through the door." He tapped the top of the wooden door with the spear.

Nat tried to turn the rusty knob with a free hand. It didn't budge. "Can you open it?" she asked. Like the knob, the guard did not budge. Nat eased Soris against the opposite wall. He gasped as his hand banged against the stone. "Hold on," she whispered. "I think we're almost there." Soris lifted his head and gave her a small nod.

Nat tried pushing against the door. She held the knob and gave the door a few kicks. The door creaked open. Light and fresh air filled the stuffy landing. One more kick and the door sprang open. It led to an enormous inner courtyard. A long, low stone building occupied the middle of the courtyard. A garden curved off to the right, and a wide overhang shaded the front of the building. A stocky guard sitting on a tiny bench jumped up as they approached.

"What's this, then?" he asked, pointing to Soris and Nat. Nat noticed he was backing up to the middle one of the building's three carved wooden doors.

"Mudug's orders. The Chemist's services are needed." Their guard gave Soris a slight push with the back of his spear, sending him sprawl-ing onto the packed dirt beneath the overhang.

"He's not going to like—wait a minute, are they bastle herders?" The stocky guard took a step back.

Nat scrambled over to Soris, encircling her arms around his waist. She looked up at both guards. "Did you know bastle fleas can jump long distances?" she said. "I've seen it myself. One jumped ten feet from a bastle and landed right on my little sister's nose. Biggest bite I've ever seen." She helped Soris stand and took a small step toward the guard that had pushed him. "Don't do that again." He gave her an indifferent look but took a step back. With the guards now yards away, she carefully lifted Soris' chin. "Are you okay?"

"Been better." His green eyes were bloodshot, and his broad cheeks were flushed. "That was a big bite on our sister, wasn't it? I'd forgotten all about that one," he said loud enough for the guards to hear.

Nat gave him a quick smile. "He needs to see the Chemist now," she demanded, the smile gone from her lips. When she turned to the guards, she noticed the dried bunches of flowers hanging from the wooden slats of the overhang. A cluster of tiny white flowers with long stems hung above her. She looked closer and examined the leafy stems. *Poisonous skunk cabbage,* she thought. As she slowly scanned the rafters, she recognized no less than five more clusters of poisonous plants, including the pinkish belled foxglove and the death camas with its small petals. She wondered how much healing this Chemist did.

"I've orders that he's not to be disturbed. He's tracking," the stocky guard said, glancing nervously at them. "He won't like being interrupted." He shook his round head back and forth as if it were on a spring.

"Doesn't matter what he likes. Mudug's orders," the other guard responded as he pulled the folded parchment from a slit in his tunic. "He wants the Chemist to look at the boy." He waved it in front of the guard. The two stared at each other for a moment before the stocky guard snatched the parchment. Grumbling, he tapped lightly on the wooden door. After a moment, he tapped again. The knob let out a sharp squeak. Nat looked away from the dried plants toward the door. Benedict appeared in the doorway, his eyes filled with fury. "I told you not to interrupt me!"

She gasped. It was all over. The guards would be on them as soon as Benedict gave the word. How had Gennes and Barba not known that he was a liar, that he was the Chemist? She frantically looked around for some way to escape. The only obvious way out was the way they'd come.

"S-sorry, Your Chemistness—I mean, sir—but you are to see them on Lord Mudug's order."

Benedict snatched the parchment from the guard's outstretched hand and read it. His eyes fixed on Nat and Soris. Nat noticed the fullness of his face, and as he stepped over the threshold, his legs were exactly the same—no short, atrophied limb. She stared in wonder as she realized she was looking at Benedict's twin.

"Pory bite?" the Chemist asked in a calmer tone. Nat glimpsed the cluttered room behind him. She caught sight of a long table before he shut the door and gestured for them and their guard to follow him. She gave Soris a questioning look, and he nodded. The gesture looked innocuous enough, but Nat understood that the Chemist had come from the room she needed to get into.

"Are you deaf? I asked if it was a pory bite."

"Yes, sir—I mean, no, sir, I am not deaf. It is a pory bite," Soris said between quick breaths.

"Bring him in here and be quick about it." His voice had a smooth drawl to it. He strode past them toward a door at the other end of the building. They entered a clean room lined with shelves of bottled herbs and liquids. A crude wooden table stood in the center. "Get him on the table," he told the guard and hopped nimbly up onto a step to retrieve two bottles from an upper shelf. Nat stared, watching his every movement. There was no way Benedict could move like that, but the resemblance was uncanny.

"You have something for me, girl?" the Chemist asked without turning from his shelves.

"Yes, I . . . um . . ." Nat pointed to the door.

"Well, go get it," he said. "And hurry. I want this boy gone before this place is infested with fleas." He slammed the bottles on a metal table and retrieved a beaten bowl from a cabinet. Nat hastened toward the door. "No, no. Stay here and help me," the Chemist barked at the guard, who was a step behind Nat. The guard pointed to his chest in question. "Yes, you." His irritation was growing. "He'll start thrashing the moment I apply this, you need to hold him down." The guard reluctantly returned to Soris, whose moans now filled the room. He rolled slightly to his side, glanced at Nat, and gave her a wink. She slid through the door. The Chemist's voice rose over the sound of Soris' moaning. "Easy there, hold him down by the shoulders. Stop worrying about bastle fleas and hold him now!"

She closed the door. She dug into the tight folds of fabric around her hip and pulled out the thin resin packet. She had just enough time to open the seal before the stocky guard saw her.

"What are you doing out here?" he demanded. Soris' scream sounded from the other side of the door.

Nat faked a stumble and reached for the guard's hand. She grabbed him to steady herself and pressed the resin against his skin. He backed up, but she clung to his wrist for a moment before letting go. His eyes rolled, and he swayed back and forth on his thick legs.

"Are you feeling okay?" Nat asked innocently.

"My head is feeling . . ." He brought his hand to his forehead and crumpled in front of the bench. She lunged to his side and tried to push him into a sitting position. He was short but broad, and Nat could hardly move him. She'd just have to risk it and leave him where he lay.

The middle door creaked open. Her eyes adjusted to the dim light coming from a window covered by a shredded curtain. Books were strewn across the floor and chairs lay upended. A wooden table sat in the middle of the room. She picked her way over the piles and stared at the enormous map covering the table. The forest she'd first come through was in the center. Beyond the forest lay a coastline running south before sweeping dramatically to the west. Rivers, cities, mountains, and even small caves appeared on the map. She scanned it quickly for Gennes' camp and let out a sigh of relief. The canyon wasn't even on the map. Her attention turned to several tiny orbs hovering in a circle about an inch above the map. They were an eighth the size of

Barba's, and each had a distinctly colored tint. All of them hovered in place except one green orb that spun erratically, settled onto the plains below the cliffs, then started spinning again. *Annin,* Nat thought. *That orb must show Annin.*

The wall adjoining the exam room vibrated as Soris let out a ripping scream. Her hands trembled as she unwrapped the fabric around her wrist and retrieved another thin packet. The markings on her forearm peeked out beneath the loose wrapping. She slid her finger into the packet and pulled out a pinch of translucent suix-stone powder. The powder floated down upon the orbs and along the edges of the map. The orbs dipped slightly. The green orb dropped and ceased its erratic motion.

"A little more on the far end will do." A woman stood in the corner of the room next to a narrow window Nat hadn't noticed. Her black hair was pulled loosely away from her face, but a thick strand fell over one eye. She picked at the seam of the rough brown tunic covering her thin frame.

"I was j-just looking," Nat stammered, her heart pounding.

The woman leapt over a pile of books, grabbed her wrist, and twisted it painfully. "Old band, not Emissary," she mumbled to herself. Nat yanked her arm away. The woman's blue-gray eyes focused on her. "If he finds you here he will kill you just like the rest of them he brings in. Be quick about it. A little more there." She pointed to the other end of the map. "Do it!" she hissed. Nat sprinkled more of the powder over the map and glanced at the woman. She nodded in encouragement as the color of each orb faded slightly. After the last orb dimmed, the woman stepped away from the map and over piles of books. Nat could see bruises and red marks on her thin, bare legs as she made her way back to the window.

"Will you tell him? The Chemist—will you tell him?" Nat asked.

The woman's lips hardened into a thin line and her eyes narrowed. "Go now." She pointed to the door, then pulled a book off a shelf and slammed it against the far wall. "Go now!" she cried.

Nat held the packet of suix stone to her wrist and hastily rewrapped the fabric. She ducked. A book flew above her head. The woman kicked an overturned chair and knocked a row of bottles off a far table. One shattered above her head as she hurried out the door. She stumbled over the unconscious guard. Something crashed against the wall. Nat fumbled in her cloak pocket and retrieved the vial Matilda had given her. She uncapped it and waved it under the guard's nose.

He coughed, inhaled deeply, and coughed again. "What . . . ?" He looked around, confused.

"You tripped and hit your head, I think," she said, pointing to the overturned stool. The guard stood slowly with Nat's help. Another crash sounded, then breaking glass. His face drained of color as he turned to the door, which shook as if a heavy object had just hit it. "I need to get back to my brother," Nat said, easing away. But the guard took no notice. He stood transfixed in front of the door as the crashing continued. Nat remembered the riven. She pulled the packet from the folds of fabric around her inner thigh just as the Chemist, the other guard, and Soris emerged from the exam room. A metal scale came sailing through a window set high above the door. Splintered glass fell around them. The Chemist's expression transformed from confusion to horror. He pushed past Nat, who held out the packet of riven.

"Here's what Lord Mudug wanted." She extended her hand.

"Leave it," he said hastily. "Get them both out of here!" he shouted to the guard by Soris.

Nat flung the packet of riven onto the ground and ran after the guard and Soris. She glanced back. A flash of black flew past the doorway before the Chemist slammed the door shut behind him.

"Move!" yelled the guard. He ushered Soris and Nat through the old wooden door leading into the castle.

"What was that?" Nat gasped.

"None of your business," he said gruffly. When he turned to face them, he swallowed hard and poked Nat with his spear tip. "Move!"

Nat tripped on a stair and scrambled to her feet. Soris was a few steps ahead of her. Either his strength had returned or the spear was enough to urge him on. The guard continued to glance over his shoulder as if he expected something to come after him. Nat exchanged looks with Soris. He shook his head.

They traveled down hallways and stairwells until they entered the hallway above the kitchen. Nat stopped and began to scratch the back of her neck.

"Keep moving," the guard said impatiently.

"I will, I just have this . . ." She began to twist her body as she scratched. "I thought I'd gotten rid of all of them." She scratched herself once more and pinched her fingers together, bringing them in front of her face. She pursed her lips and flicked the imaginary flea toward the guard. "Where there's one, there are always more." She began flapping the bottom folds of her cloak, trying to shake out imaginary fleas.

The guard backed away, holding the spear protectively in front of him. He gestured toward the door leading to the kitchen stairwell. "Out! Get out now before I—" He nervously brushed at a dark piece of lint on his arm.

"Through here?" Nat asked in feigned ignorance. She pointed to the same door.

"Yes! Get out now!" the guard yelled as he stumbled away from them.

CHAPTER THIRTY-THREE

The door hit the wall with a bang. Nat and Soris flung themselves onto the landing above the kitchen. Taking three steps at a time, they raced past Beatty. She dropped a stack of dishes as they ran by her. Crockery showered over the stairs and splintered into hundreds of pieces on the kitchen floor.

"What in the blazes?" Beatty said as she surveyed the crockery strewn on the floor. "You get back here—" Her threats met an empty kitchen.

Nat and Soris raced through the pungent courtyard behind the kitchen, retracing their steps down the alley. Soris grabbed Nat as she hurtled into the lane beyond the bricked-in garbage enclosure. A carriage rolled by, missing her by inches. "Watch it, there!" the driver yelled at them as they rounded the back of the carriage, pushing through the thick crowd.

Soris pointed past the edge of the crowd to a narrow, uncongested lane. Nat took his hand and they dived into the mass of people. A small fountain bubbled in the middle of the next intersection. "Down here." He steered her toward an alley. They zigzagged through a series of alleys and backstreets until Soris stopped short behind a crumbling brick wall covered in vines. He bent over, breathing hard.

"How are you?" she asked, cautiously touching his back.

He coughed. "Give me a second."

Nat looked up the alley. No sign of anyone. She peered over the vine-covered wall. Other than a scraggly chicken pecking at a pile of dirt, the small yard was empty. She leaned against the spongy vines and observed the few recessed doors that lined the alley.

Soris stood and spit in the road. He wiped his mouth. "All that for nothing." He spit again. "It was a crazy plan from the start, but at least we got away." He put his hand on her shoulder. She glanced at his hand and smiled, waiting for him to finish before she shared the good news. "Don't feel bad, Sister, we'll figure something out."

"But I did it, Soris. I put suix stone all over the map and the little orbs faded. It worked."

His jaw dropped. "What was all the crashing and banging, then? One minute I was yelling, and the next minute it was like an explosion coming from next door. When the Chemist heard the noise, he dropped a vial and ran outside. I figured something had tripped you up."

Two guards passed the entrance to the alley. Soris pressed Nat against the wall. His hands tightened around hers, and she felt his heart thudding against her chest.

"It's clear," she whispered in his ear. His cheek brushed hers when he looked down the alley. "I'll explain what happened when we're away from here."

He nodded and loosened his grip on her hands. Her fingers lingered in his as they jogged down the alley. "Where're we headed?" She skirted an enormous rat rummaging in a pile of garbage.

"I think it's too risky to go back to the bookstore. You saw the crowds at the entrance to the street. We need to find a way to get out of Rustbrook."

Nat nodded in agreement, then paused in front of an iron gate and peered through the bars. "What about our clothes? I didn't notice any other bastle herders in the crowds today. We stick out like a sore thumb."

Soris put a finger to his lips and pushed gently against the gate. It gave easily and swung open into the back courtyard of a three-story house. He pressed his arm against Nat and waited. No voices, no barking. They passed through the gate.

"How's this for a new set of clothes?" he asked, grinning at a tall pole with branch-like arms standing in the middle of the courtyard. Shirts, sheets, underwear, and tunics hung from the wooden arms. Soris pulled a pair of blue pants and a dark-brown tunic from the drying pole and tossed them to Nat. "Use the ties on the sleeves, they should hide your markings."

Nat turned the clothes over and examined the long tabs on the sleeves. She glanced up just as Soris pulled off his tunic. His chest was pale and broad. He looked up to find her staring. "What, did the spear tip get me? I don't feel anything." He craned his neck, checking for gashes.

"No, you don't have any cuts." Feeling foolish, she stepped behind the drying pole. When her legs were free of the wrappings, she pulled on the loose blue pants. Her brown hair fell around her shoulders as the last of the wrappings dropped from her face to the ground. She had no choice but to unhook her cloak to put on the tunic. She slid it over her head and fumbled with the sleeve ties.

"Need some help?" He slid his hand under her forearm, and she watched as he expertly twisted and tied the tabs at her wrists even with a damaged hand. She inspected the swelling and noticed that the bright red lines around the porc-tree punctures had already faded. "You really did it? You really got the suix-stone powder on the map?" he asked as he tied the next tab.

"I did, but there was a woman in the room."

"What woman?" He stopped tying the tabs and looked up with concern.

"I don't know who she was, she just appeared. One minute I was alone, the next she was right behind me, then she was throwing books and glass across the room. As bizarre as it sounds, she seemed to want to help. She warned me to get out before the Chemist found me. I don't know, Soris, it's hard to explain. It was like she went crazy breaking stuff to cover up for me so the Chemist wouldn't know I'd been in there."

"But what if she tells him? She saw you near the map—"

"She was ripping that room apart and destroying everything. I didn't get the sense that she was working with him."

He furrowed his brow and finished the knot. "I'll have to ask Gennes, maybe he knows who she is." He held her wrist. "Too tight?"

"No, it's fine." She pulled her wrist away. "What about your face? I haven't seen many bare chins around here." He wore a dark-green tunic, a blue vest, and breeches, but nothing to hide his lack of beard. He rubbed his jaw, then looked at the laundry. He pulled a short hooded cape off a low pole and swung it over his shoulder. Nat couldn't help but laugh.

"What's so funny?"

"I think that's for a child."

"Oh." He replaced the cape and reached for a long sash. "Here." He handed it to Nat. "Wrap this around me." She obediently wound the long sash around his neck and layered it until it covered his lower cheeks and chin. She bent down, grabbed a handful of dirt, and gently rubbed it in below his cheekbones. She stood back and examined her work. The dirt looked like the edge of a beard from a distance. If he kept his chin in the sash, it would work. "How's it look?" he asked, tilting his head toward the sky.

"Better than the cape. What do we do with these?" She held up the wrappings and her cloak.

"There's a garbage bin down the road. We'll stash them there. I think our best plan is to blend in with the crowd and try to get out through the main gate."

"You want to go into the crowd?" she asked as they jogged over the uneven cobblestones toward the reeking garbage bin.

"We don't have much of a choice. We'll be noticed for sure if we try to leave by the dock." Soris lifted a wooden lid off a garbage bin and shoved in their old clothes. Nat used a stick to flip rotten lettuce and grayish clumps over the clothes. He slammed the lid shut. They hurried away and merged with a stream of people moving down what Nat recognized as Wesdrono Street. She paused as they passed a store vestibule. It was the same one where she'd seen the orb earlier in the day. It was dark and empty. She shook her head. Her eyes must have been playing tricks on her. If Mudug was going to hang a Sister today, this would be the last place any Sister would want to be.

They pushed through the crowd. Sweaty bodies pressed up against her as they approached the square. A couple of gossiping women cut her off from Soris.

"Heard the Sister told the Nala where those unguarded traders were traveling," said a thin woman with a ruby-colored kerchief tied around her head.

"I heard that, too. And the Nala killed them all, each and every one of them. And to think my dear husband used to believe he was safe with a Warrior Sister guard. Probably just luck he never ran into a pack of Nala. We need more of Mudug's guards traveling with the merchants." The woman clutched a stained cloth to her breast and bumped into Nat.

"Excuse me," Nat mumbled as she pressed her right arm tightly to her side and passed between the women. She kept her head low until she caught up with Soris. She tugged at his hand. "We've got to get out of here." She looked around. They'd come up behind the newly constructed gallows. The crowd had grown in size. The air was heavy with the smell of pine and unwashed bodies. Nat spotted a short iron fence between the flow of people and the wide windows of a cheese shop. "Over there," she said, pointing to the fence.

"I've never heard of him having an apprentice. What did she look like?" Soris asked, his mouth pressed against her ear as the crowd squished them together.

"What?" she asked as she tried to squeeze past a man with a small child on his shoulders.

"The woman in the room with you. What did she look like?"

Before she could answer, a woman pushed past them and tried to climb onto the narrow ledge of the fence. She tumbled to the ground. Her legs were too short and her skirts were too heavy. "Boost me up, will you?" the stranger asked Soris, motioning to her posterior. "I can't see a thing and the Sister is coming." She grasped a bit of protruding brick on the adjacent wall. Soris looked at the overly wide drape of her skirt. "Well, come on. Push me up," she demanded. He shrugged and hoisted her onto the ledge. She wobbled back and forth, then pointed down the street. "There she is!"

The crowd parted, pushing Nat and Soris against the brick wall. A rough wooden wagon pulled by a lumbering draft horse passed in front of them. The Sister stood in the center of the wagon with her long, muscular arms tied to a post above her head. The sleeves of her tunic had been ripped off, revealing the delicate markings of a vine and a sword. Nat shifted from side to side, trying to get a better view between the heads blocking the way.

"Traitor!" Someone in front of Nat hurled a potato toward the Sister.

"I never thought I'd see a Sister from a Warrior House trussed up like that," the woman said, looking down at Nat and Soris. Nat tucked her arm close to her body, praying her sleeve stayed in place. "Hard to believe the Sisters are in cahoots with the Nala, isn't it?" She looked at Soris for affirmation. He ignored her and clasped Nat's hand. He pointed to two rows of castle guards following the wagon. Nat recognized one of the guards from Mudug's hearing room. She ducked her head and followed Soris. He stepped over the fence and behind a graying tree trunk. She stuck close to him and kept her eyes trained on the ground.

"Watch it!" a man looming in front of her yelled. Nat scuttled back. "You just stepped on my foot."

"Sorry." She maneuvered around him. They inched around the perimeter of the square toward an opening between two buildings. Nat squeezed Soris' hand to keep from getting separated.

"Coming through. She's about to vomit. Give her a little air," Soris barked. A small void opened and Nat hurried to his side. She held her hand to her mouth. They were met with looks of revulsion and distaste as they continued toward the entrance to the alley. When their progress slowed, Nat made a retching sound and the path cleared again. They pressed through the crowd blocking the alley. The farther down the alley they went, the fewer people they encountered. Children, trying to glimpse the wagon, clung to window ledges projecting above them. The wagon rolled past. Soris' scarf hung around his chest and Nat swiftly wound it back into place.

"Thanks. Let's get—" His eyes grew wide. Nat turned. The end of an arrow sank into the top of the wagon post, splitting the rope that bound the Sister's hands. Another quickly followed. Nat traced its origin to the top of the limestone building they'd just passed. Cries erupted as arrows rained down from the buildings fronting both sides of the alley. A sword dropped from above into the wagon. Flashes of silver exploded in the air. The crowd surged toward them, fleeing the arrows. Soris led her down the cobblestone alley ahead of the mob. They sprinted onto a main street, and a cloaked figure flew across a rooftop in front of them. People poured out of alleys like sand from a broken hourglass.

"Forget the main gate!" Soris yelled. "It'll be shut before we get there." He changed direction and they skidded down the slippery walkway leading to the dock. When they reached it, they found it deserted except for two guards stationed near the entrance. Cries and shouts erupted from the main gate. The two guards abandoned their post and ran to the center of the action. A handful of guards strained against the main wooden gates, trying to close them as the crowd streamed past.

"Here, untie this." Soris threw a thick rope in her direction. He jumped into a skiff tied up next to a wide-bellied cargo boat. She fumbled with the rope, untying it from the rusty dock ring. She jumped in as Soris rammed a long pole against the dock. They pushed against the cargo boat until the tip of the current caught the skiff and propelled it down the river away from the gates. Soris pulled a canvas tarp from the bow and flung it over Nat. He crouched next to her in the shadows under the tarp. Cries echoed down the river, and the river slapped against the side of the boat.

After a few minutes of silence, Nat lifted an edge of the tarp. The castle and Rustbrook disappeared as the skiff rounded a bend. Soris dug through a pile of long poles resting in the center of the boat and pulled out a cupped oar. "Take this." He thrust a pole into her hand. She sank the long pole into the water while Soris steered the boat to the far shore. When the pole hit mud, she strained to free it from the ooze and then set it closer to the boat again.

As they neared shore, a delicate smell filled the air. Slender white flowers covered the riverbank. Nat planted the pole as close to the flowers as she could and pushed the boat toward land.

"That's enough. Jump out," Soris commanded. The pole clattered against the wooden hull. Nat joined Soris in the knee-deep water. They shoved the skiff up the bank, crushing the flowers. "Unless they caught the Sisters, this river will be filled with boats in minutes." He scrambled up the slick rocks and damp moss and grabbed the bow. "We have to move the boat farther in so no one can see it." Nat glanced upstream and then pushed and shoved with Soris until the skiff lay hidden beneath the low bushes. Voices mixed with the sound of the river.

They ran past the bushes into the dense forest, her heart pounding with each step. A dead branch scraped her cheek. She caught flashes of the black soles of Soris' boots running through the dry leaves. She followed his lead, wiping a bit of blood off her face. The ground became steeper and rockier. Soris slowed his pace and came to a stop next to a moss-covered tree. Nat leaned against the spongy green moss as she caught her breath. Soris doubled over.

"Put your arms above your head." She gently straightened him and raised his arms. He winced slightly. His hand was still a little puffy. "It helps with the breathing."

"Thanks," he panted. "We have to work our way back round and pass over the road leading to the city."

Nat looked up the slope. "I figured that was where we were headed. How far from where we stashed our things?" She hoped it wasn't far. Her stomach was tight and her mouth felt like sandpaper. Too many adrenaline rushes and no food or water.

"Depending on what we run into, two, maybe three hours if we stay near the river. It leads to the road."

She wanted to keep moving far away from Rustbrook. She closed her eyes and visualized one of Estos' maps. If they continued southeast, she could be home in a matter of a few days. The thought seemed crazy.

"We have nothing right now—no weapons, no food," Soris continued. He looked up into the darkening canopy. "But I'd rather take my chances with the Nala than with the soldiers searching near the roads . . ."

Nat lifted her ripped sleeve. The fabric fell away, exposing the green vines on her pale forearm.

"Use my scarf." He unwound it from his neck. "The soldiers won't ask questions if they see those. After today, they'll just kill us." He started to wrap her forearm.

She pulled her arm away. "Leave it until we get closer to the road. If we run into a Nala, I want to be ready." A dim shaft of light fell on her face.

"Okay," he said hesitantly, "but at least let me tie it up." He knotted the ripped strip of fabric hanging from the sleeve. He held her wrist and looked into her eyes. "I can't believe we did it," he said. A wide smile spread across his face, and he leaned in to quickly kiss her lips.

"We did," Nat responded and glanced away, trying to keep from blushing.

He turned and took off into the woods. Nat touched her lips a moment, then followed him.

CHAPTER THIRTY-FOUR

The sound of splashing water filled the air. Nat retrieved her cloak from under the exposed root of the enormous tree. *Soris must be getting a drink,* she thought. She licked her lips. Water could wait until she pulled out the rest of their things.

The tree was a monster with roots like arthritic fingers reaching up from the ground. She leaned against one root and unwrapped the cloak. She traced the shape of the crossbow, loaded an arrow, and set it close to her side. The orb rolled out onto the soft ground. She placed it in her palm. It emitted a faint light in the darkness, and warmth spread through her frigid hand. Given the events of the day, she didn't care much about bringing Barba's old wardrobe back in one piece. The orb was different. Only now, after seeing the Chemist's tiny orbs, did she truly understand that the orb held a piece of Barba. She carefully slipped it into the cloak pocket and hastily changed out of her borrowed clothes back into her old tunic and leggings. The Sister's cloak fell securely over her shoulders. She adjusted her bag, grabbed Soris' satchel and the crossbow, and headed for the river.

"Anyone else?" a gruff voice asked. She froze and pressed herself against a tree trunk. She heard footsteps and then the rustle of brush.

"Nothing. Thought I saw something, but it wasn't anything," another voice answered. A Rustbrook Guard stepped out of the brush onto the riverbank. Nat slid to her belly. Soris was on his knees with his back to her. His hands were bound with a coarse rope. The guard who had spoken first held a torch that flickered weakly. He kicked Soris, knocking him to his side. Nat squeezed her eyes shut. This was not happening—not now, not when they were so close to going home. Opening her eyes, she slowly shifted the satchels off her shoulder and eased farther into the brush.

"Leave him. We're wasting time. He doesn't know anything about the Sisters. Just another one that took off with half the city," the guard on the riverbank said.

"Look at his face." The guard by Soris pointed with his boot. "No beard."

"So what? Mudug hasn't outlawed a naked face."

The guard's boot came down on Soris' chin. Nat positioned the crossbow, securing the hilt against her forearm. She'd have little time to load the second arrow—even less if she missed.

"Don't tell me you're jealous because your arse is hairier than his face?" The guard on the riverbank grabbed the torch sputtering on the ground near Soris. "Do what you want with the beardless boy. I'm done searching the forest. Leave him for the Nala." Gravel crunched under his boots as he walked down the bank.

"You're deserting the search!" cried the guard. "You'll be in the stockades by morning."

"I'm not deserting the search, you imbecile. The road needs to be searched, too, and I won't have to keep looking into the blasted treetops for those blue demons," the other guard called out as he disappeared around a bend.

"Coward," the guard mumbled as he turned his attention to Soris. "What kind of man shaves his beard?" He kicked Soris again, pushing him onto his back. Soris groaned. Nat looked through the crosshairs. "A man with something to hide, I say." The guard raised his sword.

A hand clamped down on Nat's and a finger slipped between hers and the trigger. The woman's face was blackened with dirt and bits of crumbled leaves. She pressed a finger to her lips, then turned and pointed toward a tree to her right. A shadow, perched in a crook halfway up the tree, loosed an arrow. It flew over the bushes and pierced the back of the guard. He landed with a thud facedown next to Soris. Soris twisted his head frantically, looking for the archer. The shadow dropped silently and was joined by another woman holding a curved sword low at her side.

An orb appeared in front of Nat's face, circled her head, then whizzed down the bank after the Rustbrook Guard. The bulge of Barba's orb pressed into her side. If Barba's orb was in her cloak, where had the other orb come from? Nat glanced at the woman at her side. Her dirt-encrusted face broke into a tight smile as she easily wrested the crossbow from Nat and motioned for her to follow. Two cloaked figures approached Soris and the dead guard. Nat scrambled toward the bank but felt an iron fist clamp down on her thigh.

"Your friend will be fine. Come with me now," she said to Nat. Her voice was low and barely audible.

"No, he's coming . . ." The look on the woman's face stopped her.

"He will be fine," she repeated.

They walked uphill for several minutes through the dark trees until they reached a small rocky outcrop at the top of a hill. The woman pulled out an orb and jumped from rock to rock until she reached a ledge. She jumped onto the ledge and disappeared. *They must be the Sisters from Rustbrook,* Nat realized as she stared at the ledge above her. She twisted around and looked down the valley to the river. Swaying treetops obscured the riverbank. Soris was nowhere to be seen in the starlight. She lurched up the last rock and discovered the entrance to a cave. It smelled like something wet and moldy had recently died.

Avoiding the sharp, jagged edges, Nat collapsed in the center, close to the entrance.

The Sister, leaning against the curved mouth of the cave, regarded Nat. "Do you have any food in there?" She gestured to the satchels.

Nat unhooked her bag and rummaged until she found a crumbling packet of biscuits. She pulled one out and held it up as her stomach growled. The Sister plucked the food from her hand. Nat turned her attention back to the satchel. Pretending to search for more food, she tucked her short dagger under her cloak sleeve and pulled out another biscuit. A corked water skin was dangling in the air in front of Nat when she looked up.

"Please, take some," the Sister said. Nat's lips twitched. She took a long drink and handed the skin back. The Sister gripped her wrist tightly. "Hold your arm straight." She beckoned her orb. It hovered above Nat's arm, emitting a bluish light. A few loose strands of mud-encrusted hair fell into her face as she traced Nat's markings with her finger. The mask of dirt and leaves hid her features, but her cheeks were sunken and thin. Nat tried to stop the shaking in her hands as the Sister inspected her arm. After a moment, the Sister dropped her arm and looked at her with curiosity. Her eyes shone in the dark. Nat waited for the accusations of fraud, but none came. "You were in Rustbrook yesterday morning on Wesdrono Street." It was a statement rather than a question.

"Yes," Nat replied. She glanced at the mouth of the cave, wondering where Soris and the other two Sisters were.

"What brought you to Rustbrook on a hanging day?" Her tone was light, almost as if asking about a holiday.

"We had business there," she answered. A feeling of uneasiness came over her.

"Business?" the Sister replied. "With Mudug?" Maybe she thought they were working for him.

"No—well, yes, but nothing to do with Sisters. I needed his help." Nat decided a little truth would be better than a total lie.

"No one helps a Sister these days, especially not Mudug." Her voice was cold. She turned and faced the entrance. The wind gently spun her hair around her head. She kicked a small rock and walked out of the cave. It clattered down the hill, ricocheting off the rocks below. A light wind tossed her cloak haphazardly around her legs. A storm was moving in. Thick, bumpy clouds appeared briefly with a flash of lightning, then disappeared into the darkness.

"I almost left you and your companion after the guards' ambush," she said as she turned around. Her voice was low, blending with the rustle of the leaves. "We've had more than our share of trouble today. I wasn't keen on more." She pulled the edge of her cloak away from her leg. An irregular, dark stain marred a strip of gray cloth wound around her thigh.

"Why did you help us, then?" Nat asked. The conversation was going downhill fast, but she tried to keep her tone relaxed.

"You pulled an orb from the tree, which makes you either a thief or a Sister. It's my practice to punish an orb thief. I also make it a practice to help a Sister in need. It's something we do." She stared at Nat, her eyes hooded and black. Fat drops of rain randomly pelted the rocks near the cave entrance. The wind kicked up puffs of dirt around the Sister's leather boots. She tilted her head toward the sky. Thin rivulets of dirty water ran down her cheeks, washing away some of the muck.

"I'm not a thief, and I was doing fine on my own," Nat said, trying to hide the shaking in her voice. If she hit the Sister head-on, she might have enough force to push her over the ledge. Or maybe she could use her dagger. She felt its hilt under her cloak. But then what? How would she find Soris or get home?

"I am not sure what you were trying to do, but you were far from 'doing fine.' Do you really think you would have hit the guard and saved your friend?" The Sister wiped her cheek and flicked a clump of dirt off her finger. She stepped into the cave out of the rain.

"Yes." Nat's voice wavered.

The Sister raised an eyebrow. "Doubtful. Your angle was wrong. Your friend would be dead right now if we hadn't helped." She folded a long leg and sat on a little ledge. *So much for the head-on hit,* Nat thought. The Sister untied the dirty dressing around her injured thigh. Her orb bobbed up and down near the wound. "Sheath your blade," she said to Nat while examining the gash.

Nat ducked her head to keep the flush in her cheeks from showing. She pulled the sheath out of the satchel, slid the dagger in place, and attached it to her belt. If she could find Soris so they could get on their way, she wouldn't have to second-guess everyone and everything. Sighing, she pulled out Barba's orb and whispered to it. The orb joined the Sister's, casting a brighter light on her wound. "You're right," Nat said as she pulled out a rolled-up strip of linen containing herbs. "We probably would be dead." She shivered as she looked for the silvery-white herb Ethet told her to use on open wounds. She held it up for the Sister to examine.

"I haven't seen that in a while," the Sister said as she carefully took the thin stalk from Nat. She rinsed the wound with water and crumbled the herb into the open gash. Little bits of silvery-green covered the wound.

"Were the other Sisters injured?" Nat asked.

"Once I got the sword to Camden, she was as safe as a Warrior Sister in a nest of Nala. Sister Pauler broke a rib jumping from a roof. She'll mend." The gash was long and bloody.

Nat remembered another ointment Sister Ethet had given her and pulled the small opaque glass container from her bag. "Here." She handed it to her. "This should help with the bleeding and infection. Is Sister Camden the one they were going to hang?"

The Sister nodded, turned the lid, and sniffed the contents. Her head jerked back. "Where did you get this?" she demanded.

"From a Sister—a Healing House Sister. It's perfectly safe. I'm not sure what she put in it, but I'm not trying to poison you. Here—see?" Nat dabbed some onto her finger and smeared it across the cut on her cheek. The Sister eyed her suspiciously, then took the balm and began applying it to her wound. She finished the application, tightened the lid, and handed it back to Nat. "Keep it." Nat held up a hand. Maybe generosity would get her out of this mess. "Are there any Sisters from a Healing House still around who can help you with that? It's going to need stitching."

"They're all gone," she said flatly as she took the clean linen cloth Nat offered and rewrapped the wound. "Mudug rounded up Healing House Sisters first, before any of us understood what was going on. Those who are still alive are either too frightened to practice their art of healing or are too far out on the fringe to do anyone any good." She met Nat's gaze. "You must be from the fringe if you still have contact with a Healing House Sister." She leaned against the stone wall and waited for Nat's response. When none came, she shrugged and continued. "You're an odd one." She stood and adjusted her heavy cloak. "You command your orb by voice and not thought. Your markings are antiquated." She reached for Nat's forearm and ran a finger over the markings. "They're so old, maybe as old as—"

A shrill cry like a night owl cut through the sound of the rain. The Sister dropped Nat's arm. "Let's go." She stepped out into the rain. "If you want to see your friend again, that is." She disappeared over the ledge. Nat grabbed her satchels and orb and hurried behind her. Despite her injured leg, the Sister was already halfway down the rocky slope. Nat managed to keep her in sight by ordering her orb to follow her and emit a low light. They pushed through a thicket of bushes with long, thin branches and pointed leaves.

"Put your orb out, you fool!" the Sister hissed when she realized it was following her. "Do you want the guards—or worse, a Nala—to see us?" She let go of a branch, and it whapped Nat on her uninjured cheek. Another trickle of blood streamed down her face. Feeling utterly foolish, she pocketed the orb and hastened after her. The rain barely penetrated the upper canopy, but the forest floor was slick. Nat struggled over the wet rocks that protruded through the spongy ground. The Sister ran faster despite the conditions. They reached the edge of a forest along the riverbank. Nat, now breathing heavily, thought that they must have traveled at least two miles upriver from where she and Soris had first met the Sisters. The Sister let out a shrill call similar to the one Nat had heard in the cave. A cloaked figure stepped out of the woods onto the bank ahead of them. They wound their way through the trees, keeping to the forest, as they made their way to the figure.

Soris lay unconscious by a large tree. Nat brushed past her companion and rushed to him. A large red welt the size of an egg pulsed at the base of his skull. She looked up angrily at the Sister standing over him. Her straw-colored hair was tucked into a dark hood, her cheeks were hollow, and dark, heavy circles hung below her blue eyes. "What did you do to him?" Nat yelled.

"Hush!" The Sister from the cave clapped her hand over Nat's mouth. "You are louder than a flock of geese. Between your breaking every wet branch you stepped on—how you managed that I'll never know—and lighting your orb in the forest, and now this outburst, it's a wonder Mudug's guards or the Nala haven't shown up." She dropped her hand. Nat futilely swatted her arm away. "Camden, before our young Sister here cries out again, tell her what happened."

Sister Camden pursed her thin lips and glared at Nat. "They must be a pair. By the time we had him unbound and on his feet, he was shouting and yelling, 'Where's the Sister, where's the Sister?'" She quietly mimicked Soris' voice and waved her arms. Despite her haggard appearance, she sounded forceful. "He was thoroughly uncooperative and a risk to us all. So I knocked him out, and then Pauler helped me bring him here. We should have left him to the guards. Pauler was in no condition to lug someone through the forest."

Sister Pauler pushed the bushes on the riverbank quietly to the side and joined the four of them at the base of the tree. She held her arm tightly against her ribcage. "Good to see you, Rory. It took us longer than expected to get here, and I'm sorry to say we weren't able to get any information from him before Camden knocked him out." She handed a water flask to Camden.

"Any sign of approach?" Sister Rory asked. Nat listened carefully to the exchange while she examined Soris.

"No," Pauler replied. "But the rain is letting up. They'll be on us again soon."

Soris rolled over and groaned. He pushed against the muck and found himself staring into Nat's face. "What happened?" he asked.

"We were rescued, I think." Nat gave Sister Camden a nasty look and addressed Sister Rory. "We need to be on our way. Thank you for your . . . help." She tugged at Soris' arm, dragging him to his feet.

He wobbled and slapped a hand against the trunk to gain balance. "This has not been my day," he muttered.

"You're forgetting something, Sister." Rory took a step to the side, so the Sisters created a line in front of them. "You never told me what business you had with Mudug. No Sister is foolish enough to travel through Rustbrook, let alone work a deal with Mudug with that on her arm." She pointed to Nat's markings. Pauler and Camden leaned in for a closer look, and Nat instinctively pressed her arm to her side.

"He never found out I was a Sister. We needed something from his Chemist and brought riven in exchange."

"What did you need from the Chemist? Think before you say medicine or healing services." She pointed to her leg. "You aren't lacking access to either."

Nat took a deep breath and looked at Soris. He nodded slightly. A bug landed on her lip, and she brushed it away, giving herself a moment to figure out what to say. "The Chemist had created a way to track my friends. I adjusted it slightly. We used Soris as a ruse to get to the Chemist by claiming he'd been bitten by a snake."

Rory and Pauler exchanged glances, and Pauler silently disappeared into the brush. "You said a way to track your friends. Do you know if he was tracking others?" Rory asked.

"If he was, it will be difficult or impossible for him to do it now," Nat replied. "It should take him a while to figure out what happened." She thought of the crazed woman smashing vials, and the glass raining down like a sleet storm. "There was a disruption that allowed us to get away, and I believe we ruined his ability to track."

Camden adjusted her sword and disappeared in Pauler's direction. Rory, her face still half-covered with dirt, glared at Nat and Soris. The sound of the river punctuated the silence. Nat glanced up toward the trees, half expecting to see Pauler or Camden with bows trained on them.

Finally, Rory exhaled and pointed upriver. "Mudug's using the Nala to control the trade routes from the coast. He has guards scattered from Rim Town to Rustbrook who serve as protection for the merchants, but he's got some kind of agreement with the Nala to let them move through the corridor undisturbed. Without a Warrior Sister in tow, the band could be taken out by the Nala in minutes, Rustbrook Guards or not. I'd avoid that area for now."

She faced Soris. "You look a little like your brother Gordon, Soris." His eyes widened. "I am amazed you made it through Rustbrook with no one noticing the resemblance. I was an apprentice when Emilia attended our Warrior House, and I met Gordon on more than one occasion. Their loss was . . . felt by us all." Rory placed a gentle hand on Soris' shoulder, then turned to Nat.

"When you meet up with your Sisters, let them know there are a band of us in the North. I've heard of a House deep in the forest between the Meldon Plain and the coast, but other than that, Mudug has been true to his word and destroyed any of us that he could find. The Nala have had free rein on those from any House. I know of only a handful still in this area. Travel safely. Travel free."

She was near the brush when Soris called out, "Sister, there is refuge south of the copper mines in the canyons."

"Thank you." Rory paused and looked at Nat. "You have an obligation that comes with those markings, even in these times. Don't forget it." She disappeared through the brush.

CHAPTER THIRTY-FIVE

The fire crackled and popped. Soris stirred the black pot and ladled stew into a wooden bowl. He nodded at a woman straddling a log next to the fire. Her eyes flickered in his direction as she scraped with a knife one of the rabbit hides Soris had exchanged for the meal and the earlier ride on her wagon.

He skirted the collection of fires and rough-looking merchants speaking in low tones. The free travelers' wagons formed a semicircle around the camp. A few travelers were already banking the fires, choking the flames with dirt. The grass brushed Soris' calves as he passed the long poles penning the shaggy horses. He ran up a small hill toward Nat. "It'll be cool enough by now," he said and handed her the wooden bowl. "You'd have thought she'd give me two bowls after all the rabbits I dropped at her feet." She scooted over, making room for him on a bedroll tucked against a slab of pale rock. He pressed close to Nat and wrapped the bedroll around his side.

"Beggars can't be choosers," she said and brought the bowl to her lips. The stew tasted gamey. She bit into a sweet root and passed the bowl to Soris.

"That's an odd expression." He swallowed and wiped his mouth with the back of his hand. "Odd, but true. They didn't offer the most comfortable ride, did they?" He smiled at her and she laughed.

"If I'm ever that close to geese again, it'll be too soon," she said. They'd come across the band of free travelers a day after parting with the Sisters. A member of the caravan had reluctantly agreed to let them ride in her wagon. They'd spent the day surrounded by irate caged geese. Nat was still picking feathers out of her clothes.

"We were fortunate they let us ride at all. I've been forced to walk behind wagons a time or two when I've latched onto a band of free travelers."

"They don't strike me as the most trusting people." She took another sip and inched closer to Soris, enjoying the warmth of his body. "I think the wool merchant riding with his son saw my dagger. I caught him glancing at me and heard him muttering about Sisters. I kept waiting for him to grab my forearm." She thought back to what Rory had said to her—that she had an obligation that came with her markings. *Except for seeing Soris to the safety of Benedict's house, I'm done with obligations,* she thought. Her brow furrowed when she realized how soon she'd be leaving him.

"He has more to hide than you do." Soris interrupted her thoughts and she looked at him. His chin was now covered with reddish-blond stubble. She suppressed an urge to run her hand over his new beard. "Did you get a good look at his son?" he asked. Nat shook her head. "Pointed hand. His face looked regular enough, but I'm sure there's blue skin under that high-necked tunic of his."

"A duozi?"

Soris nodded. "Probably more than one in this group. The travelers have to tolerate a duozi's presence, and there aren't many traveling groups that would. Most would just send the duozi away, or worse. I think this band wants to avoid Mudug's guards for reasons other than evading the transport tax. From the looks of them, it wouldn't surprise me if some of these merchants move year round."

"Why do you say that?"

"The only safe place for a duozi is on the run."

They'd given Nat and Soris a ride, but they weren't willing to let them stay within the protective ring of wagons after nightfall. If some of the travelers were duozi, it made sense to her now. She thought of Annin and wondered what her life had been like when she lived in Fourline. If the images of imprisonment in Benedict's house were any indication, she was better off in Nat's world.

The stars were faint glimmers in the fading twilight. Nat and Soris passed the bowl back and forth and watched the day fade. Fire after fire disappeared in the field before them. Six burly travelers took their positions around the perimeters of the camp.

Nat watched them pace. "Are they that worried about Mudug's men finding them?" She gestured to the guards. "How much trouble can they get into for refusing to pay a tax or use his escort?"

Soris gave her a curious look. "You fringers really are out of touch."

She blushed, realizing she'd made yet another misstep. "You have no idea," she said quietly. How many times had she stuck her foot in her mouth since she'd met him? She heard the horses nervously whinny in the distance.

"It's okay," he said, taking her hand. "I didn't mean to imply you were ignorant. How are you supposed to know everything that's happened or how to react when you lived and trained so far away?" He looked at her apologetically.

She let out a little laugh, then shivered. "Will you promise me something?" she asked. Soris leaned over her, pulled the edge of the bedroll tight across her chest, then curled his arm around her shoulder. She leaned her head back, resting on his arm. She relaxed her shoulders and melted into him. For the first time in weeks, she felt completely at ease.

"After what you pulled off, I'd promise you anything," he said with sincerity.

"When you see Estos and Andris again, will you tell them what you just told me?" She tried to imagine both their faces when they heard what she and Soris had accomplished. She felt his warm breath on her cheek. Thoughts of Estos and Andris disappeared when she turned and looked at him. Warmth poured from his eyes. He gave her a questioning look. She brought her hand to his face. "Thank you for . . ."

A million thoughts raced through her mind when he brushed his lips against her forehead. His cheek felt rough under her hand, but his lips were soft and full. He kissed her slowly and entwined his fingers in her hair, loosening her messy braid. She momentarily lost herself in the sensation of his kiss, forgetting where they were and who he was. She pulled away, slowly, and smiled. His breathing sounded labored, but he gently brushed a lock of hair behind her ear. She opened her mouth to tell him the truth, to tell him everything. A muffled cry sounded behind her. He shifted his gaze from her eyes past her shoulder toward the caravan.

"Natalie."

She tensed at the tone of his voice. She looked down at the field and saw a flash of movement. "I see them," she whispered.

One of the travelers guarding the camp bellowed. Nala poured over the camp. Their blue bodies crawled over wagons and flew through the air, landing on top of fleeing travelers. A few travelers formed a circle, slashing outward with long blades. But the Nala sprang over them and landed in the center of the ring.

Soris yanked her arm, pulling her away from the nightmare playing out below them. He shoved her satchel into her hands and pushed her behind the rocks. The wooden bowl clattered to the ground. Nat peered over the narrow lip of the rock and recognized the wool merchant in the fighting. He slashed at an approaching Nala with a curved blade. The tip sliced through one of its pointed arms, and blue blood spurted across his tunic. The wool merchant's son stood motionless next to his father with a dazed look on his face. *Why isn't he helping him?* Nat thought, watching in horror as the wounded Nala stuck one of its pointed limbs into the wool merchant and brought him crashing to his knees. She drew her dagger and moved toward the edge of the rock, but Soris clamped a hand down on her shoulder.

"We can't help. There are too many of them." He hooked his arm around her waist and pulled her away toward the cover of the long grass. More cries erupted from below. Nat spun around and saw a dozen faint figures on horseback watching the Nala attacking the merchants. Even in the early evening light, she could make out the blazing white circle on the arm of a few of the riders.

Soris stopped in his tracks. "Mudug's guards." His face contorted in anger.

"Why aren't they doing anything?"

"They're letting the Nala do their dirty work for them and take away the duozi."

Nat glanced back at the soldiers. A blur of light hovering above one of the dancing horses caught her attention. *An orb?* Soris pulled her into the grass and she stumbled after him, shaking her head in disbelief. She'd seen a Sister in the midst of Mudug's soldiers.

CHAPTER THIRTY-SIX

After three nights of skirting through forests, scanning treetops, and wading through grass as high as Nat's shoulders, the open valley that spread below was paradise to her eyes. Orange flowers, coaxed open by the sunrise, were sprinkled over the rocky ground that flowed into the valley. A dozen sheep grazed on the patches of grass that sprang around the rocks. Soris joined Nat in breathing in the sweet morning air. The memory of the Nala attack was still fresh in Nat's mind, but the calm surroundings settled her nerves.

"Better than the muck we came through last night." Soris settled into the grass. "I'm famished. What's left?" He flipped open the top of his satchel. Nat glanced at the dark forest behind them, looking for any movement. Soris tugged at her sleeve. "You need to eat something." He handed her the last bit of dried meat, and she dropped into the grass next to him.

"Benedict's house isn't far from here. I recognize those cliffs." She pointed to the distance. Home was so close. "Maybe a day or two walking till we get there." How many days or weeks had she been gone? The urge to run down the hill was overwhelming, but after nights of traveling with her neck craned to watch the treetops, she was exhausted. They both needed rest before moving on to Benedict's. She handed her water flask to Soris. He took a quick drink, then capped the flask.

"I can't stop thinking about them, Soris." The images of the Nala pouncing on the merchants played over and over in her mind.

"There wasn't a thing either of us could've done to help the merchants," he said with a grim expression.

She shook her head. They'd had this same conversation in hushed tones many times since they'd fled the massacre. She knew he was right, but that didn't make her feel any less guilty for leaving them.

"Mudug's guard could have helped," she said, remembering how passively they'd watched the slaughter.

"Mudug doesn't care what happens to them, especially since the caravan contained duozi. I wouldn't be surprised if he's happy there was a massacre. He can use it to scare more people into accepting his transports and paying his tax. He has the merchants in a choke hold, and fear will only tighten that hold."

"Do you think Estos really can stop him?" This was the first time Nat voiced her doubt.

"By himself, no. But he can rally the people's support and give the rebels someone to stand behind. We lived in peace for so long. Estos is a symbol of that peace and the balance the Sisters brought to Fourline. He's the one who can restore that peace."

Nat pulled a blade of grass. She twirled it in front of her face until it was nothing more than a green blur. "Speaking of Sisters, you still don't believe what I saw, do you?"

"I'll grant that you saw something, but a Sister riding with Mudug's guards?" He shook his head. "A Sister would have to be out of her mind to align herself with him."

She dropped the subject. She was certain she'd seen an orb and a rider wearing a Sister's cloak, but she was too tired to argue.

"We need more water," he said as he scratched his cheek. "And if Benedict isn't back, we'll need more food before we . . ." He looked at her with a worried expression. "Are you sure you want to split up at Benedict's?"

No, I'm not. The thought of traveling on without him made her feel anxious and confused. Other than holding her hand and helping her over rocks and up steep terrain, he hadn't touched her since the night of the massacre, but his presence had made her feel safe. She snuck a quick look at him, then gazed out over the field at the distant cliffs, resigned to what was to come.

"You need to get back to Gennes to tell him what happened, and I need to get to Estos and Andris. Benedict's is the safest place to split up."

He still looked concerned.

"We haven't seen a guard or the Nala in three days. Besides, I'm a Warrior Sister. Nothing to worry about," she joked halfheartedly.

"I guess you can manage on your own, can't you?" He fell back onto the grass. "Will I see you again, after you get word to Andris and Estos?" Soris rested, his eyes closed.

The realization that he wouldn't see her hit her. Her throat tightened. "Probably," she lied.

"If you can't come with Andris and Estos, then you have to come with your other Sisters. Gennes can use Sisters in the rebellion. And I . . . I'd like to see you." He shielded his eyes against the sun. She looked away. "What's wrong?"

"Nothing." The grass poked her wrists. "I wasn't expecting to make a friend in all this." She remembered the sensation of his lips on hers and pushed the thought away.

"Nothing wrong with making a friend. Just because you're a Sister doesn't mean . . ." He paused and reached for her hand, but she pulled it away, not wanting to leave him with more lies or promises she couldn't keep. He shifted away from her. "I know I stepped over the line when I kissed you. I didn't mean to imply anything, Sister. I'd just like to see you again."

"So would I, but I'm not sure it'll happen," she said deciding not to say anything about his kiss. Despite the warm sun, she felt cold. Soris sat up and leaned his head against his knees. They both watched the grazing sheep in silence. "Soris, what do you think makes a person a Sister?" she asked, wanting to think and talk about something else.

He squinted, and little lines formed around his eyes. "The training, the apprenticeship, the oath, the House. All the things a person goes through until she gets her marking and makes an orb. Just like what you went through."

Nat sat quietly and shook her head. "I told you I was from a fringe house. It was different for me." She thought of the tapestry she'd seen in Gennes' camp. "Gennes has a tapestry in the Sisters' quarters. Have you seen it?" Soris nodded in response. "It showed the beginning. Four girls, no formal training, no formal apprenticeship, and no House. They had each other—that was it." She smiled ruefully at him. "I think my training was more like theirs." She stood and brushed grass from her cloak, then traced the vine pattern on her forearm. She began to walk.

Soris fell into step next to her. "It makes no difference to me how you were trained. You're a Sister—otherwise your House never would have given you those markings, and you wouldn't have your orb."

She bit her lip and didn't respond. How could she keep lying to him after everything they'd been through? "Do you ever think about leaving Fourline? Finding some other place where you can live peacefully?" she asked.

He stopped and gazed down the hill toward the distant cottage. "No." He shook his head. "Not as long as my brother, my family needs me. This is my home. I'll stay and fight until Mudug's gone and everything is the way it was before." He picked a rock up and threw it far down the hill, where it disappeared into the lush grass.

The sun warmed her back as she stood silently next to him. A sad resignation settled over her. He'd never leave his home, and she couldn't tell him the truth. She searched for something to say. "You'll have Andris and Estos fighting with you soon."

"It will be good to see Andris again. Try to come back with them."

"I'll try." This time, the lie came easily.

"Water and rest before we move on?"

She nodded and grasped his hand, thinking how much she was going to miss the feeling of his strong fingers in hers. His hand slipped away when they stepped into the woods, each going in a different direction until they stopped in front of the same tree. After days of sleeping in the broad boughs of what Soris called a cafin tree, Nat knew precisely what they were looking for in a daytime hiding place.

Soris knelt down. "Up you go, Sister. I'll get water and take first watch."

Nat took a few steps back and ran toward the trunk. She planted her toes into the rough bark, scrambled up a few feet, and grabbed the lowest branch. "Thanks for the offer, but I am a Warrior Sister, Soris." She climbed a few more branches and called down. "Throw a stone if you need a boost!" Soris grabbed a small pebble, aimed, and threw it in her direction. She laughed and ducked, disappearing behind the wide cluster of leaves surrounding the tree where he couldn't see her smile fade away.

The bright light of her barrier penetrated the darkness of her dream space. A scraping sound, like a stick running across a metal fence, was incessant. She squeezed her eyes shut, concentrating on the barrier and keeping what was on the other side out. She heard a muffled voice. Was it Annin? The voice grew more muffled until Soris' scream tore through the air.

"Soris!" She tumbled off the branch. Her hand shot out just in time to grab a limb. The satchel flipped in the air and landed at the base of the tree. The rough bark scraped against her abdomen. She clutched the trunk, and her breathing slowed. The scream seemed so real, but it must have been a dream. Nat peered through the lower branches. No sign of Soris. He'd let her sleep too long. She slid down the tree trunk and landed near the base of the tree. The contents of her satchel were strewn on the ground.

"Soris?" she called while she stuffed the contents back into the bag. No answer. A breeze shifted the leaves and pine needles. The midmorning light danced around the forest floor. Maybe he was getting water. She looked up into the canopy. The treetops swayed slightly. A quick flash of a bird caught her attention.

"Soris?" she called again, pulling the small crossbow from the satchel. She walked silently toward the river they'd passed earlier in the morning. Light filtered through the trees. She kept the crossbow trained on the canopy. The forest floor sloped slightly, and a burbling sound grew louder. Peering through the trees, she saw Soris sitting on the riverbank. "Soris." She lowered the crossbow and emerged from the forest. "You let me sleep too long." He turned at the sound of her voice. A water flask fell from his hands.

"Behind!" he screamed. Nat dropped to the ground and a hot sting ripped through her shoulder. The Nala's pointed hand stabbed the bank a few feet in front of her. It opened its blue mouth, and dark liquid dripped from a row of pointed teeth. A low hiss filled the space between them. She tried to move, but her arms and legs weren't responding. It hissed again. At the sound of crunching gravel, it shifted to the side. Soris slashed his dagger through the air. The Nala flipped up and over Soris, landing on his back. Soris thrashed about, struggling to free himself from the snake-like constriction of the Nala's arms. A piercing scream filled the air as the Nala sunk its teeth into his shoulder. Nat scrambled to her feet. The arrow from her crossbow flew fast, grazing the creature's cheek just as it lifted its glossy head. It instantly released

Soris, and he crumpled, motionless, to the ground. She skirted to the side, keeping the Nala in front of her.

It stabbed the ground as it moved behind Soris, making punching sounds in the soft soil. Blue blood pulsed down its smooth face. "He will be the duozi." It pointed a sharp hand toward Soris. "But you"—it focused on Nat and turned a corner of its mouth into a twisted smile— "will die." It sprang over Soris, coming down just as she lunged forward to thrust Barba's dagger into its soft belly. Pushing it off to the side, Nat fell on her back to avoid its flailing arms. Her forearm shot out to break her fall, revealing the markings drawn on her skin.

Its eyes grew wide until they seemed to engulf the top half of its head. "Sister!" it screamed as it writhed on the smooth gravel. Its arms uncontrollably slammed into the hilt of the dagger, driving it deeper into its abdomen. It flipped and twisted like a fish on a riverbank until it twitched only slightly, then didn't move at all.

Nat pushed herself up onto her elbows. The only sound was water rushing by and her frantic breathing. The Nala lay motionless, curled in a fetal position around the dagger. A sharp pain shot down her shoulder. She struggled to her feet, ran to Soris, and cradled his head in her lap. A bloody half circle of punctures covered his left collarbone. His pulse was wild. She pulled her fingers away from his neck. She frantically glanced upstream, and her eyes fell on the Nala. She gently placed Soris' head on the gravel and reached for the crossbow. Her fingers fumbled as she tried to reload and the arrow dropped to the ground. She retrieved it and jammed it into the casing.

Her boots ground into the gravel, the sound growing louder as she approached the motionless blue creature. She aimed the crossbow at its chest and kicked its shoulder, pushing it flat on the ground. The creature flopped over, its pointed arms angled out like a *v*. She knelt down, trying to keep the crossbow steady. The dagger made a sucking sound when she pulled it from its abdomen. Prodding it with her feet, she rolled the body down the bank into the river. She grabbed a worn branch and stepped into the cold water. She pushed the Nala toward the fast current in the middle of the river. The tip of the branch ripped the skin on the creature's back. The flowing water caught its head and flipped the Nala around. It floated feetfirst downstream. Nat dropped the branch and walked onto the bank, the bottom of her cloak dripping with water.

"Soris." His bite was now encircled in a sickly blue. She replaced the ripped flap of fabric and pressed her hand against the wound. "Soris, you've got to wake up." He lay motionless in her lap. The branches of the trees lining the riverbank swayed as a light wind rippled across the river. Nat saw movement everywhere. She closed her eyes tightly, trying to shut it out. Tears began streaming down her cheeks. "Soris, wake up, please," she pleaded.

The treetops were still when she opened her eyes. She wiped her nose on her sleeve. She knew she couldn't leave him on the bank, just as she knew he was too heavy for her to carry very far. They'd seen a small cottage in the valley with the sheep. She had to find someone to help her. She crouched behind Soris and wrapped her arms under his arm-pits. Looking over her shoulder every few seconds, she pulled him under the cover of the trees. His heels dug into the gravel, making crooked grooves. He rested under a cluster of ferns, covered by wide fronds. She wanted him farther from the river, but her breathing was strained and her shoulder felt like a hot poker was permanently lodged in the muscle.

She returned to the riverbank and retrieved her weapons and bag. The groove marks disappeared as she smoothed mud and rocks over them. She then wrapped a strip of linen around Soris' bite. His face remained expressionless. She tucked the water flask and a dagger under his good arm. If he woke up, what was he going to think?

She pulled Barba's orb from her cloak and stared at its opaque sur-face. "Stay with him," she ordered. "Keep him here until I get back." The orb bobbed slightly, then settled near his face. Nat rearranged the fronds until she was satisfied, then took off running through the forest.

CHAPTER THIRTY-SEVEN

The cottage was on the other side of a low stone fence that separated two pastures at the bottom of the valley. The sheep she'd seen earlier in the day passed through an open gate. A shepherd on horseback, pushing a few straggling sheep toward the fence, emerged from behind a little knoll. He paused.

Nat frantically waved her arms above her head. "Help! I need help."

The shepherd kicked the chestnut-colored horse and rounded the remaining sheep through the open gate. She stepped back as a matted guard dog sped toward her with the shepherd not far behind. The dog halted and let out a low growl. Its black eyes were nothing but suspicious and threatening. She didn't move and looked at the ground. She'd met her share of livestock dogs and knew better than to try to placate the animal.

The shepherd pulled his horse up short next to the dog. His patched gray tunic was the same shade as his beard. "Hush," he bellowed as he dismounted. The dog, now silenced, sat obediently on its haunches next to the horse. The man stood between Nat and the animal, eyeing her with the same suspicion as his dog.

"I need—"

"Walk toward my horse," he said. "Slowly."

"What?" Nat asked.

"Walk toward my horse and touch her nose. Do it now," he commanded and stepped to the side, holding the reins loose. Another low growl erupted from the dog.

Frustrated with the request, Nat took two quick steps. The dog's ears flattened.

"Slowly." He stood with his arms crossed. A long dagger hung from a worn, braided belt tied around his waist.

"My friend and I were attacked in the forest," she said as she slowed her pace and extended her hand, palm down, toward the horse, exposing her markings.

"Attacked?" the man asked as he leaned forward to examine her arm.

"By a Nala." The horse nudged her hand. She placed her palm gently on the mare's sweaty neck and cautiously stroked her.

"Nala." The man spat at the ground. "I should have known. Ris and my horse have been on edge all morning." He gestured to his dog. Ris quieted at the sound of the old man's voice. "Is your friend dead, Sister?" he asked abruptly.

"No, he's not. After I killed the Nala—"

"You killed it?" The man tightened his grip on the reins.

"It attacked me and then my friend," she said defiantly. "It bit my friend, and he won't wake up. I couldn't carry him away on my own. I left him hidden in the forest." The words spilled from her as the man mounted his horse and extended a rough hand. She grabbed it and swung herself up behind him.

"I've had word that the Nala were pushing in from the east," he said over his shoulder as they rode toward the forest. "Since your like left, the vermin are spreading through this region. Six months ago, one bit my neighbor's daughter before we could chase it off." He was silent as they ducked into the forest. Ris wove in and out of the trees ahead of them. Nat pointed and he directed the horse.

"Girl's gone now, into the woods," he said more to himself than to Nat.

"What do you mean?"

"Her parents couldn't keep her anymore, Sister. They had little medicine to keep the venom from spreading. No Healing House Sisters to keep it in check. You know what happens," he said gruffly. "They had no choice but to send her off."

"Send her off into the forest with the Nala there?" Nat asked angrily. She couldn't imagine a child going through what she and Soris had experienced, only to be abandoned by those who should protect her.

"Nothing to be done about it, Sister. Not now, not in these times. She's got more of a chance out there than she would if she tried to live near her family."

They neared the cluster of ferns. "Stop here," Nat said. She slid off the saddle and whispered a command to the orb. A greenish glow appeared from behind the ferns. Nat's relief was quickly overcome by fear. She hurried to Soris, barely noticing the old man commanding his dog. "Find 'em," he croaked, followed by another round of spit. The dog went around the fern, then disappeared into the brush near the riverbank. The man unsheathed his dagger and followed the dog.

Nat pushed the fronds aside. Soris' eyes were partially open. "I was wondering when you were coming back," he said weakly. "Between the ferns stuck up my nose and your orb banging into my head every time I tried to move, I wasn't sure how much more I could take."

"I brought help, I think." She checked the bandage. Blood marred its surface. "Can you sit up?" She winced as she leaned in to help him.

"Did you get bitten?" Soris' eyes widened.

"No," she said. "I got hurt somehow during the fight, but I'm fine."

"At least one of us made it." He groaned as he sat up.

Nat felt a surge of guilt. "You're going to be okay, Soris." Her voice was hollow.

"No sign of the body, Sister."

Soris jumped at the sound of the old man's voice. Nat placed a hand on his back. "It's gone. I pushed it into the river. Here"—she gestured toward Soris—"help me get him up and on your horse."

"You killed it?" Soris asked as he struggled to stand with their support. Nat nodded. Ris continued to circle the trees around them while they managed to push Soris into the saddle.

"I've room only for myself and the boy, Sister." The old man looked down apologetically from the saddle.

Soris slumped over the horn, and Nat thought of how much he had undergone the past few days for her and the others. "Take him. I'll follow behind." The old man nodded and kicked his horse. It needed little prodding and trotted away through the trees. Nat collected the few belongings she'd left. The orb spun in circles at her side. Ris watched its movement intently. "Let's go, you two," she said. The trio flew through the woods away from the river.

"You said the Nala were pushing into the region." Nat held a thick mug to Soris' lips. He sputtered but managed to swallow the medicinal tea. "How long?" she asked as she laid Soris back on the wooden pallet set low into one of the cottage's stone walls.

Greffen, or more formally Greffen of the Tole Valley, as he'd introduced himself, ladled a thin liquid into a rough wooden bowl and dunked strips of gray cloth into it. "Been two years off and on. Before that, Mudug had a post south of here. The nearest House was destroyed five, maybe six years ago. The post was all we had after that." He carried the bowl to the pallet and pulled a stool close to Soris. Out one of the two narrow windows, Nat could see Ris resting in front of a flock of sheep with the sun setting behind them. The peaceful beauty looked so out of place. The sound of dripping liquid brought her attention back to the room.

"Unwrap that, would you?" Greffen pointed to Soris' makeshift bandage. Nat gently peeled the linen away from the wound. "Once the guards left, the Nala started moving in." He watched intently as she pulled off the last layer. He let out a low whistle.

"That bad?" Soris asked. Sweat covered his brow and upper lip. Nat forced him to drink another sip of the tea. She couldn't bring herself to look at the wound. It was her fault he'd been bitten. It had attacked him because he was trying to protect her. If she'd been thinking she could've flashed her markings and scared it off.

"I've seen worse," Greffen said as he dabbed the wound with the dennox paste he'd prepared from Nat's store. Soris winced. He leaned in and sniffed. "Yes, I've seen worse," he repeated. "But not by much."

"How much time do you think I have before I turn?" Soris looked at the bluish punctures ringing his shoulder before Greffen began wrapping them in the wet bandages.

"A day. Wouldn't you agree, Sister? About a day?" he answered, as if he were talking about how long it would take them to travel to the nearest village. Soris' head hit the lumpy straw pillow.

"You're not into sugarcoating, are you?" Nat glared at Greffen.

"Best he knows what he's in for." Greffen rose from the stool. "The medicine and wrapping will slow it down, but they won't stop it. You'd need a Healing Sister and a full apothecary to do that." He placed the bowl and unused linen on the table. "Not many of those around these days. Sorry, boy." He turned and shrugged his hunched shoulders.

"Sorry? There has to be something else you can do." Nat's anger at his resignation welled inside her.

"It's okay." Soris had opened his eyes and was staring at her. "We did what we set out to do. You need to get word to . . ." He paused and glanced at Greffen. He'd busied himself near the hearth, but both Nat and Soris knew he was listening intently to every word. "My brother and your friends," Soris finished cautiously. "I'll make my way north, back where we started. Maybe the Hermit can help," he added with little hope in his voice.

Nat watched, amazed, as he tried to convince her to abandon him. The doubt in his eyes reminded her of Andris—the way he had doubted her, the way he had told her she would fail. "Change of plans, Soris," she said curtly, making up her mind to bring him home. "Greffen." She turned and addressed the shepherd. "How soon will it be safe to move him?"

"Not until early morning. If that Nala you finished today was traveling with others, they'll be on his trail. You know their ways." He eyed her curiously.

Nat backpedaled. "Right." She calculated how far they could travel during the day. Soris' condition would slow them down, and there was no way she could or would depend on Benedict to help. "What will you take for your horse?" she asked.

Greffen let out a snort. "She's not for sale."

"You said yourself the Nala would be on him. Would you prefer we camp nearby and bring them to your front door? I'm not asking for a gift. What will you take?"

Greffen's lips were set in a thin line. "I'll take your dagger," he said finally.

Nat opened her mouth to protest but felt Soris' fingers brush her hand. "Fine. It's a deal. We'll leave before dawn, or earlier if we can." She extended a hand to Greffen and the now-familiar pain shot down her shoulder to her fingertips. He clasped her hand, nearly bringing her to tears. She turned her head away.

"Let me look at your shoulder." Greffen directed her to the stool, but Nat held up her hand in protest.

"It's nothing."

"Stubborn girl, sit, then have something to eat. It may be your last meal," he said as he moved to close the shutters. When he turned, he caught Nat looking nervously at the windows. "Don't worry, Sister, Ris will let us know if we have any visitors during the night."

CHAPTER THIRTY-EIGHT

Sunshine warmed her face. Wisps of hair twisted free in front of her face. Morning birdsong and a light breeze pulled her slowly from her sleep. She lay wrapped in her cloak beneath the dead lower limbs of a pine tree. Without opening her eyes, she stretched one arm, brushing against the tall, wet grass surrounding the spot where she'd slept through the night. Her shoulder no longer ached. She flexed her arm, testing for any pain. She pulled it back into the cocoon of her cloak and slowly opened her eyes.

The slender, curved tops of the sagebrush wiggled slightly in the wind. Other than their rustle, there was no other sound. Nat propped herself on her elbows and surveyed the trees. No birds. No birdsong. A soft thud sounded behind the thick trunk. It took only a few seconds before she was on her feet, running. She flew through an open meadow, jumping over the twisted, gnarled roots of the sagebrush until she hit another tree line. A jagged granite cliff loomed ahead, high above her. Cracks and fissures ran through the rocks. The highest point of the naturally convoluted pyramid was a boulder shaped like a gap-toothed grin. A single raptor floated far above the gap. Nat ran between the thin pines until she reached slabs of moss-covered granite that had tumbled from above. She glanced back. A haphazard line of trees shook wildly. The Nala wasn't far behind.

The slabs were slick with morning dew. She bounded over the fissures. Stubby trees shot defiantly out of the wider gaps in the rock. She passed a curled gray corpse of a tree and clutched one branch, pulling herself to the next outcropping. But she landed below the tree. With each step up the puzzle of a cliff, the split top appeared to grow farther and farther away. Hissing filled her ears. She tried to climb higher, but the rock slipped under her hands. The morning light dissipated into darkness. She could barely see the next handhold she needed to propel herself upward. She felt the rough, bumpy texture of the gap and pulled herself over the ledge into her dream space. "Lights up," she panted. Bars of light shot up along the ledge. Wild hissing sounded in fits on the other side. Sharp blue arms thrashed against the bars, but they remained steadfast.

Nat opened her eyes. Greffen's smoky hearth slowly came into view. She rubbed her face.

"It doesn't taste any better than yesterday." Soris held the thick mug in his hand and grimaced as he swallowed.

Nat sat up from her pallet and took in the room. The shutters were open. It was early. A fine gray mist had settled over the pasture, hiding everything beyond Greffen's fence. She stood slowly, shaking the remnants of the nightmare from her thoughts. "How are you feeling?" she asked.

"My chest and shoulder are a little sore," Soris said and focused on a bit of hay stuck under a chair leg. "But there's something else. I feel different."

"How?" Nat asked, knowing they needed to leave now, but the answer was important.

Soris looked up to meet her eyes. "You were dreaming a moment ago."

"Yes," she said, slowly beginning to gather their things. "And?"

"And I think I could see your dream."

The strap of her satchel dropped from her shoulder. "What did you see?"

"You were running through a strange field with silver-tipped plants. And then you started climbing up rock after rock." He examined his hands as he spoke. He curled his fingers in tightly, making two fists.

"Your brother can do that, get into my dreams," she said, trying to calm him.

Soris looked slightly bewildered. "Andris was bitten?"

"No." She retrieved her dagger from the worn table next to the hearth. "He just knew how to get into my head. Others can do it, too. Don't worry about it." She looked out the open window. Greffen strode out of the mist, followed by the chestnut mare. His soft words to the horse spilled in through the window. "It doesn't mean anything," she said, keeping her back to him. She pretended to struggle with the buckle on her satchel. But it did mean something.

She dropped the satchel as Greffen closed the door behind him. "Here." She held out her dagger. Greffen accepted the weapon and turned it over in his hands. "I'm going to get into trouble trading that for a horse," she told him as she wrapped a small bundle of bread and sheep's milk cheese in a cloth and tucked it in her bag. Greffen shrugged and examined the markings on the hilt. He sheathed the blade and placed it on the table.

They helped Soris to his feet, but once standing, he pushed them away. "I can walk," he said. Nat and Greffen followed him as he made his way out the door and awkwardly pulled himself onto the saddle.

Once Soris was settled, Greffen steered Nat toward a fence post. A halter with eye shields hung from it. He handed it to her. "She'll let you know if there are Nala about long before you see them. Put these on her before you reach the forest. She'll be less likely to throw you off if she senses Nala."

Nat took the halter. "Comforting."

"Sister." He touched her shoulder. "Did you see his chest?" He glanced at Soris.

"No, what's wrong?"

"When I changed the dressing, the venom lines were down past his abdomen. He's turning faster than I expected. If Nala are around, they may be drawn to him."

Nat fingered the eye shield as if examining the flap. "Let's hope your mare is fast, then." Not wanting any more bad news, she hurried to the horse and mounted. Soris sat behind her. The mare danced lightly to the left as she lifted the reins. "You ready?" she asked Soris.

He wrapped one arm around her waist and held the crossbow in the other. "If it's blue and it moves, I'll shoot it." He smiled wanly.

"Sister." Greffen was at the mare's side, holding up the dagger. "You need this more than I do."

"Thanks, I think." She took the dagger and strapped it to her belt. "Get word to the old Hermit near the Meldon Plain that you loaned us this horse. I'll do my best to see that the Hermit gets her back to you." She looked down at Greffen's deeply lined face. "But please, if he asks, just tell him you loaned us the horse, nothing else." Benedict was the last person who should know about Soris' bite.

Greffen nodded and Nat kicked the mare. She bolted through the gate and followed the line of the stone fence, away from the cottage. Nat heard Greffen yelling behind them. "What did he say?" she asked as she leaned forward over the mare's thrusting neck.

"Something about Barba!" Soris yelled over her head. "Say hello to Barba?"

How could he know about Barba? Nat kicked the horse again, urging it to move faster and farther away from the cottage. The mare's hooves tore up clods of dirt as they rode into the early morning mist. With the familiar cliffs in plain view and Estos' map memorized, Nat directed the mare toward Benedict's. They reached his house in the mid-morning. The sun reflected off the cream-colored stone steps leading to his door, but Nat didn't bother knocking. Bits of straw clung to the closed window shutters. A storm must have passed through and knocked the straw from the thatched roof before plastering it to the shutters. The rough-hewn enclosure for Benedict's donkey was empty. A film of white crust covered the bottom of the animal's water trough.

Soris set about slowly pulling up buckets of water from Benedict's well. They drank greedily before filling the trough for the mare. While the mare drank, Nat examined Benedict's house. Stone walls rose halfway up to meet the wooden exterior that extended to the thatched roof. The door and shutters were tightly secured. She could leave a message for Benedict tucked under a rock, but the chance it would survive another storm, or that Benedict would even find it upon his return, was slim.

Soris touched Nat's shoulder, which made her wound tingle. "She'll be good for a while now." He gestured to the mare, who was ripping long clumps of grass growing near the stubby stone fence surrounding the house. "I can make it to Daub Town by the morning if I'm lucky," he said. Nat turned and had to squint against the sunlight as she faced Soris. "You take the mare the rest of the way to wherever it is you're going," he added and crossed his arms. His normal grin was replaced with a look of resignation.

"You're coming with me. Like I said last night, change of plans," Nat replied.

"No, I'm not," he said. "Benedict's not around." He pointed to the silent house. "Who knows when he's coming back. There's no one else to get word to Gennes and the rest of them."

"What about the bite?"

"What about it?"

"You need medicine. You need treatment."

"I appreciate your concern, but it's done. I'm done." His tone was filled with anger as he swept his hand in front of his body. "Nobody is going to change anything now. I might as well do some good and get word to my brother before I have to—"

"Have to what? Walk into the woods? That's not happening. You're coming with me. We'll figure out some way to heal you." She strode toward the mare and tugged the reins, pulling her away from the grass.

"Why are you saying that? No one can heal me!" Soris' voice filled the silent air around the house. "Everything has changed. No more Houses, no more Healing Sisters." He pointed to the forest. "If you're bitten, you either die or you turn into a duozi and are exiled to the forest. There's no way around it, so stop acting like there's a way to fix it—to fix any of it."

"There are things my friends can do to help you."

"Why are you lying? Does it make you feel better? You weren't the one who was bitten, Sister—I was." His anger increased with each word, cutting into her.

"And it's my fault! If I hadn't fallen asleep. If I had come to the river with you. If I were a real—" She caught herself. "This is stupid. What do you have to lose by coming with me? We have two, maybe three hours of travel if this horse takes us all the way. The minute we get to where we are going, Estos will be on his way to Gennes' camp. He has a better chance of making it than you do." She regretted the words as soon as she said them. His face crumpled. She looked away, knowing she couldn't give up on him. "Or choose your path, but I will be right behind you the entire way to Gennes' camp, wasting precious time." She shoved her boot in a stirrup and landed in the saddle with a thud. "If you think for a minute that I'm leaving you after what we've been through together, you're insane. Get on the horse." She extended her hand to him.

He glared at her, unmoving. His eyes flickered to the forest, then settled on hers. "You put it a little too well, Sister," he said, grasping her hand and pulling himself up with a wince. "I have nothing to lose."

CHAPTER THIRTY-NINE

Nat pulled on the reins. The mare stepped out of the thin line of trees. The crooked tree came into view. It felt like ages, not weeks, had passed since her first trip to Fourline, when she'd shoved a crumpled bit of paper into the eye of that tree.

She decided to return using the original path through the forest instead of along the cliff. If the mare behaved, they would reach the membrane quickly. The cliff was safer, but they were running out of time. The blast of pain she felt in her shoulder when she lifted her arm would slow her down. She eyed the tree a moment longer before rummaging in her satchel.

"Why have we stopped? Did you see something?" Soris nervously scanned the tree line beyond the meadow. Aside from a few assenting grunts, these were the first words he'd spoken to her since they'd left Benedict's.

"We can leave a message for Benedict in that tree." She pointed to the crooked tree, torn parchment in hand. The horse backed up quickly, knocking Nat into her neck. "Can you put the blinders on her while I write this?" She slid off the saddle and absentmindedly handed Soris the blinders. "Greffen said she was easily distracted after a few hours of travel. He suggested we put these on her if she started getting antsy," Nat lied in response to the skeptical look on his face.

"Distracted? More like knowing when Nala are around." He grabbed the blinders and dismounted. "You are a pretty pathetic liar, Sister."

You'll find out what a good liar I am soon enough, Nat thought. She turned her attention to the parchment and scribbled a brief note to Benedict: *8 days since we saw you. My brother is better but moving on with me. If you find a mare, ask around for owner.* She paused. *Expect to see your friends soon.* The message was cryptic, but he'd understand. She folded the parchment into a compact rectangle and returned to the mare. The horse shook her head, displeased with her new limited line of sight. Soris looked off into the woods as she mounted the horse. She leaned over the mare's neck and whispered gentle, encouraging words.

"False promises?" Soris asked as they made their way through the meadow to the crooked tree.

"You're starting to remind me of Andris," Nat said. Maybe the venom was transforming his disposition along with his body. She kicked the mare, forcing Soris to grab her around the waist to avoid falling off. She brought the horse around the side of the crooked tree. She remembered how the soldiers had appeared near the spot they'd just left. Anyone would see the horse, but maybe not as easily if the mare wasn't right in front of the tree. The saplings and their nasty needles greeted her. *This should be easier with a horse,* she thought as she eyed the tree.

"Get off and hold her still. This will just take a second if you can keep the horse from moving around too much." She handed Soris the reins when he landed on the ground. She pulled her feet out of the stirrups and balanced on the saddle. She wobbled to the left. "Steady."

"Easier said," Soris replied.

As Nat reached for a low-hanging branch, the mare backed away. Pain ripped down her arm. She clung to the branch with one hand. The other brushed the tops of the saplings. She clasped her legs around the branch and grunted, painfully pulling herself around right above the eye in the tree. She shoved the paper in. Now she just needed to get down. "If you don't keep that horse still, I'm going to end up landing on you." She balanced herself by wrapping her good arm around the tree. She stepped carefully onto a branch.

"I'm not trying to make her move." Soris clasped the reins tighter. The mare's head jerked up as she backed away from the tree. "She's not interested in staying put." He glanced at Nat as he struggled with the horse. Their eyes met. Nat, wide-eyed, mouthed the word "Nala" and jumped. Soris ripped the crossbow from his satchel just as the Nala descended from the neighboring tree, one pointed arm wrapped around the tree trunk, the other pointed toward Soris. It made a sound like air escaping a tire before it sprang toward him. The mare reared, kicking her legs like a windmill, and took off running.

Nat struggled to her feet. Her right arm hung limp and useless by her side. With a twisted movement, she unsheathed the dagger with her left hand and lunged toward the Nala. The blade made a thin slice on its leg. She landed with a thud between it and Soris. Blue spittle dripped onto her cheek. The smooth blue head and gaping mouth hovered over her. She tried to close her eyes, to shut out what she knew would be the last thing she'd ever see, but she couldn't. Drips of venom hit her nose and ran down her cheek. The Nala jerked suddenly to the side. Its sleek body arched, altering its path away from Nat. The long grass bent as it crumpled to the ground next to her. Fletching protruded from its back and the tip of an arrow stuck out of its chest.

Nat frantically looked around for Soris. He looked confused and pointed his still-loaded crossbow toward the forest. A treetop twitched. "Don't shoot!" Nat screamed. She hit Soris' arm, sending the arrow high and right of the figure running toward them. Annin spun and brought her fist down on Soris' forearm. The crossbow clattered to the ground. She helped Nat to her feet.

Soris stood to the side, clutching his arm. "What was that?" he barked.

"No time for an explanation of defensive techniques," Annin spat. She brought a blade down on the Nala, separating its head from its body. Nat stared as its head rolled away. Annin pulled her toward the forest. "Thanks for getting my friend this far. Get after your horse and as far from here as you can," Annin called out to Soris.

"No, Annin." Painfully, Nat pulled free of her strong grasp. "He's coming with us."

Annin halted. "No, he isn't, and we don't have time to argue about this. There are at least two more Nala approaching from the south." She tilted her head in the direction they'd come. Her wild hair made her look slightly deranged.

Nat ran back, grabbed Soris' hand, and hauled him past Annin, toward the path. "He's been bitten, and he's coming with us!" she shouted and broke into a run. "Keep up as best you can, Soris, and listen to me, okay?"

Soris nodded, slightly dumbfounded, and picked up his pace to match Nat's. "Who is that?"

"A friend," Nat responded. "Duck!" A low limb stuck out as they rounded a rotted stump.

Annin passed Soris, skipped over two fallen logs, and squeezed in next to Nat. "When was he bitten?"

"Yesterday, midmorning. Ethet can help him," Nat said defiantly. The two jumped over an exposed root and Soris followed suit.

"Not everyone is going to be happy about this," Annin said as she took the lead.

"I could care less." Her stomach roiled at the pain in her shoulder.

They ran in silence. Both Annin and Nat looked back every few moments to ensure Soris was keeping pace. When the red boulder came into view, Annin fell back behind him.

"He's coming with us," Nat insisted again when they reached the membrane.

Annin scanned the rocks above and the forest around them, then addressed both of them. "It's a little different for us to get through than it is for you." She grabbed Soris and positioned him in front of the opening. She glanced back toward the path. "Not much time," she said. "Send the orb to Barba once you pass over. As soon as you see any part of him coming through, grab on and pull. Got it?"

"Why don't you go first?" Nat asked, suspicious it was just a ruse to keep Soris in the forest.

"Would you just get in there! I'm not going to leave him—he needs my help to get through," Annin said.

Nat turned to Soris. "See you in a second." She ducked her head and leapt through the membrane. The tunnel hummed. The orb left her fingers even before she whispered the order. It flashed down the tunnel in a blaze of light. Nat squared herself in front of the membrane, watching the weird shadows play over its surface. A bulge appeared, then another, until a human shape stretched against the layer. A single hand broke free, and Nat grasped his fingers and dug in her heels, pulling. Soris popped through the membrane and landed on the rocky ground. The membrane contorted again, pushing the bulges back as quickly as they pushed forward. Finally a foot appeared. She clutched the ankle with her left hand and pulled as hard as she could. She felt as if she were pulling a long rope out of thick, wet sand. Annin emerged, panting, and joined Soris on the ground.

"Help me get him up." Nat clasped Soris under his arm. "He needs Ethet now!" Annin pulled herself up and grasped his other arm. They stumbled down the tunnel.

Heavy footfalls approached. Oberfisk came crashing around the corner. He swept Nat into a crushing embrace. "Did you manage it?" he asked. Nat cringed in pain and heaved the contents of her stomach over the front of his "Fish Minnesota" T-shirt. He dropped her like a bomb.

"Annin, get him to Ethet." Nat croaked, wiping the vomit from her lips.

Oberfisk looked around, confused, and noticed Soris for the first time. "What's all this?" he demanded. "Wait, is that you, Soris? Can't be." He whirled on Nat. "What are you doing bringing him here?"

Nat stumbled past him and caught up with Annin as she continued down the tunnel with Soris. Riler was blocking the entrance of the tunnel but stepped aside quickly as the three of them tumbled into the infirmary. The room was painfully bright and empty. Annin dropped Soris on the table and hurried to the wall of vials.

"Where's Ethet?" Nat yelled.

Ethet burst into the room with Barba and Estos. She took one look at Soris and joined Annin at the marble table. "When was he bitten?" she demanded.

"Yesterday, midmorning," Annin and Nat said in unison.

"The bite's on the shoulder, we treated it with dennox and a medicinal wrap, but the venom was down his abdomen early today. I haven't seen the wound since." The words tumbled out of Nat as she watched helplessly. Barba cut away the clothing and bandage, stripping Soris' torso bare. A bluish color stretched from his right shoulder down his arm and across his chest.

Nat felt her skin prickle. She turned. Andris stood in the doorway. His eyes were black and his jaw was clenched. He pushed past Nat and grabbed his brother's hand. He closed his eyes. *"No!"* Andris screamed as he lifted his head. He turned to Nat. "Get her out of here! Now! Get her out before I—"

Nat felt all eyes on her. Soris rolled his head to the side, a look of confusion on his face. Estos touched her lightly on the shoulder and pulled her toward the door. "It's not my fault, Andris," she said. Her words sounded hollow. "It ambushed us . . ." She stopped. Andris' eyes were full of hatred. "You can fix him, can't you, Ethet?" she pleaded.

"Get her away from here, Estos," Andris said through clenched teeth. He had a murderous look in his eye.

Estos wrapped his arm around Nat's waist and lifted her. "You have to help him!" Nat cried out. He carried her away, Andris' glare burning into her. Estos kicked the door shut behind them.

The hallway on the other side of the massive door was quiet. She felt numb as he led her through the kitchen to the base of the stairs. He stopped and looked at her torn cloak and cheeks smeared with dirt. "You've looked better. Head upstairs, get some rest." He sighed. "I'll send Barba to talk to you in a little while." He turned and Nat reached out, grabbing his shirtsleeve.

"Estos, is he going to be okay?"

"I don't know," he said. "The venom is deep."

"But Annin was bitten, too, and she's fine. Ethet can help him like she helped Annin, right?"

"It's not that simple, Natalie. Annin's guardian got her to Ethet a few hours after Annin was bitten." He looked at her sadly. "His venom lines are running deep. The deeper the venom, the more difficult it is to stop the poison or the turning."

"What does that mean, you'll just send him back?"

"If Annin can erase his memory of this place. We can't risk his revealing where we are."

"So he could stay here, then," she said, frantically trying to come up with a solution. "You can teach him how to live here."

"Natalie, if he turns more Nala than human, he won't survive here. He can't survive here. Even Annin's struggled with Ethet's potions to aid her in this world. I'm sorry, but from what I saw, he'll have to go back." His voice was quiet and cold.

She stood mute. "I was just trying to help him," she said finally, tears slowly welling in her eyes.

"I know," he said, glancing down the hallway. "I need to return to the infirmary." He looked at his sleeve. Nat was still pinching the fabric.

She let go. "Get some rest. I'll send Barba to talk to you in a few hours to find out what went wrong." He turned his back to her.

Nat stood dumb for a moment, then said quietly, "We did it."

"Hm?" Estos paused by the door.

"Soris and I did it. We destroyed the map and the Chemist's tracker. Gennes is waiting for you at his camp in the northern canyon. You can go home now." *What a dismal triumph,* she thought.

"You really did?" Estos asked, his voice filled with surprise.

"We did," Nat responded and trudged up the stairs. She heard the thick wooden door slam shut as Estos ran down the hallway.

CHAPTER FORTY

The tunic, cloak, and dagger lay in an untidy heap in the corner of the bedroom. She'd done her best to clean up and remove the weeks of grime and filth from her body. Her pants and shirt stung her freshly scrubbed skin when she pulled them on. She'd examined the burning slice in her shoulder while cleaning up. It needed stitches and a round of antibiotics.

Nat tucked her phone into her backpack and shut the door to the bedroom with her left hand. The taxi would meet her a few blocks away from the costume shop near a steep embankment by the road. She wasn't sure how she'd explain her injury to the campus health clinic. She'd make something up, just like she'd been making everything up the last few weeks.

The hallway was still. She pulled her coat gingerly over her shoulders, leaving the right armhole empty. Silence met her at the base of the stairs. She imagined the hive of activity beyond the door and down the next hallway, the preparations they must be making to return to Fourline and find Gennes. After what Estos had said, she knew they'd take Soris back, too. She closed her eyes. There was nothing else she could do, and everything she'd done for him had turned out wrong.

She hesitated at the carved door. The kitchen was deserted. She silently padded along the carpet toward Ethet's lab and the tunnel entrance.

Ethet placed a wet strip of linen across Soris' torso. She put her finger to her lips and beckoned to Nat. She was the only person in the room with him. He lay with his eyes closed, looking peaceful.

"How is he?" she whispered. She pulled a stool next to him and brushed his hand with hers.

"I don't know yet. The poison is deep. I had to sedate him. It helps slow the progression." Ethet's lips were set in a straight line. "If it's safe, I'll take him through in a few days. I know a Sister who may be of more help to him than I can be . . . if I find her."

Nat rubbed her forehead, feeling helpless. "When he wakes up, will you tell him . . . tell him I'm sorry." She traced her finger over his broad cheekbone. He was going back to Fourline a duozi, and there was nothing she could do about it. She swallowed.

"You did the right thing bringing him here, Natalie." Ethet laid a hand on her shoulder.

Nat winced and coughed to cover up the pain she felt running down her arm. She slid off the stool. "Thanks," she said stiffly and walked out the door, leaving them behind.

Excited voices spilled out from behind a door opposite Ethet's lab. She heard Estos and Oberfisk and the clank of metal. She ran down the hall, away from the sounds. The doorknob leading to the costume shop felt cold under her fingers. It turned easily and she walked past row upon row of costumes. Flipping the lock, she opened the front door. The bell jingled. She looked back hesitantly as she stepped into the twilight. No one would come to see who was here. They were all heading home.

On the Meldon Plain

Book Two in the Fourline Trilogy

CHAPTER ONE

The sky reminded Nat of stone.

She turned onto a side street, running in the middle of the road to avoid the ice patches and clumps of snow covering the sidewalks. She passed a row of dilapidated Victorian houses. Smoke curled from their boxy chimneys and blended into the gray sky.

Late afternoon traffic poured onto the street. A dirty yellow truck missed hitting her by a few inches, and the driver slammed on his horn. She jumped over a sheet of ice, skipped onto the sidewalk, and continued her steady pace without giving the driver so much as a glance. Her feet fell rhythmically as she ran block after block. Each breath brought an icy ache of air into her lungs.

At the red metal bridge spanning the Cannon River, she turned onto the limestone riverwalk. She tore down the walkway, scattering pigeons and winter crows. Restaurants, shop fronts, and offices flashed by. Her lungs and legs burned, distracting her from the pulsing pain of her shoulder wound.

A second bridge came into view. Intricate circles reminding her of the vine pattern twisting up her forearm swirled around the railing. She glanced at the tip of the vibrant vine and spear peeking from underneath her sleeve. The pattern had yet to fade as Sister Barba had promised. Instead, since her return from Fourline, its hue had only deepened, just like her guilt over Soris. She sprinted to the bridge, rapidly moving her legs and arms and pushing away thoughts of her Sister markings and her friend.

When Nat reached the bridge, she quit running. She pressed her hips against the cold metal railing and watched the river flow toward her. Water rushed around ice sheets, creating little clusters of dull bubbles. She gently massaged her shoulder, avoiding the center of the wound as she followed the course of the water with her eyes.

The river snaked past the bridge, auto repair shops, industrial buildings, and a warehouse fronted by a stucco building. A sign reading "Gate's Costumes" hung from the front of the stucco structure. Nat pushed her green knit cap off her forehead and wiped the sweaty strands of brown hair from her brow. She watched the costume shop sign flicker on and off in the gray afternoon light.

Two months had passed since she'd pushed through the membrane tucked deep within the cliff wall behind the costume shop, leaving the world of Fourline and the Nala behind, but bringing her wounded friend Soris through. Her skin crawled as she remembered the humanoid Nala, with its lancing forelimbs and spiderlike fangs, slashing her shoulder and biting Soris. She placed her hands on the railing, the numbing cold surging through her fingers as memories of her quest into Fourline tumbled through her mind.

She'd ventured through the portal to Fourline to help Estos, the realm's young king, leave the safety of his exile in her world and return to his own. Estos' loyal rebel band needed him to lead the fight against Lord Mudug, the corrupt usurper who'd ordered the murder of Estos' sister, Queen Emilia. Nat had donned the garb of a Warrior Sister so she and Soris could destroy the Chemist's tracking device and create a safe passage for Estos' return to Fourline. But Soris had paid a price for accompanying her. She could only blame herself for not having protected him from the predatory Nala. Her journey with Soris had taught her that the Nala could turn humans into halflings called duozi with one bite from their venomous fangs. Unaware she wasn't a real Warrior Sister, Soris had trusted in her ability to keep them both safe.

Nat shook her hands and cupped them around her lips, blowing warmth back into her fingers as she thought of all the things she'd done wrong in Fourline. Failing to take Soris straight to the membrane after the Nala bit him was her biggest mistake. The skin around his wound had already turned blue like the Nala's by the time Annin helped pull his body through the resistant membrane. Nat hadn't brought Soris to Ethet, the Healing Sister who lived in her world, fast enough to curb his transformation into a duozi.

What exists in only one of the worlds cannot exist in the other. Her guilt deepened as she thought of Estos' words to her. He'd said Soris wouldn't survive in her world, that the Nala venom had progressed too deeply through his body for him to remain on this side of the membrane. Sister Ethet told her he'd have to return to Fourline, where Nat knew he'd be condemned to live the life of a duozi, targeted by both the Nala and the humans prejudiced against halflings.

Nat's legs, stiff from the sudden rest, cramped when she turned toward campus and ran away from the blinking "Gate's Costumes" sign. Hot tears, turning cold in the frigid temperature, streamed down her face. *I know you're gone, Soris,* she thought, feeling the familiar emptiness eating away at her. She brushed her arm across her eyes, and a sting of pain ripped down her shoulder to her arm. *You're gone, except in my nightmares.*

"How many is that today?" Viv, Nat's roommate, glanced up from her sketchbook. She scratched her face, and a black smudge appeared above her nose.

"How many what?" Nat carefully pulled her thin fleece sweatshirt over her head. An oozy gray stain from her weeping shoulder wound marred the fabric. She turned her body, keeping her shoulder away from Viv's line of sight, and tossed the garment into the laundry basket. She gingerly touched the loose bandage taped to her shoulder.

"Miles, kilometers, leagues, rods, *li*, minimarathons." Viv dropped the sketchbook on the floor and lifted herself out of the striped chair. Her blue hair was arranged in tiny topknots.

"Your hair looks cute," Nat said halfheartedly.

"You're evading my question, and I know for a fact you don't think my hair looks cute. The last time I wore it like this, you said I looked like a pincushion with zits."

"Your hair was red then." Nat shoved her head through the neck hole of a clean shirt, wincing when she brought her arm above her shoulder. *I'll rebandage the wound later,* she thought as Viv babbled in the background. Nat grabbed her new computer and slid it into her backpack.

Viv watched Nat change socks and slip on a pair of leather boots, her tangled brown ponytail skimming the floor when she tied the laces. Nat looked up and knew she wasn't going to escape the room easily, not without a roommate interrogation. Viv crossed her arms and leaned against the door, barring her escape.

"Three miles this morning and three this afternoon. That's how far I ran today," Nat responded.

"Are you kidding me?" Viv's brow creased. "Have you looked at yourself? I don't know how much weight you've lost since you got back from January term, but your clothes are hanging off of you and your face is all . . . sunken looking. If you'd J-termed in the tropics and picked up a tapeworm, I'd get it, but you were in Canada, so what's the deal?"

Nat stared at her roommate. If she had really been in Canada, everything would be different. She felt the tears well in her eyes and looked at the floor, pretending to struggle with her laces.

"You're right. I need to eat more. I've just been busy." She wiped her eyes, stood, and grabbed an apple from a dark-blue bowl on top of their minifridge. She took a bite. "I've got to get to my lab. I promise to eat dinner after."

Viv stepped away from the door. "You won't grab dinner after lab, because you're coming to Butler's. It's his birthday, remember?"

"A night with a bunch of inebriated artists. Looking forward to it." Nat took another bite to placate her roommate and lifted her jacket off the coat hook with her good arm, thankful Viv had yet to notice how left-handed she had become.

Viv plopped back into the chair. "It's the best company you'll get smelling like that." She scrunched up her nose. "You're turning me into a nagging roommate, Nat! Take a shower and eat, and you'd better be at Butler's by ten or I'm coming to find you," she threatened.

Nat slammed the door behind her. The late March wind stung her face as she plowed through the dorm's heavy doors. The half-eaten apple pinged against the side of the metal garbage can next to the entrance and landed in a clump of dirty snow. She buttoned her coat and walked with her head down, passing through the parking lot toward the Student Center. Safety lights shone brightly on the cars. She looked up, searching for a distraction from her thoughts and the pain in her shoulder.

Yellow light illuminated the wide first-floor windows of the Speech and Theater Building set behind the Student Center. A figure moved into the light of one window, and Nat halted. Sister Barba, the Wisdom Sister from Fourline who had drawn Nat's markings on her arm before sending her through the membrane, passed in front of the window. Nat veered away from the path between the two buildings. Her guilt over Soris was already ever present in her mind. With her shoulder wound and markings, she needed no more reminders of her quest. *It'll get better, she told herself. I'll forget all of them. I'll forget Soris. My wound will heal.*

The Science Center loomed in front of her. She pushed open the glass doors and slowly climbed the stairs. A rush of students brushed past her. Someone's backpack slammed into Nat's injured shoulder, and she bit down on her tongue to keep from crying out in pain. She climbed the remaining stairs and leaned against a window, pressing her hot forehead against the cool glass. When the pain subsided, she walked into the lab. A graying sunset filtered through the lab's floor-to-ceiling windows. The fading light left her with an unsettled feeling. Night brought no rest, only more nightmares.

Signe, her lab partner, looked up from their assigned table. Nat dropped her bag and jacket next to a metal stool, grabbed a pair of goggles, and pulled out her lab book.

"Testing for micronutrients, right?" she asked her partner.

"Yeah," Signe said. Standing a foot taller than Nat, she pulled her white-blonde hair back into a clip and pointed at a small container of seeds. Nat reached for the container.

"What's your rush? The teaching assistant isn't even here."

"We should check for copper, too, along with the other micronutrients," Nat replied, thinking the copper test would take an extra half an hour—time she could use to focus on something else other than Soris, her shoulder, and her nightmares.

CHAPTER TWO

The glowing red numbers cast a tiny halo around her alarm clock. One thirty. Nat turned onto her back and sucked in a sharp breath when she pressed her shoulder into the mattress. Viv snored loudly from the bunk below. Nat listened to the sound of running water coursing through the pipes in the ceiling above her. After the noise faded, she scanned the room trying to stay awake, but sleep pulled her in. Her eyes fluttered closed, and she fell into a fitful dream.

Blades of grass tickled the back of her neck. She shifted onto her side and looked past Soris, who lay sleeping in the grass next to her, peaceful and healthy. From the top of the hill, Greffen's stone cottage in Fourline looked tiny. Ris, Greffen's dog, barked wildly and strained against a rope tethering him to the gate of a sheep pen. Soris' eyes—green with brown flecks—flickered open.

"Where do you think Greffen is?" Soris tucked a strand of dirty-blond hair behind his ear.

"I don't know, but something has Ris riled up." Nat brought her hand to her forehead, shielding her eyes against the sun.

"Natalie, look." Soris pointed to a figure near the sheep pen. A Nala crept on its angular arms and legs past Ris, hissing as the dog lunged toward it. It scurried up the base of the hill and lifted its bulbous head. Even in the distance, Nat could feel its concave silver eyes settle on them with a predatory gaze.

Soris leapt up from the grass and grasped Nat's hand, pulling her to her feet. They plunged into the forest behind the hill. As they ran, the sun disappeared. Dense clusters of trees shut out all but the dimmest light. A cold darkness descended on the fleeing pair. Nat tried to hold tight to Soris to keep from losing him in the choking woods, but their hands slipped apart. Pine boughs pricked her bare arms as she ran farther into the woods, calling out his name over the sound of a nearby river. A glimmer of movement drew her eyes to the boughs of an enormous pine tree, and she stopped running.

A Nala, clinging to a bough, opened its black mouth, and a stream of venom dripped down and crackled on the dry leaves near her feet. Nat slowly eased away from the blue creature before turning on her heels and sprinting past the trees toward the river.

"Soris!" she screamed as she burst onto the riverbank. The slate-colored water roared, drowning out her cries.

Gasping, Soris emerged from the woods farther upriver and stumbled onto the gravel bank. The Nala jumped from a branch and slammed into Nat, sending her crashing into the icy water. The current pulled her feet toward the violent water racing down the center of the river. She coughed up water and called out to Soris just as the creature turned and sprang onto his back.

"Natalie, help me!" Soris shouted from the riverbank, thrashing his arm at the slick blue-skinned creature.

Leave him alone! Water poured into her mouth, preventing her from answering Soris' cry for help. Nat swam against the current, trying to reach the bank, but the water pulled her farther and farther downstream. She grabbed on to an overhanging tree branch and twisted around in time to see the Nala bite into Soris' shoulder.

Soris' cry reverberated through the river valley. Nat's hand slipped. She clutched the branch with her other hand and watched, helplessly, as Soris' skin turned dark blue, an exact match to the Nala looming over his body. The creature stood upright, exposing its arachnid-like abdomen.

"He's mine, Sister," it hissed. Nat choked, unable to breathe from the shock of hearing the familiar voice and recognizing the slanted gash in its gut.

"I killed you!" she shouted. She stared in disbelief at the creature; it was the same Nala that had bitten Soris on the riverbank in Fourline months ago. "This is a dream! It has to be!" she yelled. "I killed you!" Her hand slipped from the branch, and she fell into the water.

Nat swam blindly into the inky depths of the river, frantic to leave this nightmare for the safety of her dream space. Her fingers fumbled over the rocky river bottom, searching for the rough ledge to her haven. Her knuckles slammed into its jagged surface, and she pulled herself over. Coughing violently, she flopped onto the floor of the dark, empty space where no one—no images, no nightmares—could reach her unless she invited them in.

"Lights," she said weakly. The protective bars of light shot up along the ledge. She closed her eyes and let her tight muscles relax as the nightmare played out beyond the barrier of her dream space without her. "The Nala is dead," she said over and over, reassuring herself that the creature from the nightmare no longer existed.

The clock read 4:45 a.m. when Nat opened her eyes. The room felt stuffy. She threw her blanket off and stared at the ceiling before climbing down from the loft bed. The frame creaked under her shifting weight, and Viv mumbled in her sleep. Nat grabbed a towel and headed toward the shower they shared with the adjoining dorm room.

The hot water kicked in after a few seconds. She stuck her face under the spray and shivered despite the heat. She thought back to the nightmare. It was so similar to what had actually happened, when the Nala had attacked both of them on their return from the Chemist's quarters. But unlike in her dream, she'd killed the Nala after it bit Soris, and its lifeless body had floated down the river. *Why do I keep having this nightmare?* she wondered.

She pressed her head against the tiled wall, letting the water slide down her back. The hot stream stung her shoulder, and she stepped to the side to avoid the pain. She glanced at the wound. The ugly bluish-purple spot the length of her thumb was the same. Two months with no ebb to the ache. "The wound that never heals," she said to herself, thinking of Soris. She switched off the shower and dressed for a run.

Viv was still curled into a ball on her bed when Nat returned from her run around campus and into town. She kicked the leg of the bunk, and Viv groaned.

"I'm going to breakfast, want to join me?" Nat pulled on a pair of rumpled jeans and ducked, avoiding Viv's pillow.

"I have a headache, leave me alone."

"I told you to steer clear of Butler's punch. It lit on fire when I dropped a match in it."

"Stop making noise and go away," Viv said, her muffled voice rising from under the comforter. "Wait," she called out just as Nat put her hand on the doorknob. She emerged from under the covers, her hair sticking up in every direction. "Did Dermot ask you out last night?" She yawned.

"Why do you ask?" Nat crossed her arms.

"No reason. He just . . ."

"You put him up to it, didn't you?" Nat glared at her roommate. Viv slunk a little deeper under her covers.

"You need a life," she said indignantly. "Besides, he's wanted to ask you out for ages."

"The last thing I need right now is a boyfriend, especially one that needs encouragement from both my roommate and a drink." Nat glanced at the worn carpet. "He's not really my type, anyway."

"Type? You don't have a type." Viv tossed the comforter to the side and clambered out of bed.

"I do, too, and it's definitely not Dermot," she said, thinking of Soris' green eyes.

"Then who? The foreign guy from your theater class last semester, Estos? What about him?" Viv clutched the loft post and rubbed her forehead.

"Estos? No, he's just a friend, and I think he took the semester off, anyway." She grabbed her backpack, wanting to end the conversation. "I'll see you this evening, I've got class all morning and lab in the after-noon. I want to squeeze in—"

"Another run. I know." Viv waved her arm at Nat. "If I didn't know better, I'd think you were trying to avoid me."

"You could always run with me," Nat offered.

Viv hefted a book from her bedside table and threw it just as Nat ducked out the door. The book landed with a thud.

Nat dropped her backpack by the empty cafeteria table. The ache in her shoulder was worse. *Maybe it's time to see campus health again,* she thought as she slid her tray onto the circular top with her left hand and sat down.

A few students wandered along the buffet, filling bowls with cereal and grabbing fruit. She stared out the dining-room windows, past the dormitories to the bleak snow-encrusted fields. Clouds hung heavy in the morning sky. She played with her oatmeal, her thoughts straying to Soris and his broad smile. She tossed her spoon into her bowl and pushed the tray away. *I miss you, Soris. Maybe it would be better if I could just forget you, forget Fourline.*

But she couldn't, and Annin wasn't around to wipe her memories. Annin would be back in Fourline with the rest of the former rebels-in-exile by now, anyway. Nat had seen Sister Barba and Professor Gate from a distance a few times since her return, but no one else. *Besides,* she told herself, *I don't really want to see any of them except Soris.*

She cleared her tray and wandered out of the cafeteria. Students threaded their way past her, and she stepped cautiously to the side to avoid bumping her shoulder. From a distance, she saw Signe's tall figure pass through the Science Center doors. Nat hurried down the path. If she caught up with her, they could work through their lab notes before class. Her phone vibrated as she jumped over a pile of slushy snow. She pulled the phone from her back pocket and checked the number.

"Hey, Mom." She grimaced from the sharp ache in her shoulder and shifted the phone to her left hand.

"Nat." Her mom sounded surprised. "I wasn't expecting you to answer."

"It's your lucky morning," she said through the pain.

"Really? Doesn't sound like it. What's going on?"

"Nothing, just a busy week, that's all."

"Hmm. You've been pretty busy since January, as far as I can tell. Which brings me to the point of my call. I am officially giving you three weeks' notice so you can free up some time."

"For what?" Nat passed the library and skipped onto the path leading to the Science Center.

"Cal's decided. She'll be attending school with you next year." Her mom's voice rang with pleasure. "She has an appointment with the dance department the third week of April to meet with more faculty."

"What? Cal's not coming here." A flock of pigeons scattered at the sound of Nat's voice. "You can't afford the tuition to send her here." She regretted the words as soon as they came out of her mouth.

"Your new scholarships freed us up to help her, and the dance department gave her the Shiffer Scholarship. She would be a fool to turn it down," her mother said stiffly.

"I didn't go through everything I did to get those scholarships so Cal could leech off you." Nat's voice seethed with anger. The money for her tuition wasn't from a scholarship. Estos had originally agreed to cover her tuition in exchange for her traveling to Fourline to help him. The fact that she no longer had to worry about her tuition only served as a reminder that she'd ruined Soris' life.

"Leeching off us!" her mom yelled through the phone. "I can't believe you said that. Natalie, I stayed silent when you chose not to come home during your breaks, I even bit my tongue when I saw that absurd tattoo on your arm over Christmas, but I won't keep quiet while you insult your sister. Cal is not perfect, but neither are you. She is as deserving of the chances and opportunities you've been given. If you opened your eyes and saw how talented she is instead of cutting her down, you'd know what I'm talking about. I thought with time you two would grow close again like when you were younger. But after that comment . . ." Her mom's voice broke off. Nat's ears rang with the echo of her anger. She listened as her mom took several deep breaths. "Your sister will be there in three weeks, and you will treat her with respect, do you understand me?"

"Yes, Mom," Nat said, feeling lower than a worm. Her mom disconnected the call. Nat shoved her phone into her pocket and dropped her chin. She stormed down the path to the Science Center and brushed against someone in her haste.

"Natalie!"

Nat looked up to see Sister Barba tripping off the path. She reached for the Sister's elbow to steady her.

"You're in a rush," Barba said as she stepped back onto the path. Nat dropped her hand. The breeze lifted Barba's red hair in every direction.

"I'm sorry, Sister," Nat mumbled as she shifted from one foot to another.

"Not a problem. I was hoping to run into you. Maybe not so literally, but I did want to see you. How are you, Natalie?"

"Fine, I'm fine, Sister. Just a little distracted today."

"Hmm. I suppose you are wondering about Soris?" Nat's head shot up when Barba said his name. The lines around Barba's eyes deepened. "Ethet took him back to Fourline shortly after you returned. He is in good hands, Natalie," she said reassuringly. But Nat felt anything but reassured. She wanted to run as far from the Sister as she could.

"I need to get to class." A knot formed in Nat's throat. "It's . . . it's good to see you," she lied and pressed past Barba.

"You, too, Natalie," Barba said. Her eyes lingered on Nat's wrist when she opened the Science Center door. Nat glanced down at the edge of the vine and spear pattern, then at Barba. "There is a reason your markings never faded, Natalie. Please find me if you'd ever like to learn why." The Sister gave her a sad smile and walked away, leaving Nat so rattled her hand shook as she let go of the door.

On the Meldon Plain will be released on January 19, 2016. Preorder today.

ACKNOWLEDGMENTS

Thanks to my agent, Valerie Noble, for her belief in this story and her encouragement. Special thanks to the editors at Skyscape for all their guidance and support. Thanks to Nina M. for sharing her social-media savvy and answering all my ridiculous questions. There will be more. Thanks to John O. for responding to my questions about college financial aid without ever asking why. I have a family of the best cheerleaders imaginable. This book is dedicated to my husband, who teaches me each day that life is meant to be lived to its fullest. Thank you to my children for their support, patience, and inspiration. Finally, thanks to my mom for feeding me with books and teaching me how to tell a story.

ABOUT THE AUTHOR

Photo © 2015 Ally Klosterman

Pam Brondos grew up in Wyoming. After college and a brief stint in Asia, she returned to the wide-open spaces of the West. She is a science-fiction and fantasy junkie with a penchant for historical nonfiction. For more information on Brondos and the Fourline Trilogy, please visit her website at pamalabrondos.com.